SURVIVING EARTI

SKIES OF FIRE

LINDSEY POGUE

DEDICATION

For my post-apocalyptic readers who have been eagerly (but patiently) waiting for my next adventure. A new world, a new hell, a new hard-earned happily ever after. This one is for you.

And for Kristi. It has been a BLAST to work on this project with you. Here's to Kellen and Knox, and the epic hell we have put them through. #GertyGotUs

From the author of The Ending Series and Savage North Chronicles comes a new weather-ravaged, soul-stirring adventure about the most unlikely allies banding together to survive a crumbling, angry Earth.

As volcanoes erupt, wildfires spread, and sinkholes swallow entire cities, Knox and Ava must put a lifetime of grudges aside to survive the shifting landscape.

After an asteroid knocks the moon off its axis, scientists warn of Earth's eventual destruction. Governments, Moon Maniacs, and doomsday preppers brace for the worst, but as the years tick by, life continues mostly unchanged, and it becomes easy to fall into a false sense of security.

Ava Hernandez is no stranger to loss, heartache, and the struggle to survive. Branded a social pariah in her small town for reasons beyond her control, she's grown used to people's stares and mutterings over the years. Working two jobs while taking care of a sickly woman she owes her life to, it's all Ava can do to keep her head above water, let alone prep for "the end."

Knox Bennett is country boy royalty and infamous for holding a grudge. His mother is dead, his father has gone off the rails, his brother has abandoned him, and Ava is to blame for all of it. While he might've been fed with a silver spoon, all the money in the world can't prepare him or save his family's ranch from what comes next.

As fire engulfs the small town of Sonora, Texas, and nearby cities crumble, Ava and Knox are thrust together in the ensuing chaos. With all odds stacked against them, they must rely on each other to reach the safe haven alive.

Skies of Fire is a post-apocalyptic adventure set in the fire-scorched heartland of the American Southwest. This book is a stand-alone, with tie-ins to Waves of Fury, another Surviving Earth Chronicles installment written by K Webster.

Surviving Earth Chronicles include
(Series can be read in any order):
Waves of Fury by K Webster
Skies of Fire by Lindsey Pogue

SURVIVING EARTH CHRONICLES

SKIES OF FIRE

AUTHOR'S NOTE

Greetings, readers!

Before you embark on this heart-pounding, post-apocalyptic adventure, please note that this novel is a work of fiction. The Surviving Earth world is based on an array of scientific hypotheses and theories, which makes the setting and world-building simply that—hypothetical. While I have thoroughly researched many elements in this story to keep it relatable, I've also taken creative liberties.

Additionally, it's worth mentioning that Ava's character is not based on me, but her medical history and journey mirror my own and have only been slightly altered for the purpose of the story. While I understand that certain aspects may seem unlikely to some, Ava's mental health and medical diagnoses are inspired by real-life experiences.

And finally, a very special and heartfelt thank you to a longtime friend of mine, and sensitivity reader, Daniela Calderon, for ensuring I've done Ava's character justice.

This story has been a long time coming, and I hope you

enjoy this incredible adventure as Knox and Ava fight to survive the shifting Earth in *Skies of Fire*.

ONE
AVA

Call Dr. Jameson's office.
Call Hospice.
Check bank balance.
Pick up prescriptions.
Grocery shopping.

I RUN THROUGH MY MENTAL CHECKLIST OF TO-DOS BEFORE MY second shift, but it's suddenly forgotten the moment I see Lars through the diner window. He has new tattoos, apparently. They creep up his neck and disappear into the fringe of his greasy black hair, and he wears his holey Hill Country Militia t-shirt like it's a badge of honor.

I don't know if the plastic cup in my hand is actually dry before I set it aside and pick up the next one. Idly, I wipe it down, too fixated on whether Lars plans to enter the diner with his band of thugs trailing behind him. They're a ragtag crew of cretins, and having gone to school with most of them,

I know they only *look* terrifying. Lars, on the other hand, has always set my teeth on edge.

Leroy, a daily morning patron, clears his throat a few stools down, but I barely notice, too transfixed by the scene out the window. The tension leaves my shoulders as the guys pass the diner, headed for Lars's old Dodge across the street. Good. It's too early in the day to deal with their hostility.

Smoke billows from Lars's mouth as he opens the driver's side door, takes a final drag from his cigarette, and flicks it toward a passing car. His eyes narrow on the diner window, though, and I hold my breath. He sees me. The devilish upturn of his mouth tells me as much, but after a few heart-beats, he looks away.

I exhale only to grab the countertop as a familiar floor-shaking rumble fills the diner. The lights start swinging above the tables, rattling as the entire building trembles. But it's not a tremor this time. It's a low-flying Osprey, the first flight of many that will pass over us today.

As always, my eyes shift to the crack creeping farther up the wall. It grows bigger with every earthquake and thundering aircraft.

"Excuse me?"

I glance at a patron in the nearest booth, peering at me over the brim of his glasses.

"Can I get the check, please?" There's a tinge of irritation like this isn't the first time he's tried to get my attention, but he says it kindly all the same.

"Of course." Wiping the sweat from my brow, I flash him an apologetic smile and hurry over. "Sorry about that." He nods as I slip his ticket onto the table and collect his syrup-covered plate and empty juice glass. "Let me know if you need change." The patron opens his wallet, and I head for the kitchen to discard the dirty dishes.

Like most morning shifts at Bev's, I'm on autopilot. Today, however, I'm foggier than usual. Probably because I barely slept last night, looking after Mavey. And I didn't sleep a lick the night before that, wondering if Mitch and that temper of his might turn up again outside my house. It was only a matter of time before he went on another bender and trekked all the way to the trailer park to unleash his verbal wrath on me for all the neighbors to hear.

I set the dirty plate and glass in the tub inside the kitchen for Felix to add to his dish duty. He doesn't even notice as he drums his index fingers against the lip of the sink, rocking out to whatever noise blares in his earbuds. "Working hard, per usual," I mutter.

Pulling my vibrating phone from my back pocket, I pray it's not hospice calling with an emergency, but I'm only slightly relieved when I see an emergency alert.

Use caution on roads due to increased seismic activity. Stay indoors if possible.

Yeah, right.

It's only one of a dozen alerts I'll receive today, and I ignore it like I do every day. Do they really think people have the luxury of staying home and hunkering down for eternity? If I listened to every alert, I'd have been indoors since I was five, never seeing the sun.

Exhaling the heaviness I can't seem to shake these days, I escape the kitchen's heat. I could remind Bev that there must be labor laws about making us work in what will undoubtedly become sweltering conditions by noon, but I know she doesn't keep the air off because she's cheap. All we need is another rolling blackout; the entire diner would have to shut down, and neither of us can afford that. She has three kids to put through school, and I—well, I have Mavey to worry about. Resolved to deal with the heat, like most summer days, I tighten my ponytail higher atop my head to give my neck a breather.

The door dings as I step back behind the counter. A woman shuffles inside and peers around the diner. She's one of a few homeless regulars.

Bev spots her immediately and slips a patron's ticket onto his table with a thank you before addressing the woman. Her greasy blonde waves are pulled back, accentuating her gaunt face. I remember her, back when her cheeks were fuller and her jeans didn't hang off her body the way they do now. I know the shameful burn of hunger, how it erodes the pit of your stomach, and I empathize with the woman as much as I applaud her courage coming in here. Especially when half the jobs in Texas have withered away, just like spring has.

I continue wiping down the counter from the morning rush. The butter packets are already melting in their dishes. It's only a matter of time until they resemble Bev's potato soup, so I stick them in the small refrigerator beneath the counter.

"It's not just the coastal cities that should be concerned, though," a man says on the television. I glance at Tom, another regular sitting in the middle booth, where he sips his third cup of coffee for the morning. He sets the remote down on the edge of the table, his eyes fixed on the screen.

"The increased seismic activity throughout the entire *country* is a glaring indicator that the time has finally come," the interviewee continues matter-of-factly. He's yet *another* scientist, sitting across from Maryann Climmons. She's been the biggest name in the news world this side of the Mississippi, at least as long as I've been alive, and, well, she looks it. But lately, Maryann has become the face of every investigative report having anything to do with Gerty the asteroid and the surmounting effects she's had on Earth since her debut.

"Which, to be fair," Maryann counters, tilting her head expectantly, "many would say you've been claiming for years. In fact, while we've just marked Gertrude's fifty-year anniversary, we've surpassed the nation's debt ceiling, not by billions but by trillions of dollars because of decades of preparation."

I glance down at my crumb-wiping and the coffee rings on the countertop. "Everything is theory until it happens, Ms. Climmons. The best we can do is prepare for when it does." When I look up again, the scientist in the tweed suit pushes his glasses up the bridge of his nose. *Dr. Adriel Lightfoot, Southwest Environmental Research Specialist*, flashes on the screen beneath him. "Scientists used to think something like Gertrude was improbable. They thought an asteroid would need to be much larger than six miles wide to do much damage to a moon over three hundred fifty times its size. They *thought* that if something did happen, life would cease to exist on Earth, or we'd fall into another ice age. Yet, here we are. The fact of the matter is, everything is an educated guess because that's all we have." Dr. Lightfoot pauses for effect. "People are so worried about accumulating debt, but if we aren't as prepared for what's coming as we can possibly be, we're dead. Debt seems a small price to pay, given the alternative. And as morbid as it may be, it won't matter how *in debt* we are if extinction is how this ends."

On cue, the lights in the news station flicker, and Dr. Lightfoot points to his glass of rippling water, his tanned features narrowing. "Each tremor—each quake and unnatural surge of water—is a chain reaction. Life on this planet is precarious. There's a balance, and that balance has been shifting for years. As unpredictable as things are now, it will get far worse. The future is here and it doesn't care about debt."

Maryann has the decency to look slightly more humbled as Dr. Lightfoot crosses his legs. He looks as if he's settling in for a story. "You seek more proof?" he continues. "It's in the numbers—in New York's scramble for sandbags during last year's unprecedented monsoon and the parts of Florida buried in snow the past three winters. This week alone, entire communities along the Gulf of Mexico are being relocated. We've already had record flooding, so it's not some radical conspiracy—*these* things are happening. *These* things are not hypothetical. So do we continue to squabble over money or do we continue to prepare for the inevitable? Because the one thing all scientists have been able to agree on since Gerty hit is that life on this planet *is* forever changed, and if people aren't prepared for it by this point, it's their own fault."

I roll my eyes. Not because I don't believe Dr. Lightfoot and the many scientists who have come before him, but because not all of us have the time and money to pour into preparations; not all of us can be preppers when we're simply trying to survive as it is.

"Christ." Leroy grumbles my shared sentiment from his stool. "Turn that shit off, would you?" He glowers at the television. "Just another Moon Maniac posing as a scientist." The wrinkles around Leroy's tired brown eyes deepen, and he rubs his stubbled chin. Unlike him, I don't remember life before Gerty hit the moon, so the Moonies, preppers, and doomsday scientists are all I've ever known.

The shift of the moon's orbit after the impact has been the topic of conversation and most headlines since I could read.

Yes, the shift will *eventually* send humanity back into the caveman days. But the longer it takes, the less imminent it feels. Here we all are, years later, still scrimping to survive. It's easy for climatologists to tell us to prepare for the end of the world that "will happen one day," but actually doing it when every day is already a struggle is another matter entirely. It's all most of us can do to make ends meet and get through the week with a semblance of sanity still intact.

I eye Leroy's folded newspaper on the counter—*Sutton County militias at an all-time high*—then give him a sidelong look, sure he's part of one because everyone is. Not only is this Texas, but everything here is falling to shit, more than most states, because of the influx of seismic activity over the years. Tourism is non-existent, and the people who can afford to leave have already fled. Those remaining are too stubborn to leave, no matter the cost, or are waiting for it to get worse before uprooting everything they've ever known. I'm neither, just someone stuck in this hellhole.

"More scare tactics," Leroy grumbles. "More hypocritical bullshit." I don't typically agree with the grumpy old man about much of anything. He's constantly muttering and cursing at the world, but I find my attitude is oddly similar this morning, which means the world really is ending.

I pull out my notepad and clear my throat. "Breakfast?"

He meets my gaze, something he rarely does because his best friend is Mitch Bennett, and it's no secret Mitch wants me to crawl back into whatever hovel he thinks I came out of.

"You know," Leroy starts, ignoring the notepad in my hand, "when this shit happened back in '73, it took years for the chaos to die down." He gulps the last of his coffee and runs his bottom teeth over his graying mustache. "People hoarding food and water, abandoning their jobs and disrupting supply and demand—the economy *still* hasn't recovered. And don't get me started on those sons of bitches looting my gun shop. It's not like we're in for the zombie apocalypse! All this talk is doing is stirring shit up again. And all of those prep facilities, evacuation centers, and water treatment plants the government is pumping money into—where are they at? Cause they ain't here."

I don't know what it's like in big cities, but here, in Texas, towns are bled dry by the military, and our roads are nearly too pitted to drive on from years of neglect, so again, it's hard to argue with the old coot.

I rest my hip against the counter. "So, no breakfast today, then?"

Leroy is about to respond when the door dings again.

Dread fills me the instant I look up. "Fuck," I rasp as Mitch Bennett steps inside. The ease of the diner siphons away, and my stomach roils.

Mitch rarely comes to the café. So why today, of all days, when I'm already an exhausted mess, is he here? He glances around as I refill Leroy's coffee mug. I don't want to be standing here when he sits down.

Shoving the coffee on the warmer, I turn back to Leroy. He scratches his jaw, perusing the daily specials written on the wall. "Get me a fried egg sandwich on wheat." I'm about to turn away as Mitch approaches. "Oh!" Leroy growls. "And bring me some of that Tapatío I know Bev has back there somewhere. None of that Cholula shit."

I busy myself, scribbling Leroy's order down as I scan the room for Bev, praying she notices Mitch so she can deal with him while I take an extended break. But she's still in the back, getting food for the homeless woman, completely unaware of our newest patron.

Panic, hot and loathsome, flushes through me as I brace myself.

Two nights ago, when I saw Mitch, he was in a drunken rage outside my trailer, cursing my existence and waking Mavey from her medically-induced sleep. And that will continue to be my reality until I can finally get away from this town because the cops won't do anything other than drive him home when he gets like that. The Bennett family is untouchable—they are a legacy in Sonora. And Mitch isn't only the patriarch, his reputation as the biggest asshole in the state of Texas precedes him, and those two things combined give him a free pass for just about everything.

Turning my back to the counter, I clip Leroy's order to the carousel. I gather what little politeness I can muster, inhale a deep breath, grip my pen until it's biting into my hand, and turn around to face Mitch as he pulls out a stool beside Leroy.

Mitch's dark eyes meet mine before he shakes his friend's hand. He's in Wranglers and his typical Bennett Family Ranch t-shirt—not a single wrinkle or sweat stain, though I'm sure he's been up for hours.

For a man in his sixties, he's terrifying—tall with salt-and-pepper hair that pokes out from beneath his hat, broad shoulders, and the same menacing glare his son Knox inherited. But I don't show my fear, I refuse to—I don't even blink. Instead, I stare right back at him, pen poised on my ticket pad.

Mitch removes his Stetson, setting it on the counter beside him, and his cloying aftershave wafts toward me. His gaze, dark as coal, shifts to me again, hard and unrelenting.

Generally, I have no problem throwing shade back at people who disrespect me—who try to intimidate and bully me. But Mitch is different. He has been the exception to every hard and fast rule I've adopted over the years in order to look out for myself: give no shits, and never be someone else's punching bag. But deep down, part of me can't blame him for hating me. His reason for being angry at the world is valid, and though I know it's not my fault, I'm tied to his past whether I want to be or not.

He taps his blunt finger on the countertop, silently commanding a cup of coffee.

Glad he's refraining from further unpleasantries, I tuck my notepad into my apron and flip a clean mug up from the stack to set on the counter. With surprisingly steady hands, I fill his mug to the brim.

"Where's that boy of yours?" Leroy asks, but I don't wait to hear what they say next as I set the coffee back on the warmer and push the kitchen door open, disappearing into the back. My hands are clammy, and I can feel sweat thickening on my brow.

"I'm taking ten," I call over my shoulder, though Felix is too busy air drumming, and the cooks probably can't hear me over the ventilation fans and sizzling griddle.

Grabbing my messenger bag from the hook near Bev's office, I hurry out the back door and into the sunny morning. It's barely eight a.m., but the dry heat is already suffocating.

A gust of hot wind swirls around me, tugging at my pony-tail as a plastic bag flies out of the dumpster and plasters itself against my leg. Only half aware, I peel it off, my pulse pounding far too quickly for comfort as my feet begin to tingle.

"No—no. Not now," I groan. Mitch always makes me uncomfortable, but this is different.

Hurrying to the rickety picnic bench by an ash tree, I frantically search my bag for my meds. When I hear the pills rattling around, I allow myself a bit of relief. Popping one into my mouth, I pull the water bottle from my bag, take a gulp, and then another, washing the pill down. It's already too late, I know that, but maybe I won't be a complete zombie when it's over, so I can make my afternoon shift at the farm store.

As my entire body prickles with unease and sweat breaks over my skin, I fumble to untie my apron, pull it over my head, and ball it up to use as a pillow. Leaning my head down, I wait for the chills to spread and the world to fade to black.

TWO
KNOX

STANDING IN THE KITCHEN, I DOWN AN ICE-COLD GLASS OF tea. It's uncharacteristically warm, but the seasons have become more erratic over the years, so I shouldn't be surprised. And after the morning I've had, dealing with a sick steer, I can only imagine how the rest of the day will go.

Setting my glass on the granite countertop, I wipe the sweat from my brow and glance around the immaculate, industrial kitchen we rarely cook in, then into the living room decorated in earth tones and plush seats that are never used around the giant stone hearth. A house once filled with laughter and bodies is empty now and has been for years.

Predictably, my gaze lands on the only family photo displayed on the mantel. My eyes shift over my mother—too painful to linger on—then my father before resting on Kellen, standing beside a younger version of me. Kellen's dark hair and strong features make him the spitting image of our father, despite how much they resent the resemblance. Any similarity stops there, though. In fact, it doesn't only stop, it screeches to a halt that can be heard four counties over.

A college-educated, big-city businessman, Kellen

couldn't get away from the ranch fast enough after Mom died and couldn't have gotten farther away from me.

My gaze shifts to the framed image of our mother beside it. Her glittering green eyes look directly at me. She's crouched with the first calf she ever delivered cradled against her, smiling up at the camera. Her cowboy hat shades part of her face, and her smile fills my chest with an all-too-familiar ache.

The sound of Dad's dually rumbles up the gravel road, and I pour what's left of the iced tea into my thermos to take with me, grab an apple from the fruit basket, and settle my Stetson back on my head.

Biting off a hunk of crispy fruit, I exit the screen door. The faint scent of sulfur fills my nose, more potent than I'd noticed before, and Lucy, my Australian shepherd, leaps to her feet. Her mismatched eyes are wide and excited as she follows me toward the stable.

"I thought you were branding today," my father grumbles as he climbs out of the truck. He glowers at me as he slams the door. Lucy lowers her head and keeps her distance as she trots past him.

"I was." I don't bother to slow down as I head for the stables. "But some of the steers are missing."

"What?" His shoulders stiffen. "What do you mean, they're missing? I'm supposed to deliver seven of them tonight."

"Yeah, I know. Tony and I will ride to the northern pasture to wrangle them in." I bite off another hunk of apple, hoping my father will get the hint I'm not in the mood to talk, but he doesn't. Or rather, he doesn't care.

"Stop and look at me when I talk to you, boy."

Clenching my jaw, I turn to face him. Lucy stops a few paces away, watching protectively over me. I don't bother reminding my father I'm nearly thirty as I stare at him, bored and impatient.

He strides closer with that look in his eyes, the one I was afraid of when I was younger—when I was scrawnier, less imposing, and softer. The look that told me to brace myself for what comes next. But I don't cower around him, not anymore. I stopped being afraid of Mitch Bennett when I was twenty and threatened him within an inch of his life. I haven't been his punching bag since.

"If you forgot to clear out that old barbed wire you tore up last week," he warns, "and those steers are injured—"

"The old fencing is gone," I bite back. "They aren't injured. Some of the steers got separated from the herd in the night is all. Probably coyotes. I'll bring them in."

"You better pray," he says so low I barely hear him.

"Or what?" I taunt him because my ego and impatience won't allow me to ignore his prodding, it would seem. I step closer and look down at him. He's only an inch or two shorter than me, but it's enough that I can loom over him if I try to, a reminder that I am no longer a trembling little boy. He made sure of that. "I said I'll take care of it, and I will. Not for you, but for the client."

I can guess who put my father in such a foul mood this morning. Resentment is all he's known for so long, he places himself in Ava's path so that he has a reason to be angry on a daily basis. But I don't have time for his shit right now.

Horses stomp out of the stable as Tony leads them into the sunshine, saddled and anxious to go. "Ready, boss?" he calls.

My father's laser glare finally releases its hold on me.

Taking another bite from my apple, I glance in Tony's direction and give him a terse nod. "Anything else?" I ask my father, crunching the apple between my teeth to irritate him.

His hard, dark eyes narrow ever so slightly. "Get those

steers ready for transport. I want them loaded by noon. I have a long drive ahead of me." And with that, my dad turns and marches toward the house, flings the screen door open, and disappears inside.

Already anxious about the missing steers, I crack my neck, exhale deeply, and stride over to Tony with Lucy at my side.

Tony glances between me and the house. "He's a tub of fun, as usual."

I don't bother replying and hand the thermos up to Tony, sitting in Poppy's saddle. My mother's old bay mare sniffs Lucy before the apple catches her attention. I rub her face as I take two final bites, then toss the core into the pigpen. "Next time," I promise her. The last thing I need is my mother's horse choking on an apple core with a bit in her mouth.

"You know," Tony starts, hesitant. "This whole thing with him and Ava is getting—"

"Don't." I glare at him as everything inside me, already coiled with tension, tightens. Tony might be happy-go-lucky most of the time—the honey to my vinegar in our friendship —but now is not the time to lecture me on Ava or my father.

Tony holds up one hand in defense. "I know it's a touchy subject, but at some point, you and your dad need to—"

"Shut it, Tony. Stick to livestock, would you? And stop calling me boss. You make me sound old." I run my hand over Lucy's head. I know I'm being an asshole, that's all I seem to be anymore, but I can't help it. I don't want to think about Ava. Her name alone brings out the worst in my father, and whether I agree with his hatred or not, her family has been the cause of too many long, shitty nights in the Bennett house. "I just want to focus on the steers and getting them back to the barn safely."

"Fine, consider my lips sealed," Tony mutters. "But just

because your dad's a dick doesn't mean you have to be one too . . . boss." Tony stares at me as I climb onto Rooster's back.

I glance at him and it's all I can do not to roll my eyes. "Noted. Now can we get on with it?" Rooster's sorrel body expands as he inhales, and I settle into his saddle and take the reins.

Tony dips his head and flicks the brim of his hat. "After you."

With a click, I grab hold of my hat, and our horses step into a trot before we gallop away from the ranch toward the outer pastures. Lucy lopes beside us, her tongue hanging from her mouth and her gray-and-white coat catching the sunlight. What I wouldn't give to feel as free as she is right now.

"So, what are you thinking?" Tony calls over the beat of horse hooves. "We heading to the pond?" Like me, he's apprehensive. I can hear it in his voice.

"Yeah," I call back. "The ash grove just beyond it." I know every inch of the two hundred acres the Bennetts have owned for four generations, and I have a feeling the steers are taking refuge in the shade, out of the increasing morning heat.

The smell of sulfur thickens as we ride farther out, and my unease multiplies as it becomes harder to ignore. I focus on the arid breeze and the pasture stretched out before us. The terrain is primarily flat with prickly pear and desert scrub dotting the landscape. The ground is dry and the horses stir up dust as their strides devour the distance between the farm and the pond over the ridge. Coyotes don't usually cause too many issues, but it's not unheard of and I ready myself for what we may find on the other side.

As the pond comes into view, Tony and I slow the horses, not wanting to spook the cattle. Lucy slows, staying close and awaiting my command. But I don't see any stragglers around the pond.

"Well," Tony utters, readjusting his hat on his head. "They've gotta be in that thicket over there."

We trot closer, around the rocky lip of the natural pond that has watered our livestock for over a century. Rooster knows where we're headed, and I drop my hand to the saddle horn and let him take the lead. The horses slow as we reach the trees, and it's all I can do not to gag at the pungent scent of sulfur. Even Lucy's eyes squint against the aroma, and my unease solidifies to dread.

"Jesus," Tony groans, raising his arm to cover his nose. "That is *strong*." He nudges Poppy into the ash grove, and Rooster, Lucy, and I follow.

The instant a few of the missing steers come into view, the tension in my shoulders eases. But my relief is short-lived.

"Luce," I warn, calling her away from the cattle.

"Um, Knox . . ."

We watch as a steer wanders in confused circles, lowing anxiously. Clenching the reins tighter, I spot another with his head pressed against the trunk of one of the ash trees.

"Boss!"

"What?" My attention snaps in Tony's direction. It takes my brain a second to register five more steers lying down near the water's edge. Some of them look as if they aren't even breathing.

I stare at the pond. The sulfur in the air is suddenly villainous.

"It looks like polio," Tony murmurs, slowly putting the pieces together. But I already have. My jaw aches so tight, I think it might break as I look from the dead steers to the ones soon to follow.

"From sulfur poisoning?" He looks dumbfounded. "They were fine yesterday."

I don't waste my time wondering how or why. Instead, I focus on what I must do. Muttering a *goddammit*, I turn for the rope strapped to my saddle with my shotgun. This is the part I hate about ranching—the part where nature is cruel, and I have to take matters into my own hands.

"Let's rope this one." I eye a male that looks borderline too ill to save, but our livelihood is these steers; I have to try to save it.

Tony nods, equally uneasy about what we must do, and unclips his lasso. Gloves already on, we each toss our rope over one of the steer's horns and lead it away from the herd.

Head hung low, Lucy brings up the rear. She nips and yips, ensuring the rest stay in line. The steer tugs against us, but there is little muster in it, and once we're clear of the woods, Tony takes over.

"Keep them moving!" I call. "I'll catch up."

He nods again, if a bit reluctantly, and I dismount as Tony and Poppy lead what's left of the herd up the hill away from the pond.

When they're a ways off, I walk Rooster to one of the trees and wrap his reins around a low-hanging branch. Even he seems to feel the strangeness in the air, but while he hangs back, Lucy follows protectively at my side.

"Stay," I tell her. She watches me, her tongue hanging from her mouth and doggy eyebrows lifting as I unstrap the shotgun. I stare at her, shaking my head because I wish I didn't have to do this. Turning on my heel, I head back for the thicket and into the trees.

Each step is a crunch in the quiet and the ringing of a death procession. With a final glance to ensure Rooster and

Lucy are far enough away, I lift my shotgun, aim at my target, and pull the trigger.

THREE
AVA

I'M SWEATING BY THE TIME I PULL INTO THE BACK LOT OF THE farm supply store. The heat is killing me today, and getting a popped tire didn't help in the slightest. My bike screeches to a stop in the delivery bay, and I hop off, removing my suffocating helmet. I'm already late for my shift, but Scott should be grateful I made it here at all after the day I've been having. Hanging my helmet on my handlebar, I grab my empty water bottle and head inside.

"Shit—" I stop mid-step. I forgot to call the house to check in. I always call after Mavey's noon nap to make sure she doesn't need anything. Swinging my messenger bag around, I hunt for my phone. When my screen lights up, another emergency alert is waiting to be read, but I swipe it away. I have a missed call too, but it isn't from Mavey or hospice.

Julio's name fades from my screen as I debate whether to listen now or when I get off work, but I call my voicemail before I can talk myself out of it.

"Ava." His hesitant voice is gruff. "It's been a while, and I wanted to make sure you are okay . . . And see how Mavey's doing. I know you don't plan on coming this way, but with the direction things are headed, I hope you reconsider." He pauses. "I worry about you, kid. I know you're busy and you don't want my help, but . . ." Julio sighs, and after another pause, he continues, "I'm here. You always have a place with me if you need it. And I want to help if you'll let me." Then my uncle hangs up the phone.

Damn. I hadn't expected the ever-present knot in my stomach to worsen upon hearing his voice. Then again, there's a reason we don't talk much.

Forgetting about Mavey, I shove the phone into my pocket and pull open the back entrance to the store. The air-conditioned interior is blissful as I hurry into the stockroom, through the swinging door, and onto the shop floor. The warehouse is large, but having worked here for three years, I know it like the back of my hand.

"Ava, you're late!" Scott calls from the corner of the store. I hurry to the checkout counter, fighting the cloud of exhaustion that's lingered since my episode this morning.

"I know, sorry. I got a flat." I flash a smile at the customer standing at the counter, waiting to be helped, while Scott assists someone else. I cram my stuff between the trash can and a box of extra bags at my feet and straighten. The rubber pad beneath my boots alleviates some of the pressure on my tired feet, and I sigh. "Sorry to keep you waiting."

"Things happen," the older man says. The wrinkles around his eyes crinkle with a kind smile. "I hope you got it all sorted."

I huff a laugh. "Luckily, I always carry a spare tube. Learned that lesson years ago."

He chuckles, exposing coffee-stained teeth, and tosses a pack of jerky on top of a pair of leather work gloves, a package of bungee cords, and the batteries he's already set on the counter. "I'm also picking up three fifty-pound bags of chicken feed," he adds.

"You got it." My fingers clack the buttons swiftly. "Did you need help loading the chicken feed?"

The man shakes his head. "I can manage."

"All right then. Your total is $143.76, please."

The man already has his wallet open, and while he inserts his credit card, I bag up his odds and ends for him. Like most of the ranchers around here, his hands are tanned and calloused, his nail beds dirty, and he smells like a mixture of earth and sweat with a subtle hint of aftershave.

"I've heard a dozen stories about goats getting polio in my time," Scott says to the customers in the back. "Not steers, though."

As the receipt prints for the man in front of me, I strain to listen.

"I thought it was rabies at first," a familiar, lighthearted voice replies. "But the boss knew right away what it was." Tony always comes in to buy supplies for the Bennett's ranch, so it's no surprise that he's here. I've known Tony most of my life. He and Knox were older than me in school, but always on the periphery. And we used to have Sunday school together at church. After seeing Mitch earlier, though, thinking about any of them makes my pulse quicken.

"Knox had to put four of them down this morning." Tony grunts like he's heaving something onto one of the loading carts.

His words are . . . shocking. I've heard of polio in hoofed livestock, a brain-altering disease that makes them act a bit loopy from lack of vitamins in their bodies or some such thing. But it's curable *if* you catch it early enough.

I smile at the customer in front of me. "Here's your receipt." I offer it, waiting patiently as he takes his bag.

"Thank you for coming in. You can grab your chicken feed on the way out."

The older man dips his head, all southern and polite. "Have a good day," he says, then walks out the door.

I allow myself another sigh as I catch my breath from rushing to get here, settling into my six-hour shift. I pull my apron out from the cupboard below the dewormers and spermicides on the wall behind me and slip it over my head. While this apron might not be covered in dried ketchup and jam, it's just as dirty, with bits of straw and smeared grease all over it. I welcome it, though. I'm not sure why I love the smell of the farm store, but something about it is comforting. The aroma of leather and wood and grease all mixed together.

Tying my apron behind my back, I eye a bag of Southwest-flavored pretzels hanging on the rack beside me and decide that will have to be my dinner since I didn't have time to pack anything. I ate a few bites at the diner anyway.

"Thiamine injections are behind the counter. Ava will grab what we have in stock and ring you up," Scott says from the back. "We'll get this loaded for you." The loading bay doors swish open and the sound of the squeaking cart wheels disappear outside.

Anticipating Tony, I turn around and scan the vitamin supplements on the wall for Thiamine. Two brands, two different prices, and three quantities of each. Unsure which one Tony will prefer, I grab both. As his cowboy boots clomp on the cement floor, I turn around. I'm not met with Tony's kind and smiling brown eyes, but Knox's hard hazel ones, fixed directly on me.

"You've got to be kidding me." The words escape my lips before I can stop them, and I clamp my mouth shut, praying nothing else mortifying comes out of it.

Knox's eyebrow lifts slightly as he stops at the counter.

The scent of sunshine and leather rushes off him, and a hint of something enticing and crisp, like his deodorant, maybe?

I swallow and silently chide myself because it doesn't matter in the slightest what his deodorant smells like. Knox's expression, on the other hand, does matter, and that tightly set jaw of his and broad, squared shoulders say he's none too happy to see me either.

"Thiamine," I prompt, pushing the two brands toward him. "I'm not sure which one you want."

"All of them," he says without bothering to look at the boxes. He tosses a pen of crazy glue from the rack next to him onto the pile.

"All—both kinds?"

He looks at me in answer. He's just as unnerving and maddening as his father. And yet, I find I can't detest him quite as much, even if he's trying to eviscerate me with his stare. I can't hate Knox because I know what it's like to lose a mother, and somehow I'm the lucky one because I don't have reminders of her death every time I see him.

The scanner beeps over each box as I move through them, and Knox pulls out his wallet. "They're loading two rolls of barbed wire, twelve and a half gauge. Plus two hundred-gallon troughs."

I nod and enter the item numbers into the register. Working at one of the few farm supply stores that serve this area, we sell to everyone in a two-county radius, and I know most SKU codes better than my phone number. "Anything else?"

Knox shakes his head, and I can feel his eyes on me as I total his purchase out, pretending not to notice. "It comes to $531.92," I tell him. Opening a bag for the meds, I set them carefully inside and add the tube of crazy glue. "I'm sorry to hear about your cattle," I say honestly, surprising myself. Not because I don't care but because I've never been one for small talk. Knox must be surprised too, because his brow twitches ever so slightly as our eyes meet.

His jaw clenches under his five o'clock shadow—more golden than brown in the sunlight—and as expected, Knox Bennett says nothing else as I drop his receipt into the bag. He slides his wallet into the back pocket of his Wranglers and, leveling a final hard look at me, he curtly dips his head because it's the polite thing to do, grabs his purchase, and strides out of the store, leaving me a tightly wound mess in his wake.

Once Knox is outside the sliding door, his shoulders deflate a little, if I'm not mistaken, and he removes his Stetson. His short hair is slightly matted from his hat and he makes his way toward his truck.

Tony hollers something, and when I hear the tailgate slam shut, I hurry to the window. I tell myself it's to see Tony and perhaps give him a wave if he happens to look in my direction. But that's a bald-faced lie because my eyes don't leave Knox as he hands Tony the med bag and opens the driver's side door of the F-250.

Knox sets his hat inside and turns to Scott. Whatever Knox says is too low to hear, but it doesn't matter anyway. I wouldn't have heard him. Not when all I can think is I've known Knox my entire life, and he's hated me for a better part of it.

He shakes Scott's hand, and not for the first time, I appreciate what hard work on the ranch has done to Knox's arms. I lie to myself again, as if I might actually believe that checking him out is totally natural due to the lack of men in this town who are my age and still have their teeth. But there's always been something about Knox that's drawn me to him, even if I wish there wasn't.

A faraway memory niggles up from beneath the persistent darkness, and I think of him at church again when we were little. He always wore his dark jeans, t-shirt, and shit stompers, just like he is now. Only back then, he smiled. And he talked to me. More than that, he and Tony stood up for me when they saw Lars bullying me.

Now, Knox doesn't talk to me at all, and I'm not sure what's worse—his silence and the unfading animosity in his eyes, or the wistful hope that if he'd simply tell me off and get it out in the open, I would feel a thousand times better. Holding my breath and waiting around for him to detonate is torturous.

As his truck rumbles to life, Scott heads back inside. The automatic doors open for him and he looks at me, startled to find me standing by the window. "How did his cattle get polio?" I ask, watching the truck pull out of the lot onto the main road.

"Sulfur poisoning from that pond of theirs. He's already lost a dozen of them."

I frown. "That's . . . scary." And it is, especially knowing there are over two hundred now-active volcanoes throughout Texas. Large or small makes no difference. They cause the ground to shake, and now they could be poisoning the water?

Scott grabs a discarded clipboard on the other side of the counter. He's all hard edges and seriousness to look at, but Scott's a softy with one of the biggest hearts I've ever met.

A brown curl falls into his face as he flips a page over with a huff. "Here." Scott shoves the clipboard at me, and his cheeks lift in a facetious, dimpled smile bearing slightly crooked teeth. "Time for inventory."

I groan. "That's what I've been doing all week. Where's Martin?"

"He's in New Orleans."

"What?" Counting inventory might be easy, but every-thing eventually blurs together; I actually miss manual labor at this point.

"Martin's parents retired there last year," Scott explains. "Now that everyone is being relocated along the Gulf Coast, he has to move them back here."

"That's . . . rough. I know his father hasn't been doing well either." An unsettling thought strikes me. "Hey, Scott?"

"Hmm?" He lifts one of the boxes stacked beside the counter and sets it on top.

"You follow all of this Moonie stuff more than I do."

He huffs a laugh. "Moonie stuff?"

"You know, preparedness and survival stuff." Being ex-military, it runs in his blood. Scott's eyes meet mine and I consider how much I don't want to know the answer to my question. "Should we be worried about this relocation? I mean, we're not *that* far from the coast. It's only a few hours away. We'd be safe from a tsunami, right?" I think about bedridden Mavey. Of how screwed I'd be if we had to leave with no money and only one option of where we might be able to go. Not to mention how we'd even get there.

"It's something I've thought about," Scott admits, and he starts tagging each individual pack of vegetable seeds. "But then I remind myself it's the volcanoes we need to be worried about. If they ever do more than grumble, we're not only screwed, we're dead." Though Scott says it lightly, it's the truth, and his amusement quickly fades when he notices my expression. "If anything ever happens, I'll help you and Mavey as much as I can, Ava," he promises, his brown eyes softening with reassurance.

It's then I realize Scott, nearly twenty years older than me, might be the closest thing I have to a friend in this place, and I flash him a watery but grateful smile. Though he hasn't opened up much about his personal life over the years, I know his wife left him when he got out of the army, and this store has been his life ever since.

"All you need to worry about," he continues, "is how many nuts and bolts I have in Hardware." He winks at me.

"Yeah, yeah." I groan for effect. "I'm going."

"Thank you, Ava," he singsongs.

"Yeah, yeah," I repeat playfully. "You can pay me back by giving me Tuesday off."

"And why would I do that?" His voice carries down the aisle.

"Because I have a doctor's appointment in San Antonio. And with the way the bus runs, it will take me all day to get there and back."

"Fine," he says. "But you better bring me another jar of your pickled okra. A fresh batch, nothing you have shoved in the back of your fridge like last time."

I smile to myself. "Deal. I'll even—"

A rumble, so low and deep it's disorienting, emanates around me, and the earth begins to shake under my feet. It's not a helicopter this time. The shelves creak. Glass shatters. Metal clanks against metal—and the windows rattle in a cacophony so deafening I have to clamp my hands over my ears as I run for the door.

Shelves cave in. Chains jangle against each other. Supplies tumble from the walls, and one of the halogen lights suspended overhead snaps loose, swinging back and forth.

When the rumbling ebbs and the shaking ceases, the squeaking, swinging lights are all that fill the sudden quiet.

Scott and I stare at one another, eyes wide and chests heaving. "Are you all right?" he rasps.

I nod, raking my fingers through my hair, swallowing thickly. "Yeah—yes. That's the third time this week."

"Only bigger," Scott adds, and the look in his eyes is one of dread because we both know that's not likely the last or biggest either.

With a curse, Scott peers around his store, now in complete shambles. He's known for years it might only be a matter of time before Mother Earth decides to wreak havoc on our little sleepy town—we all have. But after all this time, it's starting to feel more real than ever.

"Come on," I say, bending down to pick up the cans of cat food that have fallen around my feet. I'm well aware it's better to keep myself busy and my mind from spinning.

Until now, skepticism about what the future holds has been relatively easy, but it's getting harder to ignore. The increased earthquakes. The water at the Bennett's ranch. What's next? I hastily stack can after can as panic nudges the edge of my mind, all the things I'm not prepared for taking shape.

"Ava."

What about Mavey? I can't move her. She's too sick.

Julio's call earlier resurfaces.

"Ava," Scott says more firmly, and I stop, my arms full of Purina One, and look at him.

"Go home," he says gently, peering down at me crouched on the floor.

"But . . . your store."

"It will all be here tomorrow. You should go check on Mavey."

My eyes widen. "Mavey." I nod. Yes, of course, I should go check on Mavey. Rising to my feet, I run my sweaty hands down my apron. She's probably terrified.

"Call me if you need anything," he adds, and quickly, I untie my apron as I step over supplies strewn throughout the aisle. I'm already counting down the minutes in my mind that it will take me to ride home as I reach for my bag and phone under the counter.

Scott takes my arm. "Ava."

I look at him, unaware he was even beside me.

"Be careful, okay?" Suddenly, Scott doesn't look forty-two. He looks years older than that and beyond exhausted, as if he's already lived through whatever comes next. He squeezes my arm like he might never see me again, and another wave of dread washes over me.

"You too," I whisper. "I'll check in when I can."

Scott nods half-heartedly, and without another moment's pause, I run for the back, heading for my bike, and pray Mavey is okay.

FOUR
KNOX

TONY HAS BEEN GONE FOR HOURS, AND THE SUN SETS AS I stretch the last of the barbed wire around the final post in the west paddock. The last thing I need is any of the sick cattle endangering those who haven't shown signs of disease yet.

I crank the wire stretcher two more times, feeling the burn in my arms after a hundred yards of installation. I'm accustomed to hard work—it's all we do around this place—but the day seems to have crawled by, and now that all I can do today is done, exhaustion settles over me. My t-shirt is drenched with sweat, my hair is matted to my head beneath my work hat, and a cool shower and ice-cold beer in my hand has never sounded sweeter.

When I'm finished wrapping the final piece of wire, I rise to my feet, sighing as I tip my hat back and wipe the sweat from my brow with the back of my arm. All it took was three hundred feet of barb pricks through my gloves and scratches down my forearms, but I'm done, and I scrutinize the fence with tired eyes. It's not my best work, but the steers are safe from drinking the pond water that's been poisoning them for days.

Running my teeth over my lip, I toss my pliers into the crate on the back of the ATV and roll what's left of the barbed wire spool around the spinner on the back. Finally finished, I pull my gloves off and glance at the six steers I gave injections to today as they mill around in the corner of the paddock.

While a part of me thinks I should've seen the signs of sulfur poisoning sooner, I know there's only so much I could've done. And with the increased earthquakes, I have a feeling the sulfur levels in the groundwater worsened only recently and fast, if the twelve dead I already have are any indication.

Removing my hat, I run my arm across my forehead and temple again and squint toward the house. The lights are on, which means my father is finished loading the four Angus steers we have left for San Antonio. I just pray they don't start showing signs of poisoning by the time they get to the client. He's already behind schedule as it is.

My gaze shifts to the sick cattle again. Two of them pace, acting confused, but they aren't getting worse, which is all I can ask for at this point. Each steer we lose is one to three grand we'll never recoup, depending on size and breed, and with the way the economy is going, we can't afford to bleed more money, or we'll lose this place entirely.

I glance at the pump house by the barn. The well is filtered and separate from the pond, but the scent in the air is a constant reminder of how bad the sulfur has gotten, and I'm not sure how long the filtration system will be enough to keep our drinking water safe.

One of the steers snorts in the pen, stirring my thoughts. If I had any energy left, and my muscles weren't heavy with fatigue, I would burn the dead cattle tonight to keep the scavengers away—I *should* burn them—but I'm spent. And with

Tony down south to help his mother, whose house was damaged in this afternoon's quake, I'm all I've got.

Chugging what's left of the water in my thermos, I make a mental note of a few final things to do before I can call it a day.

I check the gate, keeping what's left of the herd separate from the sick, and I climb onto the ATV to head back toward the barn. I'm about to switch it on when my phone rings in my back pocket. Pulling my cell out, I glance at the screen. One missed call and a picture of Tony with a shit-eating grin from over a decade ago flashes with his name.

I answer with a frown because if he's called me twice now, there's something wrong, or he'll be longer than he thought. "Everything all right?"

"I was about to ask you the same thing." His voice is reedy with apprehension.

My frown deepens, and I glance toward the house. "Why?" He hesitates so long my skin crawls with unease. I'm not sure I can take more bad news tonight. "Tony—"

"Haven't you seen the news?"

I glance around the ranch, cast in inky dusk. "I just finished the fence. Why? What happened?" When Tony doesn't answer, I can't turn the quad on fast enough. "Tony!" I bark.

"A tsunami hit the West Coast," he finally answers, and I can barely hear him over the drone of the engine.

"What?" I pull the phone away from my ear and stare at the missed call in the notification bar, clicking it to see who it's from. Not Tony, *Kellen.* My brother's name stares back at me, and my heart plummets. The near-constant sadness and anger filling me since my brother left is drowned out by relief.

"He called me," I rasp, putting the phone back to my ear.

"That means he's okay." I say the words aloud to reassure us both.

"Good. I was hoping you'd heard something from him."

"I gotta go." I scan the ranch through a new lens. "I'll call you later."

"Do that. I'm serious."

"I will. Thanks." Ending the call, I shove my phone into my back pocket, turn the throttle, and haul ass down the dirt road. Even if Kellen is okay, he might as well be a world away in San Francisco, and nausea churns as I reach the house.

The quad skids to a halt. I jump off and jog for the front door, flinging the screen open as I barrel inside. Then, I stop short. My father stands in front of the seventy-inch flat screen with his coffee thermos gripped in his hands, staring at an aerial view of San Francisco. It's gone, and I gape at the submerged city in horror.

1,700-foot tsunami decimates the California coast.

The ticker flashes at the bottom of the footage, and I read it over and over, trying to comprehend.

"Wait," I say, stepping closer. The footage time stamp says it was this afternoon. "No. No. No." I pull up Kellen's missed call from lunchtime, and my eyes blur. He'd called me before the tsunami, which means . . .

My mind numbs over as I stare at images of toppled high rises, floating debris, and overturned ships in the city drowned in gray seawater.

The news flashes images of Los Angeles next, then Seattle, and back to San Francisco.

I tap my home screen to life. My mind spins a million miles a minute as I press send, hold my breath, and begin to pace the living room, waiting for my brother to answer. It rings and rings, and all the while, my father stands statue-still in front of the television, wordless.

There's no voicemail and no answer. "Come on," I urge, and ending the call, I try again. I glance at the ham radio on the bookshelf. Kellen doesn't have one, and I'm not sure ours is powerful enough to reach California even if he did, so I press CALL on my phone again.

"Don't bother."

I pause mid-step, phone partially to my ear, and look at my father. "What?" His back is to me.

"No one can survive that." He says it with a shocking level of indifference.

"You don't know that—"

"Don't be a damn fool." He points to the aerial shots of the coast.

"Kellen might not have been in the city. He might've been somewhere else," I grit out, trying to convince us both. But I'm too astonished to think much of anything as I realize my father even *looks* unaffected. "Are you seriously going to pretend you don't care in the slightest that Kellen could be injured or dead?" The words barely croak out of me as I step closer to him in his silence—so close he has no choice but to look at me. "You can act like a coldhearted son of a bitch all you want, but you're the one who is a fool." I point to the washed-up city. "He is your *son!*"

"Was," my father corrects with a bone-chilling sharpness. "He chose to leave—"

"You all but shunned him from this family!" I shout.

When my father looks at me, a smirk lifts the corner of his mouth, sending chills over my skin. "Then why don't *you* ever speak to him?" He jabs his finger into my chest.

Fear, anger, and regret knot inside me with each of his words.

"Why the hell are you so pissed at him if it's all my fucking fault? Huh?" My father's eyes shimmer with emotion, but not the good kind. "Why do you act like he abandoned you and never answer his calls?"

I hate the truth of my father's words. "Because he *did* abandon me!" I shout back, my chest heaving. It's the first time I've admitted out loud that my brother ran away and left me here, alone with our father and enough grief to fill every room in this giant fucking house.

"That's what I thought," he mutters.

"Stop it!" I demand, tired of Mitch Bennett's heartless bullshit. "Stop acting like you don't care. Like you're indifferent that your oldest son could be dead—"

"He's *not* my son!" Fisting the neck of my t-shirt, my father shoves me into the wall, his coffee-laced breath a sweltering punch in the face. "He's not my son," he repeats. His gaze is wild as it shifts over me.

"Because he's gay. Say it, at least. Say the words," I insist.

But he doesn't say it. My father is scared, no matter what he says. I see it in his eyes—the fear of admitting to himself his regrets are insurmountable and he's drowning in them.

His fist tightens in my shirt as his body vibrates with rage and all the grief he's never been man enough to face.

"Hit me, old man," I dare him. "Take all your self-loathing out on me, like you used to. But remember, I hit harder than you do now."

I can hear the protest of his teeth as he grinds them together, battling the urge to pound on me. With a final shove, my father steps away, his jaw sharp as glass and his chest heaving. Without another word, he stalks to the front door, grabs his Stetson and leather jacket, then he flings the screen door open and stomps out into the night.

"Really?" I call after him. "You're *still* going to San Antonio?"

But my father doesn't reply.

"At least keep your radio on!" I shout.

His dually roars to life, the trailer creaking as it jerks into motion, and only as he disappears down the drive do I allow myself to exhale. Tears burn the backs of my eyes as I lean against the wall, my shoulders slumped.

I can't keep doing this. Every day it eats away at me, and I get further and further away from the person I want to be and the life I want to live. I'm tired of cleaning up my father's messes and running a ranch that is barely afloat.

I don't know how long I stare at the muted television and the helicopter view of San Francisco submerged in murky water. But it's long enough that I feel the heaviness of it all piling up and weighing me down. Irrepressible rage and utter helplessness consume me as I realize how alone in this I actually am.

My gaze darts to our family photo on the mantel. I think of life ten years ago and life now. First Mom, then Kellen.

Ava's face comes to mind. Those amber eyes have looked at me with anger, sadness, and regret. The face of someone whose family is responsible for what's become of mine. A woman who evokes so many conflicting emotions when in my presence that numbness is all I feel. And I'm so goddamn tired.

In two long strides, I pick the frame up and throw it at the hearth. The glass shatters against the stone, and miraculously, I feel lighter. But my relief is momentary and quickly swallowed by despondency. I have no idea if my brother is alive or if I will ever see him again, and I've spent the last ten years sulking.

Lifting my phone to my ear, I press CALL again. It rings

and rings before I hang up and try again. I don't know how many times I call Kellen, but at some point, I realize he isn't going to answer. Probably never again.

I walk to the bookshelf and turn the ham radio on, the volume all the way up, just in case he tries to reach me. Then I stop at the wet bar across the living room. I uncork the decanter and down a glass of whiskey. As I pour another, I tell myself that if Kellen *is* alive, he'll come home. He has to.

FIVE
AVA

Mavey's shallow, rattling breaths fill the double-wide trailer, and as I lean against the doorframe of her cramped bedroom, I stew, knowing that in a matter of hours, she will be gone.

Blair, her hospice nurse, checks her vitals, but it's only a formality. Mavey is dying, and if her steady decline in the past twelve hours is any indication, she won't last the night. It's all I can do to hold back the tears pricking my eyes since I walked in and saw that concerned look on Blair's face. Not concern for Mavey, but for me.

We've been preparing for this for weeks. It started with three dreadful words: I have cancer. And it has been inching into our lives ever since; a heavy storm cloud that fills every room and weighs down every conversation.

I thought my world had ended when I was told my mom died during a Moonie riot robbery at the mini-mart she worked at. But *knowing* death is coming and watching it eat away at the one person you love most is torture. Seeing the woman who raised me when she didn't have to lie in bed like this is the most difficult thing I've ever had to stomach. And strangely, the most relieving. No more pain. No more fretting. No more holding our breaths, wondering if she'll never wake up again.

Blair turns off Mavey's bedside table lamp, leaving her to sleep in the moonlight filtering in from the window. She's about to close the drapes when I step inside.

"Leave them, please." I glance at Mavey. She looks thinner than I realized in the shadows of night. Perhaps it's because, in seeing her daily, I haven't noticed her gradual change in appearance. Or, I simply didn't want to. "She loves looking at the moon."

Blair doesn't bother pointing out that Mavey won't be awake to see the moon tonight. She looks back down at her patient, brushes a gray strand of hair from her brow, and then Blair collects her things from the room.

I don't know if hospice nurses are supposed to be so kind and attentive—to look at their patients with affection—or if it's because loving Mavey is so easy.

Blair's features soften as she steps out of Mavey's room. "I'll stay—"

"No." I shake my head. "I know you're short-staffed and you've got other house calls to make. Besides, I know what to do, and I'll call you if I really need to," I promise. "We'll be okay."

Blair lifts her hand and squeezes my shoulder, and the faint scent of her floral shampoo fills my nose. "She doesn't feel any pain," Blair promises. Her eyes are red, and I know it's from the long day she's had, driving from town to town to check on her patients after the earthquake earlier today.

"Thank you," I whisper, grateful to see the furrow smoothed from Mavey's brow.

Blair scans the house—the small bathroom behind me, and the living room, cluttered with clean laundry I haven't had time to fold. She stares at the discarded medical supplies and equipment no longer in use. "Are you sure—"

"I'm sure." I give her a quiet, pleading look because the last thing I want to do is stand here arguing about it.

Blair concedes and glances at the old Formica island in the kitchen. "I left a few brochures for you."

"I saw," I say before Blair can coerce me into another support group. "But . . ." I shake my head. "I don't know how long I'll stay here once she's gone." And that's the truth. There will be nothing for me in Sonora anymore—nothing but painful memories.

Blair shifts her medical bag from one hand to the other. "Will you go to your uncle's?" she asks, not as a nurse but as a concerned friend.

"I don't know," I admit. "I've considered a dozen places with better job opportunities, but with everywhere getting so unstable . . . I might not have a choice." Saying that out loud only makes my heart hurt more, and fear prickles the edge of numbness. *I'll be in it all alone now.*

Blair's form blurs as tears burn the backs of my eyes again. As if she can sense it, Blair continues toward the door, giving me my space.

"Get some rest, Ava," she says, her last order of the night. With that, she steps out of the house, leaving me in a suffocatingly quiet, dim-lit trailer with the only person in the world I have left dying right before my eyes.

Wiping the tears from my cheeks, I walk into Mavey's room and pull the kitchen chair Blair had shoved in the corner closer to the hospice bed.

"So." I breathe, sniffling as I sit down. I take Mavey's cool hand in mine and stare at it. It's frail, just like she is, and her skin is so thin the veins in her hand bulge. "You would have a fit if you saw how long your fingernails are," I muse, and before I know what I'm doing, I walk into the bathroom, open the medicine cabinet, and grab Mavey's nail file and clippers.

"Julio called me today," I tell her, heading back to her bedside. Mavey's shallow breaths are her only response. "I didn't answer—well, he called while I was at the diner, but still . . . I haven't called him back." Gently, I lift her palm into mine, pull a tissue from the box on her bedside table, and flatten it beneath her hand before I start to clip.

"You used to do this for me," I remember with a smile. "You wanted me to feel pretty on the days that were the roughest." Growing up without a mom made the whole *girly thing* difficult. I had Julio, but he was a farmworker. He was always dirty, we were always poor, and we never had nice things, let alone *girly* things.

Tears fill my eyes until I can no longer see. "I know you'd want to feel pretty right now, too."

Hastily, I wipe the moisture from my eyes with the back of my hand and focus on her nails. When I finish clipping, I file the edges to smooth them, and suddenly I'm grinning. "I'm going to paint them pink," I tell her. "Fussy Flamingo, your favorite." It's the color she always wanted to paint mine, even if I can't stand a single shade of pink. Of course, Mavey never painted *her* fingernails at all, and that makes me smile even more.

Gruff as she was, though, Mavey always seemed to know when I needed her. She had a way of appearing in my life, like an angel, even if I'm not sure I've ever believed in them.

Whatever Mavey's reasons, she always kept to herself, save for when it came to an orphaned little girl. I think it's because she lost someone very dear to her before I met her, and she couldn't bear to form more relationships than she had to for fear of what might happen. For some reason, however, she took a shine to me. Or, rather, she pitied me, knowing I had lost my mother and lived with my drunk uncle in the trailer next door. When he was arrested after the accident, Mavey adopted me—didn't even think twice about it. And it's been the two of us ever since.

Nostrils flaring, I blink tears away, blow the file dust from her hand, and analyze my work. The tips of her nails are square, the way she likes, and the ends are flush with the tips of her fingers.

"It's nice to see they are still clean," I tell her, and rising to my feet, I head back into the bathroom to search the drawers for the horrible pink nail polish I know is in here somewhere.

I try to be quiet as I rustle through the cupboards, even if I know it doesn't matter; Mavey is on enough morphine that she'd sleep through the end of the world without stirring. After the big earthquake today, there's an immense sense of comfort in that.

"Ah-ha!" I smile when I find the bottle, and wiping a rogue tear from my cheek, I walk back into her room. I re-situate myself beside her hospice bed and can't help my grin. "Oh, to see your face," I tease her, but it takes all the elbow grease I have just to open the damn bottle that's been dried shut for years. When I finally break the seal and pull the brush out, it's thick and goopy with old paint. It makes no difference, though, and I start with her pinky finger first.

"I don't think I can go to Julio's," I confess, my thoughts drifting back to my uncle. "I know it's the easiest thing to do, at least until I get my life on track, but I don't know if I can handle dealing with the past on top of everything else. Not yet, at least." I'm not sure there's ever a good time to reunite with the man who single-handedly ruined your life, anyway.

Though I've never been great at coloring within the lines,

let alone painting fingernails with any sort of finesse, I take my time, determined to make Mavey's nails look as good as I can. As I watch the paint strokes, my mind drifts to *after.* After Mavey is gone. After there is nothing left for me here.

We knew it was coming, and even if I have little to no money saved, it's a lot easier to care for my own needs when I don't have to worry about Mavey's too. I'm twenty-five. I'll figure it all out. Still, my chest squeezes, and I straighten, clearing my throat as if it will chase the emotions away.

When I'm finished painting, I pull back and assess the damage I've done. "Absolutely horrendous." I scoff at my lack of ability to do even this. "I think we can safely cross a nail salon job off the potential career list."

The moon rises higher in the sky and the shadows move through Mavey's room. When her fingernails are the color of the wild freesias that grow by the front steps in the springtime, and I've cleaned up the paint on her cuticles as best I can, I cap the polish and set it on her bedside, suddenly exhausted.

"You won't be too sore with me if your toes don't match, will you?" Mavey responds with another rattled exhale in her blissful sleep, and I study her profile. Strong features—Roman in a way that makes me wish I could see what she looked like in her youth. But she never had photographs. I didn't realize how strange that was until I went to summer camp, and the girls all had photos of their families, friends, and pets. That was the first and only year I ever went to camp. I wasn't the most popular kid in town. Having the same blood running through my veins as the man who killed one of the town's most beloved schoolteachers made me tainted to everyone but Mavey.

Carefully, I take her palm in mine, avoiding Mavey's

drying fingernails as best I can, and trace the protruding veins in her hand.

"I'm going to miss you," I confess. I've thought about it a million times, but Mavey and I didn't talk about feelings, so I never actually said the words out loud to her.

Kissing her hand, I let the tears fall because I know I can't stop them. I don't *want* to stop them, and a part of me wishes I could crawl up there with her, fall into a deep sleep, and never wake up again. It would be a kinder fate than whatever's left of this cruel place. Where people are hateful because they can be. Where you can't earn a decent wage or access the healthcare you need without running yourself into the ground to get it.

Resting my forehead against Mavey's hand, I let the sound of her rattled breaths and my sobs fill the room until I can no longer keep my eyes open.

SIX
KNOX

Daylight pours through my bedroom window, practically blinding me as I peel my eyes open.

I cringe and run my palms over my face. Today's going to be rough—I have a splitting headache, and I haven't even gotten out of bed yet. Groaning, I sit up and glance around my room. My clothes are discarded on the floor, my hat is dangling from the chair in the corner, and a mostly empty bottle of Buffalo Trace sits on my nightstand.

"Great," I grumble, pressing my palms into my eyes, thankful I had the wherewithal to keep my boxer briefs on so that Liz, our housekeeper, doesn't get an eyeful of something she can't unsee when she pops her head in to check on me. That she hasn't yet is surprising, especially since I'm usually up before dawn. But I'm too groggy to care.

Rising to my feet, I scour the room for my phone. It's not on the charger or my side table, but a part of me can't think about it right now. I have to piss like there's no tomorrow, and I drag myself into the bathroom to take a leak.

The last thing I remember is finishing what was in the decanter and searching the cupboards for another bottle. It's one of three things my father is never short of—a curled lip, coffee, and bourbon.

Gripping the wall to hold myself upright, I rest my head on my bicep, groaning because peeing has never felt so euphoric. When I'm finished, I brush my teeth, feeling slightly less dead, and head into my room for a pair of sweats. I shut my drawer and pull them on before heading into the kitchen for a glass of water.

"Liz!" I call out. Aside from the low chatter on the radio, the house is far too quiet and empty. She's not singing in another room or walking heavily and hastily through the house as she cleans or does the laundry.

Lucy pads up the porch and she nuzzles the screen door open, which apparently I never shut last night. "What trouble have you been getting into?" I rub her ears and face as she sidles up to me for morning affection, and I pause in the living room. I take in the disarray from yesterday. The broken frame and disheveled couch. The empty decanter on the coffee table. The television is still cycling through devastating images of what's happening around the world, and suddenly, I recall the depressing reality of my life.

Lucy leads me to her food bowl, which I fill before searching the house for my phone again. How many times did I call Kellen last night before giving up? And it's obvious Liz hasn't been here at all this morning, which makes me frown. Every day, like clockwork, she is here. Save for Tony, she's been the most consistent person in my life for the last ten years.

Instead of going down that rabbit hole again, I walk into the kitchen and pull a glass from the cupboard. Only, I stop short and stare out the window toward the steer paddock. I should have fed the animals already. I should've checked on the cattle to see if they are getting any better, or worse.

Scowling, I fill the glass a quarter full before I pause again, this time bringing the glass to my nose for a sniff. It doesn't smell like sulfur yet, but I'd rather not test my luck. Dumping it out, I turn for the fridge and grab the Brita filter Liz always keeps filled to the brim.

I chug the entire glass down, desperate for the cool water to slake my parched throat. It's perfection and rejuvenating, and I'm tempted to pour another glass, but I second-guess the decision. We need to take stock of our water situation before I start drinking all the filtered water we have.

We. I shake my head. I can imagine my father's face when he returns from San Antonio to discover one more problem to wade through.

Setting the glass on the quartz countertop, I turn for the television. Images of Yellowstone and the smoking volcano are downright terrifying. But I'm not surprised; people have been evacuated for miles surrounding the national park for over a year. And Moonies have been waiting for the damn thing to erupt for decades.

The earthquakes, the tsunamis, the erratic and severe weather patterns, and the rumbling volcanoes breathed back to life—the warnings have been circulating my entire life. Still, it's unsettling because I never thought any of it actually *would* happen. At least, not until I was old and gray, long after my father was buried in the earth.

I imagined the end would come out of nowhere. I'd probably be sitting on the porch and abruptly consumed by one of the lava pits underneath me opening up and swallowing me whole. I hadn't anticipated the earth's turmoil to show up now, and like this. That I would be two years shy of thirty. That I would have the weight of the ranch on my shoulders, facing the possible death of my brother, and what it would feel like—how full of regret I would be that I had blamed him for so many things.

I never considered we might lose the ranch and cattle. And now, our clean water supply. I never considered so many things, and suddenly, it's all happening far too quickly, and despite the weight of it all bearing down on me, it's as if my mind is barely catching up.

An urgency to inventory our supplies and batten down the hatches for the shitstorm I feel growing on the horizon grips hold of me. I walk to the couch to search for my phone. My Uncle Mason and Aunt Beth have been preparing for this for years. I always thought they were the crazy ones—Moonies of epic proportions, like many others who were alive when the asteroid hit. Only now, it's them I want to speak with the most. They'll know what I should prioritize. They will help me sort through my bubbling panic. I'll have a plan in place when my father returns, and we can divide and conquer.

More aerial views from around the country flash across the television, and hope rears its dangerous head as I wonder how many survivors have been found in San Francisco since last night. I lift the cushions, searching each cranny for my phone, and glance at the television again. An entire city has fallen into a sinkhole.

I drop the cushion in my hand. Trees, homes, roads, cars, buildings—it's a never-ending view of a crumbled city. When I recognize the Tower of the Americas protruding from the rubble, I grip the couch as I stagger down. Mind in a fog, I feel for the remote discarded on the floor and turn the volume up with a shaking hand.

"—it extends the length of the city," a female voice reports from the helicopter hovering over San Antonio. "It's so wide, I can't see where it ends from here." The horror that rings in each word echoes through my head, and I inhale a ragged breath. "From what we've gathered so far, which is very little," she adds, "the sinkhole is easily fifty-miles wide—that's the breadth of San Antonio itself. Some say the hole is up to a dozen-miles deep. It's devastating and there is no doubt it will take search and rescue months to sort through the rubble."

"No." I don't know if I say it or if it escapes as a breath. Before I can fully process, I'm tearing the couch apart and shoving furniture out of the way, searching for my phone. I sprint for my room and pull the blankets from my bed until I finally spot my cell phone in the twisted sheets. Only eleven percent battery and no missed calls. Nothing from Tony or Kellen. Nothing from my father or Liz.

The phone is slick in my sweaty hands, and I can barely catch my breath as I plop down on my bed and dial my father's number, certain he's too goddamn stubborn to die and that his phone will be on. After what happened to my mother, neither of us ever turn them off for fear we'll miss an urgent call. But when I press send, the call goes straight to voicemail.

"Fuck!" I brace my elbows on my thighs, raking my hands over my face and through my short hair. "No, no, no, no, no!" I try calling him again because my father is right; I'm a fool, and it goes to voicemail just like before.

"You stubborn son of a bitch," I grumble. Hurrying to the radio, I turn the volume up and listen to the call signs coming through and their conversations. The chances of hearing my father's voice or him hearing mine are slim, but I wish with every fiber of my being that, for once in his life, he actually listened to me and left his radio on in his truck.

He'd have to be in his truck.

"—city is in chaos. Over."

"Copy that, N5TXY. I'm in Austin, just a couple of hours away. Communications are down here too. Over."

"I haven't heard from anyone in San Antonio since it happened. Have you? Over."

"Negative, N5TXY. The Texas ARES has designated 147.180 MHz as the primary repeater for emergency communications. They've gotta have more information for us. I'm going to check it out. Over."

"Roger that. I'll switch over to 147.180 MHz and standby."

I switch over as well, but it's more chatter, people trying to figure out what is going on but having no idea, and I'm wasting time standing here.

I might hate my father most days, but he's all I have left. I pull on whatever discarded clothes are on my floor, keenly aware my only option is to go to San Antonio—whatever's left of it—to find him.

SEVEN
AVA

MY EYES BURN AND MY VISION IS BLURRY. NOT BECAUSE I'M crying—I've cried all I can since Mavey passed in the night —but because I haven't closed my eyes to sleep in over twenty-four hours.

At first, she looked like she was only sleeping, tucked snuggly in her bed with her painted fingernails lifeless at her side. But as the morning ticks by, and the sun rises higher in the sky, something about her appearance changes. Or is it my perception of her? My head yells at me to stop standing in the doorway, staring at her.

Mavey loathed the idea of anyone seeing her in night-clothes, so I dressed her in her favorite gardening top and braided her hair back. Now, waiting for the paramedics to come take her body away, I feel empty. Listless.

I glance at the digital clock at her bedside and realize it's been nearly two hours since I called for someone to come. It's only then I consider the quake early this morning might've had more ramifications than I realized. Had it even broken a five on the Richter scale? Or had I been in too much of a daze to fully grasp how big it was? It took four tries to reach an operator, and considering Mavey is already gone, I question whether she's a priority right now and if they are coming at all.

A pounding at the door makes me jump.

Exhaling, I glance at Mavey one last time before I allow the paramedics to take her from our home forever. My heart squeezes at the thought. This is real. She is really dead.

Barely able to breathe, I wipe an errant tear from my cheek, and bracing myself, I open the door. Immediately, I straighten. "Scott?"

He takes the sight of me in and his face crumples.

"I know this is Texas," I start, running my hand over my nose, raw from wiping the snot away. "But why is there a pistol holstered at your hip?"

"Because I don't trust anyone," he says. Glancing past me, the wariness in his gaze prickles over my skin. "Is she gone?" he asks solemnly.

I nod, my brow furrowing with concern. I don't like the tension creasing his brow and deepening the lines webbing his eyes. "What happened?" I step aside for him to come in the trailer. I have no idea if that's a weird thing to do with Mavey's body in the adjacent room, but if Scott minds, he doesn't say anything.

"We need to get out of here." He scans the living room. "San Antonio is gone."

I balk at that. "Gone? What do you mean, *gone*?"

"That quake this morning was from the growing sinkhole that swallowed the whole damn city."

I don't know if the color drains from my face, but whatever numbness I was feeling is replaced with anxiety instead.

"People are fleeing Fredericksburg, Junction—even

Austin," Scott explains, running his hands through his shaggy hair. Had he any family here, he would be worrying about them right now, but he doesn't. Scott's here, making sure I'm okay, and I've never been more grateful because I'm not okay —not in the slightest. As my mind swims, trying to catch up, I feel like I might throw up. Or break into pieces. Or both.

Scott helps himself to a glass in the kitchen. "We're getting inundated with people passing through, and terrified people are dangerous." He takes a gulp of water, then sputters and practically drops the glass as if it punched him in the face. "Sulfur," he murmurs, and when his eyes meet mine, they are grave and weary. "Ava, if you have a place to go, you need to leave. Now."

Unbidden, my eyes shift to Mavey's room.

"She's gone," he says gently. At least as gently as he can, given the circumstances. "She wouldn't want you to stay here and put yourself at unneeded risk. Things are going to get worse."

"How do you know?" I breathe.

"Two tours in Afghanistan, and having a veteran father who spent the last twelve years of his life panicked about scarcity, that's how."

My vision blurs. If I leave this trailer, I won't ever see Mavey again. Even if a distant part of me screams that I wasn't going to anyway.

"Ava." Scott gently takes my upper arm, and I squeeze my eyes shut to hold back the tears. They eke out anyway, and a cry bubbles from my throat. "I know," Scott whispers, pulling me into his arms.

It's a gesture I didn't realize I'd needed so desperately, and I grip Scott's t-shirt in my fists. "It hurts," I tell him as the emptiness threatens to swallow me whole.

"I know it does," he whispers, leaning his cheek against

my head. "But you're going to be okay." He says it with such certainty, I huff a laugh and let go of him. "Do you have a place to go?"

Wiping more tears from my eyes, I take a deep breath and think about Julio. He's all I have left now. "Yeah, I do. But —" I shake my head, wondering how long of a bike ride that will be. Then I realize I can't leave yet, and panic starts clawing into place. "I need my prescription." I imagine hordes of people between me and the pharmacy and my pulse races. "Scott, I have to get my meds."

He rubs my arm. "We'll go get them," he promises. "You go to the Pharm House, right?"

I nod.

"Good. We'll take the back roads to get to the plaza. The militias are out. I've heard them all over the radio, so the fewer people we see, the better." Scott's words are tinged with more than caution, they're filled with fear. I tilt my head, uncertain I want to know why. Still, I ask. "What happened, Scott? What did you see out there?"

"Other than swarmed gas stations and more traffic than I've *ever* seen through the center of this town? Road rage. A man trying to break up a fight and getting knocked out with a tire iron. People with guns strapped to their hips and across their backs. None of it makes me feel warm and fuzzy inside," he says. "We'll get your prescription and supplies and get out of town."

"But, your store—"

"Aside from the supplies it allows me to take, it can't save me, Ava. Not from whatever is coming next. I heard some folks saying the sinkhole is getting bigger," Scott continues, nodding outdoors. "I have no idea if that's true, but with the water turned to shit"—he glances at the faucet— "and everyone coming this way, we're no longer safe here.

We need to get out of town as soon as possible. It's only going to get harder the longer we wait. I'll take you wherever you need to go."

"But what about you?" I shake my head, refusing to be more of a burden to this man than I've already been the past three years, between my special medical needs and unpredictable work schedule with Mavey being so sick.

"I have a brother in Missouri," he explains. "But I'll take you where you need to go first."

"Julio's place," I confess. "In Sweetwater." Assuming it will still be there. I don't say that part out loud though, too worried to give the thought voice.

Scott swallows, his scruffy cheek clenching. "Is that where you want to go, to Julio's place? You can always come with me."

I shake my head. "No, I—I should go to Sweetwater. Julio has a small orchard there, and he's been asking me to come for years."

Scott stares at me, skeptical.

"He's the only family I have here, Scott. Even if I knew my mom's family in Mexico, how would I get there?" I shrug. "I have to go to Julio's. It feels wrong otherwise."

Scott knows my determination and must realize it's not worth arguing about. He lets the matter go and holds up my messenger bag. "Pack whatever you need and say your goodbyes." He glances toward Mavey's room.

The tension in my neck dissolves, and my shoulders sag at the reminder. I nod and take my pack from him.

"I'll wait outside." Scott turns to leave.

"Thanks, Scott." Pursing my lips, I try to smile. "For coming. For checking on me." Gratitude, acute and overwhelming, settles in the longer he stares at me, and I swallow the emotion growing thicker in my throat.

"Of course." With that, Scott leaves me in the trailer that has been my home for the past ten years.

Striding through the living room, I stop in my bedroom doorway and stare at my things. A bed hastily made when I woke up at dawn yesterday for my shift at the diner. A hamper of dirty laundry at the foot of the bed and a basket of clean clothes beside it with days-old wrinkles. The lingering scent of my shampoo from my last shower fills the air. Or is that only the memory of it?

Scott's Jeep Wrangler rumbles to life outside, reminding me he's waiting, and I stride to my dresser and collect the necessities, dropping them into my bag one by one: deodorant, lip balm, hair ties, and hand cream I know I'll regret leaving behind.

I turn for my bed and kneel down, reaching underneath it for a backpack I haven't used since high school. Unzipping it, I pull the old loose-leaf papers and a notebook out, then walk back to my dresser. Pulling the drawer open so hard it nearly falls out completely, I stare at my things.

I need underwear, I tell myself, and grab a handful. Then a few sports bras because they're the most comfortable, socks, and a handful of well-worn tank tops and t-shirts. Already wearing a pair of jeans and my combat boots, I grab a pair of shorts and an extra pair of jeans from the next drawer, then stuff in two long sleeves, praying my pack will zip closed.

What sort of clothes does one need when fleeing the end of the world? What's the point if we're all going to die? If I'd had the extra funds and time to invest in bug-out bags, insurance plans, and survival classes, I might actually know what to do. But I have no idea.

When I finally get my pack zipped, I hurry into the bathroom for my comb, toothbrush, minty paste, and razor before

I scour the drawers and shelves for whatever meds I can find that aren't already in my bag. The fact that I only have enough for another day or two at most puts me on edge, so I would gladly take an expired stash at this point. But I find nothing other than expired birth control from three years ago.

I glance at the shampoo and soap in the shower, wondering if I have room for them. Deciding I'll regret it if I don't bring them, I grab them from the shower, then snag a fresh bar of soap from under the sink.

As I turn to leave, I catch sight of myself in the mirror and stop. I look more haggard than I ever have, with dark circles under my brown, red-rimmed eyes. My tanned cheeks are smeared with mascara from crying. My hair is a tangled mess. It looks like I've neglected myself for a week straight.

I hastily wipe the makeup from under my eyes and do a final scan of my room and all I'm leaving behind. It looks like a whirlwind came through in a matter of minutes, but I'll never be in this place again to care about that.

I stare at the photo of my mom and me taken on my seventh birthday, a few months before she was shot during the robbery. I don't care that I never knew my dad, or that I don't have a picture of Julio, but that I don't have one of Mavey to take with me makes my heart ache with sadness all over again.

Refusing to slow down or dwell on anything else that will break me, I cross my room in three strides, pry the backing off the picture of my mom, and toss the frame onto the bed. I slip the picture into the outer pocket of my bag and grab my bomber jacket from the closet. The baseball cap Mavey got me two birthdays ago glimmers on the top shelf. *Toxic Positivity* taunts me in bold, rainbow lettering, and I take that with me, too.

With a final glance behind me, I drape my messenger bag

across my chest and shrug into my backpack, don my cap, and then head out of my room.

I don't look at Mavey's room, knowing it will only make things harder, and I force myself out the door, locking it shut —for Mavey's sake, I tell myself—behind me.

EIGHT
KNOX

I GLANCE INTO THE REARVIEW MIRROR, ENSURING LUCY ISN'T following me as I speed down our private drive. Even if a part of me prefers the comfort of her in the seat next to me, I have a feeling it will be a long day—maybe even the longest of my life, depending on how bad things are the closer I get to San Antonio. Lucy's better off at the ranch with her overflowing food bowl, open pastures, and the comforts of home.

I swipe away the beading sweat on my brow with the back of my arm. The wind whips through my open window, and the morning sun is already unrelenting as I drive through the gate, still open from my father leaving last night. The desert scrub and fence lines are a blur as I accelerate toward the interstate.

It's all I can do to keep my eyes ahead as I scan the local radio stations for information. It's two hours to San Antonio without traffic, and I'm guessing it will take triple that to get as close as I can in the frenzied aftermath of the sinkhole.

Most of the stations are garbled country music or static . . . because San Antonio is gone, I realize. I switch to AM and scan again. More static. Some indistinct chatter. And finally, the seeker stops.

"—the antichrist is coming. Therefore, we know it is the last hour." Immediately, I scan again, knowing that, despite what my mother always taught me, the gospel will not help me in this. I veer onto the interstate, unsurprised to see a steady flow of traffic headed northwest. Seeing so many cars strapped with luggage and belongings, however, makes the dread settle even deeper.

I speed down I-10, my eyes flicking between the windshield and the radio. I need to find a station with news. I need to know what I might be up against getting to whatever is left of San Antonio—which roads I should avoid, the evacuation centers being used. Alive, injured, or dead, I need to know where to look for my father. I can't handle the uncertainty of not knowing Kellen's *and* my father's fate.

Cars speed past me in the opposite direction, but other than looking for a familiar truck should my father have gotten out of the city, I barely take notice of them. My attention shifts to a male voice breaking through the static.

"—continues spreading. Damien Quipp, a geoscientist at the University of Texas at Austin, says it's only a matter of time before Austin itself could fall through the fault line, fissuring the state."

I stare at the radio, unblinking. The sinkhole is spreading to Austin? That's an hour and a half from San Antonio.

My gut sinks as I glance up. A truck speeds toward me in my lane. The driver isn't passing slower traffic; he's using my lane as a personal runway, and I have to swerve into the shoulder to keep from hitting him.

"Piece of shit," I growl as dust balloons around me. The fucker has the nerve to honk at *me* as he races onward. Once my heart starts working again, I inch back onto the road, exhaling a steadying breath.

I pass two cars pulled over. The drivers argue in the grassy divider, shouting and arms flailing at one another. My instincts scream at me to turn around—that nothing good will come of heading into the madness, but I can't turn back.

Drawing closer to town, the oncoming traffic slows to a near stop, and honking and a distant helicopter are all I can hear. A sedan pulls into the grassy median as I pass. Then another ballsy driver plows through the grass and pulls into the northbound lane, coming toward me.

Hugging the shoulder out of instinct, I slow and let the sedan pass me, a CRV not far behind it.

"Fuck this." At the next turnoff, I exit the interstate. As much as I don't want to drive into Sonora, the line of cars heading this way glints in the sunlight as far as I can see. There may be more news I can gather from town anyway— maybe from Wyatt at the county sheriff's office—before I make it farther south and I'm unable to get back.

I follow the bend in the road and slam on my brakes. A Peterbilt is stopped dead in front of me. My F-250 screeches to a halt just shy of hitting the semi-trailer. "Christ," I hiss, loosening my grip on the steering wheel. The muscles in my shoulders tense as I rest my forehead on the steering wheel to catch my breath. *This is insanity.* Blowing out a deep breath, I stick my head out the window to peer around the big rig. Traffic is backed up, leading toward the gas stations.

Glancing in my rearview, I make sure no one is coming up behind me, and I inch onto the shoulder to creep around the semi. I don't need gas, I need information.

As I continue down the shoulder and around traffic into town, I try calling my father and brother again. Having them both at the top of my call log makes it easy, and I dial Kellen first. This time, it doesn't even ring. There's a busy signal. Gripping the phone tighter, I try my father and bring the phone to my ear. Busy. They could be trying to call me, but they are unable to get through. That would make sense. But even as the slightest bit of hope returns, the mass of cars fleeing southern Texas makes it difficult to hold on to.

San Francisco is gone.

San Antonio is gone.

What are the odds that both my brother and father are gone too?

The steering wheel creaks under my grip. My heart isn't only racing anymore; it cinches in my chest, and my eyes blur. I don't like my father. I'm not certain how much I even love the man, but there's a gutting, suffocating void in knowing that he could be gone forever. That my brother might have died thinking I hated him.

Dropping my phone onto the seat beside me, I wipe away the tears. I won't know until I know. Until then, I have to try. Clearing my throat, I focus on the road. Route 277 is a shit-show. There are more people on this side of town than I think actually live in Sutton County. This town is inundated, and if I'm going to get anywhere before nightfall, I need a better plan.

Gas station central is swarming with campers and cars, and the lots are jammed on both sides of the street. People pour out of the 7-Eleven with bags of food, and fleetingly, I consider calling my dad's friend Leroy, who always has his ear to the ground. He might be my best chance to learn what I've missed in the past twelve hours.

Scott, from the feed store, stops at the curb across the street from me, trying to pull out. He sees me, his eyes widening slightly before he glances around. I'm not sure what he's doing as he reverses back into the parking lot, waving at me to follow him.

He's the first friendly face I've seen, so I don't think twice about it. I turn into the bike lane, drive over the curb and into the parking lot, and follow behind Scott as he passes the Pizza Hut and Quality Inn. Dust billows around his Jeep as he goes off-road in the direction of his store.

I don't question it because, in actuality, it's the smartest place to go. And since Scott is ex-military and still has a lot of connections, he'll undoubtedly have more information than I do.

The warehouse comes into view at the end of the road. John Deeres and Bobcats line a section of the parking lot. Galvanized water troughs are stacked alongside pallets of planting soil and bark.

He doesn't park out front, though. I follow his Jeep around to the back, and he comes to a screeching halt at the loading bay. Just as quickly, he's out of his Jeep, and our eyes meet. I climb out of my truck.

"You come to town for supplies?" he asks.

I shake my head, uncertainty making my chest feel hollow. "Headed as close as I can get to San Antonio to look for my father."

The lines around Scott's eyes tense.

"He left for a delivery last night. I haven't heard from him."

Scott tugs his baseball cap off and runs his fingers through his curly hair. "You can't get to San Antonio, Knox. No one can."

"I have to, Scott. I—" I stop myself. "Whatever's left of it. I need to know."

"It's gone, kid. And not just San Antonio—Pipe Creek,

Kingsbury. If he was on his way back, he would be here by now. The fact that he's not—" Scott mutters a curse. His gaze holds mine. It's firm, and his voice is calm and reverent—protective in a way, like he's willing me to accept the truth, as difficult as it is, and fast. "I'm sorry."

Although I've already entertained the idea my father could be gone, I've clung to the hope that, if I went looking, I would be one of the "lucky" ones. But the sympathy in Scott's eyes and his resolute warning have my pulse pounding like I might pass out.

"*If* he's alive," Scott continues, "he'll get in touch. Or"—he glances at the phone I check for the thousandth time—"he'll find a way to get home. Your father is nothing if not a stubborn son of a bitch."

"It's not just him," I admit for the first time aloud. I hate the strain in my voice, and I clench my fists, steeling myself. "I haven't heard from my brother."

Scott's brow lifts ever so slightly, as if he forgot all about Kellen. My brother's been gone for so long, I can't say I blame him. "If he's anything like you, Knox, he'll get to safety. He'll find a way to reach you."

A thought strikes me. "Or my Uncle Mason," I tell him, hope budding, just a little. Kellen would know to go there. Hell, if my father is alive and can't get here, he would head to Kansas, too.

I push through the lump in my throat. "What else do you know?"

Scott shakes his head. "Camp Bullis, Lackland, Fort Sam Houston—all military bases in the San Antonio area are gone."

The words hit me like a rubber mallet. "We have no military?" That's a terrifying thought, if for no other reason than far too many people have been waiting for this so they can take matters into their own hands.

"None that are coming to help us in little ol' Sutton County," Scott says.

My head falls back as I peer up at the metal awning above, and I inhale a deep breath. All the state's money has gone to the military in preparation for this. They manage the relocation plans and staff the evacuation centers. It's why the draft was nearly reinstated with so many men and women needed to fill the roles and positions created for the end of the fucking world. "It's all been for nothing." The words are sour and angry, and I grit my teeth.

"Seems that way, at least at the moment. And that water situation of yours—it's everywhere. Filters will only last so long, especially if the quakes continue to crack the pipes. Soon, there will be complete anarchy, and I'm not interested in sticking around to witness it."

That same thought has lingered in the back of my mind since yesterday, the possibility that I will have to leave the ranch for good. But I'm not ready to give up. Not yet. Not when that place is literally the only thing I have left.

"Come on," Scott says, waving for me to follow. "Regardless of what you're going to do, you'll need supplies." He peers longingly at the rolling doors. "Take whatever you need because I'll never see this place again. Ava and I are headed out of town."

"Ava?"

Scott grabs his shotgun from inside his Jeep. "She's getting something at the Pharm House while I load up." I must be frowning because Scott continues. "I told her I'd get her as far as I could. Once the power grid goes down, shit is really going to hit the fan. It's only a matter of time before

Sonora is infested with looters and trigger-happy mother-fuckers."

My eyebrow raises of its own accord.

"It's Texas," he explains, and I question whether to grab my pistol from under my seat.

Scott's eyes meet mine as he jogs up the steps to the back door. "Come on, Knox. You've always been my best customer. Consider this a parting gift."

NINE
AVA

"Hello—Mal, are you back there?" the woman in front of me calls, ringing the bell on the counter impatiently. My fingers tap at my sides as golden oldies play on the radio throughout the dimly lit pharmacy. It feels ominous being in the still space with only the two of us while it's complete madness outside. In the distance, an impatient driver honks his car horn on cue.

Exhaling a deep sigh, I shift on my feet, feeling naked without my shoulder bag and the pack I left in Scott's Jeep.

"I need to get back to the house. Herb is waiting," she calls, dinging the bell again. It grates on the last of my nerves, which are shot from the past twenty-four hours.

The woman dings the bell again, and I grimace.

"Are you sure someone's even here?" I grit out, but then someone whispers in the back.

Mallory walks out in her white coat with a tense, very forced smile on her face. "I'm sorry to keep you waiting, Sandra, but we are going to have to close—"

"No."

"Yes," Mallory continues, coming out from behind the counter. "We're closing up early."

"Wait," I blurt. "Can you at least help us first?" I can't quell the pitch in my voice as panic sets in again.

"Hurry up!" a man calls from the back.

"I'm sorry," Mallory says, and I see that she's torn, but she's afraid, and that clearly wins.

"But—" the customer stammers. "Herb needs his ointment—"

"Here." Mallory grabs a box of something off the shelf on her way to the door and shoves it into the woman's hands. "Take it, please. It's on me. No charge."

"But this isn't—"

"Dammit, Sandra. Get out!"

Sandra's expression is difficult to read, but she huffs and practically stomps toward the door. As if remembering herself, Mallory inhales a deep breath and straightens her shoulders. She opens the door and waits for the customer to exit. "I am—"

"Goodbye." Mallory closes the door on her mid-sentence, then peers beyond the glass. Her hands shake as she runs her fingers through her hair. This woman is going to throw me out too, and I can't leave. Not without my prescription.

I don't move, afraid Mallory will remember I'm here, and I need a minute to think.

"This isn't happening," she murmurs, scanning the parking lot. "You need to go too, Ava," she says, but she turns the lock as she surveys the hubbub outside.

"But I don't need *ointment*," I say, and I have to control the bite in my tone, knowing it will get me nowhere with her. "I need my anti-epileptics. They were ready for pickup yesterday, but I had to rush home because—" I can't bring myself to say the words. "Because . . ." I shake my head. "Look, I'm here now." I push thoughts of Mavey away, but my chin quivers despite myself. I hate that I have to rely on this woman's kindness if I'm to have any reprieve for the next few weeks. "I need my meds, Mallory." I inhale shakily. "Now, more than ever—you know I do. Please." I force her to look at me. To hold my gaze. "This might be the last chance to get meds at all."

I must look and sound pathetic enough because Mallory disappears into the back with a resolute sigh.

"Thank you," I call. Exhaling my relief, every coiled part of me eases slightly and I feel a million pounds lighter.

When Mallory returns, she pulls two pill bottles from a white bag.

Beyond relieved, I pull my credit card from my back pocket and slide it onto the counter, then groan. My head hangs of its own accord. "Shit." It's a desperate hiss because last time I used my card it was declined, and I haven't had the time or the wherewithal to go to the bank or ATM in the chaos.

I glance up at Mallory, knowing this is not some five-dollar generic ointment she would just hand over to me. "I've been having issues with my card," I explain as calmly as I can. "And—" I gesture to her disorganized shelves, disheveled from yesterday's quake. "I'm not sure I will be able to get it sorted with everything that's going on." I pull what cash I have out of my pocket, which is nowhere near enough, and slide it over to her, my fingers trembling a little. "This is all I have on me." I sound like a fiend, an addict, but I can't help the clawing fear that borderline suffocates me as I imagine the world all but ending while I am left in my own personal hell of half-consciousness and dysfunction. I can't even promise her I'll pay her back because, after today, I won't ever see her again. "I need them. *Please.*"

Mallory drops the pill bottles into the bag. "It's fine," she says in a rush. She clearly wants me out of here. "I know you have Mavey to worry about too."

I take the bag, leaving my cash on the counter. "Mavey is dead."

Mallory's eyes widen just as the lights flicker, and then the room goes dark. The radio dies away, the hum of the halogens ceases, and the outside commotion fills the room in the deafening silence. The only light inside the pharmacy streams in from the windows, and a man shouts a curse from the back.

My stomach rolls with dread. Once the power goes out, the real panic sets in. That's what Scott told me, and the churning disquiet I've felt humming in the air since I stepped out of my double-wide this morning is already flirting with hysteria.

The world rumbles to life again as a backup generator starts up, practically growling in the silence. Mallory lets out a deep sigh, and quick and heavy footsteps precede a man who emerges from the back of the pharmacy. Phillip, the man who helped me last time, pushes his glasses up his nose, only for them to slide back down again, and his forehead shines with sweat. He stops short at the counter when he sees me. "I told you to close up, Mallory. Now—"

"And *I* told *you* we shouldn't have even opened the shop today," she snaps back.

He waves her retort away. "I can't get a hold of Sammy," he continues as if I'm not even standing there anymore. "You should go see if she's okay. I'll deal with the generator and secure things here."

"Traffic is really bad," I warn them, and though I hate to be the bearer of bad news, I'd want to know if I was trying to get to someone.

Mallory's brow furrows and Phillip looks at me. *Really* looks at me. "You're the one who always orders Depakene."

I don't have to answer. He clearly remembers me. "You better get home to whoever is waiting for you," Phillip tells me, not unkindly. He looks me up and down, not in a creepy way, but in a concerned way, like he would have for his own daughter. "Come on." He glances toward the door and grabs the keys off his belt loop. "I'll let you out."

"Thank you again," I tell Mallory over my shoulder, and without wasting another minute, I follow Phillip toward the door, shoving my cash back into my pocket. Tightening my grip on my bag of meds, I flash a grateful smile to Phillip and step out into the summer heat.

The sun is blazing, and I lower my sunglasses from the top of my head and survey the parking lot. Traffic is backed up on the I-10 westbound. Every car is stalled on the overpass in the distance, and the Sunoco station next door is packed with cars, gassing up for the trip ahead. Lines of waiting vehicles stretch from each entry as far as I can see.

As I step off the sidewalk, I spot Lars at one of the diesel pumps. He climbs out of the driver's seat. His oily black hair glistens in the afternoon sun, and his t-shirt and jeans are so tattered and faded they might be the only set he has. Rick and Ty step out of the passenger side. Rick pulls a cigarette from between his lips, laughing at the guy cursing at them, who they apparently cut off at the pump. Ty kicks the man's bumper, daring him to get out and do something about it.

They are the last people in the world I want to see right now, and as I'm about to turn in the opposite direction, Lars spots me across the lot like a damn beacon. His eyes lock on me, and a chill unfurls over my skin. There's something about the darkness in Lars's gaze—a loathing so much more fiendish than anything I've ever seen in Knox's expression.

Or even Mitch's, for that matter. Because Lars isn't a bull gunning for red, he's a predator zeroing in on his prey.

Heart pounding with dread, I turn down the road in the direction of Scott's store, and Lars's voice reaches my ears.

"There she is," he calls. "I was wondering where you were and why your house was empty—well, not *empty* but . . ."

Fury fills me and I whip around, glaring at him. "You went to my *house*?" I seethe, more shocked and angry than I am unnerved by it.

Lars steps around his truck. There's a parking lot between us as he leans against the fender with a shrug. "I wanted to make sure you were okay." A salacious grin fills his narrow face. "Boy shorts," he muses. "I'm not sure why I had you pegged as a thong underwear kind of girl."

Bile rises up my throat in disgust at the thought of him going through my things.

"Had a talk with your friend Mavey—well, she listened, I talked," he adds with a shrug. "It looks like you really are alone now."

My stomach curdles. "Fuck off, Lars." I turn back for the road. My strides eat the pavement, and all I see is red, even as a tendril of fear slithers over me.

"Where are you going?" Lars shouts. "Don't you know you shouldn't be wandering around on your own?" I can hear the smile in his voice, but I ignore him and continue in the opposite direction, willing the universe to give me this one grace. Just this once.

"At least let us give you a ride." His words are laced with a dangerous intrigue, and the moment I hear their truck doors slam shut, the dire need to flee takes over and I run.

TEN
KNOX

"There were no cops or roadblocks," I muse, passing the generators and heading for the animal feed.

"You noticed that, did you? My guess is Wyatt and the local officials are scrambling with their own problems, and no one else is coming."

I glance at Scott as he lugs a tow hitch onto his cart. "I might regret it," he says, glancing down. "I'm making myself a target, driving with a trailer of supplies, but—" He scratches his head. "I know I'll regret not taking everything I can, seeing as how we don't exactly know what we're up against. It's hard enough, leaving so much behind."

"Better to take what you can," I agree. "You can always ditch it later."

"True." He looks at me. "What's your plan? You staying at the ranch?"

My shoulders sag a little and I shake my head. "For now," I say, because I don't know what to do at this point.

"Well, feel free to take a few flats of water," he says, disappearing down an aisle. "I'm going to load my trailer up with the rest."

"I will, thanks." My voice is hollow as I stack horse feed and dog food onto my trolley cart, and I lose myself in a haze of thoughts. About the ranch and what happens to it if I leave for Ransom, Kansas. About where my father and brother will go if they are alive. The ranch, hoping to find me there? Or Kansas, hoping I was smart enough to head that way too? A part of me says to hold out for as long as I can here to see if either of them show. Another part of me screams how insane it is to linger.

The metal clank of jerry cans echoes through the warehouse as Scott lugs some into his pile. "You should take a few of these. I'm thinking that Sunoco—the one on the other side of town—might be a good place to fill up. People off the highway won't know it's there. We could get them filled before we leave."

I nod. Though I have ample fuel at the ranch, it never hurts to have more, especially since we have no idea how long the town's supply will last. Or how much I'll need to get to Kansas if I go. *When* I go, I correct myself. I know it's only a matter of time before I'll have no other choice, and that alone sends my mind down another rabbit hole.

I never considered having to leave the ranch and what that would entail. It's one thing to prepare to hole up at home where I have everything I need and know my surroundings like the back of my hand—where I can prepare to die in the comfort of my own home if it ever came to that. But if I leave, there's no telling what could happen along the way or how to prepare for it. And I have a ranch full of animals to worry about on top of whatever uncertain journey lies ahead.

"I have to keep reminding myself I'm packing for two," Scott mutters, mostly to himself. He tosses two pairs of gloves onto his pile.

"How is that, exactly?" I ask, unable to stop myself. "I

know Ava works for you, but you're traveling together?" Fleetingly, I wonder if there is a different sort of relationship between them, and I've just prodded into territory I don't want to be in.

"Mavey."

"Mavey?" I frown, confused. "Her grandmother?" I know they aren't technically related, but I'm not sure what else to call her.

"She died last night. I went to check on them this morning. Ava was still waiting for the paramedics to come. They weren't going to, of course."

Before I can process that, a door slams in the back of the warehouse, followed by the heavy, quick clomp of rubber soles on the cement floor.

Scott and I straighten. I strain to listen and hold my breath as Scott's hand hovers over the pistol at his hip.

Ava rushes in from the back, weaving around the aisle of gardening supplies. "Scott—" Her chest heaves as she catches her breath, her eyes immediately widening when she sees me. "Knox?"

"What's wrong?" Scott says, taking a step toward her.

Ava braces her hands on her thighs as she draws in a ragged breath. "Lars," she rasps. "He and Rick—they were following me."

"Following you?" Scott parrots.

She nods. "The son of a bitch went to my house looking for me, so I ran. I cut across the old hay mill."

"Then you don't know for sure if they followed you," I clarify.

Ava glares at me and tucks a loose hair from her ponytail behind her ear. "Let's just say they were until they couldn't any longer," she deadpans.

Lars has always been a juvenile delinquent, bullying kids back in school, and he never grew out of it. I've seen him picking on Ava a few times over the years, though I never understood why he seemed to zero in on her.

"I knew I shouldn't have left you alone." Scott hands her a water bottle.

"Thanks." She uncaps it quickly. "It was fine until he saw me walking by the gas station."

Scott strides over to the front of the store, stepping over the debris strewn throughout the aisles from yesterday's earthquake, and peers out the window. His hand still rests on his pistol like he's braced for what's coming.

"What does Lars Pennington want with you?" I ask, glancing back at Ava.

She throws up one arm with a final chug of water, then heaves a breath when she's finished. "His dad hated Julio?" she guesses, licking her lips. "Lars's mother abandoned him, and he was stuck with his shitty father while I had Mavey after Julio got locked up? I'm Mexican? I don't have a dick? Who knows with him. Take your pick." She discards her bottle on a broken shelf and eyes Scott.

He walks back to us, his gaze leveled on her. "Did he see you come here?"

Ava glances between us, and I can tell she wants to reassure us he didn't, but she shrugs ever so slightly. "I don't know," she admits. "I mean, I didn't see his truck after the hay mill, but he's not an idiot. He knows I work here. Where else would I go?"

"Great," I mutter, knowing Lars and his friends love nothing more than picking a good fight.

"I didn't have much of a choice," Ava snaps, misunderstanding my frustration as I head toward the back of the store for my truck. I knew I should have grabbed my gun. I've barely stepped onto the loading dock when I hear glass shatter inside the warehouse, feel a blunt hit to the back of my head, and I fall to the ground.

ELEVEN
AVA

THERE'S A LOUD CRACK AT THE FRONT WINDOW, AND I nearly jump out of my skin. Scott and I spin around.

Lars and Rick are standing on the other side of the automatic door, a baseball bat twirling in Rick's hand. Though he's more fat than muscle, compared to Lars's scrawny frame, I wouldn't want to mess with him.

The sliding door is powered off, and the glass is not shattered enough for them to step through unscathed. But something tells me Lars doesn't care about that.

His chin is angled down, his eyes fixed on us. On *me*. A strand of hair falls into his face, but he doesn't seem to notice. Whatever hatred Lars has always bore for me, it's more hair-raising and sinister now and I fear what thoughts play behind those dark eyes of his.

"The lights are off," Lars sings, "but it looks like you're home." He points to the broken door. "Are you going to let us in?"

"What do you want, Lars?" Scott says, his shoulders squared as he steps toward the door. His voice is calm, as if he knows Lars is a ticking time bomb that needs no prodding, but he holds his pistol at his side. It's not aimed at either of them. Yet.

"I wanted to get some shopping in," Lars says. He mutters something inaudible to Rick, who then takes the end of his bat and breaks the rest of the glass loose so they can step inside.

Scott lifts his pistol. "You already vandalized my shop. If you take another step inside, I will shoot you," he warns.

Lars grins. "I doubt that very much."

Where the hell is Knox? It's all I can do not to glance toward the back in search of him, but I don't dare take my eyes off Lars. Knox probably drove away, not wanting to deal with me and the drama he knew followed me here. I can't say I blame him, though a part of me resents him for it too.

Lars's smile turns sinister and his attention shifts in my direction again.

"Wait—" Just as I remember Ty was with them, I hear the crunch of boots behind me too late. A heavy arm wraps around my middle, and I shriek as it bars me against a hot, hard body. The smell of stale cigarette smoke is nearly suffocating.

Scott spins around, fear flashing in his eyes, and he aims his pistol at the guy behind me.

"You're outnumbered, man," Lars says. "Drop your gun." He points a pistol of his own at Scott for added encouragement.

"Let go," I grind out, loud enough for Ty to hear. My heart pounds as I pull uselessly against my unseen assailant.

Half turned, Scott glances between me and the gun in Lars's hand, the seconds ticking by in a sluggish blur of commands and movement.

"Do it," Rick warns him, twirling his bat for added effect.

Finally, Scott tosses his gun onto the pallet of dog food bags a few feet in front of him.

Lars seems appeased enough, and his smile returns. He peers around, making a show of appraising the fully stocked, if disarrayed, warehouse of supplies. "So, this is where the goodies are." Lars whistles with approval. "Don't mind if we do. It wasn't why we came here, but—" He shrugs.

"What are you doing, Lars?" Scott asks. He sounds like a disappointed father figure. "You're better than this."

"I told you," Lars says with a sneer, "we're shopping."

"Take whatever you want then—"

"*Whatever* I want?" he clarifies, glancing at me.

"Whatever *supplies* you want," Scott amends.

Lars huffs a laugh. "Gee, thanks. But I was already planning on it."

"Don't do something you'll regret, Lars. You might be an asshole, but you're not a killer. Or a—" Scott's words peter out, and that piques Lars's interest.

"Or a what?" His gaze shifts to me again. "A rapist?" He steps closer to Scott until he's standing only a few feet away. "Is that what you were going to say?" The playfulness in Lars's tone vanishes with his smile, and canting his head, Lars crosses his arms over his chest and looks Scott up and down. His pistol tightens in his grip. "You know nothing about me, asshole." Again, his gaze skirts to me, and the loathing glint in his eyes returns.

Clearly irritated, Lars looks at Ty behind me. "We don't have all day," he chides, and Ty holds me tighter. Rick walks over, grabbing a rope from the aisle along the way, and I exchange a pleading look with Scott. I can tell he's silently strategizing as he assesses the situation.

My shoulders drop and I stop struggling. "What is your

problem, Lars?" I rasp. Ty's hold on me shifts, his arm coming around my throat this time.

Rick heads for us, nearly stumbling on a fallen rake as he unwinds the rope. Distraction is all I can think of to buy us more time.

I glare at Lars. "Why do you hate me so much?"

His lip curls. "What makes you think this is about you?" He flings his arms out, incredulous. "Why does *everything* always have to be about Ava Hernandez?"

"Then why are you doing this?"

"Because," he says flatly, "you've always been the center of attention—the topic on everyone's wagging tongues, and it's time to see what all the fuss is about."

"You think I *want* any of that?" I hate that it comes out like a whimper. "You think I've wanted to feel like a social pariah my entire life?"

Lars shakes his head with a cruel smile. "Ava is sick at school and gets special attention. Ava has her bodyguard Knox to protect her when mean 'ol Lars is picking on her—"

"*Knox?*"

"Ava's drunk uncle *kills* a teacher, and she doesn't get shoved into the system. Even your goddamn mom died. Mine? She fucking *chose* to leave. You didn't have to deal with an abusive family. No, you got the nice old lady down the street to take you in."

My eyes well with tears despite myself. "That's how you see my life?"

"Fuck you, Ava," he spits. "Don't act innocent. You've got everyone fooled—even Captain America here, whisking you away as the world falls to shit. But I won't make it that easy for you."

"Son—"

Lars lifts his gun up and points it at Scott's head. "*Don't* call me son," he seethes.

"So, you're going to what?" I say, forcing Lars's attention back to me. "Kill me? Beat me? Rape me to teach me a lesson—to prove how horrible you can really be?"

He shrugs. "You know, Ava, I haven't decided yet. None of this was planned. Again, you're always assuming the world revolves around you. I simply saw an opportunity and took it."

Rick reaches for my hands.

"Drop it." Knox's low voice rumbles by my ear, and all attention shifts behind me as he slowly cocks a gun. It practically rings through the warehouse in everyone's silence. Ty's grip loosens, and I tug out of his hold while I have the chance.

Lars and Scott are a flutter of movement as they lunge for Scott's discarded gun. I crouch, pull a broom from the toppled display, and whirl it around, hitting Rick in the side. The broom's wooden handle breaks in two, and we both stumble backward. Rick loses his footing, giving me a single moment's reprieve, and then a shot rings out.

Scott lowers his pistol, and Lars's steps falter. His gun clatters to the floor as Lars grips his side, liquid red glistening on his fingers. "Fuuuck!" he bellows, his eyes wide with shock.

Knox wrestles with Ty, and I lunge for Lars's gun as Rick grabs me from behind, flinging me onto the cement floor like a linebacker sacks the offense. My shoulder screams in pain. The sound of bones crunching and flesh on flesh meets my ears from where Knox and Ty grapple with one another.

Groans and grunts and a whimper of my own fill the store as Scott swings Rick's discarded bat. Once. Twice. A third time. Then Scott tosses the bat aside and grabs my arm with one hand, yanking me up. He aims his gun at Rick with the other. "Don't think about moving," Scott growls.

Rick moans, crumpled on the floor at our feet as he clutches his side.

Footsteps echo behind us before a shoulder meets with my back, and Scott and I are shoved forward as a deafening roar fills the warehouse. I register the metal shelf and the quarts of oil lining it a split second before the cold steel meets my head, and its contents collapse around me.

TWELVE
KNOX

CRINGING, I DROP THE SHOVEL IN MY HAND AND PICK UP Lars's gun that skittered across the floor. My jaw, ribs, and temple scream with pain that's so distracting, I can barely focus.

I see Lars ram into the back of Scott and Ava too late. He's a bull in motion as he shoves them into the maintenance aisle, the shelves already broken from the earthquake. What's left of the displays collapse entirely, the crash resounding through the warehouse.

"You piece of shit—" Lars rasps as he struggles to get to his feet. His face is red with rage and contorted with agony as he leans against a generator box. His side and hands are covered with blood, and he can barely stay on his feet as he reaches for an axe hanging on the hook beside him.

Adrenaline whirs through me, and without a second thought, I lift the gun, aim it at his back, and pull the trigger.

Lars cries out, grabbing onto the generator box before his hands slip off and he crumples into a heap on the ground.

My arm falls to my side as I catch my breath, but my

relief is short-lived because Lars isn't the only one not getting back up.

"Scott—" My mind flurries faster than my legs will carry me. I hurdle over a toppled seed stand and a broken broom, nearly stumbling at Lars's dead body. Ava is unconscious, though I dare not think she's dead, and Rick whimpers as he tries and fails to lift one of the generators off his middle.

"Help me, man," he implores, tears in his eyes. His voice is reedy. "Please."

But it's Scott I can't look away from. He sputters where he sits, staring down at the broom handle protruding through his stomach, then at me as he tries to catch his breath.

"Knox—"

I fall to my knees beside him, hands hovering where he's been impaled, uncertain I've ever seen so much human blood. And I know he doesn't have long. "What do I do?" I ask in a rush, because I know I can't remove the wood without him bleeding out even faster.

Scott shakes his head and chokes on his breath. Blood gurgles from between his lips, and his eyes are filled with tears. "Ava?" he says hoarsely. He peers dazedly around.

"You gonna help me man, or what?" Rick whines, but the fight is gone from him.

I crawl over to Ava, ignoring Rick as I check her pulse. "Unconscious but breathing," I reassure Scott. He swallows thick and loud and leans his head back on the shelving unit behind him, like he can no longer keep it up. "Take her and get out of here," he chokes out.

I shake my head as I scurry back to him, thoughts racing and numb all at once. "Just—let me think. I can't leave you like—"

Scott grips my arm, forcing my eyes to his. "The . . . militia."

"The militia?" Confusion fades quickly as I peer around his shop with new eyes—at the mess, and Ty's mangled, bloody body, then at Lars and Rick. The cops would believe me if I told them what happened here, but the rest of Lars's crew and all his friends are in the militia. I don't want to take a chance on what they would do.

"Go," Scott gurgles. He drops his arm, no longer strong enough to lift it. "Take supplies." He swallows. "Do it. And take Ava with you." Silent tears stream down his cheeks, and even if I am too overwhelmed to cry, I feel as if the ground is shattering beneath me. I've always respected Scott, and he's shown me more kindness in the past two days than I ever had a right to.

"Please," he whispers.

"Yes—I will. Of course I will."

Scott's chin trembles and he exhales a ragged breath.

I glance at Ava again, my mind reeling as I sort through the past thirty minutes. I don't know why this man chose to help me today or how I've ended up here with Ava, of all people. Whether it's sadness, the shock of having just killed someone, or relief it wasn't me when so many times I thought it might be, my throat tighten with gratitude.

"Thank yo—" My breath catches when I look at Scott again. The light in his eyes is gone. He's gone.

THIRTEEN
AVA

My head hits the window and the pain shooting through my temple jostles me awake. I groan, my body aching with the slightest movement, and I open my eyes. The sun is so damn bright it's painful, and panic flares inside me as I try to discern where I am and what's happening.

I blink an empty field of dry grass into view. It stretches around us as we drive down a dirt road. *I'm in a car.*

I think of Scott and his Jeep and squeeze my eyes shut as a barrage of images and memories slowly come back to me. Only when there's movement in the driver's seat do I open them again and glance over. My breath lodges in my throat when I see Knox. I blink again, trying to focus beyond the pain in my skull.

"What—" I croak, and I clear my throat. "What's going on?"

His chest rises and falls before he answers. "We're taking back roads since the highway is gridlocked." His voice is low and level—he doesn't even look at me, like being together in a vehicle is a regular occurrence.

"Taking back roads to where?" I swallow thickly.

"Where's Scott? Why am I with you?" I sit up straighter, rubbing my pounding head as I take in the cab of an unfamiliar truck. Of *Knox's* truck. My messenger bag is stuffed between my feet. It's bulging, barely closed, and my backpack is also packed haphazardly beside me. "Did you go through my things?" I snap, scowling at him.

"Your stuff was dumped out in the Jeep. I had to grab it in a hurry."

Alarm zaps through me and I practically tear my backpack open, pulling my clothes out and searching through it. When I don't find my meds, I unpack my messenger bag in a flurry.

I can feel Knox's eyes on me, but I'm too focused on keeping the panic at bay. "There was a bag," I rasp. "I tossed it into Scott's Jeep before I ran into the feed store."

"There wasn't a bag when I gathered your things."

"There has to be." I pull the last of my clothes out, praying my meds are at the bottom. "It was right on top—"

"It wasn't there."

"Yes," I say flatly. "It was white with two pill bottles in it—"

"Ava—" Knox's hand clamps down on mine and my eyes dart to him. He glances from me to the road angrily. "There was no bag." His words are slow and clipped, and while I'm prone to continue arguing with him, I know he would have seen it if it had been there.

My chest heaves. If my stuff was dumped out, they went through my things. Then I remember Ty coming in through the back of the store. "He must have grabbed it," I breathe. "We have to go back."

Knox shakes his head.

"I need that bag, Knox."

"Are you going to die without it?"

"No, but—"

"Then I'm not going back to that place." His gaze shifts to the rearview mirror, and the hair on the back of my neck rises.

I stare at Knox and consider my next words carefully. "Why not?" As soon as the words fall from my lips, though, it all refocuses.

The look on Lars's face.

Ty's hold on me.

The scent of cigarettes.

The gunshot.

I shift in my seat, searching the side mirror for followers. "Are they chasing us? Is that why we're driving through a field?"

"No," Knox mutters solemnly. "They aren't chasing us."

I massage the side of my throbbing head. I feel nauseous, but it's hard to say if it's car sickness from the jostling, or, as I recall how hard I hit the shelf, from a concussion. I pick at what feels like dry blood on my temple, and the moment I look at my hand, my heart palpitates a little.

"I figured it would do no good to take you to the hospital," Knox explains, and I think he's probably right after everything I've seen today.

"Then . . ." I peer out the window again as we pull out of the field onto another dirt road, cacti and shrubs dotting the landscape. "What's going on?" A question clings to the back of my throat and I stare at Knox's profile. "Knox, where is Scott? Why am I riding with you?"

Knox's fingers grip the steering wheel so tight, the leather audibly cracks beneath them. "Scott didn't make it."

It takes a minute for his words to resonate, and my fingernails rake over my thighs, clawing into fists. "He's dead?"

Knox's silence is all the answer I need, and my hand flies

to my mouth. I turn for the window, away from Knox, as tears fill my eyes. I blink them away as best I can, taking a few shallow breaths to steady my voice before I can bring myself to speak again. I clear my throat, watching more cacti pass as we drive by. "What about the others?"

My heart is beating so wildly—so savagely—I can barely hear my own question, and when Knox doesn't answer again, I force myself to look at him. The man with whom I've barely exchanged five words in the past decade. Whose glare has kept me up at night and haunted my dreams. Now, he sits beside me with his lip swollen and crusted with dry blood, and his eyebrow split. *Because of me.*

"Everyone else is dead," he finally says. The heaviness of what he's done—what he had to do while I was unconscious hurts my heart. Regret? Relief? Complete and utter disbelief? It's hard to sort out how I feel. I'm the last person Knox would ever want to get stuck with during the end of the world, and on top of that, he had to kill someone today, maybe two someones. *Because. Of. Me.*

His dad could probably stomach something like that, but not the kid I watched from the sidelines growing up. In fact, I want to ask him so many questions about what transpired while I was unconscious, but I can't bring myself to. Knox might be strong in all senses of the word, but like me, he looks as if he's barely holding it together, and I won't prod him for the missing pieces. Not yet.

"We're going to bury him," Knox says over the diesel engine as he accelerates down a private drive.

Unexpectedly, I huff with relief, grateful I get to say a semblance of goodbye. But the wave recedes just as quickly, and I wrap my fingers around the seatbelt strapping me in. "Where are we going?"

"To my pla—"

"No," I grip the armrest. "No, Knox. Your dad is going to freak out. I can't deal with that right now. Please—"

He stares at me and every word on my tongue withers away. "There's nowhere else to go," he says coolly. "Besides . . . he's gone."

My heart pounds in my ears as I watch Knox's profile. I don't know if he means his dad fled Sutton County, or if he's dead, like so many others today.

"Is he . . ." I let the words fall away, unable to utter them. I have no love for Mitch Bennett, but for Knox's sake, I would feel sorry if he lost his dad, having already lost his mom too.

"I don't know." His voice is so quiet I barely hear him.

For obvious reasons, I can tell he doesn't want to talk about it, so I say nothing more and focus on exhaling the anxiety that's alive and slithering around inside me. Before the sun even rose, I lost Mavey. Now, Scott is gone, and so are Lars and some of his crew. And beside me is Knox, who only yesterday wordlessly glared at me from the other side of the checkout counter.

I stare at stretches of barbed wire fencing, the world blurring around me. "Is there anything else I need to know?" I ask softly, the energy completely draining from me. "I might have a heart attack if there are any more surprises today."

Knox makes a derisive noise. "You and me both." He rests his elbow in the window, rubbing his stubbled jaw anxiously.

I risk a glance in the side mirror. Now that I know Scott must be in the back, I'm afraid to check. But having slept through Knox loading Scott's body and everything else on his own, forcing myself to look is the least I can do. I'll have to at some point anyway.

But when I look, all I can see are the tops of gas cans, a

flat of water, and the edge of a few crates, so I focus forward again.

The gate of the Bennett Family Ranch comes into view. I've seen their insignia a hundred times, but I've never been here, and my stomach roils with how wrong it feels.

Knox pulls through the open gate and brings the truck to a stop just inside.

"I'll do it," I offer, knowing he's going to close it behind us.

"No." Knox shoves his door open. "You shouldn't be walking around until we know how bad your concussion is." He gives me no time to respond and strides over to the barred metal gate and pushes it shut.

I watch in the mirror as he drapes the chain around the post before he locks it. I realize Knox is in a basic white t-shirt and jeans, both spattered with dirt and blood. No hat today, which I've rarely seen. Instead of turning back for the truck when he's finished, Knox stands there with his back to me. I watch and wait until, finally, Knox leans forward and braces himself on the bars. His t-shirt tightens over his expanding body as he heaves. Tears blur my eyes again, and my heart feels a dozen times heavier, knowing the part I've played in Knox's momentary breakdown. I look away to give him privacy. I owe him that much.

Wiping my eyes, I search my bag for sunglasses, praying they will help with my headache. I worry they've also been left behind when I find them in the bottom of my bag. I consider it a win and wipe the smudges off before slipping them on.

I can't help the direction my gaze drifts, but I feel slightly better when I see Knox straighten in the mirror. He wipes his face on his bicep and turns back for the truck. His eyes are glassy and red, and I face forward as he climbs into the cab, pretending I saw nothing at all.

Knox doesn't look at me, and he says nothing as he shifts the F-250 into gear. We continue down the drive a quarter mile in silence before a lodge comes into view. I assume it's his house, as grand as it is, and as the homestead opens up, the barns and stables and some paddocks sprawl along the right side of the property.

An Australian shepherd runs out from the shade of a tractor, barking and butt-wagging as it trots closer. Knox continues past the barn and stables, past a few paddocks with steers, before he finally stops at a large redwood shed.

"Wait here," he says, shutting off the engine. I don't argue as he climbs out of the truck, greeted by his dog.

"Hey, girl," Knox murmurs. He rubs her ears and bows his head, and with an excited whimper, she licks his face. The dog can barely contain her excitement, and Knox seems to soak it in, like it gives him strength.

Finally, he rises to his feet, pushes the driver's side door shut, and heads for the shed. His four-legged friend follows after him, prancing and hopping around by his side. When they emerge again, Knox has a shovel and pickax clutched in his hands. He lays them carefully in the back of the truck and climbs back into the driver's seat.

We continue past the shed, leaving the homestead behind us, and I take in the land surrounding the ranch. Low hills and some flatland grazed down to nothing. There are ash trees and prickly pears scattered here and there and fence lines off in the distance, but nothing more than that. We head toward a cluster of Texas oaks, and when we reach their shade, Knox brings the truck to a stop.

I open my door to get out.

"Ava."

I look at him.

"You were out for nearly an hour. I'm not a doctor, but I'm guessing you have a bad concussion. You're not helping me dig a hole."

"Of course I am," I counter. Climbing out of the truck, I realize it's higher off the ground than I thought, and I grip the armrest to steady myself as my feet hit the hard earth. My headache is loud and proud, but the nausea ebbs a little now that we're no longer moving. "I'm not letting you dig a hole for my friend while I sit back and watch," I say, and as I shut my door, my eyes fix on Scott's body wrapped in a painting tarp in the back. My heart drops. My hands begin to sweat, and I feel like I might be sick. Boxes and crates and supplies are stacked around Scott, almost protective in a way, and all I can do is stare at him.

Metal clangs against the truck bed as Knox lifts the pickax out.

I swallow the returning nausea, along with the sob threatening to bubble up inside me, and walk around the tailgate on mostly steady feet. I lift the shovel out. "I want to help," I tell him, meeting his hazel eyes. My voice is strained, but Knox doesn't argue. He only stares at me a second longer, then heads toward the trees. "It's this way." His voice is a low rumble, barely audible above our footsteps, but I follow him around a sprawling oak.

The afternoon is hot and humid, and it feels like every bit of dust that lifts with each step sticks to my sweat-dampened skin. Unlike town, where the scent of fried food and magnolias fill the air, it smells like sunbaked soil out here, and as a slight breeze picks up, sulfur too.

When we get to a small plot of grave markers, I realize we're burying Scott in the Bennett family cemetery.

Knox leans his shovel and pickax against a tree trunk, and

I pause behind him. His mother is buried out here, and discomfort prickles over me. The nights Mitch came to my house in a drunken fury because of his dead wife flare to life. Now, I'm looking at her headstone, and it makes me sick to my stomach, like I'm trespassing where I don't belong. "It feels wrong to be here."

"Then go back to the truck," Knox says tersely. He's staring at me, the pickax half lodged in the ground.

Instead of trying to explain myself or arguing with him, I start to shovel out the earth he has loosened with the axe. Who Knox buries here is his business, but I won't leave him to bury Scott alone.

I feel the bruised muscles of my body with each heave of the shovel, but I work as hard and fast as I can, trying to keep up with Knox. With each swing of the pickax, he gains momentum until I imagine it's my face he's picturing, or perhaps Lars's, and he continues to upturn the hard ground until it's loose and malleable.

I pause once to grab us each a water bottle from the back of the truck so we don't die of thirst on top of everything else. Then we continue to make quick work of the hole in silence. I don't know where Knox's mind drifts, but I realize I'm staring at the earth, awed by how long it's been here—far longer than us. If the fate of this planet is truly altering, whatever happens, the dirt will remain long after we're gone. And soon, like Scott, we'll be a part of it too.

Knox pauses, assesses the human-sized hole, and drops the pickax. Without ceremony, he turns for the truck. "Come on." He calls for me to follow, and I steel myself for what comes next.

Dropping my shovel, I walk to the tailgate where Knox tugs Scott's canvas-wrapped body from the back, careful but intent. Knox's arms strain, his hands trembling a little, and I know it's from utter exhaustion. I imagine him wrapping Scott's lifeless body and lugging it into the truck alone. And him having to load the supplies and then worry about me and my things on top of everything else.

"Take his feet," Knox says. His muscles strain some more under his bloody t-shirt as he lowers Scott's upper half from the back of the truck, taking the brunt of his weight. His jaw clenches and Knox nods toward Scott's final resting place in the ground.

All I can think as we carry Scott to his grave is how heavy he is and how I will never forgive myself if I drop him. My arms tremble, but my grip tightens and I hold fast, using every ounce of energy I have left as we clumsily lay him to rest.

Both of us stand there, heaving for breath. This morning, Scott offered to help me, and now he is dead. "Thank you," I whisper, squeezing my eyes shut. "For everything." My chin trembles because Scott deserves more than this, and yet, words fail me. He has been more than a boss since the day I started working for him—the closest thing I had to a protective male figure in my life. He made me laugh and feel seen, and I will miss him.

When I realize Knox is staring at me, I meet his gaze.

"Ready?" he asks quietly.

Exhaling, I nod, and Knox pushes piles of dirt back into the hole with the head of his pickax. I use the shovel and we fill the earth in around him.

The sun is setting on the longest day of my life by the time we're finished, and as the sky turns rose gold, I find I'm strangely grateful to be standing here with Knox. Or maybe I'm grateful to be standing here with anyone. I'd be alone otherwise. Julio and Sweetwater are all I have. My chest aches with the need to cry, but no tears come. I'm too exhausted. Too numb.

I give Knox a moment as he stares at the older graves a few yards away, then ask, "What happens now?" I'm at Knox's mercy out here. On his land. At his home.

Slowly, he shakes his head. "I don't know." He rubs his dirty hand over his face. "We'll figure it out tomorrow. You can stay here tonight." It's a statement more than an offer, and I can tell I'm not exactly wanted here. I can't say I blame him after all the trouble I've laid at his feet. He had to kill a guy today because of me. More than one, if I had to guess. But I don't have the guts to ask him to relive what happened while I was unconscious quite yet.

"You don't have to do that," I tell him. I rake my fingers through my blood-crusted hair and lift my face toward the slight breeze, drawing in a deep breath.

"Yes," Knox says, "I do." His dog comes traipsing from behind the trees, bobbed tail wagging and utterly oblivious to the heaviness suspended between us.

"The roads," I realize.

Knox picks up the tools and turns on his heel, walking back to the truck. "Come on. I'm tired." *I don't want to talk about it* he really means, and as I watch Knox trudge away, I contemplate what to do. My options are limited at this point, but to rely on Knox?

The longer I stay around him, the more he will grow to hate me at the end of all this, and I am not sure I can stand it.

FOURTEEN
KNOX

Bracing my hand against the marble, I let the water singe my skin, rolling over my shoulders, back, and arms, and take the vestiges of this fucking awful day with it. My eyes sting with exhaustion, my mind and muscles ache, and my chest burns with the all-too-familiar remnants of grief.

Memories flood my mind, vivid and as clear as if they happened only yesterday.

The house phone ringing when I stepped out of the shower, having cleaned up for dinner.

The color draining from my father's face as I walked out of my room.

Kellen's stiff shoulders as he stared at me from the kitchen counter, unblinking.

The look on Sheriff Wyatt's face as the three of us pulled up to the accident on the frontage road . . . his words sounding so far away as I stared at my mother's car smashed into an oak tree.

"*She's gone.*" The regretful sound in his voice—even the cold emptiness that nearly swallowed me when I saw her body covered in a sheet on the pavement—is so achingly vivid I wish I could live one single day without remembering it.

But more than my mother's lifeless form, I remember the look on Julio's face as the police car drove away. The way he was staring at her, like he couldn't take his eyes off what he'd done before they shifted to me, red and strangely vacant.

I lean my forehead against the shower wall and squeeze my eyes shut. This nightmare can't be my life, and yet, death has stalked me for so long it feels inevitable, too.

Every night my father came home so drunk, I thought it might be my end.

Every time the phone rang in the middle of the night.

Every time I've had to look a steer in the eyes before shooting him square between them.

And every time I've woken to an ominous red sky at morning, I've fought the urge to hold my breath. Now, here I am, in the center of chaos that feels like both the beginning and the end.

I clench my fist, recalling the crunch of cartilage against my knuckles as Ty fell to the ground after I'd surprised him in the aisleway at the warehouse. Then I exhale the image of Lars's pallid skin drenched in crimson. And worse than the echo of Rick's agonizing cries as he tried to lift himself, only to fall back into a broken heap, is the memory of Scott's final, ragged breaths and his plea for me to take Ava.

When her bloodshot, amber eyes flash to mind, I can't help but find an acute, unexpected solace in her presence. Relief that her slight frame is no longer crumpled and unconscious on the cold cement floor and that I am not alone. Even if another part of me wants to blame her for all of this, I am not my father. Shitstorms may follow Ava wherever she goes, but to blame a child for a grown man's drunkenness is wrong, no matter what my father has always chosen to believe.

Even after today, when all I want to do is curse her, I can't. Not when I experienced Lars's insanity for myself. When I heard the hatred in his voice, it was clear he was on a mission, and I was uncertain how it would all end.

Another memory forms, this one distant and disjointed at first. A memory I haven't thought about in years. A younger Ava, maybe thirteen or fourteen, waiting for a ride on the middle school campus long after everyone had gone. I was in high school, and Tony and I were walking to his house after football practice. It was before the accident, but still, Ava looked so alone. I don't know why I remember her tattered backpack or the way her dark hair fell in her face like a shield as she toed the gravel in the parking lot. But I do. Something happened that gave me pause.

Lars. His scrawny form comes into focus. He shouted at her from his group of friends, smoking under a tree on the adjacent soccer field.

Tony and I stopped, but I don't recall what Lars said.

Opening my eyes, I watch the water circle the drain at my feet, searching my brain for the rest of the memory.

"*Poor Ava, all alone. Did your drunk uncle forget about you again?*" Laughing, Lars took a drag from his cigarette like he thought he was untouchable. "*Too bad your mom can't come get you because she's dead.*"

"*Hey! Leave her alone.*" Grip tightening on my backpack straps, I took a step forward and glared at him in warning.

Lars's attention snapped to me, and his friend at his side looked uncertain he should get mixed up with us. We were older than them. Bigger too.

"*Yeah, or what?*" Lars taunted, but it was false bravado. "*You'll beat me up?*"

Tony stepped up beside me. "*Are you offering?*"

Lars sneered, his eyes shifting between us as he considered the outcome. Flicking his cigarette in Ava's direction, he scoffed. *"I've got better things to do,"* he muttered, and the two of them went back to the three girls waiting for them under the tree.

My eyes locked with Ava's. Her relief was in the glassy sheen of her eyes. She muttered a thank you and hurried off in the other direction. I don't know where she went, but I was both curious and concerned.

How could I have forgotten about that?

Mom died after that. That's how. My entire world was upended.

I consider what else I might've forgotten until I'm numb to the sting of the water, and registering the tinge of sulfur filling the shower, I shut it off and reach for my towel. The glass is partially fogged, but I can see my outline well enough. A crescent darkens one of my eyes and my busted lip is slightly swollen. But I am alive, which is more than I can say for everyone else I know.

Wrapping the towel around my waist, I open the glass door and step onto the heated tile floor. It shouldn't hurt so bad to put on my deodorant or shave, but after lugging bodies, fighting, digging, and the sheer tension that's been coiled through me all day, each monotonous task feels like a chore and all I want to do is sleep.

Running my hand over my spiky, wet hair, I head for my room. Lucy looks at me from where she's curled at the foot of my bed, and I'm about to cave in, climb into soft sheets, and pass the fuck out. But the floor creaks above me. A clatter follows, and with a groan, I hurry from my room, making my way upstairs.

FIFTEEN
AVA

MY HAPHAZARDLY PACKED BAG TOPPLES OFF THE TOILET LID onto the floor, but I barely register it as I stare at myself in the mirror in the upstairs bathroom. The bruised face staring back at me is indistinct and hazy. My dark hair is as scraggly and unruly as the bits of the day that all run together, and it's the headache that registers the most. That and my discomfort standing in Knox's fancy bathroom on a fancy memory foam rug beneath my boots, gazing into a mirror over a fancy vanity. I've never felt so out of place, and with every creak of the house, I think Mitch will appear in the doorway.

Blinking, I stare at my overnight bag. For the first time in my life, Mitch might be the least of my problems. I have three pills left in my bag, and when they are gone . . . I'm afraid of what will happen.

My hand flexes at my side and the blisters on my palm sting. Glancing around the bathroom, I dare to hope I'll find a Band-Aid or rubbing alcohol.

I open one of the dark-stained cabinets framing the mirror. This en suite is part of a man's bedroom. Or, at least, it was at some point. Its sharp edges and masculine grays and blues scream as much, so I hesitate as I open another cabinet, uncertain of what I might find.

Hair products, an old toothbrush, and tweezers. A dusty, half-used bottle of mouthwash. Unable to see everything on the top shelf, I rise onto my tiptoes and feel around, knocking an electric razor off. I cringe as it hits the counter, then continue searching. My fingers brush a pill bottle that rattles, and an unexpected hope swells to life. I snatch the bottle with the tips of my fingers. Tylenol. *Expired* Tylenol.

I sigh, though I don't know why. I already know there's no stash of Clobazam or Depakene, but I can't help but look all the same.

When I'm finished searching the top cupboards, I scour the bottom ones. There are no pill bottles, only clean towels and extra toilet paper, and a comb, dental floss, and nail clippers in one of the drawers.

The floor creaks behind me and I look up in alarm. Knox stands in the doorway, freshly showered and staring at me in the mirror. His bare chest is heaving slightly, and his hand clutches the towel around his waist tighter. I swallow thickly.

Knox's shoulders sag a little, maybe with relief, but then a scowl hardens into place. "Looking for something?"

"I—uh." A wayward droplet falls from the tip of his hair and carves a path between his pecs.

"Ava?"

My gaze snaps to his as his hazel eyes narrow, and his eyebrow arches skeptically.

I lick my lips. "I was just—"

"Just what?" he snaps, a sharp edge of distrust filling each word.

My speechlessness subsides, and I grit my teeth. "I was looking for a Band-Aid." It's mostly true.

Knox makes a derisive noise, and my hackles rise anew.

"What did you think I was doing? Stealing from you or something?" Rolling my eyes, I hold up my blistered hands. His absence of an answer is all I need. "You know what, forget it." I lift my bag from the sink and shove what's left of my meds inside as I gather my things.

I can see Knox staring at the pill bottle in the mirror, and I can only imagine what else he's thinking—what poison his father has spread about me. Or maybe he hasn't had to because Knox already assumes the worst.

"They're prescription," I reassure him, even if it bothers me that I feel the need to explain myself at all. But I am in *his* house, and Knox *is* helping me after essentially saving my life . . . even if it's begrudgingly. His hard gaze meets mine in the mirror and we stare at each other until I can't take it anymore. "God," I mutter, "stereotype much?" I bend down to grab my backpack so I can get the hell out of here.

"*What*?" he grinds out.

"Just because my uncle has an addiction problem doesn't mean I do." I've been offended by his family enough to last a lifetime, and if these are my last days in this world, I won't be spending them under his judgmental glare.

Pulling my bag strap over my shoulder, I brush past Knox and head for the stairs.

"So, I saved you hot water for nothing?"

I stop, staring over my shoulder at him in surprise. Slowly, he turns to the side and looks at me, his expression unreadable. When Knox said I could get cleaned up here, I didn't realize he meant I could actually shower.

The tension in his jaw softens, along with his features—only slightly—and he runs his hand up the back of his head, sending a few more droplets flying, as he lets out a deep breath. "I assume you saw the towels during your search?"

The thought of a shower sends chills over my skin. I nod and glance at the bottom cabinet ravenously.

"I'll get you a first aid kit with bandages from downstairs," he says. "Do you"—his gaze rakes over me from my soiled t-shirt to my boot-clad feet—"need anything else?"

I shake my head with far too much enthusiasm to be normal in such close proximity to Knox Bennett. "No." I sound more astonished than I mean to, but I'm grateful he isn't being a total dick about this situation we're in. "I have what I need. Thanks."

With a final survey of me up and down, Knox passes me in the hall, careful not to let our shoulders touch. The crisp scent of citrus and deodorant wafts behind him, and squeezing my eyes shut, I tell myself to ignore it and focus on getting through the next hour without making anything worse.

The water smells mildly sulfuric, but it's a small price to pay as it washes over the rawest parts of me. I never thought I'd want a hot shower in the dead of summer, but the heat is soothing, and I let my weariness consume me. I'm too tired to feel, too wrung out to cry, and I welcome the exhaustion.

After the crusted blood is washed from my scalp and the dirt scrubbed from my skin, I linger under the spray for only a few moments more to wash the suds away. The water starts to cool as I shut it off, and I pull down the towel I'd flung over the glass door. It's the plushest towel I've ever used, but I miss the rougher, well-worn ones I've grown so accustomed to at home.

I try not to think about home, though, because it's not real, not anymore.

Drying off, I glance at my clothes strewn around the bathroom. It looks like a bomb detonated in here from trying to find my shampoo and shower stuff Knox shoved haphazardly into my bags with everything else. I make a mental note to sort through my things tomorrow, to see what else Ty might've stolen with my meds. But that's a task for a fresh mind, when my head isn't pounding and it doesn't hurt to blink.

I wrap my hair in the towel, ignoring my headache. Clicking the shower door open, I step onto the memory foam mat awaiting me. *That* is a feeling I could get used to, and I find I can't stop thinking about the bed in the other room, wondering if the mattress will feel as magical when I finally get to lie on it. Since the Bennett family is one of the richest, oldest families in Sutton County, I expect sleeping on their plush bed in the extra bedroom will be the best night of rest I've ever had.

I pull on a pair of underwear and pajama shorts, then a tank top, before I collect my things from the shower. I leave them in the sink to drip dry, and I gather my dirty clothes. The pants and shirt I wore earlier today are stained with blood, and while I would prefer to throw them away, my wardrobe is limited.

I contemplate asking Knox if I can wash them, then drop it all again where I stand, resolved to deal with it tomorrow when I can see straight.

Tugging the towel from my head, I drape it over the shower door to dry, then brush through the tangles. It's mundane and routine, but it's never felt so good. The seconds pass, and when I hear a noise downstairs, I stir again. Blinking at myself in the mirror, I notice the circles under my eyes look more like bruises, and the pink cut across my cheek stings a little in the cool air. But even if I look like hell, I feel a thousand times better.

More content than I could have hoped to be only hours ago, I toss my brush onto the counter and turn for the door. The instant I open it, sleep is forgotten. A first aid kit sits outside the door, but that might as well be forgotten, too, the instant the scent of bacon hits my nose. My stomach turns with a savage hunger, and while it might be presumptuous to think Knox is down there making food for both of us, I can't recall the last time I ate something, and I pad down the hall and then the stairs on bare feet.

My stomach rumbles again. If Knox isn't prepared to share, I'm not above begging. Or at least scouring his cabinets for crumbs.

The wooden stairs are sturdy and don't make a sound as I wind my way down to the living room. The house looks and feels less like a home and more like a lodge with its warm tones, rich woods, and plush furniture. While most of the house is devoid of personality and looks unused, the sitting room attached to the kitchen looks lived in and comfortable, like this is where Knox and Mitch spend their time. The rest of it—the fancy dining area and library and the living spaces upstairs, are all just furnished rooms.

The wood floor is cool beneath my feet as I pad around the couch toward the open, industrial-grade kitchen. Cricket sounds hum through the screen door, and Lucy, or so I've heard Knox call her, lifts her head from her dog bed by the stone hearth. Her butt wags happily, but she doesn't get up.

I pause in front of the giant, muted television mounted above the mantel. Images of flooded cities and smoking volcanoes flash across the screen, but I don't want to think about any of that right now so I continue to the island in the center of the kitchen.

Knox moves seamlessly from the counter to the stove, and if he notices me, he doesn't bother looking up. Seeing him in a faded Dallas Cowboys t-shirt, black sweats, and bare feet feels strangely intimate, and having already ogled him tonight, I look away.

Plates sit on the quartz countertop, and my gratitude mixes with relief. *Two* plates.

"I figured you might be hungry," he says, still not meeting my gaze. Knox shuts the gas stove off, and lifting the pan, he scoops a fried egg out for each of us.

"I'm starving," I admit.

Knox removes a paper towel from another plate on the countertop, exposing a row of fried bacon, and my stomach rumbles again, loud and overly obnoxious. This time, Knox does look up, his eyes scanning me, briefly landing on my stomach before lingering on my chest. Catching himself, he clears his throat and meets my gaze.

I blush, feeling more naked than I ever have in a tank top and pajama shorts. "Can I—uh—help with anything?"

"You can grab a couple of waters from the pantry," he says, glancing toward a closed door on the other side of the kitchen. "It's not safe to drink from the faucet anymore."

Nodding, I walk around the island and stop short so I don't run into Knox as he passes in front of me, headed for the toaster. The pantry is stocked with cans and boxes of food —not so much food that I think he's a prepper or a Moonie, but enough that I can tell he and his father have been prepared to hole up here for a little while if need be.

Grabbing two plastic bottles, I take a final look around, curious if Knox means to stay here until he's forced to leave, then head back into the kitchen.

With a sigh, Knox sets a butter dish between our plates, then scans the counter to ensure he's thought of everything. Tapatío, salt, pepper, and a bottle of ketchup are clustered in the center, and when he pulls silverware out of the drawer behind him, I begin to salivate all over again.

"Thank you," I breathe, staring at this unexpected gift. Eggs, bacon, and toast—so simple and yet so mouthwatering. I lift onto a padded stool at the breakfast bar.

"Sure." He climbs onto the stool beside me.

As I butter my toast, Knox squirts ketchup on his fried egg in silence, then drizzles some Tapatío on it, followed by a dusting of salt and pepper. I don't usually like ketchup, but he makes it look amazing, so I do the same, wanting *all the things* on my plate. Then we dive in.

The food is orgasmic against my tongue: ketchup, eggs, bacon, wheat bread—none of it has ever tasted so good.

At first, I'm content to keep quiet, trying as best I can to not eat like a complete savage. But as our silverware scrapes our plates and the intermittent chatter on the radio fades into the background, our silence feels expectant, even if Knox hasn't looked at me once.

I swallow a bite of toast. "I've never had breakfast for—" I glance at the microwave clock. I knew it was late, but I didn't expect it to be nearly ten. "An almost-midnight snack."

"It's the best," he replies simply, and licking his lips, Knox opens his bottle of water and chugs it down.

"I know you have limited supplies, so I appreciate you—"

"It's fine," he says, wiping the water from his lips with the back of his hand instead of his crumpled napkin. "I'm not a total dick. I wasn't only going to make food for myself."

"I know, but after everything that happened today, I'm just—I'm really grateful. You didn't have to bring me here at all, but you did. And now I'm having what is probably the best meal I've had in weeks."

He looks at me, skeptical. "You work at a diner."

"Yeah, well, Kyle's breakfast never tasted this good." I bite off a hunk of bacon, and with a huff, I shake my head, completely incredulous of our situation.

"What?" Knox shovels the last of his egg into his mouth.

"Oh, nothing, other than the fact that, before today, we haven't spent more than twenty minutes in the same vicinity. Now, I'm in your house, eating your food."

"Yeah, well, everything is upside down. So, it seems fitting."

I snort. "True."

His eyes dart to me and then we eat the rest of our breakfast with the noise of our crackling water bottles and scraping silverware filling the kitchen. Lucy yawns audibly from her bed, then walks over to her kibble bowl by the back door.

With a yawn of his own, Knox rests his elbows on the countertop as he runs his hands over his face. "Where were you and Scott headed?" After the day we've had, I can only imagine how much his body hurts—probably worse than mine.

My meal, barely settled in my stomach, threatens to churn as I meet his gaze—a beautiful mix of copper and green that's fixed directly on me. "He was heading to Missouri."

"And you?" He stares at me, and Lucy comes up to sit beside his stool. "You were going to Missouri with him?" He reaches down and rubs her head. It's disarming that a man with a stare so sharp it could cut glass can seem so utterly gentle at the same time.

I discard my napkin on my empty plate and push it away from me. "Scott was taking me to Sweetwater," I admit.

Knox waits a beat before asking, "Who's in Sweetwater?"

There's something about his tone that makes me think he already knows. And of course he would. His father didn't start coming to the trailer park, cursing my existence in a drunken rage until Julio was released from prison. When Julio never came back to Sonora, for obvious reasons, it was as if Mitch needed to take his aggression out on someone, and Julio's only kin seemed to suffice.

Regardless, I knew this question would come eventually. I just hadn't wanted Knox to ask it so soon, not when we are on somewhat common ground at the moment.

Bracing myself, I tell him. "Julio." I can't bring myself to look away, needing to see Knox's reaction. Disgust at the thought of my uncle's face? Regret for helping me? Fury at the gull I have to think Knox might take me there? But it's none of those.

Knox's brow, tanned from working in the sun, twitches, but other than that, he looks deceptively unfazed. Then again, anger has never been Knox's MO. He's always kept himself closed off around me instead.

"I don't know what your plan was, bringing me here," I start, preparing myself for whatever he decides next, "but I get it if you want me to leave." I step down from the stool and collect our dirty plates.

Knox doesn't answer as I set them in the sink. "I promised Scott I would help you," he finally says.

"What?" My eyes snap over my shoulder to him. "What do you mean, you *promised* him?"

Elbows still perched on the counter, Knox rubs his hands over his face again, scrubbing his hair like it pains him to answer. "It was the final thing he said."

I collect the dirty pan and spatula, swallowing the emotion thickening in my throat. That Scott would be worried about me in his final moments is almost too much to bear right now.

"You've already done enough, Knox." Roughly, I clear my throat. As much as I hate to think about being on my own, it's true. He's helped me more than I ever could have hoped for today—he even fed me.

"So, you're going to, what, take the bus?" he asks dryly.

"I'll figure something out." I'm nothing if not a survivor. At least, that's what I tell myself, and I let the faucet water run over my fingers as I wait for it to warm. "He shouldn't have asked that of you."

"I'm going to take you to Sweetwater, Ava." Exhaustion riddles the sigh that follows, and his stool scrapes against the tiled floor.

"Knox—"

"We can argue about it later." His eyes don't meet mine when I look back at him. "I'm going to bed. You should have everything you need upstairs."

Without another word, Knox disappears down a hallway, and Lucy trots after him. The moment I hear his door shut, I turn the water off and brace my hands against the counter like it's the only thing keeping me upright.

Staring at the dirty dishes, I try and fail to keep the tears at bay. I learned a long time ago not to rely on anyone other than Mavey, and this was why—this unbearable weight in my chest, knowing the burden I've become. I felt it with Scott, but he didn't have the reluctance in his voice that Knox does. There was no convoluted history to wade through, and I didn't have to wonder how much Scott resented and hated me every time he looked in my direction, or avoided meeting my gaze.

Now, the person I know wishes me miles away is the very person I have to rely on. Again.

SIXTEEN
KNOX

I WAKE WITH A START. MY ROOM IS AWASH WITH DAYLIGHT, the heat of midday seeping in. I could sleep for hours more, but I've already been in bed too long.

Sitting up, I reach for my phone on the nightstand. "Shit." I climb out of bed faster than my body is ready for and nearly stumble back onto the mattress. It's nearly one p.m., and I should have fed the animals hours ago.

Yanking on my jeans, I scan my room for Lucy, but she's not here. No wonder I slept so long without her to pounce on me at dawn for breakfast and a bathroom break.

I tread into the bathroom, registering the distant hum of the backup generator. The fact that it's on means the power went out, which isn't comforting. I take care of morning business in a rush, and after I've brushed my teeth and splashed cold, sulfuric water on my face, I know I need to do something about the water situation today. As my list of priorities multiplies in the few minutes I've been awake, reality quickly sets in, and my shoulders feel heavy again.

Hurrying back to my room, I open the middle drawer of my dresser, pull out a clean, white t-shirt, and tug it over my head. Grabbing a pair of socks in my top drawer, I plop down on the mattress to pull them on. My boots are next, and my mind wanders to Ava. I have no idea what she's been up to while I've been sleeping the day away. The thought of her awake and roving around the house makes me uneasy. Not because I don't trust her per se, but because it's Ava and it's weird that she's here at all.

Boots laced, I shove off my bed and swing my bedroom door open. Bracing myself for whatever I might find, I make my way down the hallway, and stop. Ava is crouched by the mantel in the living room. I hear the tinkle of broken glass and remember the portrait of my family shattered there from the other night.

My gut reaction is to bark at her to leave it alone, but I hesitate, watching Ava's thoughtful expression instead. Her dark ponytail falls over her shoulder as she lifts the glassless frame, and she stares at the image of my family for so long my chest starts to ache. What is she thinking? I'm anxious to know, but the moment she brushes the tip of her finger over my mother's face, I can't take it anymore, and I step into the living room.

Ava jolts to her feet, her face reddening. "You're awake."

I stalk over and take the photo from her hands.

"I was just cleaning up the glass," she says in a rush.

Setting the frame on the mantel, I glance around the living room. It's neat and tidy. So is the kitchen. "You cleaned my house?"

Ava shoves her hands in her back pockets with an emphatic exhale. "I wanted to help, somehow. To thank you. And when I let Lucy out, I fed the animals, too."

My gaze snaps to hers. "You fed the animals?" I ask dubiously. I'm not sure if I should be grateful she took the initiative or upset she had the audacity to assume she should.

I don't know if it's my tone, but her uncertainty fades away, and her eyes harden on me in response. "I knew how tired you must've been." Her words are pure acid. "And I wasn't sure how long you would sleep." Her gray tank top is smudged on the side with what looks like dried horse or cow slobber, and her jeans have dirt on the thigh. Dark wisps of hair frizz around her bronze skin, and her amber eyes twinkle in the sunlight filling the room. She's finished my morning chores and then some. And now, I feel like an ass.

"Obviously, I don't know what you feed them all," Ava continues. "So, I portioned out the pellets you buy from the store."

I watch her, feeling somewhat baffled by this woman. Half the time I don't know if I'm put out by her or if I am intrigued.

"Don't make it weird, okay?" she says in my silence. Ava rubs her forehead. "I know you would prefer I wasn't here despite your misguided obligation to take care of me. I was having a hard time finding things to keep me busy that wouldn't seem overly creepy, or like I was overstepping, like doing your laundry or something." She shrugs as if she'd really considered it. "You were exhausted, and I wanted to help. It doesn't have to be a *thing.*"

I've always known Ava feels bad about what happened to my mother. She's barely held eye contact with me since her uncle was put away. But I'm starting to get the impression she thinks I dislike her a lot more than I do. First, she thought I would leave her at the farm supply store after being attacked. Then, that I would rather her be God knows where on her own instead of having her safe here with me . . . especially when the truth is, it's comforting not to be alone.

"All right," I say, and her brow lifts with surprise. I hate that my gaze shifts to her mouth before I look away.

"All right?"

I nod. "Is there anything else I should know about?" I turn for the front door to make my rounds. There are sick livestock to check on, supplies to inventory, and decisions to be made about what happens next.

Pushing the screen door open, I stop on the porch and inhale the sulfur in the air, more potent than yesterday. The day is hazy but the heat is already cloying as I step into the sun. As it beats down on me, I realize I forgot my hat, but that's the least of my worries.

Lucy scurries out from the shade of the tractor by the garden shed and lopes over, her body trembling with excitement. "Hey, pup." I give her head a good rub as she follows me toward the stables.

"The power went out sometime in the night," Ava offers, her strides nearly as wide as mine to keep up.

I pause and look at her. She worries her bottom lip in thought, her hands still in her back pockets. I try not to notice the way her shirt hugs her curves but fail miserably and look away again. "I noticed the backup generator was on."

"Do we have to worry about it running out of fuel?" She falls into step behind me again.

"No, it's piped into the natural gas," I explain, grateful that's one less thing I have to worry about today.

"About the water—" Ava starts again as we step into the horse stable. Poppy, Rooster, and Loca all poke their heads out of their stalls in greeting, eyes wide and ears forward.

"What about it?" Our footsteps echo against the cement walkway.

"With the sulfur issue, I didn't know what you'd want to do, so I didn't refill any of the troughs."

"Okay, I'll get it sorted." I've never had to bleach the

animals' drinking water, but I'm not sure I have another option at this point.

"And the sick steers," Ava adds more hesitantly. Reluctantly, I meet her gaze. "One of them looks pretty bad."

I glare in no particular direction, my hope of sidestepping death today extinguishing. "I'll take care of it."

Ava looks as regretful as I feel, and her amber eyes shift over me. "Is there anything I can do to help?"

I'm about to tell her no, there isn't anything she can do unless she wants to shoot a steer between the eyes, but then another thought strikes me instead. "Inventory. Whether we stay here for a while, or get on the road to Sweetwater, we need to know what we have."

She nods. "I can do that."

"Unload what you can from my truck, mark down our supplies and anything glaring we may still need. When I'm finished, we'll see what I have stocked in the pantry and shed."

Ava doesn't need more direction than that. With a renewed sense of purpose, she marches back the way we came.

"Hey, Ava?"

Hands in her back pockets again, she spins around to look at me.

"Thank you."

She visibly swallows, and if I'm not mistaken, relief fills her eyes. "Of course." Her voice is soft, and with an absent stroke of her hand over Poppy's brown muzzle, she strides into the sunlight.

By late afternoon, the air is thick with the scent of smoke, and I've checked the ham radio four times for news and gleaned enough to know the sinkhole mayhem continues to spread. Martial law has been enacted in bigger cities like New York and Washington DC as more and more people panic. And with everyone fleeing the southern part of the state, northern counties all over Texas are in chaos. Some of the families in locations that are inundated by travelers try to stay hunkered down, while some of them have fled perfectly good homes to head farther north, not wanting to see what will happen next in the Lone Star State. Most disconcerting are the wildfires spreading from New Mexico toward Balmorhea and Mentone, though chatter says firefighters may have them under control. The more I dwell on it, though, the more uneasy it makes me, so I focus on ranch tasks instead.

By six p.m., most of what I wanted to accomplish is done, and Rooster and I head back to the stable. Dirty and exhausted, he clomps faster, anxious to get back to his paddock. I've filled five steel drums with water, cleaned and chlorinated for the animals to drink over the next few days, and led the sick steer over the ridge to put it out of its misery. I still haven't burned the bodies, though. Not only do I want to avoid drawing unwanted attention to us out here, I have more immediate concerns. Especially if we're not going to stay at the ranch.

I pull Rooster to a stop at the hitching post, and Lucy, panting and exhausted from traipsing around the property, runs over to the water trough for a drink. I glance around for Ava. From what I can tell, she's unloaded most of the supplies and arranged them neatly inside the stable, safe from the sun. But I don't see her.

Rooster lets out a heavy sigh, and I climb down from the

saddle. I go through the motions, removing his tack, and all the while, my thoughts drift to Sweetwater.

If Sweetwater is where Ava wants to go, I will take her. But my gut tells me staying here is best, and I can't help but wonder how that would work—the two of us holed up here for the foreseeable future. Or if Ava would even be willing to stay.

Surely, she would see sense in the idea that we are safer here than facing whatever the unknown might have in store for us? We have plenty of food, and access to water, even if it will eventually need to be treated. I can protect us here better than on the road, and maybe—just maybe—my father and brother, even Tony, might surprise me and return to the ranch at some point. It's obvious how uncomfortable Ava is here, so convincing her to stay won't be easy, but I know I have to; it's the smartest thing to do for now, even if it's . . . awkward.

It's been years since a woman lived in the house—ten years to be exact—and that Ava, of all people, might become a permanent resident is the most ironic turn of events yet. The image of her standing at the island last night, freshly showered in her pajamas, flashes to mind, and my body heats instantaneously. It's a mindfuck is what it is, and I push all those thoughts away.

When Rooster's sorrel coat is brushed down, and he's watered, I lead him back to his stall. With a final pat on his rump, I nudge him inside to rest and close him in. My stomach rumbles with hunger. Craving a ham sandwich with extra mustard and a side of kettle chips, I head for the house to make us something to eat, scouring the outbuildings for Ava along the way.

The truck bed is completely empty. And those feed sacks were anything but easy to move, especially in the blaze of the Texas sun. I shake my head, imagining Ava straining as she unloaded everything on her own, and know I have to give her props for that. If nothing else, she's got grit and gumption, which she'll need on the ranch.

Wiping my sweaty brow with my shoulder, I notice the garden shed is open.

"Ava, take a break." I stride over. "I'm making foo—" I stop at the tractor. "Ava?" A bone-chilling dread rushes through my veins. She's crumpled on the ground against the shed. "Ava!" I fall to my knees beside her. "Ava, can you hear me?" Her eyes are open and glazed over, her lips slightly parted, and her face is pale. "Ava, say something," I demand, but I don't touch her, uncertain what to do. Finally, she blinks, but it's lethargic, and her breathing is ragged. "What do I do?" I plead. "What's wrong?" Heat stroke? Side effects from her concussion?

I don't wait for Ava to answer as I scoop her into my arms. "I'll get you inside where it's cool." Her body is limp, her skin sticky with sweat. "Ava," I breathe as I march toward the porch, "say something. Please."

Lethargically, she lifts her arm and splays her palm across my chest. "Sleep," she murmurs so quietly I barely hear her over the creak of the screen door as I fling it open. "Water and sleep."

I take her to the couch and lay her down. "I'll get you water," I promise, brushing the sweaty strands of hair from her face. Rushing to the fridge and back, I tell myself she is fine—everything will be fine—and kneel beside her.

Ava blinks a few more times and licks her lips as the color slowly returns to her skin.

"You already look better," I say, more for myself than for her benefit. Twisting the top off the water, I put it to her mouth, offering her a drink.

Ava's hand comes up, but she doesn't take the bottle.

Instead, her arm drops to her chest, like it's too heavy to hold up and she lifts her head as much as she can to sip from the bottle.

"Ava, what the hell is happening?"

Closing her eyes, she takes a few small drinks. "I'll be okay," she rasps as she drops her head. Her cheeks flush, but it can't possibly be with embarrassment, and she averts her gaze. "I just need rest."

All I can do is stare at her as she turns over to face the couch cushions.

That's it? That's all she's going to give me? I nearly had a heart attack, thinking she might be dying, and now she's going to sleep? What if sleeping is the last thing she should be doing? What if she's dehydrated and needs more water? What if she fell out there and hit her head again?

I rise to my feet, heart racing, fear and confusion tangling like bramble bushes as I peer down at her. What the actual fuck just happened?

SEVENTEEN
AVA

I WAKE ON KNOX'S COUCH, A BLANKET DRAPED OVER ME, and only a small lamp illuminating the living room. I don't know when the sun set during my dozing in and out all evening or what time it is, but there's a chill in the air, so it must be late.

The house is quiet, save for the distant hum of the generator, and for a moment, I think Knox has gone to bed.

A horse whinny carries in from outside, and I sit up. I can see the moonlit barn through the screen door, then I hear Knox's voice, a low murmur too quiet to comprehend. The porch creaks next, and my cheeks heat as I realize he has likely been outside, waiting for me to wake up.

Untangling from the blanket, I right myself, my boots hitting the rug with a soft thud. I should have warned Knox this might happen—that it *would* eventually happen. I rally myself to go out there.

Epilepsy is not a topic that comes up naturally in *any* conversation, especially not in the chaotic mess of the past two days. I have to explain it to him, though—he deserves far more than that—and I force myself to get up.

Grabbing the half-empty water bottle from the coffee table, I walk to the door. I'm still fully dressed, but my tank top covers little, and the chilly night sends goosebumps over my exposed arms as I push the screen open. The tinge of smoke in the air is barely noticeable because all I can think about is what Knox will say next.

But he says nothing. Knox doesn't even look at me as I step outside. His hand pauses its ministrations on Lucy's silky ear, though, and her head darts in my direction.

"Hey," I say dumbly. I walk over to the rocking chair next to his.

"Hey." Even in the night shadows, I can tell his gaze is fixed on the stables and inky horizon—anywhere but toward me.

"I should have warned you." It's all I can think to say as I lower into the seat, pulling my legs under me.

Finally, Knox looks at me, playing with Lucy's ear as she dozes off again beside him. I think it comforts him as much as her. "So . . . you *did* know that would happen."

I nod. "I assumed it would, eventually."

His jaw clenches in the moon shadows, and I know he's angry. Still, he gives nothing else away. "Was it the heat?"

Turning the water bottle around in my hand, I shake my head. "No—I mean, the heat doesn't help, but it's not solely that. If anything, it just makes it worse."

Knox stares at me for so long I begin to itch under his gaze, uncertain of what he's thinking. I want him to ask me all his questions, simply to fill the awkward silence that seems to settle between us so easily. And finally, he grants my wish. "That happens a lot?"

I bite my lip, considering what *a lot* means to him. "It comes and goes in waves, but it's worse when I stop taking my meds."

Knox rubs his forehead. "The pills in the white bag."

I run my finger over the grooves in the chair arm.

"And that bag, the one you can't find, was all you had?"

"I have a few pills left, but silly me," I say caustically, "I thought I could ration them." I uncap my water and take a drink for something to do—movement to disperse the anxious energy buzzing through me. "I know better."

Knox's gaze bores into the side of my face as if I'm not squirming enough already.

"I'll survive without them," I promise. "It just sucks, is all."

"It's why you don't drive," he muses, and wordlessness finds us again. Crickets and the pacing horses in the stables fill the night.

"Usually," I start, "I know when they are coming and can prepare for them. Well, as much as you can prepare for something like that. But today, I don't know. It came faster than I'm used to." I shake my head. "I wasn't ready for it."

"Ready for what, exactly?" In my periphery, Knox shifts in his seat. "What happens?"

"Some call them absence seizures, but it's more than that." I search for a way to explain it to him. I've never talked to anyone about my spells other than Scott because it's happened at work a few times, and Mavey, of course. I feel exposed having it happen around Knox when two days ago, we weren't even on speaking terms.

Placing my hand on my chest, I force myself to find the words. "It's like I feel a void coming to life inside of me. That's the only way I can think to explain it." With a huff, I shake my head. "You'd think *knowing* a spell is coming is a good thing, but sometimes I think it makes them worse. I can't stop them, so I stew and wait for them to come."

Lucy snores softly at Knox's feet, and when I glance at

him, he's staring out at the darkness. "You were looking right at me," he murmurs, and there's a trace of horror in his voice. "You looked dead, Ava."

I lean my head back against the chair, slowly rocking back and forth. There are cobwebs on the slatted porch ceiling, and I make a mental note to clean them for Knox tomorrow. "I don't know how to explain it," I say. "But it's like being paralyzed. Sometimes, I can hear and see things, but I can't move. Other times, everything tunnels away, fading completely until I can't see or hear anything at all. It only lasts for seconds, I think. Maybe a few minutes, but afterward, it feels like the life is drained from me."

Knox leans his head back in the chair, stoic and thoughtful, and the more I watch him, I think he's being careful with his words, too. "How long have you had them?"

"All my life," I whisper.

Moonlight stripes Knox's face. His brow is furrowed, his jaw tight again. And that pensive look of his is quickly becoming maddeningly dependable.

"It was hard to diagnose when I was little," I continue. "Even now, my doctors argue what it is. I've gotten so many tests done, but they are always inconclusive." I snort a laugh. "I'm not sure what that says about me," I mutter.

"Since you continue to have them," Knox says flatly, "I'd say whatever they're doing isn't working. You need to see a specialist."

I laugh again.

"It's not funny, Ava." His chiding voice makes me bristle, and the smile falls from my lips.

"You don't think I know that?" I sit straighter in my chair. "I'm the one who has to live with it. But money doesn't grow on trees, Knox. At least not for me. I've barely been able to pay my medical bills as it is—a specialist is out of the question. Just getting to the city is an obstacle in itself, and leaving Mavey overnight—" My voice cracks, and I grit my teeth. "There have been more important things to worry about. Especially now."

The water sloshes in my bottle as I rock back and forth, exhaling the weighty memory of Mavey. Of how different my life was only a handful of hours ago. "I hate losing control of my body," I confess. "Especially when it happens in public. Being conscious and incapable of speaking, moving, or even seeing sometimes—" I say in a rush. "Obviously, I would fix it if I could."

With a hefty sigh, Lucy stretches out on the porch, and the horses move restlessly in the stables.

"I wish there was a better way to tell how bad things have gotten in town," Knox mutters.

I've wondered the same thing a dozen times, and every time I think of town, I imagine what's left of Lars's crew looking for the one who killed their friends. Because my gut tells me if any of them learned what happened in the supply store, they'd know it had something to do with me.

I shake my head. "I know what you're thinking, Knox, and it's not worth it. Especially because we—" A familiar rumble roars in the night, instantly followed by the quaking earth. Lucy scrambles away in fear, the horses neigh, and the wood around us creaks in protest.

Remotely, I notice strange lights flickering in the distance as I grab onto the arms of the rocking chair to push myself up and run, but Knox and I are barely standing when the world stills again, and the rumbling ceases.

We wait for an aftershock with bated breath, and when nothing comes, I meet his wide-eyed gaze.

"You'd think I'd be used to that by now," I rasp, wiping my sweaty hands on my pants.

"Same." Knox stares toward the paddock where Poppy paces. "I should've realized that was why the animals have been so anxious tonight."

Lucy comes scampering back from around the house, and Knox steps off the porch. "I hooked the antenna up earlier. See what you can find on the TV. I'm going to check on the livestock."

"Yeah," I breathe. "Okay." I move for the screen door, watching the way Knox's strides consume the distance to the stables, once again filled with purpose. Our reprieve, it would seem, is over.

EIGHTEEN
KNOX

WHEN I'M FINISHED CHECKING ON THE HORSES AND THE steers, I head to the shed to find my father's old radio from the days he used to work in the fields. With the ham radio overloaded with civilian chatter, the phone lines down, the power out, and the scent of fire on the breeze, it's my last-ditch effort to figure out what's happening at the government level.

Once I find the radio, I switch the flashlight off to conserve the battery and head back. The intermittent moonlight illuminates the generator idling on the side of the house, and I thank God we spent an obscene amount of money to install it a few years ago.

When I step inside, Ava is in front of the television, her stance wide and one hand on her hip as she scans for news. "Only one channel will come in," she says, peevish. Sweat glistens on her brow, lit by the screen and the single lamp on the side table. "And it's not entirely helpful." I read the prompt plastered across the television.

The following warnings have been issued for the state of Texas. The National Weather Service has issued a wildfire alert for all counties in the Great Plains region. All residents in affected areas should evacuate immediately.

I'm not surprised by the alert, having smelled smoke in the air all day.

"If the wind shifts, it could easily come this way," Ava murmurs. "And we have no way of knowing."

Refusing to let my mind spiral, I lift the radio. "Maybe this will help." I drop to the couch, and clenching my hand at my side, I brace myself and click the radio on.

When Ava plops down beside me, the faint scent of her apple shampoo I smelled last night at dinner wafts off her, and I clear my throat.

"Here—" She extends the antenna for me, and we both seem to hold our breath as I scan the stations. Static. Static. Muffled music. Static. Static. Static.

" . . . evacuate immediately." The monotone voice is scratchy, and I angle the radio for a better signal. "Due to increased wildfire events, warnings have been issued for the southern and Great Plains states. Evacuation may be required. Please be advised."

Ava watches me closely, gauging my reaction, no doubt to temper her own.

"Due to severe wind events in the Midwest, a shelter-in-place order has been issued. Tsunami warnings and mandatory evacuation orders have been announced for all coastal states. Evacuate to the nearest safe shelter immediately." The voice pauses before continuing again. "Due to unprecedented winter storm events in the Northeast, shelter-in-place or evacuation may be required. Please be advised. Locate the nearest safe shelter immediately."

Silence stretches for a moment before the broadcast starts again. "The National Weather Service has issued the following statements. Due to unprecedented and severe weather patterns, the president of the United States has declared a state of emergency in the following regions. Please be advised. All coastal communities should find a safe shelter and evacuate immediately. Due to increased wildfire events, a warning has been issued—" I turn the volume down as the broadcast loops and stare at the dusty radio.

"So much for staying here as long as we can," I mutter.

I lean back against the couch, and Ava does the same, her shoulder brushing mine as we stare at the television screen, its glow almost haunting in the shadowy room.

"We don't know where the fires are exactly," Ava points out. "Just because we can smell them doesn't mean they are coming this way. The wind can carry the smoke for miles."

"True, but our luck isn't that good." I close my eyes as I consider how quickly we should pack and get out of here. But go where? And what about the animals? The truth is, we have no clue where the closest safe shelter is since half of Texas is already gone. And I know that whatever we do find will be inundated with people.

"I don't know if Sweetwater is any better off," Ava says quietly, "but at least we have a direction to go." Once again, Ava waits for my reaction, but I don't have the energy to care about Julio right now.

"What did it say about the Midwest?" I ask instead, thinking about my uncle's farm in Ransom. I've been so focused on trying to stay here for as long as possible I wasn't even paying attention.

"Wind events," she recalls. "Shelter-in-place, I think."

"Tornadoes," we both seem to realize at once.

"That's not entirely surprising, I guess." Pulling my phone from my back pocket, I find Mason's number in my contacts and press the call button. The recorded operator comes on immediately, and with a groan, I toss my phone onto the coffee table with a clatter. "Pointless."

I fail to exhale the tension coiling through every inch of me, and Lucy must feel it too because she patters over and licks my hand. Her blue and gray eyes draw together with concern.

Sitting up, I set the radio on the coffee table. "What do you want to do?" It's a selfish question, but I'm tired of making decisions and want her to decide for both of us.

Ava looks at the television, her gaze lingering before shifting back to me. She chews the inside of her cheek, which is something I've never seen her do, and I wonder if it's a new tick or just one of a million things I don't know about her.

None of that matters, though, and closing my eyes, I lean my head back and sort through more pressing thoughts.

"I think," Ava drawls, as if her thoughts are still forming. "I think we spend tomorrow finishing the inventory I didn't get to today. Then, maybe we prepare everything we'll need if the time comes and we have to leave at the drop of a hat. Otherwise—" I meet her gaze again as she hedges. Her lips are pursed, her expression uncertain. "Otherwise, we stay here for as long as we can, where we're safest. For now."

This close, Ava's eyes gleam like smoky quartz in the lamplight. I see fear in their depths. I see exhaustion. But I see her determination and strength too. I can feel it radiating off her, even as she bites her cheek with uncertainty, and unexpectedly, a calmness eases over me. All her life she's been surviving, and if she can look at me, composed and levelheaded after the hell we've gone through in the past twenty-four hours, I know I have to be solid too.

"Then," I start, unable to resist another glance at her lips, "that's what we'll do. Tonight, we get some rest. We can worry about tomorrow when the sun comes up."

"Yeah, okay," she agrees, and with our next steps decided, I lean back into the couch again. We both stare up at the exposed beams in the ceiling. The wind chime jingles outside, the low murmur of the radio and the distant sound of the generator fill the room, and still it feels too quiet between us.

"What did he do?" I ask suddenly. Ava seemed far too close to jumping out of a moving vehicle when she realized we were at the ranch.

"What?" She blinks at me, but I can tell she's tracking because she clams up almost immediately.

"Why are you so scared of my father? I know what a mean bastard he is, but the look on your face yesterday—" My jaw tightens. "It hasn't sat right with me since."

Ava's dark eyebrows draw together and she looks down at her fingernails. "He started coming to the trailer park a few years ago."

I frown. I hadn't expected her to say that. "What for?" My fist clenches at my side.

"To remind me how much he hates Julio—and me, I guess." She's thoughtful as I sit up and angle to face her fully.

"What was my dad doing at your house, Ava?" My voice is quiet but filled with dread and rage and disappointment as I wait for her to explain. And maybe there's a little guilt for having known none of this.

"Yelling, mostly. He didn't come inside or anything. He never tried or even knocked at the door. But he would stand outside, cursing Julio and shouting all the things he wanted me to tell him next time I see him. Sometimes, it was me he seemed mad at. It just depended, I guess, and I think learning Julio had gotten out of prison pushed him over the edge."

I can think of a handful of nights over the past few years when Wyatt brought my father home drunk. I'd thought it was because he didn't want my dad to drive home from the bar, but had it been an escort from Ava's house every time?

"The sheriff apologized but never did much more than that. I know he and your dad were friends—"

"So what? He's the fucking sheriff." I glare into the empty fireplace. "I knew my dad made comments to you sometimes—he blamed everyone for all his problems." I shake my head. "But I never knew about that."

Ava pulls her legs in to her chest, nestling into the corner of the couch. "It doesn't matter now. It's over—all of it is over."

It's what she doesn't say that hangs in the air between us —Mavey is gone. My father is gone. Hell, the whole town may be gone for all we know. Still, imagining Mavey and Ava alone in that trailer and my father bullying them makes me hate him all over again. As reluctant as she seems, I know Ava isn't telling me everything, either.

"I'm sorry he did that to you. That you had to worry about my father on top of everything else."

"It's not your fault your dad's an asshole, Knox," she says, far too forgiving. "Or . . . was."

"Still, I spent so much time ignoring him as much as I could . . . I should have paid more attention."

"Honestly," she says with a brittle laugh. "I would take your dad harassing me over this shit any day." And while I appreciate her making light of it, I can't find it in me to do much more than smile.

"If I'm being *really* honest," she continues, glancing around my house, "I thought you hated me as much as he did.

That's why this is so . . . weird." My eyes meet Ava's for a second before her cheeks redden a little and she looks away. "Maybe you do and you're just better at hiding it."

Though I can't blame Ava for thinking I'm so much like my father, it still rankles me. "I've never hated you." The words form easily. "But I've resented you at times, even though none of what happened to my mother and my family has ever been your fault." Only as I speak the words aloud do they actually feel true. "None of this should have ever been a burden on you." I stare at the broken portrait on the mantel. "My father destroyed this family after she was gone. Or maybe it was headed that way all along. My mom was the glue holding us all together. When she died, everything imploded." Deep down, that feels most like the truth. "Kellen was always going to be gay and my dad was always going to punish him for it," I confess. "None of that had anything to do with you or Julio, or even my mom, for that matter. None of that would have been any different if she were still alive."

"Is that whose room I'm sleeping in? Your brother's?"

I glance toward the stairs. "He hasn't been home in ten years. Not since my mom—well, you know."

Ava picks at a loose thread in the seam of her jeans. "I'm sorry, Knox." The sincerity in her voice tears at my heart a little because, like me, Ava has lost her entire family too. "Where's Kellen now?"

A knot forms in the center of my chest, tightening as I try to speak. "Dead, I think. In California."

Leaning closer, Ava rests her hand on my shoulder, and I feel the warmth of her handprint through my shirt. "I would say I'm sorry again, but the words seem pointless the more I say them."

My gaze flicks to hers, then lowers to her pursed lips. "Thanks." Her eyes glisten with unshed tears, but I don't know who they're for. Me? My brother? For my family? For both of us?

It might be the summer heat or the world ending, but the air between us feels thick and charged, and my instinct is to move away and put more distance between us. But I don't. I sit there, staring at her and remembering her when she was a kid, with her knobby knees and long dark braid that reached her lower back. Her knees aren't so knobby anymore, and the shyness in her eyes holds far too many emotions to fathom. She licks her lips, and even they are fascinating.

Her hand falls away.

I clear my throat.

"We really are orphans now," she muses, and her voice is so quiet, I almost miss it as I blink myself out of my daze.

The television flickers, drawing her attention, and the glow of it illuminates her profile.

"I haven't heard from Tony in two days," I admit. I don't tell Ava so she feels sorry for me, but because I know they were friends. "He was with his mother in San Antonio. Then, the sinkhole—" I try and fail to swallow the growing lump in my throat. "I have no idea if he's alive."

Nostrils flaring, Ava inhales a deep, ragged breath and bobs her head. Slowly. Resigned. "I wondered," she admits, and when Lucy groans with a stretch, stirring the mood again, Ava rises to her feet. "I should probably get some sleep if I'm going to be worth anything tomorrow."

I stand, and Lucy hops to her feet too. "Do you want to take a sandwich up with you?" I'm not sure I'm even hungry, but the words come out all the same.

"I'm okay." She grabs her battered water bottle from the coffee table. "Thanks, though." With a watery smile, Ava makes her way to the stairs only to stop at the bottom. "Hey, Knox?" She looks back at me. "Thanks for taking care of me today." Gratitude cracks her voice, and knowing what she's been going through with Mavey and her own doctors, I wonder when someone took care of Ava last.

"I'm just glad you're okay."

She huffs a sad sort of laugh. "Hopefully this isn't a trend, my having to thank you every night for saving me in some way."

I want to tell Ava that she has saved me too— my sanity, if nothing else. But I don't, and she disappears up the steps.

I'm not sure how long I stare at the darkened staircase before Lucy whimpers at my side, licking my hand impatiently. Groaning, I run my hand over my face and head, peering down at her. "Food. And then sleep," I tell her, knowing we both desperately need it.

NINETEEN
AVA

BETWEEN MUDDY DREAMS AND INCOHERENT THOUGHTS, I hear voices and see shadows behind my eyelids. It's all in my head—the fear and bated breath in which I wait for Lars's crew to find us, hell-bent on retaliation. I calm myself with the growing confidence that they have far more urgent things to worry about, the same as the rest of us.

The plush mattress keeps me up rather than helping me sleep. It's a constant reminder I am in Knox's house and of the conversations we shared today. I had no idea he'd lost so many people, and after what happened with Scott, I can imagine Knox is barely holding himself together. But he is, for me. Just as I'm sure I would have lost my shit by now if not for him. But unease slithers over me, ever-present. It's only a matter of time before the ground shakes again, and what's to stop the earth from finally giving in beneath us, swallowing the ranch whole?

Lightning flashes in the distance, as it has been, off and on for a couple of hours, but I try not to worry about fires right now. Lucy and the anxious horses outside will alert us to anything approaching if the time comes. But when I'm not thinking about sudden evacuation, I'm listening to the creaks and groans of the large house settling in the wind.

Amid my tossing and turning, I try to imagine a world different from this one. A world where people don't have to worry about the shift in gravity or the impending effects of an asteroid collision with the moon. A world where everyday concerns are not consumed with what cataclysmic event will hit next. Where Gerty is the name of a little girl on the playground and not the harbinger of death, the bringer of chaos, and the eventual end of us all.

I roll onto my back and inhale a deep breath, willing myself to go to sleep. I need to maintain at least a little sanity to deal with reality tomorrow. But when the floorboards creak beside me, my eyes fly open.

At first, I think the form looming next to my bed is only a sleepy illusion, but as a man's broad-shouldered outline sharpens, I scream.

Scurrying out of the tangled blankets, my heart pounding, I flatten against the wall across the room and shove the blinds over, allowing the moonlight in. It swaths Mitch Bennett in a haunting, almost otherworldly blue.

"Ava!" Knox's voice booms from the first floor as he barrels loudly up the stairs.

I have a distant thought to gather my things and rush out of here, knowing I am the last person on Earth that Mitch would ever welcome into his house, but I'm stunned in place. Confused. Horror-struck at the sight of him. He's just standing there, silent and motionless.

Mitch's dark hair is disheveled and his eyes are sunken in. His cheek is streaked with grease or dirt—maybe even dried blood. His black t-shirt with the Bennett logo is torn, and he has a hole in the knee of his Wranglers. But the dead look in his eyes is what pins me in place. His gaze is empty, not glazed over like he's drunk. He doesn't even seem angry to see me cowering across the room from him.

"Ava—" Knox lurches to a stop in the doorway, his bare chest heaving as he takes in the sight of his father. "Dad? What—" Knox steps into the room, his hair tousled and his face lined from sleep.

Mitch doesn't answer, and his stare doesn't waver from me.

"Dad," Knox tries again, sterner this time.

Having never seen Mitch Bennett so still and quiet before, I swallow another scream, uncertain of what he'll do next. "I —I'll go," I stammer, afraid to move.

Knox moves to stand beside his father. "Dad," he repeats carefully.

Finally, Mitch looks at him and his features soften a little. "Knox." His voice is rough and breathy.

Knox assesses his father up and down. "What happened? I worried you were dead."

Mitch's eyebrows draw together, the lines in his forehead deepening, and then his eyes fill with something I have never seen before. It looks a lot like sadness. Relief, maybe. But instead of answering him, Mitch's shoulders droop; he turns on his boot heel, and leaves the room, a slight limp in his step.

Knox meets my gaze, a flustered, frantic sort of confusion furrowing his brow. Turning, he stalks after his father. "Dad, Jesus—tell me what happened."

Without Mitch's invisible hold on me, I start collecting my things in a rush, knowing I cannot stay here now that he's returned. A pang of sadness is quickly chased away by desperation, and I hurry into the bathroom. I fumble, grabbing what few things I have, and return to the room as Knox strides in.

"What are you doing?"

"Leaving, obviously," I bite out. "I can't stay here—not now. I shouldn't have been here to begin with. I knew this would happen."

"Ava, you can't go. Where—"

"I won't stay where I'm not wanted."

"He hasn't said a single thing about you—he hasn't said anything at all," Knox amends.

"He doesn't have to, Knox. Your dad has wished me dead for the last ten years. That feeling doesn't just go away."

"You're assuming—"

I spin around to face him. "Assuming? The entire trailer park knows it," I snap. "No, the entire *town.*"

Knox glowers and rubs his temple, and I see the weight of every minute and hour and burden in his tired eyes. "Look, whatever happened in the past doesn't really matter now, does it? Everything changed the minute the sinkhole swallowed half of Texas. If you leave now, you have no way to protect yourself, and no way to get to Sweetwater."

"I'll figure it out." I pull a sweatshirt over my head. "I have to."

"No," Knox says, grabbing my arm gently. "Ava, you don't. You're being stubborn. You don't have to do anything. Not yet."

I meet his gaze, my body trembling.

"At least wait until the sun is up so I can give you supplies." He motions down the hall. "He's in his room. If you feel unsafe up here, you can keep your things downstairs with me." The words must taste sour because Knox struggles to say them. But he's right, no matter how desperately I want to flee and risk the wrath of the world from here to Sweetwater, I have nothing—no water, no transportation, and no protection. I need a few minutes to think things through and come up with a plan, not a death wish.

"I'll help you figure it out," Knox promises. "Just—let me think for a second, all right? Two minutes ago, I thought my dad was dead."

That steadies my swirling thoughts. "Yeah. Sure." I suddenly can't stop nodding. "Of course. You should try to talk to him. Make sure he's okay." As much as Mitch unnerves me, he didn't look okay, not in the slightest. Exhaling, I shake my head, dislodging myself from my self-centered flight mode, and lick my lips.

Knox flashes me a grateful look I don't quite understand, and then he pulls my pack over his shoulder. "You can stay downstairs in my room. I'll sleep up here."

I swallow, glancing into the hallway as my nerves settle a little. "I'm sorry."

He stops halfway to the door. "For what?"

"For this being one more thing you have to worry about."

His gaze lingers on me for a minute, but he doesn't reply as he heads out of the room and down the stairs.

I finish shoving my things into my messenger bag and step into the hallway. But unlike Knox, I hesitate. I stare down the hall at Mitch's closed door. He is not tearing his room apart. He is not crying, at least not loud enough to hear. I don't know if it's years of conditioned fear or waking up to a man in the house looming over me, but I feel more terrified having Mitch here than of what happened with Lars yesterday.

Lucy's claws tap on the hardwood downstairs, and blinking, I tear my gaze from Mitch's bedroom door. With the fleeting thought that it was strangely comforting to be here while it lasted, I make my way downstairs.

TWENTY
KNOX

I RAP MY KNUCKLES ON HIS BEDROOM DOOR. "DAD?" I'VE never seen him so still and silent, and I am beginning to worry he is more than exhausted, he's broken. When he doesn't answer, I peek my head inside. He's sitting on his perfectly made king bed, fully clothed, facing the window that overlooks the stables and the pastures that extend beyond it. With his back to me, I can't tell if he's crying or simply staring, but I go in anyway.

"I brought you water and toast in case you're hungry." I inch around his bed. His eyes are dry, exhausted, and red-rimmed in the dawn light. He blinks but doesn't look at me as I set the plate of food and a water bottle on his nightstand. "Pop—"

"Why is the Hernandez girl here?" he asks. His voice is rough from disuse, but he doesn't look away from the window.

I eye him as I consider my reply. "We ran into trouble at the supply store, and she was hurt. So, I brought her here." Lowering myself into the chair adjacent to the window, I stare down at the sheepskin rug at my feet, where my father has tied his boots every morning for years. Even the chair cushion is molded to fit him. "Scott's dead," I add, trying not to relive all that again. "I brought him back here to bury him."

Finally, my father looks at me. "How?"

"Lars and some of his guys. Scott was helping us get supplies when Lars came looking for Ava." I rake my fingers over my head and lean back in the chair, exhaling the emotions sharpening with every image. "It was bad, but . . ."

"But what?"

I meet his gaze. "At least they are dead now too."

My father's brow twitches slightly. I can see the questions in his eyes, or maybe it's relief that I'm alive? Even in his altered state, it's hard to tell with him. Seeing my angry, obstinate father browbeaten and barely speaking is so unsettling it brings the sting of tears to my eyes. "What happened?" I whisper. "When I heard about the sinkhole, I was going after you—"

"You shouldn't have done that."

I swallow the bitter words that start to form on my tongue. *Why, because you wouldn't have?* I want to say it, but as much as I think that might be true, the sudden lift in his shoulders and the terror in his voice, clipped and edged with a hint of desperation, make me think otherwise.

"There's nothing left, Knox. There's nothing south of here. The things I've seen—" When my father's voice cracks, he looks away from me as if he can't stand to show such weakness. "It's over—all of it. I don't care what they've been saying for years. There was no preparing for what's happening . . . It was stupid to think we could."

"Tell me," I urge. "Tell me what you saw—what are we up against? We're limited to generators and the radio. It's all I can do not to drive to town to get Ava's meds, but I don't know what's out there."

Mitch Bennett frowns at the mention of Ava, but I don't think it's with hate or censure. If anything, he looks surprised. Whatever curiosities he has, however, he locks away and blinks out the window instead. My father is quiet so long I think he's refusing to answer me.

"I always knew death was a bitch," he finally mutters. "But . . . I never thought it was evil." His voice is barely a whisper. "I never knew it was alive—a parasite spread through the wind. The ground shakes and swallows a man whole, but it's the people it doesn't swallow that wreak the most havoc. Fear—all it does is unleash the devil."

I think my father has finally lost it. That he's snapped past the point of repair. But the stoic horror in his voice that borders on awe is the most sober I've ever heard him. He's not raw and riddled with guilt and anger like every other day of his life, and I run my clammy hands over my basketball shorts, holding my breath as I wait for him to continue.

"I stopped for the night in Kerrville," he says, his voice a million miles away. "I woke up to a quake so bad, I heard the walls splitting, and everything went black after that. I don't know how many hours I was out, but gunfire—" He swallows thickly. "Gunfire woke me again, and I was half buried in rubble. My leg was pinned under a shelving unit, and before I could really gain my bearings, I had to watch three men shoot an old man without a second thought—to *put him out of his misery*, they said."

My father's voice breaks. "But I heard the old man begging—I *still* hear it. Just like I can still hear the amuse-ment in their voices when they told him it was better this way and pulled the trigger. I knew right then if they found me alive, I was going to be next. So, I lay there, pretending I was dead for what felt like hours, while I watched them through the rubble, tending to their own injuries. They planned what to do next, like it was just another day," he bites out.

Elbows on his knees, my father clasps his hands behind his head and peers down at the floor. "And the whole time," he says hoarsely, "I knew the old man was just out of sight. Dead, with who knows how many others."

My chest squeezes, imagining my imposing father reduced to a terrified child, hiding in the rubble.

"My truck and the steers were gone when I finally got out," he says, which is why he didn't try to reach me over the radio. "So, I walked. I looked for survivors. For information —trying to figure out how bad it was beyond Kerrville. There were no evacuation centers I could find. The town was leveled by sinkhole tremors." He shakes his head, disbelief pinching his features. "After hours of walking, I spotted a group of people surrounding a car. I heard the breaking glass before I registered the people inside were screaming." He pauses. "They were trying to keep the others out."

There's a long stretch of silence and sunlight brightens the room before my father looks up again, his eyes hollow. "I wanted to help them but couldn't get my feet to move," he admits. "What would I have done? They were desperate—all of them. The people who broke into the car and the people who were trying to keep the others out. There was no stopping them. Why didn't they just drive away?" His voice pitches. "Why didn't they leave?"

I want to reach for my father, to comfort him in some way, but that's not how we are, and even now it doesn't feel quite right. "You couldn't have helped them," I say instead. "Not one against many. Not without putting yourself in danger." I'm not sure why I feel the need to reassure my callous, cruel father of anything, but I do, and his eyes shift to me like he's as shocked as I am.

"It was all for nothing," he murmurs. "Four people against two. They pulled that couple out of the car, beat them enough to immobilize them, and sped away . . . And I just hid behind a tree, waiting for it all to be over. And in the end, it was all for nothing." He sneers at that, a huff of disbelief escaping him. But as the moments pass, his eyes glaze over once more. It's like I can see every moment replaying in that mind of his. In the way his eyebrows draw together. The way his chapped lips press into a hard line and his scruffy chin trembles. It's like he's searching each scenario for answers he'll never find.

"They were dead too."

I frown. "What do you mean?"

"I found the car later, in a ravine just down the road. And when I looked down . . ."

My father pales again, and tears fill his eyes and roll down his cheeks when he blinks. I want to know how he got the Prius parked haphazardly in the driveway, and I have a dozen other questions, but I'm scared to learn the answers. Scared of what reliving it all again will do to him.

"What about the roads?" I ask instead, focusing on more pressing information. "Are they drivable? If we have to get to Ransom—"

"No." My father's head snaps up. "You stay here where it's safe, Knox." He says it like a command, and it fills me with unexpected relief to know my father is still in there, somewhere. Not entirely broken. "Leaving is too dangerous."

I lean my head back on the chair and squeeze my eyes shut. It doesn't matter if my father thinks we should stay here, because I don't know what Ava will want to do, and the ranch might not be a viable option forever.

The bed creaks and my father unties his boots. Each movement seems a chore, and I can only imagine how exhausted he is. One boot has blood on it. It could be his; his clothes are ripped and soiled. But it could be someone else's too.

I clear my throat. "We heard a report about fires in the north. Did you see anything?"

"No." My father pulls his boot off. "But I've smelled them for days. Now—" He drops it on the floor beside him. "Leave me alone, Knox." It's a half-hearted command, but I know better than to prod the bear.

Clenching my hands into fists, I rise to my feet, hesitating for only a moment as I brace myself. "I'm glad you're alive," I admit. "But—" I let the word hang in our silence, and when my father finally looks at me, I continue, "If Ava decides to stay here, and I find out you're bullying her or pulling *any* of the shit you have been lately, we're going to have problems."

At least my father has the decency to look guilty as he averts his gaze. That's enough for me, for now. As I reach the door, I barely hear my name above the turning handle.

"Knox?"

When I glance back at my father, he's staring at the boot in his hand. "Have you heard from your brother?"

The regret in his voice is unmistakable, and I shake my head. "No," I whisper.

Thunder rumbles in the distance as if it's heralding a new day of uncertainty, and I close the door behind me.

TWENTY-ONE
AVA

EARLY MORNING OR NOT—SLEEP DEPRIVED OR NOT—I HAVE so much nervous energy, I know I have to keep busy or I'll quite literally freak out. Dew glistens on the spiderwebs that cling to the rafters of the barn, shimmering in the cool morning breeze.

I fill one of the buckets with the water Knox treated yesterday and lug it to the horse trough. Knox has been upstairs so long, I have no idea what's being said between him and his father, but every minute that passes makes the knot in my stomach tighten. Instead of throwing up, though, I laugh.

Rooster, Loca, and Poppy all look at me like I'm crazy, their ears shifting to the sound of my escaped hysteria. "I am," I admit, shrugging. "I'm losing my damn mind. It's finally happening." I scratch my forehead. I don't know what's worse, the wave of nausea when I consider leaving and being on my own, or the absolute certainty that Knox would leave with me before he let that happen, whether he wanted to or not. Because that's who I've learned Knox is, duty bound to a fault.

"It's a little early for chores, isn't it?"

I startle and spin around to find him leaning against the steel drum, a clean shirt tucked into his Wranglers and a baseball cap on his head, like it's just another day on the Bennett Family Ranch. He reaches out, rubbing the old, brown mare's face lovingly.

"I needed some air," I admit. Turning back to the horse trough, I empty the rest of the bucket, using my knee for leverage. I hadn't even realized I'd pulled on shorts in my haste to get dressed and out of the house. Water splashes on my legs, sending a wave of chills over me in the cool morning air. Or is it the way Knox is watching me?

Lucy scampers up, her tongue hanging out of her mouth after making her morning rounds.

"It's going to be fine," Knox tells me, and I know what he's referring to.

I nod because I know he wants me to believe him, but I don't.

"I'm serious."

"I know, but . . ." I set the water bucket beside him, exchanging it for the feed scoop instead.

"Ava?"

I turn for the grain barrel. I should call Julio. We haven't tried that yet. Just because Knox couldn't get his phone to work doesn't mean mine won't.

"Ava—" He takes my arm, the flannel of my shirt bunching in his grasp, forcing me to stop. When I look up at him, he glances at his hold on me and lets go. "My father won't bother you. I promise." I hear his determination as much as I see it in his eyes, but all of this is so much bigger than Mitch Bennett.

Suddenly, every wound up part of me deflates, and the

feed scoop hangs at my side. "It's not just that, Knox. Being here—it puts you in a weird position."

"No, it doesn't—"

"Not to mention your dad."

"What about him? He's got his own issues to worry about, and he knows where I stand with you."

My head tilts of its own accord as I consider what, exactly, that means.

"I told him that if you decide to stay, he has to accept it."

"And?" I deadpan. "He's totally fine with that?"

"He doesn't have a choice. But no, he didn't argue with me about it, if that's what you're worried about. So, we stick to our plan. We work on the inventory today. We prepare for —" He shrugs and readjusts his ball cap on his head. "Whatever the hell happens next."

Even though I refuse to acknowledge the way his muscles flex, my eyes linger a little too long on his arm.

"Ava?"

My gaze snaps to him. "Yeah?"

"Are we good?" There's a pleading look in his eyes I don't expect to see.

Before I can find the wherewithal to argue, I nod in answer. "Yeah. We're good."

He gives me a sidelong glance. "We are? You aren't just saying that?"

"Yes, Knox." This time, I can't help a small, mostly sane laugh. "We're good," I promise. "Thank you."

His gaze narrows slightly before he seems satisfied, and with a heavy sigh, he peers around the ranch. "We'll finish with the animals, then wrap up the inventory before it gets too hot."

Though the cloud cover is gray, the air is turning muggy already, and I peel my flannel off. I glance at the beat-up

Prius in the driveway. "I didn't peg your dad as a hybrid guy," I say in jest. Knox tears his eyes away from me, and he stares over his shoulder.

"I don't know the story behind it, but I have a feeling it saved his life."

Though I never thought I'd care one way or another what happens to Mitch Bennett, I can tell Knox is anxious and concerned about his dad, and suddenly, I worry a little about him too. "Is he going to be okay?"

Knox glances up at his father's bedroom window on the second level. I half expect Mitch to be looming in it, watching us with a menacing glare, but he's not. "I think so," he murmurs.

Without thought, I reach for his arm this time. "Are *you*?"

Knox looks at me with tired eyes, too shadowed for me to see the green and gold that usually brighten them. "I'm fine," he murmurs, but something passes over his features before he grabs the feed scoop I dropped. "We'd better get to work."

Despite the thick, gray clouds, the afternoon is sweltering. It smells of smoke, and sweat dampens every part of my body —even my palms. Dust and grime embed in my nails and the creases of my hands, and I want nothing more than a cold shower and an even colder beer.

Knox slams the F-250's tailgate closed. Thunder rumbles in the distance, punctuating the strange charge that's been filling the air all afternoon. But still, no rain comes, despite the stormy day.

"We should take a break," Knox says, as exhausted as I am. "Get something to eat and see how we're feeling after." He nods to the trailer. "If we have to leave, I'll want to take the horses. Which means I need to make sure we have supplies for them too."

I glance at Loca's buckskin head hanging over the rail of the paddock, watching us intently. "Do you think they know?" I ask, because it feels like the horses have been watching us all day.

He watches the mare as she begins to pace along the fence. "They know something's up—like they think we're going somewhere." The corner of Knox's mouth curves up, and he leans his forearms against the truck, smiling at me. "Do you even know how to ride a horse?"

Knox is *smiling*. At me. It's stunning and gives me pause.

When I realize he's waiting for an answer, I lick my lips and look at Loca again. "No. Well—I mean, I've never done it before."

For some reason, that makes Knox chuckle. A throaty sound that dissolves my unease and makes me grin. I smack his arm. "Why is that so funny?"

"I don't know, maybe because you live in Texas of all places."

"So? What reason have I ever had to ride a horse?"

"Not even in sixth grade? Did you go to the ropes course and dude ranch with Mr. Thomason's class like the rest of us had to?"

I shake my head. "I was out that day, apparently."

"Well, we should go for a ride, then," he says, sobering a little. "You need to know how."

As reality settles over us again, our smiles fade, yet I feel the lightest I have in days. Even with Mitch here.

The screen door squeaks open. "Come and get it!"

Knox and I turn toward the house as the screen slams shut again, Mitch disappearing inside. My heart thuds, and my palms feel clammier than before. It's one thing to know Mitch is inside, but another to be in the same room with him.

Knox looks at me, his brow lifted in surprise. "I guess grub's on," he says, and with a shrug, he heads for the house.

This is the moment I have been dreading all day. The first meeting since I woke to find Mitch looming over me in bed. I could refuse, but it would only make things more uncomfortable, especially for Knox.

Reluctantly, I follow him into the house, steeling myself for whatever comes next.

Lucy trots up, her butt wagging like it might be time for her lunch too. Knox pets her as he opens the screen. "You hungry, pup?"

It smells like Old Spice the instant I step inside. Mitch's back is to us, his hair damp and combed like he's just showered and donned clean clothes.

Knox doesn't give his father a second glance as he heads for the table that's only had stacks of mail and unused placemats on it until now. I keep a safe distance behind him. Three sandwiches are plated, and a few bags of chips are in the center. A half pitcher of iced tea sits beside a stack of napkins.

"I didn't know what you wanted," Mitch mutters, bringing over a jar of pickles. "But we only had roast beef in the fridge, so that's what you get." When I look up, Mitch glances away from me, his freshly shaven jaw ticking slightly.

My lungs burn from holding my breath, and exhaling, I glance at my sandwich with an erratically pounding heartbeat. "Uh, roast beef is fine. Thanks."

Knox meets my gaze with a look that's both stoic and encouraging, and I pull a chair out across the table from him.

Finally, Mitch finishes whatever he's doing in the kitchen and comes to join us. I bite the inside of my cheek, waiting for a comment to slip, or a disgusted look to be cast in my direction, but Mitch doesn't say anything and he doesn't look at me again. He simply pulls out his chair, sits down, and takes a giant bite of his sandwich.

Knox crunches on a crisp pickle, oblivious to my internal freak-out as I pick up my sandwich. This is happening. The three of us are eating lunch together as if the past doesn't exist here.

"Eat," Mitch commands, eyeing the bread squishing in my firm grip. "You two have been out there all day. You can't work on a ranch and not have food in your belly."

I take a bite because Mitch Bennett tells me to. "It's not poisoned, is it?" I joke, but the instant the words are out, I wish I could shove them back in. Knox and Mitch both look at me, mid-chew.

My cheeks burn, and internally, I chide myself for bringing more attention to the absurdity of this situation. "Sorry. Bad joke." I brush the crumbs from my lips and, this time, I take a huge bite so no other words will sneak out.

"I thought you would be resting," Knox eventually says, breaking the awkward-as-fuck silence. He eyes his father over the brim of his glass and takes a gulp of tea. "You didn't have to make us food."

Mitch shakes some barbecue chips onto his plate. "I don't want to rest all day. Too much thinking." He plops one into his mouth and bites down with a crunch. "I was going to do an inventory, but it looks like you've already done it." Mitch's gaze shifts from Knox to me.

I look away, licking my lips. "Well, thank you. I didn't realize how hungry I was."

He grunts. "It's just a sandwich."

Just. A. Sandwich. I take another huge bite to stifle the hysteria.

The longer we sit in the tension-filled room, the greater sense I have that something more lingers in the atmosphere of things unsaid. Whatever relationship Knox and his father have, it isn't a great one, and Mitch's return hasn't seemed to change that. They are stilted around one another, and what I thought might be a wordless standoff of sorts feels more like the crossroads of what was and what will be moving forward.

"After the past couple days," Knox finally says, only this time he looks at me. "We need to be prepared for anything." I don't know if he's considering what happened at the supply store, our water situation, Scott, my episode yesterday, or his dad's sudden return from the dead, but Knox exhales and shoves a chip in his mouth.

"We." It's a quiet, almost breathless word, and Knox and I both look at his father. Mitch swallows a bite of sandwich. "You two—you're . . . *a thing* now?" Mitch might sound concerned or confused—or maybe a mixture of both—but he doesn't seem outraged by the idea. Still, I'm wary of his calmness.

"No," I say. The expectant silence and myriad of thoughts Mitch is probably thinking is too much to bear. "We just happened to be at the wrong place at the wrong time, is all. Knox has been stuck with me ever since." It's another awkward joke, and it falls on deaf ears.

Knox watches his father closely, but Mitch has no outward response as he takes another bite. "At least he hasn't been alone," Mitch mutters. Knox's brow lifts slightly in shock.

And just like that, the past ten years of drama between our families is squashed. At least for now. I eat my sandwich and chips until all hunger pains are sated, and Knox does the same. Each time a piece of roast beef falls from his sandwich, he feeds it to Lucy, sitting semi-patiently at his feet.

"This medicine you mentioned," Mitch says, scooting his chair out. He plops the last chip on his plate into his mouth and walks toward the sink. "Is it something Britton might have next door?"

Knox shakes his head, swallowing his final bite. "Not unless he has epilepsy." The thought of Knox and his father talking about me at all is unsettling, but it feels acutely personal that they were discussing my health.

Mitch looks at me and tosses his napkin into the trash compactor. "No." He moves to the counter and caps the mustard. "I don't think he does."

I busy myself rolling the chip bags. "I'll be fine," I reassure them. It's not terminal, just really inconvenient. I won't let it be a burden to you." But the instant I say it, I know that's not entirely true; yesterday with Knox is proof.

Mitch strides past the table and grabs one of a few Stetsons hanging on the coat rack. "You two clean the kitchen," he says, settling his hat on his head. He stares through the screen. "Your mom has some medical books on the shelf in the formal living room, Knox. You might find something useful in there." He elbows the door open. "I'm going to check on the generator." Then he heads out, the screen slamming shut behind him.

Knox and I look at one another. "That exchange was . . . bizarre," I say, taking my plate into the kitchen.

He watches his dad pass the living room window, headed around back. "Yeah. It was. Especially mentioning my mom like that. He never talks about her."

"Should we be worried?"

Knox doesn't answer at first, then shakes his head. "I don't think so. If anything"—he meets my gaze—"it seems like he's finally waking up."

TWENTY-TWO
KNOX

MY BODY ACHES WITH EXHAUSTION, BUT MY MIND, NO matter how heavy, won't shut off. I can't sleep in my brother's room without dwelling on whether he's alive or dead, so I make my way downstairs. The house is still, save for the sporadic gusts of wind that shift the rafters.

Lucy looks up from her bed by the door, her bobbed tail wagging tentatively, but she doesn't get up. "It's too early," I commiserate. "I know."

Taking my hoodie off the back of the couch, I glance at my bedroom door down the hall. Of course, it's closed. I don't know if Ava is asleep or not, but I would bet the door is locked to keep unwanted visitors out. Obviously, nothing is okay between her and my father, but cohabitation is the only choice we have. At least they are making it work. For now.

Cracking my neck, I reach for the front door, open it quietly, and step onto the porch. I'm immediately hit by the scent of fire on the breeze. It's been inescapable all day, so I don't know why I thought tonight would be different. Still, the smoky, muggy night air is better than the confines of my brother's old room and the tension-wrought house.

The porch creaks as I move one of the chairs closer to the railing to better see the stars. Only after I bunch my hoodie behind my head for a pillow do I realize there isn't a single star in sight on such a cloudy night. Of course there's not. Even so, I'm content to listen to the rustle of the sagebrush instead of the yawning silence of Kellen's room.

Ava. She fills my thoughts again. Imagining her asleep in that very room before my father appeared, wondering what she must've felt. Ava asleep in my bed while I'm out here stewing. I want to know if she's awake. If she was only placating me earlier when she promised she'd stay, or if she'll leave, regardless of how reckless that would be.

I tell myself Ava should do whatever she wants to, that it shouldn't matter to me either way. But it does. I don't know when it happened, exactly, but I *do* care for Ava—at least, I care *about* her. My promise to Scott is only one of many reasons I don't want her to leave.

As I try to sort through my thoughts—the feelings I've been ignoring and what they might mean—I close my eyes and inhale a deep breath.

She thought I've hated her all this time. While I don't hate Ava and never have, I've gone out of my way to avoid her for ten years. All because I didn't want to deal with my own shit. In that way, I guess I'm more like my father than I thought, and that frustrates me even more. Especially as I consider how disappointed my mother would be if she were still alive. She'd have told me years ago that Ava, an innocent girl thrust into this as much as I was, isn't to blame. And more than that, she had no mother or father to take care of her, not even an uncle, when it was all said and done. She had none of the people who should have been loving her and caring about her. Meanwhile, I avoided her like it might make my life easier somehow. It didn't.

I heave what feels like the heaviest sigh of my life and nestle deeper into the chair, glad when the hard wood cuts into my back to stir me from depressing, unwanted thoughts. None of that matters anymore.

Instead, I revel in the small comfort that none of the sick cattle worsened today. With my father being strangely okay with Ava staying here, and not having to shoot another animal between the eyes, I take the win.

My mind drifts from one distant thought to another as my body finally eases and the hope of sleep inches its way in. One of the horses stirs in the stable, and a steer grunts in the distance. Remotely, the sensation of something soft kisses my skin, then another whisper of a touch tickles my nose and I wipe it away. A flake catches in my lashes as I open my eyes, and blinking, I shoot up. The rail is dusted in ash, and when I look down at my lap . . .

"The fuck . . ."

The horses nicker again, drawing my attention toward the stable and beyond it to the brightening sky. I blink, over and over, praying that isn't a mixture of orange flames and black smoke on the horizon.

"Da—" I clear my throat. "Dad!" I shout, the hoodie dropping to the ground as I jump to my feet. "Dad! Wake up!" I fling the screen door open and rush into the house. "Ava, get up!" I call, barreling down the hall. I push into my room for my clothes, but it's locked. "Ava!" I pound on the door.

The light flicks on as Ava flings the door open, wide-eyed and blinking at me. Her chest heaves and her hair is mussed around her face. I nudge past her to collect my boots and pants and she stumbles back.

"Knox?" Her tremulous, sleep-laden voice barely cuts through my frantic thoughts. "What's wrong?"

"Fire," I rasp.

Ava runs to the window, pushing the curtain away. "Shit."

All I can think about are the animals. Our supplies. The house . . .

"Knox!" my dad calls from the living room.

"The fires!" I call. "They're coming this way!" My dad must see the wildfires cresting the pasture because his heavy, hurried footsteps boom around upstairs.

Ava pulls her clothes on as we rush around my room. "What do you think?" She grabs her things from my bathroom. "An hour before it gets this far?"

"Less with this wind." My stomach drops, knowing there is nothing we can do to save this place in what precious minutes we have. Nothing but save ourselves and leave the ranch behind.

I meet her worried gaze as I hurry out the door. "I'm letting the steers and the pigs loose," my dad calls as he jogs down the stairs, his boots not even laced all the way.

I nod, thinking the same thing. "They have a better chance on their own. I'll get the horses loaded in the trailer."

My father stops at the couch and looks behind me. "Ava—"

She rushes out of my room, dressed and ready to help, but her eyes are wild and filled with fear.

"Grab Knox's bags. Get everything loaded in the truck."

She nods before disappearing into my room again. "They're in the closet!" I call.

Lucy bumps the screen door open and leads the way as my father and I jog toward the barn. The approaching fire is almost mesmerizing, close enough I can see the flickering flames consuming the earth as it creeps closer. Even the smoke thickens in the air, making my eyes burn.

"Knox!" my father snaps. I meet his hard stare. "Focus." He glances at the pacing horses.

"Extra supplies and food for the horses are already loaded in the trailer," I tell him, continuing toward the paddock. Loca, Poppy, and Rooster follow me along the fence line as I gather their halters. I go in for Loca first. She's skittish as I lead her to the trailer, but she's been loaded enough times that she doesn't fuss too much.

My father gestures and hollers at the steers in the corral as Lucy helps herd them to freedom, and I halter Rooster and load him into the trailer next. He's as anxious to flee the frenetic charge in the air as the rest of us, and he doesn't fight me.

As I turn back for Poppy, my father emerges from the shadows, his eyes on the approaching flames. The wind brings the fire closer with every gust.

"You have food and water?" he confirms.

"We do."

"Guns? Ammo?" He looks me squarely in the eyes.

"Yeah, I've got fuel, and the camping stuff too, if we need it."

My father nods, but the deep furrow in his brow is unchanged. I sidestep him for Poppy's stall, but my father grabs the gate. He grips the metal tighter, pushing against my pull so hard his knuckles whiten. "I'll let her go."

"Let her go?"

He glances at the trailer. "Caring for two horses is enough, Knox, and Poppy's old. She tires easily. Leave her with me and I'll let her go."

Ava jogs closer. "Everything's loaded in the truck. I grabbed food for Lucy too." Ava sounds out of breath, but I don't think about her or Lucy as my father's glare narrows on me, and the meaning of his words sinks in.

"No," I say, as a sickening feeling fills me from head to toe. "You're not staying. You're coming with us."

My father's eyes shift to the growing flames. "I'm not leaving, son." He sounds as determined as he sounds regretful.

"Dad—"

"I won't leave, Knox," he says more firmly, and, this time, his eyes meet mine. "This is our home. Where your mother is buried—"

"Tomorrow this whole place will be ash—"

"Son," he says, the calm firmness of his tone giving me pause. I've never heard my father sound or look more resolved than he does at this moment, looking directly at me. "This is my decision. You and Ava, you two get to Ransom. Stay off the main roads as much as you can, and don't trust *anyone* along the way."

I gape at him. "But Dad—"

"You have the horses if you need them. And you've got a good head on your shoulders. I know you'll be fine."

"You can't be serious," I croak.

"I am. I knew the moment I returned home, I would not leave this place again."

Acid burns my throat. "But what—what about Kellen? If he's alive—if he goes to Ransom too—"

"Then you two will have each other. And you can tell him . . ." My father's words catch in his throat, and I see the pain in his eyes, even though he tries not to show it. "Tell him I'm glad he's okay when you see him." Not *if* but *when*.

My body feels cold and yet everything burns—my chest, my lungs, my goddamn eyes I can barely see through. "You're really doing this?" My voice cracks like when I was a child, small and helpless.

"Knox," my father says softly, and I don't have to break down in sobs to feel like my world is crumbling all over again. I wipe the tears from my eyes to no avail. "Go, son. Get Ava out of here." When I don't move, he turns to Ava. "Go on," he barks at her. "Get that truck started—get out of here!"

She wipes the tears from her cheek and runs to the cab of the truck.

My father grips my shoulder. "Go, Knox. Please." The words are clipped and mournful, and as much as I can't stand the man standing in front of me, I don't want to leave him here—I can't imagine it.

"If you change your mind—" I lick my dry lips. "You'll come to Ransom, right?"

After a beat, my father nods, if a bit sadly. "I'll meet you in Ransom, if I change my mind."

"You're insane," I mutter, shaking my head. But as much as I hate his decision, a part of me understands it too.

"Go on now," he growls out this time. "Get." He shoves my shoulder toward the truck. "Ava, get him out of here!" he shouts. "And take care of him for me." His voice cracks as he turns for the back of the trailer to lock it up.

Ava hurries to me, taking my hand in hers with a squeeze. "Come on." Her voice is soft but urgent. "We have to get the horses out of here."

I let her lead me to the passenger door, but as my father steps away from the trailer, I tug my hand from hers. I can't leave him, not like this.

Turning, I backtrack and wrap my arms around his shoulders, pulling him in for a hug. The last one I will ever get. I exhale emotions so painful it hurts to breathe and inhale the scent of him. "I love you, you stubborn asshole."

Mitch Bennett's arms wrap around me, tightening as he

kisses the side of my head. "Your mother would be proud of you, son. *I* am proud of you."

I squeeze him tighter, holding my breath as if it might freeze the moment. When my lungs burn so much I can no longer stand it, I finally let go, and turning away, I force myself toward the truck without looking back. Every step is excruciating, knowing deep down I will never see my father again, but I push it all aside and walk around the truck, side-stepping Ava. "I'll drive."

"Knox, I don't think—"

"I said, I'll drive." I climb in, gripping the steering wheel so hard my knuckles ache, and wait for Ava to get Lucy into the truck. As soon as the door is shut, I brave a look at my father for the final time. Only he's gone, his form disappearing into the shadows of the stable. Cursing him, I put the truck into gear and we leave the ranch.

TWENTY-THREE
AVA

I THINK WE'VE BEEN DRIVING FOR ONLY A HANDFUL OF minutes, but it feels like an hour. And I have no idea where we are, only that with San Antonio worsening to the south, we needed to get around the fires to continue north. Even on the periphery of it, though, the world smolders. The fields smoke with cinder and the horizon glows behind us.

Ashes cloak the windshield, and the wipers hiccup across the glass, clearing them away. The AC hums, circulating the air in the cab of the truck, and the trailer creaks over each bump in the frontage road. I don't know if it's a harmony of horrors left behind or horrors yet to come.

Shivering, I glance at Lucy in the backseat. She braces herself on the bench, our packs piled up around her as her mismatched eyes dart between the windows. Another pothole jostles the truck, and Lucy nearly flies forward.

I sneak a look at Knox. His attention is fixed on the road, but it's clear his thoughts are back at the ranch; he checks his side mirror constantly as if Mitch might have changed his mind and rode after us.

It feels like I should say something to him, to comfort

Knox in some way, but I can barely process my own thoughts. I'm still in shock, my adrenaline racing.

We continue in silence, Knox driving slowly—carefully —and while I know I am not an experienced driver, I still feel useless, with no way to help now that what was left of Knox's life has been ripped away from him.

Knox's grip loosens on the steering wheel with a deep sigh, and I think he's resigned to the fact his dad isn't coming.

"Hey," I whisper. His jaw ticks, so I know he's heard me, but his attention remains on the road. "Obviously, I don't have my license, but maybe we should switch so you can process everything. I'll drive slow."

He blinks out the window, saying nothing.

"Knox?" I place my hand on his where it grips the center console like it's a lifeline. That stirs him enough that he finally looks at me. The interior lights illuminate every contour of Knox's face. His eyes are red-rimmed, though he hasn't broken down since saying goodbye to his father, which scares me.

Knox looks at my hand on his before fixating on the road again. "I'm fine," he mutters. "I need something to focus on anyway."

I nod, reluctant. "If that's what you want." His fingers curl into a fist beneath mine, and I realize I'm stroking my thumb over the back of his hand. Immediately, I let go, but Knox's fingers grab mine, squeezing hold of them in a silent request. Still, he doesn't look at me, but it's obvious Knox is barely holding himself together. His deep, steadying breaths and the quiver of his chin give him away . . . and I don't know how to help him.

I squeeze his hand in return, sit back in my seat, and try to keep my own emotions in check. If holding Knox's hand is all I can offer him—if it's all he'll take from me—I'm here for it as long as he needs me.

A few cars pass us as we drive on, but Knox hasn't seemed to notice. We continue another hour or so, slow and steady, through the back and frontage roads until the sky begins to lighten in an orange haze that looks otherworldly. Only then is the true extent of the devastation obvious. The landscape is grisly in the daylight, as equally shocking as it is devastating.

Like a plague ravaging the land, the fire has consumed everything—one field after another as far as the eye can see, scorched in black. Smoke rises from the rubble. The ash-covered road is all that's left unscathed.

My eyes blur as I process the aftermath. "This wind is feeding the fires," I whisper. I've never seen anything so hauntingly grim as an incinerated world. The charred remains of a tree glint with embers as we drive closer. A gas station just beyond is nothing more than its cement foundation and scrap metal. The Mike's Auto sign is covered in soot and half buried in debris, and I squeeze Knox's hand tighter. "Do you think they got out of there?" The thought is so sudden, I'm not certain if I say the words or think them.

"If they were smart," Knox says, his voice rough from disuse, "they left long before the fire got here." Despite the lack of radio and phone communication, I have to hope Knox is right, or the thought of all these people burned to dust—their final moments—might finally break me.

"There would be more cars," Knox adds. When I look at him, he meets my gaze. "If people hadn't fled," he supplies.

It's sound reasoning, so I nod and offer him a weak but grateful smile. Regardless if it's true, the thought gives me the slightest bit of comfort as we drive past what little is left of the farms and pastures that stretch beyond us. Brick chimneys, steel drums, metal piping, and water troughs are all that's discernible in the ruins.

A speck on the side of the road ahead becomes a van as we drive closer. My heart rate ticks faster as I notice it's parked and two guys are standing outside of it. They straighten when they hear us approaching, and I assume Knox will slow down to talk to them—to help them—but he doesn't.

"Hey!" one of the guys calls as we continue past them.

I turn in my seat, watching them quickly fade into the distance. "Knox, why didn't you—"

"Because my dad told me not to trust anyone," he grits out, and a lump forms in my throat. "And if two young guys my age can't change their own tire, or are too dumb or lazy to hoof it to safety instead of hanging out on the side of an abandoned road, we don't have time for them." He grits his teeth. "We don't have room for them, anyway, and I won't risk your safety and what little we have left for two strangers."

I blink as Knox's words sink in. "All right."

His exhale fills the entire cab of the truck and he runs his hand over his face. "If we're going to Sweetwater," Knox says, changing the subject, "we'll have to get on the highway soon." He doesn't sound happy about it, and I can't blame him. Mitch warned us to stay off the roads. Knox's safety was paramount in their final moments together, and once again, I am struck by the reality that Knox is sacrificing what he truly wants to do, because instead of heading directly to his uncle's place in Kansas like his dad *thinks* he's doing, Knox is changing course. For me. Guilt hollows my stomach, but as much as I wish I could tell Knox to keep driving, I need to be with Julio. I need him to know I'm okay and to see that he is too; he's the only family I have left.

I refocus out the window, acutely aware of how complicated this situation is about to get. Julio and Knox in the same space? I get heart palpitations thinking about it. "Thank you," I murmur. "I know my uncle is the last person you want to see right now."

A heartbeat passes. "I told you I would take you," Knox finally says, but the stilted tone of his voice gives me pause, and I look at him, studying his pensive profile. "We don't know what condition Sweetwater will be in, Ava," he adds carefully, and I realize it's hesitation in his voice, concern even. "I doubt it will be unscathed." His gaze shifts over my face, lingering a beat before he refocuses on the road. "Just . . . prepare yourself for whatever we find."

Picking at my fingernail, I peer out the window again. I've thought the same thing, I just haven't allowed myself to stew over it. Not when the world is literally burning to ash around us, and Knox just left Mitch to whatever his fate will be. So, I keep my eyes ahead.

As the farm road veers toward the highway junction, my stomach drops again. Cars, or what's left of their metal carcasses, clutter the turnoff and shoulder. "Do you think the fire blocked the road?" I wonder aloud. Knox and I stare at the carnage and it feels like a moment of silent mourning. The odds that every car in the gridlock was empty are slim to none.

"Maybe," he breathes.

Bile inches its way up my throat, knowing people might've been stuck inside. I can't imagine it—I don't *want* to. And yet . . . it's impossible to think of anything else.

"Shit." Knox brings the truck to a stop where the vehicles thicken. I scour the congestion stretching in all directions, looking for a chink in the soot and steel maze.

"That big rig," I say, pointing a quarter mile ahead. Sitting up straighter, I attempt to gauge the distance between it and what few cars are spread along the shoulder. "If we can get to it, there might be a way around it to the off-ramp. Maybe another farm road on the other side we can take." Tapping my finger on the console, I assess the obstacles in our way of getting that far. "It'll be tight, though."

Knox looks at me—more like stares through me as he weighs our options, but there aren't any others.

"We have to try," he finally says, and he glances back at the horse trailer. It's heavy and bulky and the horses are going to freak if we aren't careful.

"Do you want me to get out and find a path—"

"No," he says quickly, scanning the sea of cars. Most of them are only remains, though it looks as if some were miraculously spared by the flames.

"Stay in the truck." Knox climbs out, leaving the engine running and the AC circulating as he shuts the door behind him.

Lucy whines and jumps into the front. She steps on me, oblivious to her weight as she shoves me against the passenger window. "Back, Lucy. Sit." It's a feeble command, and she doesn't listen. She only pauses, moving around to lick my face with a whine before her eyes search for Knox in the maze again. He surveys the road and landscape as he makes his way farther down the highway. Suddenly, Knox's steps falter. He does a double take at one of the cars, and I cringe, certain that is *not* a good sign.

Lucy and I watch as he continues through the gridlock, walking around the vehicles like he's avoiding headstones in a graveyard, beelining for the big rig. Some of the trucks are only half the size they once were, their tires gone and their bodies melted.

Eventually, Knox disappears behind one of them. I don't realize I'm holding my breath until he reappears around a diesel rig in the distance and makes his way back to us. Knox's eyes meet mine through the windshield. I don't know what his expression is trying to convey, but he passes the driver's side and continues to the horse trailer.

Lucy whimpers as she jumps into the backseat again, watching him and impatiently waiting. The trailer shifts a little, the horses' heads bob in my side mirror, and before long, Knox jumps into the truck bed, scouring our supplies for something. He pulls out a package, jumps out again, and climbs back into the driver's seat. The scent of smoke wafts off him, and he hands me a N95 mask. "Put this on. The wind is picking up, and this is going to take a while."

Knox and I pull the elastic over our heads, positioning our masks. It's a little suffocating, my own breath hot on my face, but I don't like the thought of all this smoke in my lungs either.

Knox leans forward, peering out at the sea of cars again. "I think I can get us through. I might have to nudge a few cars out of the way, but it's doable."

He sounds slightly uncertain, but I trust Knox. "What can I do?"

He glances in the rearview mirror like he can actually see past the horse trailer. "Roll your window down. I need you to watch the front right bumper and make sure I don't clip anything harder than I have to. And the trailer." Knox rolls his window down and leans out, assessing the road in front of him as he puts the truck in gear.

With a slight press on the gas, the F-250 starts forward, the engine revving just a little. "If I can carve a path from what's left of that minivan over there to the hatchback, and over to the shoulder, I think I can get to the Peterbilt and inch my way past that Dodge on the off-ramp."

His eyes shift to me like he needs the extra encouragement. "Yeah," I say. "Good plan." I brace myself as he locks his jaw with pure determination and starts weaving his way through the vehicles.

It's slow going at first. Like Knox, I lean out the window, guiding him as best as I can. He nudges a car out of the way. The sound of screeching metal makes me flinch, but it's what's inside the vehicles I try not to notice. Some of them might be empty, but others likely aren't, and I do all I can to not look too closely.

We're halfway to the eighteen-wheeler when the trailer takes more of a hit than I think he expected as he maneuvers the path of least resistance through the tight turns.

"You're close on this side," I say over my shoulder. "But you can make it." The bumper barely skims the front end of a Tesla. Or rather, what's left of it. "You can—"

A deep rumble fills the eerie silence. Lucy perks up, and Knox and I look at each other as the ground starts to shake. Like a wave cresting a stretch of beach, an earthquake rolls through Route 87. The trailer shakes, the horses stir, and Lucy whimpers as the cab creaks and groans, along with all of our supplies rattling in the bed of the truck. If the world opens up and swallows us whole, there's nothing we can do about it, and Knox and I both seem to hold our breath.

The entire highway is riddled with movement. Steel skeletons crumble, and a body in the Tesla beside me falls forward, the skull and charred flesh of some hapless victim hitting the windshield. I jerk away from the window, covering my mouth.

"Ava—"

Knox grips my arm. "Look at me," he urges. I drag my gaze away and peer into his hazel eyes, which are so easy to get lost in. Strong. Stoic. Quiet Knox. His hand is warm, his gaze hot like a brand as the seconds pass, becoming more like minutes, until, finally, the rumbling fades, the shaking dissipates, and the world is eerily silent again. I will my heartbeat to steady as I take a deep breath.

"Are you okay?"

"Yeah—" I nod. "Yes. I'm fine."

Knox peers beyond me at the Tesla, and the worry etched in his brow softens a little.

"I know," I say before he can remind me. "I'm going to see much worse. I just—I wasn't prepared. That's all."

Knox lets go of my arm and refocuses on the highway. He reaches back, stroking Lucy's head to calm her, and probably himself too. "We need to keep moving," he says more urgently this time.

When he accelerates again, Knox applies more pressure to the gas pedal, and we move through the metal graveyard with less precision.

I reclaim my place as sentry in the passenger seat, guarding the right side of the truck and trailer as we force our way to the semi. If Knox sees bodies as we weave our way through the gridlock, he has no visible reaction. So, I keep my moans and groans to myself and stay as focused as I can.

It feels like an hour has passed before we're finally through the obstacle course. Knox stops the truck, running his hands over his jeans. He clenches his hands into fists like his fingers ache and exhales an unsteady breath. "It's been a while, but I think I remember how to get to Sweetwater from here." He cracks his neck, glancing up and down the shoulder of the off ramp. It's mostly clear—easy money compared to what we just waded through—and he drives on.

We aren't a dozen yards ahead when the road clears up a bit and Knox can actually accelerate. "This should take us to another frontage road."

We roll up our windows to keep the smoky air out and

settle in for the last stretch of the journey. The road feels endless as it winds between pastures, finally getting to Highway 70. The land here is fire-scarred like elsewhere, and I realize how long the flames must have been burning to have spread so far—a couple of days at least. The stronger the wind, the more ash fills the air, and I wonder how much farther the fires will spread before there is nothing left to consume.

Mitch's face, shadowed and resigned, flashes to mind, and I glance at Knox. At least I know for certain Scott and Mavey are gone, but Knox will always wonder if his father is.

As we drive closer to town, utility poles line the road again, and the fire scars covering the earth disappear with the burn zone behind us.

"Look!" I point to the silhouette of wind turbines on the horizon. The skies are clearer here, and a little bit of the tension in my shoulders abates. "We're getting close." I catch myself smiling in the mirror and my smile grows a little wider.

But as the turbines grow taller and the hazy morning clears, patches of sunlight illuminate a world riddled with fissure scars, broken turbines, and toppled water towers—collateral damage left in the wake of so many quakes.

Sweetwater. Dread creeps a little closer as I try to focus on the open road and clearing skies instead. We pass a crumbled silo and empty green pastures, only slowing as the cracks in the asphalt worsen. Untouched by wildfires, the outskirts of town look livable, and eventually, the sporadic farmhouses and businesses we pass become many. Instead of being happy, I feel unsettled—anxious and reluctant.

I look at Knox. Once we get to Julio's, he'll go his own way, and I'll never see him again.

Knox gives an overturned big rig a wide berth as I

swallow the conflicting emotions thickening in my throat. "So," I start. "I was thinking—"

A herd of elk rush from behind the semi into the road, and Knox slams on the brakes. The trailer tires lock and screech, the weight of our haul pushing us forward. The cement wall of the creek bridge stops us from going over as we hit. The airbags deploy, and we lurch forward. I'm flung back, and my head hits the passenger window. Lucy collides with the dash, and Knox curses—a thump meeting my ears—before everything stops. The truck and trailer settle back into place as much as the pawing, anxious horses will allow.

Gaping and frozen in shock, I blink. Again and again until the world refocuses. "Son of a bitch," I hiss, squeezing my eyes shut. Pain sings through my head and I reach for the warm blood in my hairline and cringe.

"You okay?" Knox rasps.

I think I nod, watching four elk retreat into the foliage along the creek. Knox's door squeaks open and Lucy scrambles out. Cramped and a little claustrophobic, I can't get out of the truck fast enough either. I reach for the seatbelt, only I never put it on after helping Knox maneuver through the gridlock. "Epic fail, Ava." I groan, and I reach for the handle as my door opens on its own.

Knox is so close I can feel the warmth of his body beside me. "You're bleeding." Slightly frantic, he takes my face in his hands, assessing the wound. I know it can't be too terrible if I'm still conscious.

"I'll be fine," I reassure him, and I step down from the truck. I stumble and Knox grabs onto my arm for good measure. I stare at the way his fingers press into my arm, the roughness of his palm against my skin. We're both trembling, I realize. Adrenaline buzzes between us, and squinting against the sunlight, I peer up at him. This time, I reach for his face. "That's going to hurt," I warn, my fingers hovering just above the knot forming on his temple.

"Who says it doesn't already?" he mutters.

With a nervous laugh, I loosen my hold on Knox and take a step back.

He gestures for me to grab onto the truck. "Wait here while I check on the horses. You might have another concussion."

"Me?" I glower at him. "You're the one with a persimmon on your head."

He glances at me over his shoulder, but Knox doesn't reply.

With a shoulder-loosening sigh, I close my eyes and lift my face up to the sunlight, grateful a few cuts, bumps, and bruises are all we have to worry about. My eyes pop open, snapping to the crushed front of the truck. "Shit."

"Yeah," Knox mutters, reaching into the back of the truck to pull out a water bottle for each of us. "Shit is right." He hands me one, his eyes fixed on the front end.

Since there is steam coming from the hood, I assume we're screwed. I sneak another look at Knox to gauge just *how* screwed we are. "I know it's bad," I start. "But like . . . how bad are we talking?"

"Fucked," he says tersely. Knox tries to open the hood, but it's jammed. "I'm assuming we have no radiator at this point."

Groaning, I fold my arms on the edge of the truck bed and lower my head. "We were so close." The longer my body trembles, the more I question whether it's subsiding adrenaline or if I'm about to have a breakdown.

"We have the horses," Knox reminds me, then chugs his water. "And the longer we all stay out here in this shitty air quality, the worse we're all going to feel—the horses included."

Knox tosses his water bottle into the cab of the truck.

"We're *riding* to Julio's?"

Knox walks to the trailer gate. "It's why we brought them." He unlatches the back. "Saddle up."

TWENTY-FOUR
KNOX

HORSE HOOVES ON THE ASPHALT, CREAKING LEATHER, AND clanking food cans fill the late morning as I saddle Rooster. It's muscle memory at this point, and I go through the motions while Ava sorts through our provisions. With nothing more than our backpacks and horses to carry supplies, everything has to be reassessed, and quickly.

Lucy and the horses eat the last full meal they'll likely get for a while, and though we should probably eat something as well, I'm too nauseous to think about food at the moment. Too . . . numb.

I figured the horses might come in handy, but we've barely started the journey and we're already truckless; most of our supplies will be left behind. My mind is elsewhere as I slide Rooster's bit into his mouth, grateful the horses are okay, even if our prepping and planning has been for nothing. Half the shit I got from Scott is useless. Everything happened at the warehouse and him dying was for what, exactly? Because we're in the middle of fucking nowhere with who knows how long to go before we get to Julio's, and hundreds of miles still before I get to Mason's.

All of this feels pointless, and the more I think about it, the more my hands tremble, the more my chest burns, and my throat begins to close. Eventually, I can't even see the damn cinch belt.

I step over the trailer hitch and cross the road, marching under the bridge where I can lose my shit in private, because it's all too much. *"Goddammit, Knox."* I can hear my father's voice like he's hot on my heels. I should have been more careful. I should have driven slower. I should not have come to Sweetwater to begin with—we should've driven straight for Kansas.

I stop at the edge of the creek and tear my baseball cap off, pressing the heels of my hands into my eyes. Gritting my teeth, I will the acidic burn of defeat and disappointment away and I blow out a breath, then another, and crouch by the water's edge. The sound of a babbling brook should be peaceful, but it's only a reminder that we can't even rely on drinkable water.

Elbows on my knees, I hang my head. I should be grateful I'm not alone in this, but it's only a matter of time before I am, and the reality of that hits the hardest.

Lucy trots over and nudges my arm with her wet nose, licks the side of my face, and nestles her way into my hold. She's a lifeline I never knew I needed, and I wrap my arms around her neck, holding on as tightly as I dare as I soak her energy in.

"Come on, Knox," I mutter. "Get your shit together." I exhale, wiping the dampness from my eyes. One task at a time. Just like I have been doing since all of this started. I need something to focus on—one single purpose to fulfill. I need to get Ava to Julio, and I'll figure out my next step after.

I fill my lungs with a long, tension-easing breath, welcoming the burn as I wait for the lump in my throat to subside. With all the determination I can manage, I adjust my ball cap and hike back to the road, wiping my eyes for a final time.

Ava averts her gaze when I get to the trailer. She's not dumb. Ava knows I'm barely holding myself together, and I appreciate that she keeps her unsolicited reassurances to herself. We both know the past four days have been the worst of our lives, and words change nothing. For now, her presence is enough, even if it's only temporary.

"Ready?" I tighten the cinch on Loca's saddle and move to Rooster's next.

"Ready." Ava hands me my N95 mask, but I shove it into my back pocket instead of putting it on. The smoke in the air is the least of my concerns right now. I take stock of my shotgun and handgun, and all the ammo and gear we can manage between our two backpacks and the saddlebags.

"Let's get the hell out of here," I grumble, and after patting the pistol holstered at my side, I climb into Rooster's saddle.

Ava dons a *Toxic Positivity* ball cap with rainbow lettering, and I almost snort. Her eyes skirt to mine as she pulls her ponytail through the back with a knowing smile. Her black hair falls long and straight down her back. "It was a gag gift," she explains.

"Obviously," I mutter.

She mounts Loca, and it's more graceful than expected for a first-time rider.

The mare cranes her neck, watching Ava curiously as she situates herself in the saddle, like the buckskin knows Ava is a newbie.

"I would be remiss," Ava starts, staring Loca in the eyes, "not to point out the fact that you have given *me* the horse named Loca."

I grin. "She's sweet, Ava. You don't have to worry about her."

Nervously, Ava licks her lips. "Remember who fed you," she says, leaning down to give Loca a pat. "And who snuck you an apple back at the ranch."

I try to stifle my amusement, though in truth, I appreciate the distraction. "Time for a crash course," I tell her, and I lift my reins. "Hold them about here so you aren't tugging back on her head while we're walking. You want to give her some slack to move comfortably."

Ava mimics my grip on the leather reins, and I demonstrate the rest of the commands. "Gently pull back to slow or stop her. Move the reins left and right, depending which way you want her to go. She'll move as she feels the pressure against her neck, and you don't have to yank."

Ava nods like a bobble head. "It's the height of the fall that worries me most," she explains.

"She's a good girl, she'll listen," I promise. "And when you want her to start walking, squeeze your thighs a little or click your tongue. It's as simple as that."

"I've seen the movies," Ava says, her brown eyes shifting between me and Loca in distrust. "What if something spooks her and she takes off running?"

This time, I can't resist a chuckle at the pitch of panic in her voice. "You hold on for dear life."

Ava's eyes widen so much their amber flecks shimmer despite the shadow of her hat.

My laugh deepens. "You'll be fine. Rooster is more likely to spook than Loca, but if something *does* happen, hold on to that saddle horn, pull back on the reins if you can, and eventually, she'll stop. I'll come after you, if it's that bad."

Ava licks her lips, gripping the saddle horn until her knuckles whiten.

"Ava?"

She peers down at the asphalt like she's peeking over a plunging ledge. At sixteen hands, Loca is a tall horse, but even if she wasn't, I imagine Ava would be just as leery.

"Ava."

Her gaze darts to me.

"You'll be fine. There's a reason my dad kept Poppy and not Loca." The truth hurts to admit. "Loca's seasoned and has a good temperament—she's used to cutting cattle and working in more chaos than this." I gesture to the empty road and sporadic trees. "This is a cakewalk for her, and I'm right here if something happens." Obviously anything *could* happen, but I don't dare say that.

"All right, then." Ava squares her shoulders with determination.

Lifting my reins again, I pull back for Rooster to reverse and turn him away from the trailer, toward the road.

"You didn't show me that one," Ava grumbles, and I flash her a smile over my shoulder. Slow and hesitant, she mimics the command, and Loca obeys, falling easily into step beside me.

I whistle for Lucy, and gritting my teeth, I glance at the truck and trailer we're leaving behind for a final time.

"Julio might have a spare vehicle you can take," Ava offers, and while I appreciate the thought, I can't think about him right now. My head aches enough already.

Lucy trots ahead, sniffing the blackberry bushes at the end of the bridge. A butterfly lands on a blossom, and as Lucy's snout nuzzles deeper, a bird flutters out. It strikes me how small pockets of the world are unaffected, at least for now, and I appreciate how normal it seems.

"My ass is *so* going to hurt after this," Ava mutters. I try not to stare as I watch her settle into the saddle from the corner of my eye. She eases her grip on the reins and pommel, and eventually, as Ava loosens up, her body sways with each step Loca takes, like Ava is part of the rhythm.

We continue around a bend with scant trees or shade for a while. The sun heats the back of my neck and arms, and soon my jeans feel stuck to my thighs.

"This heat is killer," Ava grumbles, and she knocks her ponytail off her shoulder. Sweat dampens the back of her gray tank top and my t-shirt clings to me like a second skin.

"Tell me about it."

Ava glares up at the sun. "So," she drawls, "do you want the good news or the not-so-good news first?"

Whatever tension had left my body coils back into place. "Let's start with the good news."

"All right, then. West Bradford," she starts, tilting her head at me, "the street Julio lives on, is right off this road. So, we won't have to trek through town or anything."

I stare at her, reluctant to ask, "And the not-so-good news?"

She shrugs. "It's still about two miles away."

I frown. "Why is that bad news?" I assumed we had more than a couple of miles to go.

A hint of a smile tugs at Ava's full lips. "It's not. But you looked like you needed a break from whatever that scowl was about." She mimics me with an exaggerated expression, and I smile despite myself.

"If I really look like that, please, just shoot me now and put me out of my misery."

Ava's shoulders rise with a soft chuckle, and she pats a trifold sticking out of her back pocket. "I found a map in the glove box. I figured it would come in handy since Google Maps is no longer an option."

"Smart."

Ava winks at me, and I know what she's doing. She's distracting me from myself, and I appreciate the diversion.

We fall into companionable silence, scanning every shadow, dirt road, and driveway for danger, hyperaware of our surroundings as we ride closer to Sweetwater.

The hotter it becomes, the more I pray Julio has drinkable water for us and the horses when we finally get there.

I notice Ava fidgeting from the corner of my eye, picking at the dried blood on her hairline.

"How are you feeling?" I can't see her wound from this side.

"Fine. I have a headache, but I'll survive."

"When we can take a real break, we'll put some ointment on it."

She waves my concern away. "Seriously, I'll be fine. We've been through worse."

There were never truer words, and our eyes linger on one another this time. The accident was nothing compared to what happened with Lars. "I can't believe this is our life," I mutter.

Ava snorts. "I can. It seems like my entire life has been building up to this." Her voice is filled with as much derision as exhaustion. "Like the universe has been preparing me for things to get shittier and shittier."

"There you go, touting that toxic positivity again."

Ava grins—a real one this time. "What can I say? It pours out of me effortlessly."

A distant hum meets our ears, loudening as a car whizzes down the road. Ava grips on the saddle horn tighter, and I nod for us to move farther off the shoulder, steering the horses as far away from the asphalt as we can. We pull them to a stop and wait for the car to pass. My hand goes to my pistol, and I nod for Ava to unstrap the shotgun on her saddle, just in case.

Her eyes are wide and her chest heaves in time with my pounding heart.

"If you need to," I tell her, my gaze flicking to the car as it slows, "ride for Julio's."

"Yeah—" Ava nods and licks her lips. "Okay."

I hold my breath as the Volvo station wagon rolls to a stop, it's diesel engine idling a few yards from us. The back seat is packed to the gills with belongings, and two older women sit in the front. That makes me feel slightly less apprehensive, but not much.

Tilting their heads, they peer at us through the windshield. They converse in the safety of the car for a moment, and I nod in greeting, attempting to look as non-threatening as possible.

Finally, the driver rolls down her window. "Where are you two headed?" Her gaze darts from me to Ava.

"We know someone in Sweetwater."

"It's a nuthouse," the woman in the passenger seat says, her voice barely reaching my ears over the sound of the engine.

The driver eyes us carefully. "You been south?" Her gray hair is piled on top of her head, and she's wearing a short-sleeved grocer's uniform.

"We came from Sonora."

She blinks. "And?"

"Don't go," I tell her easily. "There's nothing left."

The two women exchange a glance and look at us again. "The fires?"

Dipping my chin, I peer up the road toward town. Nuthouse to them could mean anything, so I ask, "How bad is it that direction?"

"The ground is splitting in the Panhandle Plains, our fire-fighters are deployed throughout Hill Country, our police force is too small to manage the amount of scared and desperate people coming through, and the government is threatening martial law, but we have yet to see a single uniform. They're all too busy dealing with the big cities. So, how do you think?"

"Point taken," I mutter. "And your militias?"

"Same as they've always been," she says dryly. "Present."

"Well, there is nothing for you south of here," I tell her. "Only wildfires and a spreading sinkhole. Trust me, you don't want to head that way." The instant the woman in the passenger seat breaks into tears, I feel horrible for being so callous about it.

The driver murmurs something to her and rubs the woman's shoulder before meeting my gaze. "Evacuation centers?"

I shake my head. The driver purses her lips and glances between me and Ava again. "Safe travels," she says, and then rolls her window up, continuing down the road without a single look back.

I meet Ava's gaze, and I watch the tension in her shoulders deflate as she takes a deep breath.

"Let's keep moving," I say, glancing at the disappearing car once more, and we continue down the road.

"What do you think she meant by the ground splitting?" Ava asks, sounding withdrawn and apprehensive.

"From the earthquakes, maybe?" I lift the bill of my ball cap and run my hand over my head. "Hopefully Julio will know."

We ride for a few minutes in silence, speaking nothing of what we've learned because it doesn't change anything. Instead, I stew in thought and consider our chances of getting into Sweetwater without seeing another person.

Lucy trots beside us, exhausted but keeping pace with the

horses. I can almost appreciate the eerily still world since the last thing we want is to run into people.

The horses spook as a gunshot rings through the air somewhere in the distance. Ava and I look at each other, her chest heaving as much as mine. Two more shots ring out. They are far away but hair-raising nonetheless.

"We need to get off this road," we say at once.

I lift my reins, waiting for Ava to follow suit. "Settle into your saddle and push your heels down. It's about to get bumpy." I grip my saddle horn for Ava's benefit, and she follows my demonstration as I click my tongue and nudge Rooster into a trot along the shoulder. Ava lurches in her saddle as Loca follows us with little persuasion, and Lucy lopes beside us, her tongue hanging from her mouth.

When Ava seems to have gotten the hang of it, we break into a canter, keeping to the shade trees and out of direct sight.

The road seems to stretch on and on before West Bradford finally comes into view.

"Left or right?" I call over my shoulder.

"Right!"

When we get to the fork in the road, we veer off, slowing our horses to a trot as we take in the country road. Lucy all but collapses in the shade of an ash tree as our horses catch their breath. "We're looking for lot four-eleven," Ava says.

We press the horses onward, and I let Lucy rest until she's ready to catch up. Ava and I pass fenced horse pastures and open fields. There are *No Trespassing* signs posted in some areas, and one lot looks fortified for the end of times. But all of that fades away as the weight of where I am going and who I am about to see finally, *really* hits me with a slow, cold trickle of dread.

This is the guy who killed my mother.

Julio is the man who upturned everything, and I'm about to come face-to-face with him.

The realization is paralyzing for a moment. Then anger consumes me, followed by an unexpected flood of resentment, but not because of my mom, and that gives me pause.

If it weren't for Julio, Ava and I might still be on our way to Kansas. We might still have the truck, and I wouldn't be taking her to him, only to be on my own for the rest of my journey.

I watch Ava and Loca as they take the lead a few strides ahead.

When did my future become so entangled with Ava's? When did my level of comfort and fortitude become dependent on her presence? Of all the sobering thoughts I've had today, continuing on without Ava is the most looming.

Ava pulls Loca to a stop in front of a white fence.

Rooster and I halt beside them, but I don't see a lot number. "Is this it?" I glance behind us for Lucy, who leisurely follows behind us.

"I just had this moment of clarity," she says. Her eyes meet mine. "I'm about to see my uncle, who I haven't seen since the night of the accident. And you're about to see the man who—who ruined your life," she adds more quietly.

"Don't worry about me, Ava. I'm more worried about what happens when I leave you here—that this is somewhere you should even be right now." I can't help the sharpness in my voice, because all of this feels wrong.

Ava stares at me, her eyes shifting from my eyes to my hat and then back to the white fence, but she says nothing more. What *can* she say? We've come all this way to bring her here. Neither of us knows what will happen next.

Ava worries her bottom lip like she's having second thoughts, then nudges Loca down the dirt drive.

Instead of overthinking Ava's hesitation, I un-holster my pistol, resting it against my thigh as I keep pace beside her. I don't think Julio would go out of his way to hurt Ava, but I don't trust the son of a bitch either. I heard he was on the straight and narrow since being released from prison, but that means nothing to me. Not when the world is falling to shit and Julio has a track record of selfish tendencies and zero coping skills, which left Ava an orphan.

Eventually, a house comes into view through an apple orchard. Its chipped, white paint has seen better days, and a rusted Chevy pickup is parked under a dilapidated carport built off to the side. The only thing that makes the place look lived-in are the fresh tire tracks in the gravel, and a couple of cushioned chairs on the porch.

As we ride closer, I note the large, raised planter beds and vegetable gardens that run along the right side of the house, and a dozen or so apple trees stretch beyond them.

Ava looks skeptical as she brings Loca to a stop in front of the porch. Her eyes lock with mine for only a second before she dismounts and lands on her feet with a thud. The weight of her backpack makes her teeter.

I dismount. "Do you want me to go in with you?" I help her shrug off her pack, and the whole time a part of me is screaming that I shouldn't let her out of my sight. The other part of me is wound so tight, I'm afraid to go inside for my own well-being.

"No, I'll be fine." Ava hands me Loca's reins. "Julio told me to come. He's probably been waiting for me." She nods toward a rolled-up hose at the corner of the house. "You should water the horses. I'll, uh, be out in a minute."

I nod, grateful to postpone my meeting with Julio for as long as I can, and holster my gun. Lucy sniffs around the old truck, finding more shade out of the heat, and I peel my backpack off, giving my sweaty back some air. Clothes, water, a bedroll, and first aid kit—all of it is crammed in there, filling the Osprey bag to near bursting

"Here goes," Ava mutters, and clearing her throat, she readjusts her hat. "Julio?" Ava steps onto the porch and peers through the screen door. "It's Ava." As she opens the screen and steps inside, I lead the horses to the hose by the garden. I can't help the way my heart pounds, how dry my throat is, or the way my neck is so tight, it aches to move it.

"No." I tug Rooster's reins away from the vegetables growing over the side of the garden bed. "That's not for you." I angle him toward the hose instead, occupying him with the promise of water. It hasn't smelled like sulfur since Sutton County, so I assume it's drinkable, in small amounts at least. There's an upturned water bucket with shears on it that I flip over to fill.

The horses nip at each other, battling for the water bucket, and I take their reins again. "Easy," I soothe, lifting the hose to Loca's mouth while Rooster slurps from the bucket.

Her ears perk up, and she lips at the cool spray. I'm half tempted to run the water over my head to cool myself off when Rooster's head jolts from the bucket, his eyes wide and nervous, and the hairs on the back of my neck stand on end.

I feel the press of metal against my neck, and my heart stops beating.

"I don't want any trouble," a familiar, gravelly voice says. It's low with warning, but there's a tinge of fear too.

"No? Then maybe you should remove the barrel of your gun from my neck," I grit out. My fingers itch to reach for my pistol, but Julio is too close to risk it.

"Leave my property," he demands. "Or I *will* shoot you. Just like your friend."

My blood runs cold and every ounce of bravado I have drains away. "What?"

"Come on, now. Move." The barrel presses harder into my flesh, but all I see is red.

"Or what?" I seethe. "You'll kill me like you killed my mother?" For some ungodly reason, I turn around to face him.

Julio's brow is etched with deep lines, his skin weather-worn, and his mouth agape as he stumbles back. His mustache trembles with his lip.

"Knox Bennett?" He looks horrified to see me. His tanned skin pales, and his brown eyes are . . . wrong.

"Julio," I grind out. I mean to knock the gun from his hand, but there's something about his shock—his awe in seeing me—that gives me pause. His gaze shifts over my face in utter confusion. "Where the hell is Ava?"

He stumbles back. "Ava?" Julio's eyes flare with apprehension.

"She went into the house. We thought *you* were in there." Fear grips hold of me as I imagine Ava inside with someone who is not Julio—someone dangerous enough to warrant my being held at gunpoint. "Ava!" I barely hear her name as it leaves my lips, drowned out by the sound of her scream.

Julio lunges for the front door, tripping over himself.

I bypass him and run inside.

TWENTY-FIVE
AVA

KNOX SHOUTS MY NAME, BUT HE'S ONLY A FLASH IN MY periphery as I run down the steps to the two dead bodies in the backyard, trembling as I examine their crumpled forms. *Not Julio.* Instead, it's two thirty-something men. One has a gun wound in the chest, and the other, whose head is contorted, has blood staining his back. I exhale a whimpered sigh of relief.

"Ava—" Knox barrels out the back door and down the steps.

Frantically, I scan the backyard for another body. "Where's Julio?" I only see a garden shed with the door open, potting soil upturned and spilling onto the ground. An old tractor, overgrown with weeds . . .

"I thought it was him," I squeak. "But—"

"Julio is—" Knox spins around. "He was right behind me."

There's a shuffle, and when Julio steps out of the house, I nearly choke with relief. "Oh, thank God." I hurry over as he stumbles a little, gripping the porch post to steady himself.

"I thought I'd missed one." He stares into my eyes.

"When you screamed . . ." The look on his face is a mix of elation, confusion, and sadness. Then I realize he's gripping his side, soaked in crimson.

"You've been shot?"

Julio's legs give out, and he nearly falls down the steps. "I told them to take what they needed. I didn't want trouble," he sputters, grimacing in pain.

Knox is instantly at my side.

"We need to get you out of this heat," I say. Knox and I lift Julio, bracing his weight between us as we help him up the steps and through the back door.

Suddenly, every second I'd spent looking through the small house, assessing this new life he made for himself, feels like wasted, precious time, because the manic energy coursing through me tells me we don't have much of it left.

"Over here." Knox leads us to the couch, and he helps me ease Julio down as gently as we can. Blood covers the side of his button-up shirt and spreads down his leg. My heart is racing so fast, I pray I don't have a panic attack right here and now, while Julio is near death in front of me. *He can't die.* The words loop through my head, but the way Julio looks at me, I think I've said it out loud. "We need to stop the bleed—"

"You came," Julio breathes. He gulps a breath. His brown eyes are unfocused and watery with pain and sadness. Tears glide down the deep lines of his face, and the gurgle of what I know are final breaths lodge in the back of his throat. "I'm so sorry."

"No—none of that," I tell him, and Knox appears with a handful of towels. Julio cringes as I press them to his wound. "If we'd gotten here sooner," I rasp. My voice doesn't sound like my own. It's desperate and frantic and almost hysterical. I want to scream at him to stay alive because, estranged or not, I need him. We're all we've got, and now he's leaving me too.

"There are so many regrets," he croaks. "So many things to say."

"All that matters is I'm here now. We'll get you fixed up. We'll figure everything else out later." The words pour from my lips. They are defiant and determined even if my heart is breaking on the inside.

"I—" Julio winces. "I see your mother in my dreams." Instead of looking at me, Julio slowly turns his head to Knox.

Knox's nostrils flare, and his eyes, already glistening with emotion, harden momentarily before they fill with tears.

"She asks me if you are okay and . . . I can never answer her." He struggles to swallow. "I have only . . . ever been able to ask . . . for her forgiveness."

Silent tears streak Knox's cheeks, and I wipe my nose on my arm and stifle a sob.

"Now," Julio rasps, "if I meet her again, I can give her peace."

Knox's chin trembles as he stares at the man who has tainted every part of his life. But he doesn't look at him with rage or indifference. He looks at Julio with sorrow.

Squeezing his eyes shut, Julio exhales a ragged breath. He swallows convulsively, and I grip his hand tighter. "It's as it should be now."

"Julio . . ." His name is a plea, and when he opens his eyes, his distant gaze meeting mine, Julio lifts his trembling hand and cups my face. "You look just like Maria. She would have been forty-five this month." His palm is rough from hard work, and the regret in his eyes cuts me to the core. I could have come sooner. I could have come months ago. I could have visited or called at least.

"Julio—"

"I'm so—sorry, mija."

"Don't," I tell him, but Julio chokes on whatever he is going to say next. I grip his shoulder. "No—you can't do this to me!"

Julio suffocates on his final words, and his eyes roll back into his head.

"Stay awake, goddammit!" I shake him vehemently. "Julio! Look at me—" I don't know how many times I say his name or for how long I shake him. And I don't know if my cries are borne of anger or sadness, but he is gone and death has claimed the last of my family. More than that, I never gave Julio a proper second chance.

"Ava." Knox's voice is faint, and my hands fall into my lap. I stare at the blood staining my nail beds and fingers. I have been angry and filled with grief more times than I can count, but the regret I feel is toxic, corrosive, and all-consuming.

Knox lifts me to my feet. "Did you hear me?" He squeezes my shoulders and I blink at him. "Ava? Please say something."

"I'm—" I clear my throat, forcing my tongue to work. "I'm fine."

Knox shakes his head. "No, you're not. And you don't have to be, but you were muttering to yourself."

I stare at the blood staining Knox's shirt and hands.

"Ava?" When he whispers my name, I force myself to meet his gaze. Looking into Knox's eyes is almost worse than numbness because I see his fear. It's wild and alive like my own, and the fissures riddling their way through me deepen.

"Ava," he says, more firmly this time. His thumbs rub my shoulders as he grips me harder, willing me to say something. To be strong. "Ava, *I'm* here." Knox says it like he's answering a question I don't remember asking, and I feel the warm press of his clammy hand against my face. "Julio's not all you have left." His words stir something inside me. A shred of hope? A modicum of relief? I stare at Knox, *really* look into his hazel eyes, and I believe him. I have Knox and Knox has me.

I nod, and somewhere deep down, I find a fraying thread of resolve and grab hold of it. "Okay," I whisper. I try and fail to swallow the lump in my throat. "I'm okay." I say it for myself more than for Knox and repeat the words over and over until I start to believe them.

As my focus shifts, I glance around the house—everywhere but where Julio lies on the couch. "We should stay here tonight." Resolve anchors deeper with every word. Rooster's sorrel tail flicks outside the window, and Lucy sits on the porch, panting as she watches us. "You should tie the horses up—get them something to eat."

"Ava." Knox strokes my shoulders. "You should take a minute—"

"I don't *want* a minute," I bite out. "Sorry, I just—" I rub my forehead, willing the thickness in my brain to go away. "I need to be alone."

Knox straightens, and I realize he is only inches from me. Taking a step back, he pulls his ball cap off his head. "I'll take care of the horses," he says, running his hand through his sweaty hair. "Let me know if you need anything."

I nod, but I don't trust myself to meet Knox's gaze again as he reluctantly turns for the door. He is all I have left, and it's only a matter of time before something happens to him too.

TWENTY-SIX
KNOX

THERE'S A TINGE OF ORANGE IN THE EVENING SKY AS THE last rays of sun sink behind the apple orchard. After digging a hole under one of them to bury Julio, Ava and I gave each other some space. She went inside to wash the blood from her body, and I've found menial tasks to keep my hands and mind busy, even if I'm so exhausted, I feel empty.

I pluck a few ripened cherry tomatoes from the vine and drop them in a bowl.

I resented Julio and was apprehensive about coming here, but I didn't want him to die. I didn't want to witness Ava go through that and watch her break. And I definitely didn't expect to hear him utter a word about my mother, and it nearly ripped me in two.

But it's the mixture of guilt and relief I feel now that Ava and I will remain in this together that makes me uneasy around her now. After what happened this afternoon, it's Ava and me against the world again.

My gut sours every time I picture her crumpled face, her red-rimmed, hollow eyes, and I have to relive the sounds of her shattering to pieces. So, I refocus on the ripened tomatoes, to put in our canned chili from Julio's pantry. He's got enough non-perishable food to last us a couple of weeks, if we need to take it with us.

Lucy ambles over. She must sense the mood that's settled over Ava and me because she hasn't left my side. She licks the back of my hand, and with a dramatic sigh, Lucy finds shade to stretch out in, and I continue picking.

I add a jalapeño to the bowl and a bell pepper, then head into the house, desperate for my turn in the shower. I don't question how the water is still running in Sweetwater, though I know it won't last. Not without a generator. I haven't even looked for one, but we won't be here long enough for it to matter. Ava and I haven't talked about leaving, but I can't imagine she'd want to stay here, not after today.

I consider my truck and trailer a few miles down the road. While I don't like the idea of backtracking, many of our things were left behind—more water and food, camping gear, ammo, fuel—everything too big or heavy to carry. Now that we have Julio's truck, our prospects have once again changed.

Stepping into the kitchen, I set the produce bucket on the counter and fill a glass with water, chugging it down. I don't know if we'll come across running, drinkable water again, and I take every advantage to enjoy it while it lasts.

Lucy paws at the screen door, my ever-present shadow, and when I open it, she comes in without ceremony and plops down on the cool tile floor in the kitchen, right at my feet.

"Really?" I mutter. She stretches out in answer and exhales another deep sigh. "I'll move around you, no worries." I am about to search for a can opener and heat up the chili when I realize the water isn't running anymore in the bathroom, and my attention shifts entirely. I head for the bedroom where our bags are stashed.

"Is the shower free?" I say loud enough so Ava can hear

me in the bathroom. When I push the bedroom door fully open, she's standing by the queen-sized bed, her hair long and wet down her bare back, in nothing but a pair of boy shorts.

"Shit—" I take a step back. "Sorry."

"Actually—" Ava hedges. "Can you help me with something?" She clutches a clean t-shirt to her chest. She's washed in the setting sunlight that pours through the window, illuminating the water drops on her back, still dripping from the ends of her hair.

"Uh, yeah." I swallow thickly. "Sure."

"I have a cut on my back I can't really reach," she mutters. Her fingers trace the edge of the abrasion she can't see. "I figured I should put some Neosporin on it before I'm covered in dust and sweat again." She looks at me over her shoulder. "Do you mind?"

"Yeah—" I shake my head. "I mean, no. I don't mind." I step closer and take the tube from her. Ava gathers her hair over her shoulder with the one hand, and presses the shirt closer to her chest with the other. The air stirs, and Ava's scent fills my nose. I have no idea what she smells like, but it's the most comforting smell I hadn't realized I'd missed.

I clear my throat. "Do you know what cut you?" I uncap the ointment, realizing my hands are dirty. "Wait. Hold up a sec." Tossing the tube on the bed, I hurry to the bathroom, opening the closed door, now that I know she's not in there, and wash my hands. Ava's neon orange sports bra hangs from the showerhead, dripping into the tub. Along with her black boy shorts.

Quickly, I dry my hands, open the squeaky door, and head back to the bedroom. "I thought you were still in the bathroom." I rub my hands together so they aren't cold when I touch her.

"Yeah, it won't stay open."

"Do you feel better, at least?" I squirt Neosporin on my fingertip and the instant I brush her back, chills ripple over Ava's skin. I can't help noticing the way they spread over every inch of her—the light hairs illuminated in the sunlight; a birthmark on her right shoulder blade; an old scar on the other side of her lower back that I have to stop myself from touching.

"What's the scar from?" I murmur, reluctantly lifting my hand away.

"Um—" Her voice is hoarse. "One of my episodes. It was the first time it happened at the supply store. I knew it was coming—I sat down, even—but when I lost consciousness, I slipped off the chair and cut my back on a rake prong."

I stare at her profile. "Jesus, Ava."

She huffs a laugh. "Yeah, it wasn't exactly fun."

Sighing, I exhale my frustration on her behalf. "For as long as you've been dealing with this, I guess I should be surprised you don't have more scars." Resting my other hand on her shoulder, I tilt her face toward me. "And this?" I brush her loose hair away from her forehead with the backs of my fingers. "We might as well doctor it up too."

Ava's mouth parts slightly. "Thanks." The word is hushed, filled with exhaustion and gratitude, and gently, I rub what's left of the ointment on my finger over the small, red cut on her hairline. Her body warmth at this proximity is intoxicating. "What about you?" The amber flecks in her irises are bright like liquid gold.

"What about me?"

"After you shower, we'll get those scrapes on your jaw and forearms cleaned up."

"I'll be fine—"

A soft sound, not quite a laugh, escapes her. "Nope. That's not how it works. You don't get to fuss over me and neglect your own bumps and bruises." Her eyebrow arches, daring me to argue with her.

I smile in defeat. "Have it your way." I hold my palms out, the tube of ointment between my fingers.

The corner of Ava's mouth lifts in victory, and I have a sudden need to kiss her. Instead, I take a step back. "I'll get a bandage for your back."

I open the first aid pack on the bed and pick one from the box, indifferent to the size. Ava turns her back to me again, and I carefully cover her wound—not because I'm worried I'll hurt her, but because I'm scared of what I might do if I touch her skin again.

"Done." In two strides, I'm at my pack, pulling out clean clothes before I rush for the door. "There's a can of chili on the counter, if you're hungry."

I hear Ava's "thank you" from the other room as I close myself inside the bathroom, exceedingly grateful for the distance . . . and the privacy.

TWENTY-SEVEN
AVA

JULIO'S ROOM IS SMALL AND HIS BED IS COMFORTABLE, almost too comfortable, but still, I can't sleep, even if I'm desperate for it. I stare up at the squeaking ceiling fan, thankful Sweetwater still has electricity. The night is hot and humid, but that's summer in Texas. One of the horses sneezes outside the window, and the crickets bask in their night songs. It's soothing, and yet . . .

Since waking to wildfires, our accident on the bridge, and arriving at Julio's, wave after wave of *what next* floods my mind each time I close my eyes. It leaves my heart pounding and my head filled with dread and doubt and all the troubling emotions in-between. The fact that smoke lingers in the air doesn't help, even if I barely notice it anymore.

I look at Knox lying to my right, his bare back facing me. His breathing is even, but something tells me he's still awake. A bedless spare room and the couch neither of us have touched since arriving left one option—bunkmates. "Knox?"

A heartbeat passes. "Yeah?"

"Do you really think we can make it to Ransom tomorrow, even with the ground splitting, like that lady said?" I dare to hope that by tomorrow night, we might be at his uncle's place.

Knox rolls onto his back and stares up at the ceiling, clasping his hands on his stomach like me. "I don't know. Theoretically, it's only a day of driving. But the way things are . . . it's hard to say."

"Yeah," I breathe. "I know." I stare at his profile, watching the way his chest rises and falls. The biggest unknown neither of us state aloud is whether his aunt and uncle, or even their farm for that matter, are still there. We've heard nothing about the situation in Kansas.

"Anything could happen between here and Ransom," Knox mutters, and his words only solidify the tension in my shoulders. "There's no point dwelling on it."

It's true, anything could happen in five hundred miles, but I feel so much solace in Knox's presence, I feel like we'll get through it—whatever it is—no matter what. "Your uncle will be relieved to see you."

A few more moments pass. "Yeah," he whispers.

"You seem . . . skeptical."

Knox lets out a hefty sigh, running his hand over his face. "I want to hope he'll be there and everything will be okay—that we'll get to the ranch in one piece and finally be able to breathe, but . . ."

"It feels dangerous to hope?"

When Knox looks at me, his eyes are dark and shimmery in the moonlight streaming through the window. "Yeah," he admits, "it does."

I take a deep breath, letting his words sink in, and a thought gives me pause. "Do you think—" I turn on my side to face him fully. "Do you think they will mind when you show up with another mouth to feed?"

"No." Knox says it effortlessly. "Mason and Beth will

welcome you with open arms. My uncle is nothing like my father." A pregnant silence fills the room as Mitch's fate—unknown as it may be—weighs on us.

"But we *will* get there," Knox says when I'm silent for too long, and I realize he's staring at me. "Eventually."

I offer him a tired smile. "I know we will." I'm not sure why, but I rest my hand on Knox's. I don't know how I expect him to react, but he laces his fingers with mine like it's second nature. "Is it terrible that I'm relieved I'm going to Ransom with you? I didn't want it to be on these terms, of course, but . . . Still, I'm relieved."

Knox stares at me for so long, I start to worry. "No," he finally answers. "Because I'm glad too." His thumb brushes mine. "I don't know how to do this without you."

His words aren't only a confession, but raw, filled with emotion, and comforting in a way that makes it hurt to breathe. The visage of him blurs a little as my eyes sting with the threat of tears. "Me neither," I whisper.

We share a drawn-out moment of silent understanding—Knox searching my expression for whatever he needs to find, and me willing him to say whatever it is I can't decipher in his gaze.

"I'll do everything I can to get us there safely," he promises.

I have to swallow the lump in my throat to answer. "So will I."

Knox reaches for my face and brushes a loose strand of hair out of my eyes. "Try to get some sleep," he whispers. "We should get on the road early if we're going to make it before nightfall." What Knox doesn't mention is that bringing me to Sweetwater took him off course, so our journey is longer now, and we have a lot of ground to cover.

I exhale that burden, knowing there is nothing I can do about it now. "Night."

Swallowing, Knox drops his hand, and this time when I close my eyes, sleep is unavoidable. I feel like the empty parts of me have been soothed just a little, but as levity fills me and the cricket songs fade away, Knox whispers my name.

"Yeah?" I whisper back.

"What's that scent you wear?"

His question is as sobering as it is surprising, and I open my eyes to look at his shadowed features. "You mean the sunblock?"

If I'm not mistaken, he smiles in the darkness. "Yeah, I guess. That, and your shampoo, I think. I like it."

My stomach does a somersault, and I can't help a grin of my own. "Good," I whisper. "Because you're sort of stuck with me."

We sleep until the earth starts shaking and crashing objects rattle through the house. Lucy skitters out of the room, and as groggy as I am, I know the drill. In a heartbeat, I've assessed the rocking ceiling fan, the boxes crashing on the other side of the closet door, and our bed rolling closer to the television mounted across the room that could tear from the wall in a single instant.

Knox and I scurry off the mattress for the doorframe. I expect the quake to cease but the entire house protests and the roar of the moving ground is deafening. My toes grip the floor as I brace myself for what I worry won't end when the world goes eerily still again.

Body thrumming with adrenaline, I meet Knox's gaze. His chest is heaving to match mine, and only as he lets go of my hand do I realize he was holding it at all. We stare at one another, catching our breaths. As exhausted as we are, there will be no sleeping tonight, not after that.

Knox scrubs his hand over his face with a groan. "This state is going to crumble out from under us before we can be rid of it," he mutters.

"No, it won't," I promise him. Knox looks at me. "Because we won't be here much longer."

TWENTY-EIGHT
KNOX

THE MORNING IS STRANGELY COLD, AND SMOKE IS THICKER IN the air today, enough that we drive in Julio's truck with the windows up and our N95 masks on for what few miles stretch between the house and the horse trailer.

The sun rises somewhere beyond the clouds, turning the dark sky to murky gray. It might be ominous if it wasn't so expected, but the weather is the least of my concerns. The instant my F-250 comes into view on the bridge, my stomach drops. The passenger door is open.

"Shit." I hit the steering wheel, making Ava jump. Her attention snaps to me, eyes wide, but all I can do is stare at the contents from the cab of my truck littering the ground.

I jerk the column shifter into park and the Chevy lurches to a halt. "How much do you want to bet," I say, pulling off my mask. I toss it onto the dash. "That it's *all* gone?" It isn't a question and I don't wait for Ava to answer as I shut the engine off and push the heavy door open.

"At least the trailer is still here," Ava says, thoughtful as she climbs out, eyeing what's left of our supplies.

I'm too busy cursing myself to find the silver lining. The

glove box and center console are open and the interior is a mess. The bottled waters and extra dog food in the back seat are gone. The ammo we couldn't carry that was stashed under the seat—gone. After yesterday, I'm more convinced than ever that we'll need it.

"Fuck!" I hit the fender with my hand in a sudden rage. "Why can't we catch a fucking break?" Tearing my ball cap from my head, I rake my fingers through my hair. "I should have come back yesterday. I should have—"

"It's not like we were sitting around all day yesterday, Knox. Or that we were thinking very clearly. We were in a car accident. We didn't think—"

"Exactly! We didn't *think*. And I knew better than to leave it all out like this. Now, all of our shit is gone."

"Oh, because you're a pro at this stuff? Give yourself a break, Knox."

"It's common sense!" I shout. "Of course someone would come along and take our shit. Hell, I would too if some dumbass left it out like this."

Ava reaches for me.

"Don't." I hate the way she flinches at my tone, and it takes a few deep breaths before I can meet her gaze again. "Sorry . . . I don't mean to yell at you. But I should've known better."

Chewing the inside of her cheek, Ava stares at the truck and trailer. "Maybe," she concedes. "But this changes nothing. Not really. We have the Chevy and now we have the trailer. We can still get to Ransom with the horses."

"Not on less than a full tank," I remind her. "And definitely not pulling a full horse trailer."

Ava throws her arms up. "Then . . . we'll go as far as we can in the truck and ride the rest of the way," she says, increasingly exasperated with me. "There are worse things than our stuff getting stolen. You know this."

I meet her gaze again. It's dark, narrowed, and fixed on me. My shoulders slump. I know Ava is right, but I'm growing far too familiar with the feeling of failure and defeat, and it's more than my ego and sanity can handle. "It could've been avoided, that's all."

Like reaching for a wounded creature, Ava rests her hand on my bicep. Her fingers are cool and warm all at once, and her eyes search mine. "Lesson learned," she says softly. "It's a shitty lesson, I'll give you that, but we'll be fine. I promise." Her thumb strokes my skin, just below the hem of my sleeve, and it might be the most soothing thing I've felt in years. I can't help the way my eyes drift to her lips, then the column of her throat as she swallows.

"For someone who is scared to hope," I say, my voice more husky than I expect, "you sound pretty confident." Last night she was restless with doubt, and now she's the one reassuring me.

Ava shrugs. "Toxic positivity, remember?" There's a hint of a smile in her voice. "And I believe it this time." She steps closer, her eyes holding a fierce, almost protective sort of certainty. "We have everything we need at the house. And now the horse trailer. We'll be fine." Ava's brow lifts with a silent dare to tell her she's wrong, but I won't argue with her.

Instead, I lean in and press my lips to hers. It shocks us both, I think, but Ava doesn't push me away. As her mouth forms to mine, all the burdens of doubt dissolve, relief flooding in its place. It's a slow kiss, an exploratory one that feels like a lifetime coming. Her lips brush mine and as I get a brief taste of her tongue, something tickles my cheek.

I pull away and Ava grips my arm like her knees might give out.

When we open our eyes, neither of us says a word. Her cheeks are pink, her lips damp. Her eyes gleam with wonder and, dare I hope, lust. I want to kiss her again—to feed this sudden hunger I have in her presence. But as a gray flake lands in Ava's hair, and another one on the hand still gripping my arm, we stare dumbly at it.

"Ash," she breathes. We peer up at the sky in this strangely quiet morning, and suddenly, whatever reverie we found in that single moment between us vanishes. We shouldn't be on the open road, and we definitely shouldn't be breathing this air.

"We need to go," I murmur, and begrudgingly I take a step back. "Let's get the trailer hitched and get the hell out of here."

TWENTY-NINE
AVA

WE ARE ON THE ROAD FOR AN HOUR OR SO, CRAMMED IN THE Chevy. With the uneven, cracked pavement, and the smoke hovering around us like mist, it's been slow going, bumpy, and the cab is taut with silence. Without a backseat, Lucy is camped in the truck bed with the provisions we brought from Julio's. We already had jerky, a few MREs, and protein bars in our packs, and we picked Julio's pantry and garden clean.

The more I think of him, the thicker the lump in my throat forms. As much as I wish things were different, what affects me most is how numb I feel about his death now, and the guilt that quickly follows.

I peer through the passenger window, watching the ash stir along the shoulder as we pass. It blankets the world like freshly fallen snow in a never-ending desert and mutes everything much the same. With the return of smoke comes the strange, orange haze that breaks through the cloud cover, and everything feels unnatural, down to the unexpected cold. I'd put long sleeves on when we returned to Julio's with the trailer, and despite the late morning, it hasn't warmed yet.

What would Mavey say about all this? Where would we

be right now if she was alive? I consider how much harder it would have been had she lived, and another wave of guilt hits me like a slap to the face.

It was supposed to be this way. That's what Mavey would've said. She wouldn't have wanted to live in this world, and more than that, she wouldn't have wanted to make it harder on me. In fact, I can practically see Mavey and Mitch dying on the proverbial hill together, stubborn as they both are. As stubborn as they both *were*.

Knox reaches into the bag of apples by my feet. We haven't talked about the kiss, nor are we likely to, and I'm okay with that. Whatever Knox and I are at the moment is a product of anomalies, so why would kissing him feel any different? Nothing is normal, and finding comfort and affection in Knox Bennett isn't as surprising as it would have been a week ago. And I've had far too many surprises to overthink it.

Instead, I busy my mind with pragmatic thoughts, like how long our food will last us without rationing it. Even if it's theoretically only a day of driving, it will take us longer than that to get to Kansas at the rate the road conditions are worsening. On top of what was in our backpacks, we grabbed the four jars of homemade tomato sauce Julio had made, the noodle boxes, a pot, as well as every canteen and bottle we could find, and filled them with well water. If we don't find another stove, we have apples for days, and can eat the sauce alone, if needed.

Our goal remains: stay away from people to limit risk and potential danger. And I don't even *allow* myself to consider there could be nothing for us in Kansas—that Knox's aunt and uncle are gone.

As my mind shifts back to meal planning, the world shakes. I hear it more than feel it quaking beneath us as we continue driving. Knox's hands tighten around the steering wheel, but we don't stop. Lucy's head pops up in the back, but otherwise she barely seems to care.

The earthquake is over as quickly as it started, and Knox and I exchange a look of apprehension. The earth has been grumbling more frequently, and even if we're growing used to them, the tremors linger like omens of something yet to come.

Knox maneuvers off the road and onto the shoulder, giving a large hole in the asphalt a wide berth as we continue down the frontage route.

"Do you think we'd have better luck on the freeway?"

Knox glances at the side mirror. "Maybe. We'll check it out at the next junction, see if it's cleared up at all. I figure the farther away we get from the San Antonio area, from where everyone was fleeing, the luckier we might be." He eyes the next turnoff, like he might consider taking it, but continues straight.

Turning in my seat, I check the sign before it disappears in the smoke. Amarillo. Twenty miles northeast.

If it weren't in the opposite direction, I might propose a stop in Amarillo, to see if we can find anything out about the fires that have flared up again and to check the area for more fuel. But the fuel we'd waste heading that direction could present more complications than we can afford, especially if there's nothing for us there.

So, I stare into the smoky gloom, a few hundred feet in front of us is all that's visible. I can tell Knox is driving more carefully than last time, taking special care around every turn and avoiding every pothole he can manage.

Licking his lips, he swallows a bite of apple. "These have to be new fires. It doesn't make sense otherwise."

"Agreed. I'll check the radio for a working station. Maybe a—"

"Uh . . . Ava." Knox's tone is so sober, my hand stills. Slowly—reluctantly—I look at him. He stares beyond the windshield, slowing the truck a little. It takes me a few heartbeats to realize what I'm looking at through the smoke.

The truck rolls to a stop, and both of us stare at a tear in the desert floor, barely visible save for the black smoke rising from it.

I don't know how long my mouth is gaping before I ask, "Is that what I think it is?"

"There's only one way to find out." Shutting down the engine, Knox grabs his N95 mask from the dash and climbs out. Lucy jumps out of the truck bed after him.

I follow, glancing at the horses in the trailer, and I meet Loca's gaze through one of the openings before I catch up with Knox, a few paces ahead.

Intermittent ash still falls from the sky, muffling our footsteps as we walk closer, each step more cautious than the last. The coolness in the air is chased instantly away by the heat emanating from the rift in the ground, and hardening lava spills onto the road. Like Lucy, I find my head tilting in awed curiosity.

"Stay," Knox commands. Lucy and I halt and look at him. He's talking to her of course, and bracing myself, I continue closer.

Since Gerty, dozens of extinct volcanoes around the world have been waking up, and new ones emerge with every shift in the earth. I'd watched the news footage of an eruption every morning while eating my cereal. Or a volcanologist rappelling into the bowels of the earth to study Mother Nature's advancing stages of unrest after the asteroid collision. And every week, a new theory would emerge from an award-winning scientist, or someone would win an honorific for their invention or dedication to understanding the shifting landscape. It was only a matter of time before we'd start to see the physical effects above ground.

Living in a state surrounded and inhabited by waking volcanoes, we learned all about them. Fire and earthquake drills and evacuation routes were ingrained in us. None of it prepared any of us for sinkholes swallowing half the state, and *none* of it quite prepared me for this. "This is what the woman meant about the ground splitting," I realize aloud. We stop when a strong wave of heat presses against us, and I gape at the lava trail, two meters wide. The way the lava carves through the ground right in front of me is damn near mesmerizing. "Breaking glass," I whisper.

"What?"

"I never knew lava sounded like breaking glass as it moves." The flow is so slow it's almost imperceptible beneath the hardening surface. And the heat, oppressive as it is, comes and goes with the slightest shift in the air. It's there one minute and gone the next, making chills prickle over my skin.

"These are causing all the quakes," Knox murmurs, and I look at him.

"Do you think they're responsible for the fires too?"

He nods, ever so slightly, as his gaze follows the molten river until it disappears in the haze. "New Mexico is riddled with volcanoes, and that's only one hundred miles from here."

Sinkholes or erupting volcanoes—I don't know which is worse. My brow beads with sweat, and not because of the lava inching its way through North Texas. The unpleasant and persistent question *what next?* forms on the tip of my tongue.

"We have to turn around." Knox looks at me. "We have to

get to Amarillo and find out what's going on." His jaw flexes as if he's trying to talk himself out of it, and he glances back at the truck and trailer. "If this gets worse north of here, then leaving Texas . . ." He shakes his head. He doesn't need to continue; I already know that if we're stuck here, that's a whole new wave of problems, and the day has just begun.

THIRTY
KNOX

"HOLY SHIT," AVA BREATHES. HER VOICE IS MUFFLED BY HER mask, but I feel the same hair-raising apprehension as I take in the wasteland surrounding us.

Amarillo is a charred ruin.

I eye the chipping *Gerty Got Us* graffiti on a billboard, then the train on the railroad tracks, abandoned and covered in ash alongside the interstate. It, too, is covered in spray paint—psalms about the Rapture and reunification in the dying world.

Reluctantly, I drive deeper into the city, hopeful that it's not entirely gone. Motels, gas stations, business and apartment complexes—they still smolder, as if it's only been a day or two since the fire came through, spreading toward the New Mexico border.

Metal shipping containers and lampposts dusted with soot are all that seem intact, and I slow the Chevy to a stop in the middle of the road.

When I look at Ava, she peels her eyes from our more-than-lacking prospects.

"We could turn around," I tell her. "We could keep

heading north—drive until we can't anymore. We have a quarter tank left. Then we continue on horseback."

"Or," she hedges, "we take a chance here. There have to be supplies somewhere." She glances at our reserves in the back of the truck, worrying her bottom lip. I can't help but stare at the way she tugs it between her teeth. "It's a risk," she admits. Her lip is slightly swollen and red from biting it so much. "But we have no idea what we're up against if we continue north. It's already worse than we thought. Maybe this is our chance to find out." She peers around, uncertain. "We're already here," she says more quietly, and I think she's trying to convince herself as much as she's trying to convince me. "Besides, you have your shotgun and pistol, so we're not helpless."

When Ava looks at me, I see it in her eyes—a desperation of sorts.

"Fine, but we don't stop if it's sketchy."

Ava snorts a laugh. "If it doesn't look sketchy at this point, it *is* sketchy."

I huff with the shake of my head. "That is . . . disturbingly accurate." With a combined sigh, we brace ourselves and continue down the interstate.

Amarillo seems sprawling, a long stretch of road that looks like it takes us straight through the city. "We're not going downtown," I tell her. "We stay out in the open." At this point, especially in a place this ravaged, anyone remaining will be desperate, and that itself is enough to make me turn around, wasted fuel or not.

Ava nods, her attention fixed on the ominous stretch of road out the window.

I need to let the horses out soon, but not here where there are too many places for lurkers to hide. With my atten-tion split between what I can see ahead and the baleful scene around us, I keep my eyes open for movement in the haze.

We pass a few silos and houses, a heavy equipment yard, and a mechanic shop. And as buildings untouched by fire emerge, a mixture of hope and fear swells in my chest. Hope that there *are* people here, and fear we will meet them.

"Knox." Ava taps my shoulder and points out her window as a fire station appears a few hundred feet ahead. Its windows are dusted with ash and the garage is open and empty—devoid of engines. The building, though, is intact. "We have to check it, right?" she says. "I mean, they will know what's going on more than anyone, and if we can even continue north." Ava looks at me, expectant, and she's right. If we're going to find any supplies or information, it doesn't get much better than a firehouse. "Even if they evacuated, it's worth scoping out," I agree.

I glance in my side mirror, ensuring no one has crept up behind us, and scout my route options. A median and frontage road separates us from the firehouse.

"There's a turnoff up there," Ava says, squinting.

I nod, and in spite of the familiar tension coiling throughout every inch of my body, the charge in the air buzzes with anticipation instead of hopelessness.

We make our way toward the turnoff, and I eye the businesses and buildings as I take the exit. Most of the buildings in this area appear vacant, with very few vehicles left in parking lots and driveways. As we approach the firehouse, however, a knot forms in my stomach. If I park too far away, we'll be hard pressed to get back to the truck and horses if something happens. If I drive into the lot, I'll undoubtedly be heard and seen by anyone still inside.

Gritting my teeth, I decide closer is the lesser of two evils because I'm leaving Ava with the truck, and I park just shy of the driveway on the side of the road. We have no idea who we'll find inside, or if we'll be greeted with resistance, but there's no going back now.

The truck brakes grind slightly as we come to a complete stop, and I lean toward the window to see up the flagpole. The American flag is wilted without a breeze and at half-mast, and I wonder how long ago it was lowered.

The firehouse itself is boxy, but the building facade appears relatively new, aside from the ash and soot that coats it. That could be a good thing, or bad. If the station was built within the last decade, it will be retrofitted with government mandated amenities and equipment in preparation for a cata-clysmic event and state of emergency. It would have stock-piles of food inside, oxygen tanks and masks, excess fuel, solar-powered generators, radios, an underground bunker, thousands of gallons of water stores, fireproof gear—it's a safe haven built to protect the people who would have to save humanity in the end. Which also means if people were smart, they would flock here for safety. *Or ransack it and take everything worth saving.*

The three open bay doors of the empty garage tell much of a story. No fire engines means the place is likely abandoned.

I shut off the truck and look at Ava. Her chest is heaving, her eyes wide with fear. "I'll go in first. I don't want the truck unattended until we know what we're dealing with."

She nods, if a bit reluctant, and we both get out of the truck. "Keep the shotgun with you the entire time," I tell her. "Use it if you have to. Honk the horn if you need to get my attention." I nod toward the glass doors at the entrance. "I'll be as quick as I can."

I can only hope that if someone's in there and they see me coming, they ask before they shoot.

THIRTY-ONE
AVA

MY HEART HAMMERS IN MY CHEST AS I WONDER WHAT horrible decision I've talked us into. My breath is stifling against my mask as I lean against the truck. The tepid afternoon only feeds the gathering sweat that dampens my brow and slickens my palms, and as Knox disappears into the garage, my heart lodges in my throat. My only shred of solace is knowing Lucy is with him. She'll sniff out someone before Knox can be blindsided, and bark if something goes wrong. She might be a sweet girl, but she'd maim if she had to protect Knox. I know she would.

As that familiar void and tingling sensation threatens the edge of my senses, I squeeze my eyes shut. "No. Not now," I whisper. "Pull yourself together, Ava."

I inhale deeply, exhaling as I open my eyes, and fan myself with a map I slipped in the door cubby. The breeze helps, and I lick my drying lips and try to keep my breathing steady. "You got this. You'll be okay."

Inhale. Exhale.

Inhale. Exhale.

I grip the shotgun tighter against me, trying my best to

push the anxiety that riddles every inch of me down. Apprehensive doesn't begin to cover it. Did I really suggest this?

Knox could get shot. Ambushed. *I* could get ambushed. Foot tapping, I stare up the road. It's quiet, save for a crow cawing from its perch on the telephone pole. It peers down at me, blinking its beady eyes, its head cocked to the side. Then the crow leans forward to caw again. It's incessant and makes me uncomfortable, so I look away.

Inhale. Exhale.

Inhale. Exhale.

I try to focus on anything but myself and scan the second-story windows of the firehouse for movement. *Please be empty* loops through my head, and I realize I don't want to find anyone here. I want this place to be abandoned. Overflowing with provisions and filled with answers to all my questions, sure. But people? I know not everyone is like Lars or the trigger-happy trespassers who shot Julio. But if they were?

I swallow the bile inching its way up my throat. I'm fine with it being only Knox and me until we get to Kansas.

A tinny thunk practically booms in the oppressive silence, and I jump, glaring at Loca's big brown eye blinking at me from inside the trailer. She paws at the wall again, making too much noise.

"Shh!" I whisper-chide, my eyes shifting back to our surroundings. "Do you want to be found out? Because your next rider will *not* be as amazing as me." I lift a brow, and Loca snorts in answer.

It's quiet again, and after waiting for what feels like an eternity, a cold sweat breaks down my spine. Unbidden, I feel it creeping in again—the void.

"No." It's another exhaled breath as a distant ringing starts in the back of my head, growing louder. A coldness fills my veins and spreads throughout my body. "Breathe, Ava." I squeeze my eyes shut again, willing it to go away. "*Breathe.*" But every inhale and exhale with my mask on is suffocating and I can't tear it off fast enough.

I grab the doorframe to brace myself, the fibrous mask crumpled in my grip. I drop into the passenger seat, afraid to open my eyes as I exhale—slowly. I don't want the world to be black—I can't afford this right now. I know panic only makes it worse, so I try to think about cold water and a breeze.

The longer I fan myself, the better I feel, and just as I think I might feel more collected, a whistle meets my ears. My eyes fly open to find Knox striding across the street, Lucy trotting beside him.

Licking my lips, I straighten, exhaling with relief as my mind clears.

"It's abandoned," he says. "I think they all went to Guymon."

"Wh—" I clear my throat. "Where's that?" With shaking hands, I uncap my water bottle and take a deep pull, praying it cools me off from the inside out.

"Oklahoma." Knox holsters his pistol, glancing at the horses, oblivious to my inner turmoil. Thankfully. This is not something he needs on his plate right now.

"Oklahoma? That could be a good sign," I realize, knowing our plan is to head north anyway.

"Yeah. It's about one hundred twenty miles north of here." Knox reaches through the open truck window for his water. "It looks like there's an evacuation center or research facility of some sort there."

"How do you know?"

Knox looks at me. "It's written on the wall. Literally." His brow furrows as he eyes me up and down. "Are you okay?"

It's easy to guess that my skin is more pallid than it should be.

"Yeah. Well"—I shrug—"slightly terrified you'd get ambushed, but . . ." I give him a tight-lipped smile.

Knox appraises me a second longer before he gets in the truck. He sees too much, even if he isn't quite sure *what* he's picking up on. But truthfully, I do feel a little better, and having never been able to talk myself back from the edge of a spell, I am slightly hopeful.

"I'm just glad you're back," I whisper.

"You're sure you're okay?" he says, pulling the door shut.

I close mine too. "Yeah, Knox." I sound more impatient than intended. "So, what's the plan?"

After a heartbeat more, he pulls the truck closer to the station. "It will be dark soon. Let's stay here tonight and park in the garage for now, keep everything out of sight while we figure things out."

I can't help but notice the tracks our tires leave in the ash, but darkness or maybe more ash will cover them soon enough.

"There's a basketball court in the back where the horses can stretch their legs," Knox continues. "We can take stock of what was left behind, and I can look through all the notes and paperwork that's here, see what I can make of it."

"So, coming here was a good thing," I muse, the weight of worry and potential regret lifting.

"Yeah," Knox says, throwing the truck and trailer into reverse. "I think it was."

After a couple of backward maneuvers, we're parked in the enormous garage that's more like an airplane hangar. I imagine six fire engines could fit inside, but today, it's only us.

I climb out before Knox can shut off the truck, desperate

to keep my body and mind busy so the darkness doesn't start creeping in again. Is it a logical plan? I have no idea. But focusing on everything *other than* having an episode seems to help a little.

Walking around the trailer, I reach for the gate latch when Knox appears beside me. I startle. He frowns. "Are you sure you're okay?"

I frown back. "Yeah, Knox. I'm just uncomfortable being here. And I was freaking out while you were inside, but it's all good now."

Lucy trots around, sniffing an old oil puddle before moving on to the lockers and equipment racks lining the wall. She's completely unfazed, which gives me a small sense of comfort. She'd be on alert if something was amiss.

"Okay, I'll stop asking," he mutters. Knox steps into the trailer and unties Rooster's lead rope. His hooves echo throughout the garage like a hammer against a steel drum as Knox backs him down the ramp. The sound grates on my senses and my skin crawls in response.

"Hold him, would you?"

I take the rope, and Knox heads into the trailer to untie Loca. "I need to show you something when we get the horses settled."

"That sounds a little ominous," I say, leading Rooster toward the back door, away from Loca's fidgeting that resounds through the entire garage. My adrenaline is still pounding, and it's putting every sense I have on edge. Leaning my forehead against Rooster's neck, I inhale his scent as his warmth seeps through my palm. I don't know why he's so calming, but I focus on his silky hair beneath my fingers as we wait for Knox and Loca.

"Over here."

Straightening, I lead Rooster behind Knox and Loca out

of a side exit. I'm not surprised to see the entire yard covered in ash. The covered grill area to the right, the patio set and basketball net. I stare at the fire tower in the back lot as Knox unclips Loca's lead rope and smacks her rump. She startles and trots away, playfully flinging her head. I unclip Rooster's rope, but he meanders after Knox, heading toward a garden hose a few yards down.

I notice a puddle on the ground. Knox likely checked the water during his sweep of the building. "I'll grab their buckets," I mutter, returning to the trailer. Back and forth I go, getting the horses' food, while Knox fills the buckets for them to sip from throughout the evening.

With the horses content, we make quick work of the roll-up doors. Actually, Knox does. He grabs one of the chain hoists at the closest bay, and I start on the opposite end of the garage. Knox has rolled down two of the three doors by the time I'm half done with mine. He makes it look effortless, of course. I can't even appreciate the flex of his arms because I'm too busy cringing as the screech of metal fills the garage. "This seems counterintuitive in an emergency situation," I grumble.

"The power's out." He smirks. "It's not always this arduous."

"That makes more sense."

Knox waves for me to follow him when we're finished. "Are you afraid of heights?" As we step into the back, I peer four stories up at the top of the fire tower. "Not typically. No."

"Good."

Without slowing, Knox hurries up the staircase winding around the building, taking two steps at a time. Lucy races past him with far too much pep in her step. I'm sure the exercise is refreshing for her after being cooped up in the back of the truck all day. On the other hand, I feel like I've been hit by a truck. I keep up as best as I can, wishing there was more of a breeze to counteract the still, almost humid afternoon.

I do a double take and stop on the third-floor platform. "What the actual fuck?" The last level of stairs is forgotten as I peer at what's left of the town.

"You can see it more clearly up here," Knox calls back, nearly to the top.

Heaving a breath, I hurry after him, more swiftly this time.

"That," Knox says, staring out at the lava rifts that have torn through the town, "is why I said we need a new plan." Lava fissures stretch across the edge of the town like a patchwork of deadly scars, and I hate to think about what else waits for us beyond the smoke.

"*That* is why they left this place behind," I realize.

"And according to the maps they have covering the walls inside," Knox explains, "it's like this all the way to New Mexico. We need to look at them . . . closely. Because our plan just changed."

THIRTY-TWO
KNOX

I pat Lucy's belly where she sleeps on the linoleum floor at my feet. I've been poring over maps, old government reports, and inventory lists—all the things that were left behind—for over an hour, trying to determine what's too outdated to be useful.

"It looks like everyone was evacuated south of the closest rift zone," I think aloud. "And we're right outside a concentration of them."

"Mm-hmm." I barely hear Ava as she makes us something to eat behind me in the kitchen.

I stare at the maps again, wondering why this outpost didn't take all their data with them. So we would know where to go? Or is it because the last dispatch was five days ago, and these maps are useless now? According to the three in front of me, we wouldn't have gotten another two miles or so from where we turned around for Amarillo. We would've ended up here anyway.

"I think these maps are going to show us the clearest path around the fissures, assuming they're still relatively accurate."

"Sounds good."

I glance back at Ava as she pours a box of pasta into a boiling pot on the stove. She leans against the counter, her arms crossed over her chest as she watches the steam rise. She's been reserved and acting cagey since we got here, and I have no idea why. It couldn't possibly be because of our kiss. Right? I keep wondering if she might be feeling awkward now that we're not on the move.

Desperate to pry more than two syllables from her, I try again. "Thank God for the solar generators, huh?"

Ava glances at me over her shoulder, forcing another quick, tight-lipped smile.

"Anyway," I continue, cracking the pressure in my neck, "I say we leave the truck behind tomorrow and take the horses." I run my finger along each of the Sharpie-drawn lava flows that riddle the plains and mountains to the west. "We have no choice but to go through the terrain to get to the other side, and the horses will be our best chance. A two-day ride, maybe? But it's our safest bet."

Still, Ava is quiet, and shaking my head, I spin around. "Are you going to tell me what's—"

It happens in slow motion. Ava reaches for a chair to hold onto, but she's too late.

"Ava!" Her fingers only brush the back of it as she loses her footing. I'm on my feet, sprinting to reach her as she falls to the ground, my heart in my throat. "Ava—" I barely reach her in time and pull her into my lap, cradling her head and uncertain what to do. I know it's one of her episodes, but that doesn't change how terrifying it is to watch her face slacken or the color drain from her cheeks.

Her body is clammy, but her eyes aren't open like before; she's out cold. She might be used to this, but I'm sure as hell not. It's terrifying, but I try to stay focused, to think rationally.

I reach for the nob and shut the stove off. The towel draped over the oven handle falls to the floor and I use it to pat the sweat from her brow. "Ava." Her name is a harsh whisper as I search my mind for words from what feels like a lifetime ago. What did she tell me about these things last time? It was different from this, but will she wake up the same way—tired and thirsty? I'm not sure if I should remove her long-sleeves, or leave her as she is.

My thoughts are a blur as I lift Ava into my arms, kissing her forehead as I carry her into the bunkroom. It's all I can do not to squeeze the life out of her, holding her to my chest, as if any of my strength might seep into her bones and wake her.

The bunkroom smells stale and unused, but the beds, a dozen of them split in three rows, fill the giant space. The room looks partially ransacked, the remnants of a whirlwind rush to leave. A couple of phone chargers are left on the nightstands, books are stacked beside reading lamps, and only some beds are covered with blankets.

Carefully, I lay Ava on a bed against the wall, easing her head down as gently as I can. I can't take my eyes off her face. I want her eyelashes to flutter or the color to return to her cheeks. I even lay my ear to her chest to make sure her heart is still beating. "Come on," I quietly urge, though I want to shout it as a command. It's been seconds—a couple of minutes at most—and she'll wake up soon, like last time. I think.

I remove her boots and steal the comforter from the next bed over. "I'll get you some water." In case she can hear me, I want her to know I'll be back, and I rush out of the room, Lucy at my side.

This is the second time I've been this scared in the past

week. Not even fleeing the ranch was this terrifying—at least then I had some control. Here, like this, with nothing to do but wait it out, desperation feels real and alive as it claws through my chest like a rabid wolf.

Tossing the towel on the counter, I grab two water bottles from our stash and a box of crackers in case Ava wakes hungry, and I swoop my arm through her backpack strap along the way.

I set the water and crackers down on the nightstand and drop Ava's backpack on the ground. Her cheeks finally have some color, and too anxious to sit and wait for her to wake up, I crawl into bed beside her, pulling Ava against me. "I'm right here," I whisper. I place my hand on her chest to feel each breath because it's the only salve for my nerves at this point. My arms tighten around her. "I'm right here."

THIRTY-THREE
AVA

I STARE AT KNOX, THE WAY HIS EYES MOVE UNDER HIS eyelids in the pale moonlight. The way his brow is furrowed, even in sleep.

I can still hear his voice in my mind. It's the echo of a dream, but I knew he was here. Somehow. And for the first time in my life, when I woke up it wasn't with panic, because Knox's arms were wrapped around me. I felt cared for and safe and haven't stopped staring at him since.

He's done so much for me; I only want to soothe what tugs at his brow and torments his dreams. I'm not a romantic or a creep—not a woman who would typically stare at a man while he's sleeping, let alone kiss him—but I want to. And I'm too tired to care if it's weird or what Knox's reaction will be when he wakes.

I've wanted him in some capacity my whole life. As a protector at school, a friend—as someone who looked at me with something other than antipathy. And I want him now. Even having lost everything, it feels like I have all I need in a sense, too.

The mattress creaks in protest as I lean in. The scent of

smoke clings to him, and I'm acutely aware of my heartbeat, pounding so loud I'm sure it will wake him as my mouth brushes his.

Knox's breath hitches, but he doesn't flinch or pull away, and my apprehension fades. This is not like the kiss we shared by the truck this morning, which ended as quickly as it began. It feels more intimate, more raw, and such a long time coming. So, I take my time, allowing the embers of what could be catch flame. I savor the warmth of his kiss and the faint taste of salt on his lips, the pounding of his pulse beneath his skin and the flex of his body as I kiss him deeper.

I'm all too aware of this man—the size of him so close to me, and his heat is like a homecoming. Like he is the sun in the constant gray, and I lose myself in the gravitational pull I've always felt toward him.

With a ragged breath, Knox kisses me back. His fingers lace in my hair and his tongue seeks mine, so tentative and patient—so perfectly right—I think my heart might explode. But as his hand loosens in my hair and drops to my shoulder, he gently pulls away.

"You scared the shit out of me today," he rasps, the remnants of fear and confusion still threading his voice.

Images of Knox tearing through the firehouse, trying to fix me, fill my mind, and I squeeze my eyes shut. "I'm sorry. I haven't had a spell like that in years. I was trying to fight it off all afternoon, but—"

"All afternoon?" Knox bites out. His back hits the wall as his body tenses. "You need to tell me this shit, Ava." When my eyes meet his in the night shadows, he's glaring at me.

He's right. I know he is, and heat burns my cheeks. I would expect the same. I would want to help him in any way I could. "I will next time. I promise. I just—I'm not used to—"

"To what?"

My throat tightens and I force myself to hold his accusatory gaze. "I'm not used to talking about it," I admit, willing Knox to understand. "It's my burden, you know? I'm not used to having to share it with someone. You have so much on your mind already, I don't want to burden you more with this—it's completely out of your control." I rarely spoke to Mavey about my seizures because she had her own health issues to worry about, but I don't tell him that.

"I don't care, Ava. Things are different now," he says more softly. Knox brushes a fallen strand of hair from my face, and the back of his knuckle lingers against my cheek. "We're in this together." His voice is stern but earnest and my cheeks burn hotter. I have to stop myself from leaning into his touch, from melting into his strength. "I need to know when you're not well so I can help you. So I'm not blindsided." He takes a deep breath. "You have no idea how scared I was," he whispers, and my heart squeezes so tightly I think it might burst. "I need you, Ava. I can't do this without you. So . . . let me help you, okay? Please?"

Knox's desperation, as controlled as it is, is palpable. No one has ever cared about me the way he seems to. His actions —the fiery gleam in his eyes sometimes—pierce my soul, and something inside me breaks.

"Okay," I whisper. My vision blurs with tears. "I'm sorry. The last thing I want to do is make this harder for you."

Knox lets out an incredulous laugh as his hand falls away. "Ava, you just passed out for an hour, and you're worried about *me*?"

I wipe a rogue tear from my cheek but another one falls in its place. "Sorry—I get emotional after. It's stupid, but I can't help it."

Knox pulls me into him. "Don't apologize." The roughness of his voice tears at my heart even more. "For being infuriating at times, maybe," he teases, "but not for crying."

I smile into Knox's shoulder and allow myself to melt into him. I hold on for dear life because, for the first time, I have someone stronger than me to lean on, and I don't have to bear the weight of everything on my own. It's a foreign, unnatural feeling, and yet a sudden lightness fills me.

"One time," I recall, remembering one of the worst days, "I had an episode in a parking lot. This strange wave of numbness and fire overcame me, and I collapsed. I was conscious but couldn't move, and the pavement was so hot. I can still feel the sharp asphalt biting into my cheek." I close my eyes, reliving it so clearly. "I could see the cars parked around me, and I watched someone walk right by and do nothing. They *said* nothing. It was the first time it had happened in public, and ever since that day, the panic I feel when I know it's coming is incapacitating."

"No one stopped to help you?"

My head shifts ever so slightly. "I remember thinking *that's* the type of world we live in now, and I've sort of held a grudge against people ever since."

"God, people suck."

I smile to myself, my heart aching a little. "That's what Mavey said, and that's when she got me the *Toxic Positivity* hat."

"With rainbow lettering that suits you so well," he adds dryly.

I chuckle, and Knox's arms tighten around me, our bodies pressed together on the double bed as he rubs slow circles on my back. I soak it in, listening to every methodical beat of his heart, having never felt anything like this before. "Thank you, Knox."

His hand stills, his fingers pressing firmly into my back to hold me against him. "I'm not going anywhere, Ava, wherever this journey takes us."

I don't know if he means the road to Kansas or where our paths lead beyond it, but I lift my head and smile into his neck, each word filling the bristly parts of me with warmth. "Me neither."

Knox rests his cheek against my forehead, and a rush of air leaves his lungs. "You promise?" His words are a whisper and full of uncertainty.

Slowly, I pull back and look him in the eyes. "I promise." His gaze is glassy and his predictably set jaw clenches in the moonlight. It's a reminder that Knox has had his own battles and burdens. A reminder that, like me, Knox has no one left. "I promise," I say again.

His Adam's apple moves up and down with a slow swallow, and I see it in his eyes as they shift to my mouth—the same longing that's been growing inside me for days. A need to be nearer and close the inches between us. But he doesn't move.

"Knox," I breathe. My heart is pounding so hard and so fast I think I might faint again, but it would be worth it if I could feel the weight of his body against mine, if I could revel in something good for the first time in so long. It's like I'm starved for it.

Closing my eyes, I lean in until our lips are only a hair's breadth apart.

"Ava—"

I claim his mouth, swallowing his breath before he can speak again. I don't want to know what he's going to say. The need to feel alive and full of him consumes me, and I wrap my arms around Knox's neck instead, willing him to accept this—to have me in this moment—all of me.

My body takes over and my leg inches up to wrap around

him, but Knox grips my arms, firm but gentle, and his body goes rigid against me. "Ava."

Mortification is a stomach churning, skin-singeing poison as I realize this is not what Knox wants right now. And I've just made it *very* apparent that I do.

I pull away, my elbows sinking into my pillow as I cover my face, gathering what few wits I have left. "That was . . . intense." I want to crawl under the blanket and never come out again. "*Too* intense. Sorry. I—"

"It's not that." Knox lies back on his pillow, raking his fingers through his short hair as he stares up at the ceiling. I don't know if he sounds or looks more tormented.

"Then"—I swallow my unease—"what is it?" I hate how small my voice is, but nothing has ever made sense when it comes to Knox Bennett, and I don't know if I should be relieved he's not repulsed by me, or brace myself for the *sex will make things too complicated* conversation.

"You were just unconscious, Ava. We should . . . take it slow."

I did just admit my emotions are higher after a spell like that, but this is different. This is the possibility of Knox and me, and if it's my heightened emotions giving me such courage, I welcome it gladly. The fact is, I don't feel sick or sad. If anything, I feel more well and alive than I ever have.

Leaning closer, I take hold of Knox's shirt and look him in the eyes. "Knox Bennett," I say quietly. Gently, even. "I have wanted you since I saw you all grown up in high school." His brow twitches with confusion, and I want to laugh. "If the only thing holding you back right now is that you think you'll *break* me somehow, then let me assure you, I would happily let you if that were even possible."

Knox's jaw tightens. His eyes scour mine for uncertainty, but there's none to be found. And I watch the play of emotions on his face as his reservations shatter. Lifting up onto his elbow, Knox snakes his other arm around my waist and captures my mouth with his. There's no ceremony this time. No hesitation. Knox's kiss is determined, barely restrained, and his hand slides up my neck and through my hair as he rolls me onto my back. His kisses are consuming, his tongue seeking mine as if he's been deprived of it for far too long, and my thoughts are distant and frenzied as my instincts take control.

My hands slide up the corded muscles of Knox's back. My fingers rake down his biceps, and I grab his hips, pulling him closer. My body arches as he settles over me, his thick length pressing against my jeans, pelvis to pelvis, and I groan as he grinds into me.

Each touch is frantic and greedy. His teeth score the column of my neck and his hand roams under my shirt, stopping at my pebbled nipple; my sports bra is all that denies him access. He nips at the fabric, as if to teach it a lesson, then lifts my shirt, tugs my bra down, and sucks my breast into his mouth. I writhe as the most exquisite sensation feathers through me and his warm tongue licks over my skin. His scruff against my tender flesh sends a trickle of deliciously hot chills fluttering through me.

But this intoxicating thrill and feeling him hard and pressed against me isn't enough. I want to touch Knox's flesh and make him come until every tension-filled inch of his body melts away in euphoria.

I fumble with the button of his pants and reach into his briefs, taking his erection in my hand.

"Fuuck." Knox groans into my breasts, and I smile to myself, determined to stroke him until he can no longer see straight. "Ava—" It's a guttural, almost pained word of warning, but I keep going. I want to give him this. I want to see pleasure crinkling Knox's brow instead of worry and sadness.

Knox gasps and his entire body trembles with building desire as he unravels above me. His hand grips my side, his fingers pressing my flesh with bruising pressure. With a quick hiss of breath, a groan rumbles through him. He curses as he squeezes me harder, growls my name, and comes completely undone.

His warmth pools on my stomach, and Knox pants for breath. He is slick and sweaty, and as the last of the tension seeps from his body, he drops his head to my shoulder. "Holy hell," he rasps, his chest heaving against me.

I bask in my victory and brush my lips to his ear. "You're welcome."

We both laugh, my chest rising and falling as quickly as his. I won't deny the tinge of disappointment in not having my own release or not having felt Knox inside me, but it's better this way. It negates the awkward conversation about contraceptives and the depressing truth of how long it's been since I've slept with someone, and I close my eyes, allowing myself to smile.

I wonder if Knox is aware his thumb strokes the skin above my hip as he comes down from his high. "That wasn't how I saw that going," he says huskily, inhaling another deep breath as he lifts off me. He pulls his shirt off and uses it to wipe his come from my stomach before meeting my gaze.

I don't know what I expected to see in his expression— exhaustion mixed in with a heady, sated gleam, perhaps. But there is no exhaustion. There's a glint of determination that seems almost vindictive, and a thrill of anticipation winds its way through me.

Knox looks down at me with a wolfish grin.

"Um . . ." I lick my lips. "Should I be afraid right now?"

He hums in answer and slides his hand down the plane of my sweat-dampened stomach to the zipper of my jeans. He unbuttons them more deftly than I'd managed with him and slips his fingers beneath my underwear.

My insides quiver with the promise of bliss as the pressure of his rough, hot hand inches over my delicate skin. My toes curl with anticipation, and I grip the sheets at my side.

The instant Knox's fingers sink inside me, his mouth descends on mine, swallowing a cry of pleasure as it escapes my lips.

I grab the ledge of the headboard, bracing myself as Knox's fingers fill me, and stars are all I can see.

THIRTY-FOUR
KNOX

OUR FORKS CLANK AGAINST OUR PASTA BOWLS AS AVA AND I have a midnight dinner in the living room. Lucy snores intermittently on one of the couches, and the soft light of the kitchen filters in, washing Ava in a soft glow.

Remotely, I'm thankful for the solar generators, so I don't have to worry about power right now, and the tower out back with a view of the city if I feel too unsettled and need to check on things. Together, they give me peace of mind. So, I pride myself in Ava's slightly rumpled appearance instead, and savor what transpired down the hall an hour ago.

If we were still Knox and Ava from last week, it would be awkward between us, but it feels very much the same, only . . . more. She still looks at me with a thousand thoughts behind her rich, amber eyes I wish I could read better; I still feel baffled by her presence in my life and comforted to have her with me at the same time. But now there's a secret we share—a heat in her gaze that warms my chest whenever she looks at me.

I take another bite of pasta, silently thanking Julio for this meal and the firehouse for this moment of peace Ava and I find ourselves in. I can sense her scrutinizing me, and swallowing, I glance at her. "What's that smile for?"

The apple of her cheek rounds with a smirk. "Nothing."

My eyes narrow, and I try not to smile as her smirk widens. "Tell me."

Ava forks the last bite into her mouth and shrugs. "I don't want to dredge up old stuff."

Lowering my bowl in my lap, I stare at her, expectant.

"It's just—" She licks her lips. "It's taken the end of the world for you to look at me differently is all." She discards her bowl and napkin on the carpet.

My pulse ticks with surprise, but I know what she means by that. Ava has mentioned how much she thought I hated her *five* times in the past week, and it makes me sick to think she ever believed that. "I've already told you. I never hated you or had evil thoughts about you, Ava."

She gives me a sidelong, incredulous look. "Are you sure about that? There was a lot of glaring and general displeasure when I was anywhere near you."

I avert my gaze because I can't argue with that. "That was my guilt showing is all."

"What do you mean?"

"Well," I start, scratching the side of my face, "according to my father, I was *supposed* to hate you—hell, I wanted to," I confess. "If for no other reason than to stop beating myself up for feeling sorry that you, like me, were caught in the middle of it all."

Whatever playfulness danced in her eyes becomes thoughtful—almost distant—and as much as I don't want to dredge up the past, either, I want Ava to understand.

I wipe my mouth, setting my bowl and napkin aside with hers. "I was in the farm store one day," I explain. "I saw you in the pen with the chicks, changing out their water." I watch the way Ava's fingers play with the ends of her hair as I revisit that unsettling moment that's likely molded every action since.

"You were playing with the most adorable babies, and you still looked . . . sad. More than that, you looked defeated, almost hopeless." I watched her smile wane and sadness fill her eyes, and it was gutting, even if I had no idea why. "I wanted to talk to you. I wanted to know what bothered you because you looked miserable, but I felt *guilty*. Like it was a betrayal to my dad and my family—what was left of it anyway. Julio ruined my life, and whether it was my own grief and misplaced anger or my dad's constant outbursts, I felt like you held some part of the blame, so it felt wrong not to resent you, too. But I never actually did, Ava. I stopped going into the farm store after that. I figured it would be easier not to think of you, and I'd stop feeling so conflicted if I sent Tony instead."

Her mouth quirks with sadness. "Was it? Easier, I mean."

I huff a laugh. "No. Pieces of you were everywhere, Ava Hernandez. I hadn't realized it until I tried to cut you out of my life, and then it just pissed me off. I'd still see you riding your bike around town or working through the diner window. Or my dad would bring up Julio being out of jail, or I'd have to weed my mother's gravesite. It was always something."

"Yeah, I guess that would be terrible." She picks busily at her fingernail.

"I didn't say terrible," I clarify, placing my hand on hers. She looks up at me. "It was just . . . hard. It would have been much easier if my dad had let it all go. But Mitch Bennett has never let anything go a day in his life." I lean back, my hand dropping into my lap as I think of him. Of my brother. Of Tony, wherever he is, if he's still alive. And I think about Scott and Lars and shake my head. "God, even in school, that guy was such a dick. After I graduated, I figured I would hear about some horrible thing he'd done. Probably read about it in the paper."

"Lars," Ava realizes. There's a tinge of shame in her voice that gives me pause. "He was right about one thing."

"I doubt that."

"I'm serious." Ava's gaze is unfocused and far away. "Think about it. Somehow, I've been in the center of it all—what happened at the feed store, what happened with your family, what happened to Scott." Her brow crumples. "It's like I'm the cancer and—"

"Don't *even* think that shit, Ava," I bite out. "One woman is not the cause of all of this. And Lars was a fucking idiot and a menace to society. He's had a chip on his shoulder his whole life *and* a screw loose. He made his own decisions, just as you and I have. He just ended up dead because of them. And so did Scott. That's on Lars, not on you."

Ava looks at me—*really* looks at me—as her gaze shifts over my face. I see the doubt in her eyes, like she's gauging my sincerity. "We've been through a lot together, haven't we?"

"Ten plus years and counting."

Ava spins her water bottle around on the floor beside her and I realize something. "Our lives have been entwined for as long as I can remember." I think of seeing her at church on Sundays, that day outside the school, at the diner and around town—always circling each other's lives in some way, no matter how small or fleeting.

"Small towns are like that, I guess."

"Yeah," I breath. "I guess."

It's silent as we lose ourselves in the past, unwanted as it might be. What a mess our lives have been. So much grief and disparity. So much wasted time and heartache. Then I remember what she said . . . "What about you?"

Ava looks up. "What do you mean?"

"*Knox Bennett, I have wanted you since high school,*" I parrot. Ava's brow twitches with surprise and her tanned cheeks flame red as I repeat her words from earlier. "All those years of awkward run-ins, I could always tell there was something you wanted to say. I just wasn't expecting your thoughts were anything like *that*."

She snorts a laugh and rubs her forehead. "Yeah, well, me neither, but that doesn't mean it's untrue."

"So, you were serious?" Part of me thought it was heat-of-the-moment ramblings. "I'm flattered." Ava scoffs, and once again, her water bottle is far more fascinating than it should be. "I'm serious. I had no idea."

"Well," she drawls, "now you do." I take a moment to admire Ava's profile—her bronze skin and the way her dark lashes fan against her cheekbones as she glances down, smiling shyly. Ava is beautiful and the strongest person I've ever met, and she doesn't even know it.

"Thank you," I say, and she glances over. "For telling me. I know that's not easy for you."

Her cheek lifts with a small smile and she shrugs. "I mean, you're sort of the last guy on Earth. At least it feels that way. So—"

I bark a laugh. "So, it's lack of options. Noted." Ava winks at me, and I toss my napkin at her. "Brat."

We sit in companionable silence for a moment, but the longer it stretches the more uncomfortable it begins to feel.

"Should we talk about it?"

Her eyes snap to me. "About what?" She glances toward the bunkroom. "Talk about *that*?"

I grin, unable to help myself. "We never talked about the kiss on the road eith—"

"I thought we silently agreed not to."

"Ava, I don't think that's a *thing*."

With a grumbled sigh, she turns to face me, and the quirk of a smile threatens the corner of her mouth. "Fine." She grabs a pillow off the recliner, shoves it between her back and the couch, and settles in. "Let's talk about it." She's testing me, trying to call my bluff.

Chuckling, I climb to my feet. "Calm down, turbo." I collect our dirty bowls. "I need provisions if we're going to have this conversation."

Ava gets up, grabbing our dirty napkins and her empty water bottle before joining me in the kitchen. "Provisions, you say?"

"Yeah, I could use something stronger than water."

"Ooh." She claps her hands with excitement. "I like the sound of that."

My grin widens. We've never had this levity between us, and it feels nice. Tomorrow will bring enough troubles without us having to dwell on them tonight; I'm not ready to let reality back in yet. "Don't get too excited." I set our dishes in the sink and turn to the floor-to-ceiling pantry. A bottle of wine stands on the top shelf all by its lonesome, and I reach for it.

"What exactly," Ava starts, "are firefighters doing with alcohol in the station?"

"Not drinking it, if the layer of dust is anything to go by." I angle the bottle away from us and blow the loose particles off. When that doesn't work, I wipe the label with a paper towel. "Stag's Leap. Napa Valley Cabernet Sauvignon. 2016. I have no idea if it's any good."

Ava and I look at each other, and she shrugs. "No one else is going to drink it."

I can't help that my eyes go to her ample chest as she casually shoves her hands in her back pockets, and I avert my gaze before Ava notices. "What do you think the odds are we find a corkscrew around here?"

Ava's grin turns devilish, and she holds up her finger. "Please hold." She spins on her heel and patters across the kitchen barefoot, snags the flashlight on the counter by the door, and steps out into the backyard. She murmurs something, probably to the horses, but her words are indistinct.

Lucy saunters in from her napping couch. She eyes the half-empty bowl of dog chow by the fridge as if it has a disease. "Oh, we're playing that game tonight, are we?" Rolling my eyes, I grab the gallon-sized Ziploc with her food and put another handful into her bowl. "Low and empty are not the same," I tell her. Though we've had this one-sided conversation for years, I know she can understand me. Lucy's doggy eyebrows arch, her butt wagging merrily like it's dancing to "Gotcha, sucker," and she happily munches away on her midnight snack.

Ava returns, beaming as she holds up a corkscrew. "I saw it in their grilling stuff earlier." It's old school and a little rusted, but it will work, and I pry it open.

"Good find." I raise my palm for a high-five.

Ava winks and slaps her hand to mine. It's warm and small, and I immediately think of her fingernails digging into my ass on the bed earlier. "Ah, why don't you—"

"I'm on it," she chirps, and I watch her backside as she jaunts away. Those hips were my handlebars an hour ago, her legs wrapped around me like a vise. It all happened so fast, and I barely savored any of it. Her curves and skin. That scent of hers that drives me mad . . .

"I can feel you watching me," she says, opening the cupboard across the kitchen.

Biting back a smile, I refocus on the wine. By the time I uncork it, all the cabinets behind me have been opened and shut, and Ava returns with two cups.

"Here." She holds out two mugs. "These will have to suffice as fancy wine glasses."

"Seems adequate," I muse. "I wouldn't know how to hold a wine glass anyway."

"Pinkies out," Ava drawls. "Obviously." She holds up a World's Best Grandpa mug. "I want this one."

"Which leaves me with . . ." I read the other mug. "Potter County Chili Cook-off 2003." My eyebrow raises of its own accord.

"I bet it was magical," Ava quips, and we head for the living room with our libations. We resume our seats on the carpet, slightly closer to each other than before.

"So," Ava starts, "we're really going to have this conversation, then?"

I nod as she crosses her legs and props the pillow behind her back again. "Why aren't we sitting on the couch?" I ask, perusing the giant sectional and the two La-Z-Boy recliners we could choose from.

Ava's expression dims. "Habit, I guess." She holds her mug out for a splash of wine.

"What does that mean? You didn't have a couch at home?" My chest cinches at the thought because I know she didn't have two jobs and live in a trailer park because she was made of money.

"Thanks," she murmurs when her cup is half full, and I pour mine next. "We had a couch. It was a loveseat, but it was Mavey's seat. I wanted it that way." She waves the conversation away. "Our place was small. We didn't have room for much. We can sit on the couch if you want." Ava splays her palm on the floor to get up.

"No—" I reach for her. "It's fine. I was only curious." I clear my throat before the tension can settle in, and I raise my mug. "To Potter County."

Ava's smile returns. "And good wine."

"Don't jinx it," I mutter, and we both take a sip. It's earthy and robust and makes my mouth pucker. But I don't hate it.

Ava swirls it around in her cup before taking another sip, like she's done this before. "Not bad," she murmurs. "Is it weird that I taste tobacco?"

"I taste tree bark, so I'm going with no, that's not weird at all."

We laugh and take another drink. "Delightful." Ava licks her lips, and leaning back, she nestles her mug in her lap. "So, I take it you don't drink much wine, then?"

"Is it that obvious?"

She nods forlornly. "You didn't use your pinky. So, it's *very* obvious."

"What can I say? I'm more of a beer and whiskey kind of guy."

"So I gathered." Ava's brow lifts with amusement. "When we were at your house," she supplies. "I think you'd had a bender the night before I got there, if the empty bottle and decanter in the living room were anything to go by."

"God." I shake my head. That night, my dad left, and I couldn't reach my brother. "That feels like ages ago already."

"I know, it's crazy." She picks at a loose tuft in the carpet.

"What about you? What's your drink of choice?"

Ava shrugs. "Honestly, I don't drink a lot. But my go-to would probably be vodka or tequila."

My eyes widen. "Really? Are you a party girl, and I didn't know?"

"Such a rager," she deadpans. "I did have wine on a date once. Then I proceeded to get plastered because the company was so deplorable."

I wince to cover up my disdain for this person, whoever he is. "That bad, huh?"

"Um, yeah." She shakes the bad memory away.

"Well, you're not the only one. I've had some doozies too." I will probably regret this, but I want Ava to know something about me that isn't tied to our past. "Do you remember Caroline Masterson?"

Ava frowns. "The girl who got caught giving Professor Grady's TA a blow job in the chem lab at Southwest? Everyone at the diner was talking about it." Ava's mouth quirks in thought. "Was she dating you when that happened?" My expression must say it all because her hand flies to her mouth to hold in a laugh. "I'm so sorry. That's not funny, but I laugh when I'm nervous." It is slightly humiliating, yet Ava's expression is priceless. I've never seen her smile so damn much, and I wouldn't change it for the world.

I chuckle. "It's okay. It was five years ago, and we dated for like a month. It was no big deal."

Ava shakes her head. "How did I not know any of this?"

"Ha! I didn't exactly announce it to anyone, Ava. And you and I weren't exactly friends."

"True. But still. That had to suck in the moment." Ava's eyes flick to mine, lingering a second before she picks up her mug to finish her wine. "She's an idiot for doing that to you," she mutters. Ava licks her lips as she pours herself another splash. "More?"

I hand her my cup. "Has there been anyone?" I ask, uncertain where the words come from but wishing I could stuff them back down my throat. Instead, they just keep flow-ing. "Anyone special. Someone you thought might be *the one*?"

Ava props her elbow on the couch, her temple resting on her fist. "I've been too busy working and taking care of Mavey to date. It's been a couple years, at least. In fact, the people closest to me are my bosses and coworkers. Or they *were*. It's pathetic, really." She grumbles the last part.

"Don't." I shake my head, tired of her self-loathing. "Don't diminish all your hard work and all you've sacrificed to keep Mavey comfortable, Ava. Not to mention how much you've struggled to support yourself, too, along the way." I take her hand in mind. "I'm serious."

A small, tentative smile trembles on her lips. "You're right. And I wouldn't change any of it. I mean, my health stuff, of course—and I would take Mavey's pain away if I could have, but—" Ava shakes her head. "I would never change my caring for her. I was happy to do it. I owed it to her."

"She got something out of it, too, you know?"

Ava's eyes shift to mine again, a sudden gleam in them.

"I didn't know her well," I admit, "but any woman who takes in a little girl and raises her when she doesn't have to does it because she cares. Yes, Mavey helped you, but I promise you were more to her than just a kid to clothe and a mouth to feed. She cared about you."

Ava's eyes well with tears and she offers me a watery smile. "Thanks, Knox."

"You're the strongest person I've ever met, Ava." I can't help the reverence in my voice despite trying to keep my cool. "I wish you could see it."

Her nostrils flare. "Not always."

I miss the smile brightening her face, but she needs to

hear this. "You're allowed to have bad days and doubts, but that doesn't change the fact that you're a fighter and far more compassionate than I think you want to let on." My jaw aches and I clear my throat. "Every time I think about our lives before all of this, I feel like complete shit."

"What? Why?"

"Because—" I shrug, itchy in my own skin. "If I'd talked to you even once, of all the times I'd wanted to, I would have known how amazing you are. I could have taken you to a doctor's appointment so you didn't have to ride that stupid bike that always broke. I could have helped you with Mavey or taken you on a date." I exhale a shaky breath of frustration. "I wasted so much time *hiding* from you. What sort of coward does that? All it would have taken was me saying *hi* instead of turning in the opposite direction, and we could have been friends."

Ava smiles, and I do a double take. Not a *this-is-hilarious* sort of smile, but a pleasantly surprised one. She looks at me so long and with so much softness, it gives me butterflies.

"What?"

Ava's smile curves into a grin. "You would have asked me on a date?"

I groan and rub my hands over my face. "That's what you're focusing on?" She looks almost giddy, and it's fucking adorable.

"*Duh.*" She inches closer on her knees. "I can't even imagine you asking me out on a date or what my knee-jerk reaction would've been. But," she says with a pop of her lips, "I know I would have said yes."

I grimace. "Gee, thanks. Lather the regret on a little thicker."

Ava chuckles and rests her hand on my arm. "I'm only giving you a hard time, Knox." She gives me a slight squeeze. "I honestly don't know if I would have said yes. I had a lot going on. I couldn't afford any distractions. Not to mention, trust is not something I dole out very easily." She exhales, and the lightness between us dims. I don't want to lose her to the past again, and I cup her cheek.

Ava's eyes snap to me.

"I was an idiot," I whisper. I stare at the copper flecks in her eyes I've come to memorize, and the way her long lashes accentuate her natural beauty.

"You still are," she whispers, and as Ava's eyes close, she kisses my palm. "Because even after everything we've been through, I'm right here. I haven't gone anywhere." Her lashes flit open, and her whiskey-colored gaze gleams with a wistful longing, making every inch of my body stir.

So, I kiss Ava because it's all I can think about. And since the bedroom earlier, it's been all I could do not to explore her body all over again.

My fingers thread the hair at the nape of her neck, and I inhale. Our tongues already know this dance, seeking each other out again. Ava tastes like wine and smells like citrus, and I want nothing more than to bury myself inside her. To worship her body and help her shed the worries that have always weighed her down. To show her how amazing she is and make love to her right here because we may never get another chance . . . and the reality of that burns like acid in my chest.

Groaning, I rest my forehead against hers. "I don't have a condom."

Ava strums the hair on the back of my neck, her chest heaving as she pulls away. "Well," she says with a sigh. "It's a good thing I have an IUD—it's the most reliable method with all of my meds." She looks me in the eyes. "And unless there's anything else I need to worry about with you—"

"God, no."

"Then," she says, licking her lips. Her eyes twinkle with anticipation. "What are you waiting for?" Despite Ava's bravado, I see the uncertainty in her expression. The desire in her eyes just barely overshadows her vulnerability.

"You," I breathe. I rise to my feet and gather Ava into my arms, kissing her long and deep—worried that she'll vanish before I can show her everything I can't find the words to say. "I think I've been waiting for you."

THIRTY-FIVE
AVA

I WAKE WITH A START, MY HEART POUNDING, AND I DON'T know why. I glance around the bunkroom, blinking through a sliver of light peeking through the windows. It's daytime. I have a moment of panic, like I should be doing something, then remember . . .

Last night.

My hand flies to my chest, my *bare* chest, and I peer down as it all comes flooding back. My attention snaps to Knox, asleep on his stomach beside me, tangled in blankets.

I cover my mouth, stifling a giddy laugh. Yeah, that freaking happened. I run my fingers through my tangled hair, exhaling the strange unease I woke with. When I look at Knox again, though, jubilant butterflies take its place.

I was not expecting what happened last night. Him. Any of it. *Wanting* Knox and *having* him are two very different things. And to top it off, us together felt like more than convenient sex. Much more. Like, despite our distance over the years, it was always leading to this—Knox and me together, predetermined and forever in each other's gravitational orbit.

Pulling the comforter to my chest, I lie back, sinking into the mattress. My eyes drift to Knox again, unbidden, and I watch the way his back rises and falls with each shallow breath.

When I realize I'm grinning like a goober, I know I'm done for, and I pull the comforter over my face.

A boom fills the air, and the entire firehouse shakes. I slingshot up in bed, and Lucy lurches to her feet by the bunkroom door. Knox stirs in his sleep as I grip his shoulder.

"Wake up," I hiss, scanning the bunkroom like the walls might cave in around us. "Knox—I think that was an explosion."

He turns over, scrubbing his face as I collect my under-wear and bra from the floor.

"An explosion?"

I nod, nearly losing my balance as I reach for my jeans. "Yes, at least, I think that's what it was. Maybe a few blocks away?" Something had woken me, I realize. Another boom? An earthquake?

"Stay in here," Knox says groggily. He hikes his pants up to his hip and grabs his pistol from the holster beside the bed. "Check the windows for anything." He pads out of the room on bare feet.

Grabbing the shotgun, I do exactly as he says, my heart racing as I inch my way to the shuttered window to sneak a peek.

I open it slowly with the handle crank. The day is grayed by ash clouds. The side of the firehouse is still and what I can see of the street is empty. Ash dust still covers everything, and there are no new tire tracks or creepy people peering up at me like I half expect. Nothing appears disturbed.

Moving to the back of the room, I check the other windows. Other than a well-worn path in the gray-covered basketball court from anxious horses, nothing seems out of place.

"We need a better view." Knox rushes in and plops down on the bed, hastily donning his boots.

"The tower?"

He nods as I pull my boots on, too. There's a moment when our eyes meet and linger, exchanging an "it was fun while it lasted" look, since reality has set back in with the subtlety of a cannon.

Throwing my hair up in a knot, I give Knox a brusque "I'm ready" nod, and we cautiously make our way outside. I have no idea what time of day it is, maybe close to noon, if I had to guess, and the weather is cool again without the sun. I shiver but it might be nerves and apprehension. "The ground shook," I explain. "I don't think it was an earthquake, though. I mean, it could've been, I guess, but it didn't feel like it. Not with a boom like that."

Knox scans the backyard for movement. "I think we're about to find out." We hurry up the stairs, zigzagging our way up the fire tower. We're not yet to the top when I notice a smoke cloud on the horizon.

"Either something exploded," Knox says a little breathless.

"Or someone set a fire," I finish for him. We stare at the billowing smoke, catching our breaths. "I mean, it could be a collapsed building," I hedge. "Maybe from the earthquakes?"

Knox looks at me, his pensive brow and clenched jaw predictably back in place. "I don't want to hang around to find out."

"Agreed."

We stare at each other, silently bracing ourselves for whatever comes next.

"You're faster with the horses," I tell him. "I'll gather our things."

He nods, and I recognize the disappointment in Knox's expression because it's the same way I feel: our break is over and far too soon. Thankfully, our exit plan was decided yesterday, even if we hadn't anticipated such a hasty departure.

I turn for the stairs. "I'll make sure we have everything we need from the truck."

"Grab the maps," Knox says, falling into quick steps behind me. Like the flip of a switch, we're back in survival mode, like the last twelve hours together never even happened.

Twenty minutes later, our things are packed, and what doesn't fit in our backpacks is strapped to Loca's and Rooster's saddles. They are our best hope for maneuvering around the rifts in the terrain that are undriveable.

"Assuming the maps are still accurate," Knox says, unhooking his stirrup from the saddle horn, "we'll use the frontage road along Route 87 until the fissures get bad. I think it's the best route without straying too close to New Mexico. Since we're on horseback, it should be easier to maneuver."

I adjust my *Toxic Positivity* hat. "Sounds good."

Knox's eyes shift to me. "We only use the main road when we have no other choice, just to be safe."

"Agreed." With a long stretch of uncharted territory lying ahead and only a couple of small towns and rest stops along the way, our options for water and shelter are severely limited. Still, I'm anxious to get out of Amarillo. It feels like we've worn out our welcome, and I would rather leave this place behind before my memory of it can be tarnished.

I tighten Loca's cinch the way Knox showed me, and do a final saddle check.

"Hey."

My attention snaps to Knox. He's standing a few inches from me, his hazel eyes shining with warmth.

"Hey," I breathe. When he looks at me, heat spreads through my chest up to my cheeks. Less than an hour ago, we were naked in bed.

Knox reaches for a strand of hair, fallen from under my cap, and tucks it behind my ear. "This isn't how I wanted things to go this morning," he says thickly. His face is scruffier today, and I reach for his cheek.

"I know." I don't want Knox worrying about me or over-thinking what happened between us. Not while we need to get out of here safely. I shrug it off, unable to resist a smirk. "It was fun while it lasted."

"Oh, it's not over." A devilish smile lifts the corner of his mouth, and leaning in, Knox presses a kiss to my lips. It's firm and urgent and a little desperate like he doesn't want it all to be forgotten. When he pulls away, the gold flecks in his eyes glimmer. "That fine with you?"

I nod dumbly, lips parted and a little breathless. "Um, yeah." I clear my throat. "Totally."

With a smirk of his own, Knox checks Loca's saddle again for good measure, and we mount up. The horses are anxious to get on the road, and Lucy is already exploring the route ahead.

"You good?" Knox pauses for a moment, looking me

over. And if I'm not mistaken, admiration softens his expression.

I give him a thumbs up. "I'm good," I promise. At least as good as I can be after the abrupt start to our day.

"You say that now," Knox tosses over his shoulder, "but riding all day after last night . . ." He tilts his head with a low whistle. "You're going to be *sore*—"

"Ha!" I roll my eyes. "You're such a boy."

"You think I'm joking." Knox chuckles to himself, and when he's had his fill, he calls for Lucy and clicks Rooster into a trot.

I nudge Loca after them, still grinning to myself.

We keep to the side of the road as we head north through town. The world isn't as still as it seemed yesterday. Birds are chirping in the distance, and the haze we've been shrouded in for days disperses with the breeze.

Knox eyes our tire tracks, which are still visible from yesterday.

"It's funny," I muse. "Before all of this started, I would have thought we'd be *looking* for people, not trying to steer clear of them."

"Yeah, well, I'd rather it be just the two of us than risk another Lars or Julio situation. And after what my dad saw —" Knox shakes his head. "I think it's better this way."

I nod, knowing he's right. At least until we find the facility in Guymon. I offer him a pensive smile, knowing there are no simple or easy decisions to make anymore, and we continue down the road.

We weave our way around abandoned cars and looted rubble. Gerty graffiti gleams on a water tower. This time, though, it's a cartoon mural of her sitting on the moon in a lounge chair, a long-necked dinosaur stretched out beside her, both with shades on as they watch Earth catch flame.

I might not have mocked Gertrude's collision with the moon, but I never took it as seriously as I should have either. Being born after the fact made Gerty feel more like a cautionary story than a reality. A way for parents to guilt their kids into eating all their dinner because they never knew when food might become scarce. To be grateful for what they have because another, worse Gertrude might strike, and it could all be gone. But when all you hear about are catastrophic and extreme weather events, changing migration patterns, government preparation projects, and research—it all becomes background noise.

But passing broken windows and maneuvering around abandoned cars, walking through the garbage in the streets makes it all *very* real. We pass a plaza completely lit up with Open signs flashing red, and interior lights flickering with each power surge. "Solar?" I ask Knox, feeling strangely exposed and vulnerable as we pass. I'm almost as afraid to keep staring inside as I am to look away, uncertain who might be in there.

"That would be my guess. I don't see Thai Kitchen and the laundromat being open for business on a day like this."

He points toward an off-shooting road. Another plaza is lit up, even though soot covers the side of the buildings like a small fire broke out some days back.

"Hold up," Knox hisses. He pulls Rooster to a stop before we round a corner. "Lucy, stay." His voice is low and sharp, and the adrenaline I've been trying to keep at bay starts whirring through me.

I don't have to ask Knox what's wrong because I see their reflection on the glass storefront across the street. *People.* There are four of them dressed entirely in black, their faces covered and automatic rifles strapped against three of their chests. "Military?" I whisper as they load something into a white van.

"Could be. Or a private militia."

"What are the odds they happen to be here at the same time as that explosion, yet have nothing to do with it?"

"Not good."

"Then let's go," I urge. I haven't had to shoot my gun at someone yet, and I don't want today to be that day. "If we can see them in the reflection, they'll be able to see us, and I don't want to wait for their reaction."

Knox watches them in the window a few seconds longer. I know it's a gamble either way. We stay and expose ourselves to four men with guns, or we pretend we were never here at all, and we hastily continue on our way, leaving possible help behind.

"Scott didn't die so that we could get caught up with people who look more dangerous than Lars," Knox whispers as if he's trying to convince himself. His eyes never stray from the window. "Let's go." He spins Rooster around, and I happily do the same with Loca as we change course and head down a side street. When we're a block away and less likely to be heard, it feels like I can finally breathe. We nudge the horses into a run and get the hell out of Amarillo for good.

THIRTY-SIX
KNOX

WHEN I WAS SEVEN, I SAW THE LAVA BEDS IN HAWAII WITH my family. I thought it was cool then, an endless desert of rolling black hills. But this—this is the last thing I want to see in Texas. Despite the markings on the map, the terrain is more unsteady than I'd hoped.

The horses have been on high alert since Amarillo; their eyes and ears haven't stopped shifting over the unstable terrain. The plains are a tapestry of scorched earth, lava rivers, and heat waves. It's impossible to determine which parts of the lava beds are stable or ready to bubble up again. One minute, the air is noxious. The next, it's thick with sulfur. And then randomly, it smells like nothing at all. It seems like if the horses step wrong the ground shakes.

We give the fissures as much berth as possible, but soon, the main road will be our only option.

"It's like a quilt of fire scars," Ava murmurs.

A gaseous hiss fills the stillness and Loca spooks. It's second nature for me to reach for her reins, but Ava is learning quickly. Ava might grip the saddle horn like it's all that's keeping her in the seat, but she emanates calmness, soothing Loca with slow, reassuring movements.

"You're good with her, you know?"

With an exaggerated harrumph, Ava wipes her palm on her thigh, and Loca falls into step behind me again.

"I might even go so far as to say you're getting used to riding."

"Ha. It doesn't feel like I'm *riding* so much as I'm holding on for dear life."

I shake my head because she doesn't give herself enough credit. "This is some sketchy shit, and you're riding like a pro."

Ava shrugs. "I had a decent teacher."

"*Decent*?" I scoff, repositioning my ball cap on my head. "You wound me."

Ava looks momentarily victorious, then wiggles around in the saddle, grimacing.

"You okay? I told you, riding all day after last night—"

"Yep," she grits out, forcing a smile. "Right as rain."

I grin. "Liar."

Ava laughs despite herself and rests the reins on Loca's mane, stretching out her fingers. "I'll take saddle sores and hand cramps over being dead any day."

"Well, let's hope it doesn't come to that quite yet," I grumble. "And I promise, it will hurt more if you stop riding and have to start again than if we just keep going."

Ava heaves a sigh. "I figured as much." She readjusts herself in the saddle again. "At least my ass is numb. I can't really feel the pain anymore."

I try not to find too much amusement in her predicament and take a drink of water from my canteen. We ride for another couple of hours, and the horses ease into the changing landscape. Loca's hyperawareness tapers to intermittent curiosity, and Rooster drags his hooves at a bored pace. The day is cool, the breeze slightly chilling, and in a matter of hours, night will set in and we'll need to find a place to set up camp.

"Knox."

I follow Ava's gaze up a dirt road. There's a farmhouse at the end of it, complete with a hay barn, an old windmill, and a dozen warning signs posted on the gate.

Do not enter.

Trespassers will be shot on sight.

Private road.

Keep out.

No trespassing.

Beware of dog.

Private property.

"That's . . . slightly terrifying," Ava mutters.

I glance at the shotgun strapped behind her, ensuring it hasn't miraculously disappeared since last I checked. Whether by coincidence or design, the people we saw in Amarillo might be heading this way at some point, and I haven't stopped bracing myself for whatever might happen between now and nightfall. "Let's keep moving," I tell her, and I click Rooster forward.

We continue on, veering off the frontage road to keep as much distance as we can from a fissure in the ground.

By the time we're a few miles outside the small town of Cactus, the sky is darkening and the brisk afternoon has dropped to a pink-nose sort of cold. With the ash clouds blotting out the sun, the world looks and feels almost frozen. Ava zips her vest up to cover her neck.

"Is that a pond?"

I squint through a copse of oak trees. "I think so." We pass a rotted pump house that's been neglected for what looks like the better part of a decade and continue toward the trees.

The pond is bigger than I expected when it finally comes into view, and I pull Rooster to a stop between two wild oaks. "This might be the best place we'll find to set up camp tonight. We can hunker down in the trees. We don't know what the water situation will be like in Cactus, assuming it's there at all, and we only have an hour until it's full dark."

Ava scans the distant mountains as if they hold the answers. "Our tent and the horses would be relatively hidden," she agrees, and she clicks Loca toward the water for a much-needed drink. Rooster and I follow.

"A break *and* water?" Ava sighs with relief. "I consider this a win."

Lucy overtakes us on the path as she runs for the pond. She stops at the edge and takes a step back, her ears perked and head tilted in caution.

I groan inwardly and climb down, leading Rooster a few steps closer. "Shit." Exhaling, I rock back on my heels and run my hand down my face.

"You've got to be kidding me." Ava dismounts and inches closer. The horses' heads hang low and curious as they sniff the water, but they lean away like they know better—like they can smell the death.

The water's surface is dotted with dead fish.

Ava hands me Loca's reins and crouches at the water's edge, grimacing as she steadies herself on sore legs. Her ponytail falls over her shoulder as she leans forward, and reaching out, she holds her hand above the water. Her eyes snap to me. "It's warm."

"I figured." I consider how many lava tunnels run beneath us and peer back in the direction we came.

"Do we keep riding, then?" Ava pulls her hat off and rubs her brow.

"I think we have to." I hand her reins back and climb into Rooster's saddle again. "And let's hope we find some decent water in Cactus. Otherwise, our rations will be dismal tomorrow—"

"And we still have at least a day of riding to get through," she finishes for me.

I nod, but if water is unsafe here, I have little hope it will be any better in Cactus, especially if everyone uses well or reservoir water.

Ava tugs her hat on again. "Then we better go before I can't get back in my saddle." She winces as she lugs her leg over Loca's back.

The pond starts gurgling first, and then hissing air echoes around us. The ground rumbles and shakes, and Rooster rears up. My body jolts back. The gray sky whips past me, and the sense I'm falling is the last thing I remember.

THIRTY-SEVEN
AVA

"*Knox!*" My scream is lost among the earsplitting horse cries and the bubbling pond. Crows caw as they scatter somewhere in the distance. The trees creak as they settle back into place, and I grip the saddle horn, shushing Loca in a half-hearted attempt to calm her as she spins and tugs against me, winding up to bolt.

When she steadies enough for me to climb down, I wrap her reins around the tree branch and practically fall to my knees beside Knox's unconscious, crumpled body. He's contorted on his side with his backpack and flannel bunched around him.

I shove Lucy away from his face to get a better look.

This is *not* happening.

This *cannot* be happening.

I blink, focusing on his chest, willing it to rise.

Knox is big and strong and healthy. He is fine. He *will* be fine. But despite my internal pep talk, I can't tell if Knox is breathing, and as utter terror grips hold of me, I bend over to listen for a heartbeat. His chest finally rises, and I hold my breath, waiting for it to fall. It does. Again and again. And still, distrusting my own eyes, I press my trembling fingers to Knox's wrist to confirm a pulse. His skin is warm, and the life beating inside him soothes me, though only a little.

When I'm content my mind isn't playing tricks on me, I roll back on my heels and cover my face with my hands, desperate to keep my shit together. As every horrible scenario threatens to rear its ugly head, I try to keep focused. Did he hit the tree? A rock on the ground? Was it something in his backpack that knocked him unconscious?

I examine Knox's body for obvious broken bones or traces of blood. There are no hoofprints or proof Rooster stepped on him, but those five chaotic seconds are a blur. For all I know, Knox's back could be broken.

"Can you hear me, Knox?" I press my palm to his chest, gentle but firm. "I need you to wake up."

Nothing. Not a flutter under his eyelids or a hitch in his breath. His lips don't twitch and neither do his fingers. He's completely out.

Squeezing my eyes shut, I blow out a breath, run my sweaty hands down my pants, and reorganize my thoughts again. If it's a concussion, he'll wake soon. He has to. "Knox, I know I shouldn't move you, but I need to see if you're bleeding." I swallow again, my throat suddenly dry. If he's bleeding, I'll know he hit his head, but what are the repercussions of such a blow?

I try not to consider it. Clenching my trembling fingers into fists, I take another deep breath, lean in, and pull the collar of his shirt down with one hand, moving his backpack away with the other. The moment I see blood on the dirt and the flannel collar, a sob bubbles out of me, along with an unwanted slew of what-ifs.

Falling onto my butt, I press my hands over my face and force myself to inhale. I make myself think of Mavey—of anything and everything I learned from hospice that might be helpful. But my mind is blank. All I can see is Mavey with her painted fingernails, lying lifeless in bed.

I only exhale when my lungs burn with more than fear and sadness.

In and out.

In and out.

I can't just sit here. I need to do something—take action.

Blinking back tears, I tug my pack off to look for my first aid kit. Head wounds bleed a lot. It probably looks worse than it is. Stop the bleeding and give him a moment to wake up. Everything will be fine.

I fumble with the zipper pouch, grab a roll of gauze and tear open a cotton pad to cover the wound at the base of his skull. "This will help with the bleeding." I say the words out loud so I might actually believe them. "It's not gushing. That's a good thing."

With precise movements, I wrap Knox's wound as best I can, lifting his head only slightly to get the bandage around. He's heavier than I expect, but I fixate on his warm skin and check his rising chest again, ensuring it's still moving.

Lucy whimpers, watching me skeptically. "I'm being careful," I promise for both our sakes. When I'm finally finished, I sit back and catch my breath; I hadn't realized I'd been holding it. I wipe the blood on my hands onto my jeans and rub Lucy's head—which is all I can offer her right now.

I meet her worried doggy eyes. "What do I do now?" She blinks, whimpers, and sits in wait. "There has to be some-thing." Shaking my head, I glance uselessly around us.

The water is undrinkable, and the inky sky is bordering on black; it's only a matter of time before it's completely dark. "I know I shouldn't move you, Knox," I murmur, "but—what if you don't wake up? I need to find help." Even if moving him weren't a dangerous gamble, there's no way I can get his dead weight on the back of his horse—Knox outweighs me by fifty pounds at least.

With no other option, I launch into work mode, desperate to keep my mind busy while I wait for Knox to wake up. I pour some of our drinking water into a plastic container for Lucy. When she's finished, I do the same for each of the horses. They slurp up a bottle between them in an instant but it's all I can afford to give them, for now.

Still, Knox sleeps.

I unpack and roll out a sleeping bag to cover him, then gather wood for a campfire. And still, Knox sleeps. My mind spins as I question the differences between sleep and being knocked out—what did that hit to the head do to him? What is it doing to him *right now*? I brush silent tears away as I light kindling in a small tuft of tinder I put together, blowing the flames higher when they catch. When I'm finished, I grab Knox's water bottle to place beside him, just like he does for me when I wake up from one of my seizures.

But still, Knox sleeps, and hysteria starts inching its way in.

I have to go for help.

Ignoring my sore legs, I crouch beside him, resting my hand on Knox's forehead. He's warm but not overly hot. He's breathing, but it's been thirty minutes and he's still not awake. The longer he stays like this, the worse off he might be when he wakes.

If *he wakes.*

What if he wakes and I'm gone? What if he doesn't know what happened and he's alone? What if he leaves while I'm gone to go looking for *me*?

My nostrils flare as I shove each paralyzing thought down

as far as it will go. I have to at least *try* to get help because I have no idea what's wrong with him.

I peer north through the sparse trees, at the ominous plains and unwelcoming landscape stretched beyond. There is nothing out there. Remembering Cactus, I consider riding there, banking on people still living in the tiny town and willing to help. If they all went to Guymon, though, and Knox is still asleep when I get back, I'll have to find a way to get us there too.

The farm with the trespassing signs. It's the only place we've passed remotely close to here, but they might shoot me on the spot. *Or . . .* I bite the inside of my cheek. I could get lucky, and they'd be willing to help. Maybe they won't be there at all, but a place like that might have a truck, or trailer, or a goddamn tractor for all I care, *something* I can use to get Knox to Guymon.

I stare at Lucy lying forlornly beside him. "You have to stay," I tell her. Her ears perk up as I rise to my feet. Absently, I unload everything I can from Loca's back, even the shotgun I leave beside Knox in exchange for the pistol holstered to his belt.

Grabbing one of the maps and a pen from Knox's bag, I circle the approximate location I'm headed and draw an arrow to the edge of the paper.

FARMHOUSE. WENT FOR HELP.

I write it in big, double-traced letters, and tuck the map under my backpack, propped next to him so it doesn't blow away.

I study Knox's face in the dancing firelight—his serious, sharp angles that soften in sleep. How can a man so strong and capable look so helpless? How can my heart be breaking and I don't even know if he's gone?

"I'll be back," I promise, and tuck the sleeping bag around him as best I can. "I'm going to find help."

Wiping a stray tear from my cheek, I silently beg him to be okay. I can't do any of this without him. I don't *want* to. This was our beginning, what all the bullshit we've gone through in the past decade was leading to. Us. A second chance, together. There has to be a reason we're all we have left, and I won't lose him or sit here uselessly with hope.

Before I can turn into a blubbering mess, I make sure the pistol is loaded and grab a flashlight to shove in Loca's saddlebag, the rope, and extra bullets, just in case. When it's all loaded, I climb up and give Lucy a final command to stay put.

I glance at Knox, uncertain if it's fear that he might not wake up or fear that he will and I won't be here that makes it hard to breathe.

"Come on." I kick Loca into a full run and ride for help.

THIRTY-EIGHT
AVA

I'T'S DIFFICULT TO SEE IN THE DARK, BUT I TRUST LOCA'S instincts, and her strides devour the landscape. Her hooves land solid and full of purpose, and the sound and whip of the wind drowns out all my toxic thoughts as the world blurs around us.

It feels more like thirty minutes have passed, but I'm sure it's barely been ten when I nudge Loca to run faster toward the farmhouse. The brisk air burns my eyes, and I squint in the thickening darkness. Loca stumbles here and there over rocks and uneven terrain as it worsens, but she moves with determination, like she knows time is against us.

I squint when something dots the skyline. The old barn comes into view, then the windmill, and white-knuckled fear returns as I grip the reins tighter. "I really hate you, Gerty," I murmur.

With each gallop closer, I tell myself not everyone is dangerous. Hell, if Mitch could have changed to someone less hateful after harboring that much animosity and resentment, anyone can.

We slow as we approach the gate. It's hanging off its

hinges; in fact, I'm not sure it's been properly opened or closed in years.

I scan the property with new eyes and guide Loca through, giving her a moment to catch her breath as we head up the dirt road. We walk past a pump house, which means these people are—or were—using a well. Considering our dwindling water supply, I consider whether theirs is drinkable. With so much sulfur in the air, everything smells the same, the safe barely distinguishable from the toxic anymore.

Weeds grow like beanstalks, weaving through the vehicle carcasses and up the crumbling outbuildings that line the driveway. It's a fire hazard—a junk yard—and I'm nearly convinced the place is abandoned.

With the moon tucked behind clouds, the world beyond it is lost to outlines and shadow. But as the old farmhouse comes into full view, light glows through the draped windows.

"Shit." I chew the raw spot on my bottom lip. I knew this moment might come when I'd have to differentiate my instincts from my fear of the unknown. Now that it's here, and with each sense as loud and as unnerving as the rest, I listen to my desperation. I ignore the poisonous thoughts telling me to turn around, that it's not worth it, because I've come this far, and I can't afford to waste this much time. There is no going back now.

I eye a loft barn missing its doors. What looks like a covered wood shelter is empty beside it, and as I draw closer to the house, the roof is concave on one side, like it's rotted through. The windows on the second floor are dark and boarded, and when I'm close enough to notice the blistering paint on the house, I pull Loca to a stop.

This place should be condemned and I'm more convinced than ever they can't help me.

Movement in the corner window catches my eye, and my skin prickles with unease. Someone is watching me.

"Hell—" I clear my throat. "Hello?" Something tells me they aren't the type of people I want assuming I'm here for nefarious reasons. "Sorry to intrude, but I need your help!" My voice booms in the silence and I scan the windows for more movement. "Please?" Loca and I stop at the wraparound porch.

The drapes at the window by the door rustle, and I gulp as a person's silhouette takes form. Despite the dread that fills me from head to toe, I force myself to continue. "I need your help, please." I show them my hands. "I'm not here to cause trouble. Someone is hurt. I just—" I swallow thickly. "Maybe you have a neighbor who can help me?"

The silhouette moves from the window.

The reins tighten in one hand as I flex the other at my side, prepared to pull the pistol strapped to my waist if necessary.

The knob rattles, and the front door creaks open. "We have no neighbors," a female voice croaks. "And we don't like visitors." An older woman pokes her head out. Her silver hair, done up in a conical-shaped beehive like my third-grade teacher always wore, glimmers in the interior light. She looks frail, and suddenly the house's disrepair makes sense. But even as the tension in my neck and shoulders eases slightly, my hope dwindles. This woman can't help me. Not unless she has a working vehicle I can use.

"I'll ride to Cactus," I tell her. "Maybe there's someone there who—"

"Cactus is gone," she says, and if I'm not mistaken, it's with a hint of amusement.

"Gone?" It comes out in a breath. "Was it the fires?" The last of my composure begins to fray. "Wait." I hold my hands up, gesturing to the ground as I dismount so as not to surprise her. "You said *we* don't like visitors." My boots hit the dirt with a thud. "Is there someone here who can help me?" I tug my vest down, hiding the pistol at my waist. "I have an injured friend who needs medical attention. Or a vehicle, maybe, so I can transport him?"

The woman peers warily down the road.

"It's only me, I swear. My friend is back at camp, where he was injured." I take a step closer. "Do you have a vehicle?" I try again.

"My husband's truck," the woman says. She opens the door fully and steps into view. She's in her beige nightgown and slippers. She has a shotgun nearly as big as she is clutched at her side, but it doesn't unnerve me to see it, like I expect. In fact, it's strangely comforting; I might think there was something wrong with this old woman if she opened the door unarmed to a stranger during the apocalypse.

"Can I use his truck? I swear, I *will* return it."

The woman nods, if a bit reluctantly, and again, I don't blame her in the slightest.

"Thank you," I say gently, taking a step closer. "I know you have no reason to trust me, but I'm desperate. I swear, I'm not here to cause any trouble. If your husband can help me, I'll do whatever I can to repay you both."

She looks at Loca and me again, and I imagine she's wondering why I don't have a vehicle of my own. "All right, then," she grumbles. "You can tie your horse there." She points to the porch post and her gaze practically burns a hole through me as she waits. Watching. Skeptical.

The porch protests as I head for the house, just like my aching legs and thudding heartbeat. I stop at the door a few feet from the old woman. She stands no taller than my collarbone and deep lines etch her face. Despite the gruffness of her voice, her eyes are softer than I expect and glisten in the dim light. "I appreciate this more than you know."

"Hurry now," she grouses, waving me in. "You're letting out my heat."

I step inside, but it's not the heat I feel as she shuts the door behind me. It smells like sulfur and a backed up septic tank. My hand flies to my mouth as I clear my throat, swallow, and exhale through my mouth.

"What's wrong with them?"

My head snaps to the woman as she weaves her way through the maze of boxes. This place is like a hoarder's haven.

"What?"

The woman crouches by the fire in the hearth. She's so frail, her fingers tremble as she tears cardboard into pieces and tosses them into the dying fire. "Your friend." She gives me the side-eye. "What's wrong with them?"

"Oh. He, uh, fell off his horse." I scan the room, uncertain what I've walked into. "He's unconscious," I add. There's a path between stacks of towering boxes, leading to two closed doors on the left side of the living room, and a kitchen disappears around the corner on the right. "I'm Ava, by the way."

"Sheila. Or Buttercup, to my husband."

I flash her a tight smile and continue my appraisal of the house. Every piece of furniture is vintage. Every box I see is decades old, if the outdated logos and faded colors are anything to go by. Boxes that once held laundry soap, sponges, jars, and toilet paper are now stacked empty. If I didn't know any better, I'd say they robbed a warehouse at some point. Only, it must've been nearly fifty years ago.

"I have some old medical books over there on that shelf. You can take a look at them while I get us some tea. See if they can help your friend."

"Don't trouble yourself, please," I say. I glance at the bookshelf, barely visible behind a mountain of cardboard. "I need to get back to him as soon as possible. If I could speak with your husband about the truck?" Sheila's already in the kitchen, and noting the dying fire, I crouch to throw in a few more pieces of cardboard for her. I figure it's the least I can do.

"Sheila," I say a little louder. "I really don't want to trouble you. If you could get your husband—"

"You'll have to wait," she calls from the kitchen. "Lenny will help you when he can."

I peer at the staircase, completely blocked by boxes. "And where is he, exactly?"

There's clanking in the kitchen. "Indisposed," she says, as if telling me to mind my business. I glance at the two closed doors, assuming one is the bathroom, then shove my hands in my back pocket, trying not to touch anything or knock it over. The layer of fuzz covering everything practically glows in the firelight, but the pictures framed on the mantel catch my attention.

A woman with rich blonde hair and chubby cheeks and a slender-framed man stare back at me. They're in dirty pants and collared shirts with tool belts slung around their hips. A half-constructed house is erected behind them. The very one I'm standing in. It creaks, and I scan its decrepit state, saddened for Sheila—for what she once had and what she lives in now.

The faucet squeaks in the kitchen and I continue my perusal of the place, not wanting to snoop but too anxious to stand still. I peek inside a few of the open boxes, careful not to knock anything over. If Sheila is anything like Ms. Maddison, who lived two trailers down from us, she'll know if anything in her cluttered home is out of place. Most of the boxes are empty, though, awaiting their turn for the burn pile.

I spot a stack of newspapers amid the clutter and gasp. "No way." I read the date, then the headline: *Unprecedented happenings.* I move it aside and pick up another.

How to hold out during the next ice age.

Preparing for the end.

What scientists are saying.

Catastrophic climate shifts.

A new era of survival.

Man versus Moon. The deeper I delve into the pile, the more I understand.

Gertrude changes the course of life on Earth.

"Moonies," I whisper, taking in each box with new eyes. All that they stocked up on. All that they did to prepare, and *this* is the state they are living in?

"Here," Sheila says, startling me. She shuffles into the living room with rattling china on her tea tray, her mouth pressed in a thin line of concentration. She looks like she might drop the tray at any moment, so I reach for it, not having the heart to tell her I can't stay and socialize. A dozen questions flood my mind as I set it on a doily in the center of the glass coffee table, flanked by two high-backed chairs; they are the only two spots in the entire house uncluttered enough to sit on.

This close to her, I notice the glint in Sheila's eyes is more of a glaze and wonder if she's been crying, and the hollowness of her cheeks transforms her face in the shadows. "Dammit." She wags her finger. "I forgot a spoon."

"No. It's okay—really."

Sheila waves me away. "I can't remember the last time we got a visitor," she replies over her shoulder. She turns for the kitchen again and I note the tape in her hair, near the nape of her neck, holding it in place. With the state of this house and her beehive hairdo, I'm starting to think Sheila hasn't been out in the world much lately.

I glance at the two closed doors, listening for movement inside, but all I hear are the drawers opening and closing in the kitchen and the crack of dying flames.

I carefully lift the cup closest to me and eye the purple, hand-painted roses. As I suspected, sulfur fills my nose, and gagging, I jerk my hand away. The tea sloshes over the rim and onto the threadbare rug at my feet. If there's any tea in this, I can't tell, and there is no way the old woman can miss the potent scent of rotten eggs.

I glance back down at the tray. A teapot and two cups. No sugar or honey or cream.

"Here we go." Sheila shuffles over and sets a spoon by the teapot. To use for what, I'm not sure, and when she looks at me, a trickle of blood drips from her nose.

"You're bleeding—" I look for something to wipe it with and pause, finding nothing.

"It happens," she mutters, smearing it away with the back of her hand. "It's the pits getting old." Sheila lowers herself into the high-backed chair closest to the fire and brings the tea to her lips.

"Don't drink that." I reach for her cup, but Sheila glares at me and moves it out of reach.

"I beg your pardon?"

"The sulfur. Can't you smell it?"

She glances from her teacup to me, her frown deepening. "So what? It's been that way for months."

I gape at her. "Months?" I shake my head. "Sheila, too much sulfur will make you sick." I think about the steers at Knox's ranch and how the concentration of it drove them to insanity and death.

"Beggars can't be choosers," she gripes. "You're lucky I'm sharing any with you at all." Sheila takes a defiant drink, her eyes not leaving mine. "Is that what the world has come to?" She licks her lips. "I welcome you into my home—"

"I'm sorry. I just—" I lift the teapot lid to see no herbs steeping inside. The brown water is simply that—completely undrinkable. "Sheila, this water is making you sick. Surely you understand that?" I eye her bony frame up and down, but as the old woman stares at her dying fire, I realize she's not listening to me anymore. Her hands continue to tremble and her eyes shimmer in the failing light. In my gut, I know it's too late for her anyway.

"I should go," I say, glancing at the closed doors behind me. I don't even know if Lenny exists at this point.

"I thought you needed help?" Sheila sips from her cup, her gaze fixed on the fireplace.

"I'll find it somewhere else." I turn for the door. "Thank you for—"

"Lenny," Sheila says quietly, eyes still on the embers. The fire needs more cardboard, but she doesn't seem to care. "He takes care of the hunting and fixing the house. And he was the one who would bring me news about life out there . . ." As her voice trails off, I'm unsure if it's her sudden use of "was" or "life out there" that gives me pause.

"Sheila," I hedge, glancing at the stack of newspapers from decades ago. "When was the last time you left this house?"

She takes another sip from her teacup before answering. "When we got word of Gertrude, we knew it was only a matter of time before the world fell to pieces." Her hoarse voice is faraway and thoughtful. "I didn't want to raise my child in a world like that."

Scanning the room with new eyes, I note that some of the

old boxes were filled with diapers and baby food at some point.

"You had a child in this house?" I ask carefully.

"Did." Sheila's voice is soft. Wistful. "Lyla. She died when she was a year old. I knew she was jaundiced, but we never saw a doctor, so I don't know if that's what took her."

My hands fall to my side, and I feel for Sheila—I really do—but Knox is what's important right now. Not a seventy-year-old woman who has not and clearly *will not* leave her house.

My stomach churns as the truth of that sets in. "Why did you bring me in here if you can't help me save my friend?"

"I said I didn't leave the house," she repeats, finally looking at me. "But Lenny did." She nods toward the second room with the closed door.

"Sheila?" I run my hand down my vest, ensuring the pistol is still there should I need it. "Is Lenny in that room?"

She nods. "He has a truck you can use out back. But—"

"But what?"

"I haven't been able to go in there since he . . ." She clears the trepidation from her throat. "If you want the keys, you have to get them yourself."

Sheila stands up, hip and shoulder bones accentuated as she runs her hands nervously down the front of her silky, discolored nightgown. "They should be in his coat pocket, likely draped on the back of the chair." She takes a skeleton key off the mantle and shuffles past me toward the room. The scent of rose water and powder fills my nose—not exactly horrible compared to the sulfur and mold combination in the air, but equally potent—and bracing myself, I follow behind her.

When Sheila stops at the door, her eyes meet mine. "I won't step foot in that room."

I hold my palms up. "I won't ask you to," I promise, though I have no idea how long Lenny has been in there, and I'm terrified of what I might see. I need that truck, though, and nod for her to unlock the door.

Sheila takes a step back and averts her gaze like she's as uncomfortable as I am.

Rolling my shoulders, I reach for the handle. I inhale a lungful of air, scared what smells might accost me on the other side, and push the door open. It groans as the wood dislodges, and I step inside. Light from the doorway pours in, illuminating a human-sized form on the bed. Thankfully, it's covered, and I peer around for the chair. "Where's the—"

The door shuts behind me, and I spin around, shrouded in complete darkness as my eyes adjust. "Sheila!" The lock clicks before I can find the knob. "What the hell are you doing, Sheila?"

"I told you, beggars can't be choosers," she mutters. "I'm sorry, child."

"Sheila!" I pound on the door. "Sheila, let me help you. Whatever it is, I can help—"

"I know you can."

The icy burn of dread fills every inch of me. "What?"

She shuffles around on the other side of the door as I strain to listen. "That's the only reason I didn't kill you on the spot."

"Sheila, what are you going to do?"

"What I have to." The floorboards creak as she walks away.

"Sheila! Let me out of here," I demand, but the racking of a slug in the shotgun barrel steals my breath. Whatever horrors I considered she might try with me are replaced with the certainty that Sheila is starving and desperate, and as she shuffles farther away, I know it's Loca she wants.

"Sheila, don't you dare touch my horse, or I swear to God, I will kill you myself!" I shout. "Let me help you find food. I have some back at camp. I—"

When I hear the front door open, my fear turns to fury. I am so tired of feeling desperate. Of being weak. I kick at the door and ram my shoulder into it, to no avail. Once. Twice. I glance at the boarded-up window across the room where barely a trickle of moonlight filters in over Lenny's body.

Pulling the pistol from my waist, I stand back, aim for what I can make out of the knob, and gritting my teeth, I pull the trigger. I hit the door but miss the handle by an inch. The light filtering through the hole illuminates the room more, and I aim again. This time, the door splinters in the doorjamb, busting it loose, and I yank it open.

I sprint through the maze of boxes, knocking most of them over, and head straight for Sheila on the porch as she struggles to hold the shotgun up high enough to aim at Loca. I careen into the old woman, and Loca's head jerks up in the chaos. Sheila and I collapse on the porch.

I curse.

She shrieks and wails as my weight crushes her, and before I can stand, her teeth sink into my forearm, and I scream.

Tearing my arm away, I lurch to my feet, shoving Sheila back down by her forehead as she tries to stand. She grunts and hisses as her back hits the ground, and with a wobbly arm, Sheila reaches for the shotgun.

"I don't think so," I grit out. I grab the shotgun and step out of reach. My chest heaves. My mind whirls. And I don't know if I should hate this woman or feel sorry for her.

"You don't understand," she cries, staggering to get to her feet.

"And if you didn't just bite me like a feral fucking animal, I might have more sympathy for you."

She shakes her head. "You don't know how it feels. The hunger. The—"

"Then you should have asked for help," I growl. "For a trade. I offered to help you, and now you get nothing!" I shout, angrier with myself than I am with her.

Shotgun in hand and pistol holstered in my belt, I turn for Loca.

"Wait—you can't leave me here alone. I'm sick. You said so yourself. I'm hungry—"

I toss Loca's reins over her head and mount up, the shotgun gripped in my hand. It's heavy and awkward, but I'd carry it a thousand miles if it meant she couldn't have it. Luckily, I know it won't come to that.

"You can't leave me unarmed!" she shouts, desperation tearing through her voice.

My pulse pounds in my ears, and I can barely catch my breath as adrenaline catches up with me. My hands shake, but I ignore it and walk Loca along the railing and past the porch. Heaving my arm back, I toss the shotgun as far as I can. It only makes it a yard or two before landing with a heavy thud in the overgrown weeds, but it might as well be a mile away to Sheila.

"You need food? Go and hunt something, then." And with a final glare at a teary-eyed Sheila wobbling on her feet, I kick Loca into a gallop and ride away as fast as I can, letting the wind tear over me as I hold on for dear life. I feel pride and hate myself in equal measure, knowing how close I was to something worse happening, and my entire body begins to shake.

The past twenty minutes feel more like hours, and I have no idea what to do now. Knox could be awake. Or he might still be unconscious. I have no place else to go if I head south. And the thought of running into more people—bile rises up my throat.

Loca weaves us through the broken gate, and we veer north toward the pond. We take the road this time because I'm desperate to see Knox, to ensure he's where I left him and still breathing.

Only as the adrenaline wanes do I feel the sting in my arm and remember the bite. My nostrils flare and I grit back my absurdity, fear, and utter disbelief. I don't know if Sheila broke the skin beneath my long sleeves, but that's a problem for later.

Drops of water hit my face, sporadically at first, until thunder rumbles somewhere in the distance and lightning cracks across the sky, a sudden downpour following. My clothes are drenched within seconds, my body cold and shivering even more as the wind whips over me. Visibility is even less than it was in the darkness alone, and I bite my lip to keep it from trembling.

The distance back seems longer somehow, and though it's a straight shot back to the pond, I begin to wonder if I've gotten turned around somehow. Loca slips in the mud, and I urge her onto the asphalt for better footing.

Eventually, light and shadow forms in front of us, and confused, I squint to see it through sheets of rain; it stretches along the road ahead. As the raindrops illuminate, another rumble meets my ears, only it's the sound of an engine.

"No." I squeeze my eyes shut, praying that's not what I think it is.

My wet hair is loose from my cap and whips me in the face as I peer over my shoulder at an approaching vehicle. A van. And as it gets closer, I realize it's *the* van from Amarillo and the people in black.

"No. No. No." Fear grips me anew, but it's too late to hide. There's nowhere to go and they've already spotted us. With a barbed wire fence lining the empty pastures on either side of me, I can only urge Loca faster.

The vehicle speeds up, the engine growing louder the closer it follows. "Hey!" Someone shouts.

"Leave me alone!" It's a desperate shriek as I urge Loca faster and faster. I'm pushing her to a breaking point. I can feel it in her trembling muscles, but the van drives at a constant pace behind us, and I realize I'm leading them right back to Knox.

Suddenly, numbness washes over me. Their van will outlast us, and with nowhere else to go, exhaustion wins out. I slow Loca from a gallop to a trot and, finally, a sob breaks loose. *They don't have to know about Knox.* It's my only comforting thought as I lift my face to the pelting rain, Loca's ribs heaving under me.

The van slows, the breaks squeaking as it finally stops a few yards behind us.

I hold the reins so tightly my fingers ache, and when the van doors open, I grip the pistol at my side and turn Loca to face them.

THIRTY-NINE
KNOX

IT'S THE THROBBING THAT STIRS MY SENSES. THE NUMBNESS, the tingling, and the inability to lift my arm. Peeling my eyes open is a feat of its own, and I blink at the white ceiling cast in a flashing green hue.

Soft breath tickles the skin beneath my jaw, and I register the weight of someone lying against me. The unease I woke with fades a little as I find Ava curled into my side, her head on my shoulder, her arms wrapped around mine as she sleeps.

I swallow what feels like a spadeful of gravel and glance around. We're in a cement medical room, with a glass case on the other side stocked with supplies. A monitor beeps beside me, and antiseptic lingers in the air. Pale light filters through a door cracked slightly open, but there's silence beyond it.

I look down at Ava again, searching my memories for morsels that make sense. We left Amarillo for Guymon, avoiding the road in case the people in black followed us. We stopped for water and . . .

The dead fish. I remember the quake and Rooster rearing back. I was going to fall; I knew it the instant he spooked, and then I felt a rip of pain. As the fog in my mind abates, the pounding in the base of my skull and tingling in my arm worsens.

I stare at the needle in my arm, telling myself I'm not paralyzed if I can feel Ava's death grip on me, as well as every aching inch of my body. I watch the continuous drip of the IV beside me as small, barely-there moments of consciousness flash to life.

A voice in my head asks me if I can hear them.

A feeling of weightlessness makes my stomach flip.

The jostling that rattled my teeth.

The methodical hum of an engine.

It's all a haze, yet I remember a familiar voice interwoven through it all. *Ava's.*

I have no idea how long I've been asleep, but somehow, she got me here—wherever here is—and I'm overcome with questions. And whatever Ava had to do to get us here, she figured it out alone.

Jaw clenching, I stare at her—*really* seeing Ava curled into herself. The way she's clutching me as if she's afraid I'll disappear. I'm in a hospital gown, but her jeans are bloody, and a flare of apprehension fills me as my focus shifts to what I can see of her face. Her ponytail is loose, her hair hanging over her shoulder in a knotted mess, and her down vest and long sleeves are covered in dirt. I don't think the blood is hers, and as I reach for the knot in the back of my pounding skull, I assume it's mine. My hair is matted and damp under a bandage wrapped loosely around my head. When I look at my fingers, there's no blood but a strong anti-septic smell.

Exhaling, I rest my head and let it all sink in. Wherever we are, we're safe, but the surmounting unknowns eat away at me.

"Ava?" Her name is gritty in my throat, and reaching

over, I tuck a strand of hair behind her ear, waiting for her to stir.

Ava's lashes flutter, and her lids fly open as she registers my touch. Her grip on me loosens as she shoots up, propping herself with one hand as her bleary eyes shift over me. "You're awake." Immediately, they start welling with tears.

I drop my hand with a tight-lipped smile. "Thanks to you, I think. Are we in Cactus?" I scan the room again. It's windowless and equipped with the bare essentials, not like a hospital.

Ava shakes her head. "There's nothing in Cactus."

I frown.

"We're at the facility," she murmurs. "We're in Guymon."

"Guymon?" That was a day's ride from where we stopped, probably longer. "How—"

"The people in black," she whispers, but she sounds more sheepish than anything. "They found me on the road, riding back to you." Whatever maelstrom churns in Ava's amber eyes is also thick in her voice. "I didn't want to lead them to you, so I—" She sighs, twisting her ponytail before finally meeting my gaze.

"So, they weren't dangerous, then," I realize.

Ava looks down with a sigh. "No, they were retrieving the last of the equipment they'd left behind when that building collapsed. They actually lost someone." She shakes her head, like she's at her wit's end. "We got lucky, Knox. I thought it was going to end a lot differently."

Tingling hand be damned, I reach for her, but Ava winces the second I touch her arm. I snap my hand back.

"Bruised," she murmurs, flashing me a weak smile. "But none of that matters now. You're awake, and Malia wanted me to find her the second you came to." The more Ava brightens, the more I know it's all for show. She's a rush of moving limbs as she climbs off the bed, muttering about the doctor and that she knew I'd be okay, they just had to be patient.

"Hey—" I take Ava's hand before she gets too far to reach.

She whips around to look at me.

"Slow down a minute," I say as gently as I can. I clear my throat and tug her back to me.

Ava squeezes my hand in hers, absently fingering my blanket with the other. Her brow furrows deeper.

"Are you okay?"

Ava nods before her forced smile catches up, and then her chin trembles. "I just—I'm glad you're okay. That's all."

"Do I hear chatter in here?" A female voice, soft and expectant, comes from the hall before the door opens wider. An Asian woman in cargo pants, boots, and a white doctor's coat steps into the room. She looks in her forties with a wavy, black bob that barely reaches her jaw.

"Good. You're awake." She smiles, more believably than Ava, and walks around the bed to the other side. "Knox, I'm Malia. It's nice to finally meet you." She clasps her hands in front of her. She has kind eyes that crinkle in the corners.

"Uh, you too."

"She cleaned your head wound and gave you fluids," Ava explains.

Malia nods absently, staring at my chart. "Dehydration is no joke." She pulls a penlight from her coat pocket. "Look at me, please." She holds it up for me to follow. "Believe it or not, the actual wound isn't terrible, though the swelling is a bit concerning. We need to keep an eye on it, but from what I can tell, a concussion and a few scrapes and bruises should be the extent of things." I squint in the bright light, and when Malia's satisfied, she smiles. "Any questions?"

"Dozens, actually. How did I get here?" I look at Ava. "Where are our things? The horses and Lucy—"

"The animals are fine. Our stuff is here," Ava promises. "Dillon and Andrew brought us here in the van."

"And," Malia adds, looking at Ava, "they returned a few minutes ago with the horses. That's why I came to speak with you."

Ava nods. "I'll go check on them—see that they aren't too shaken."

"Actually, Ava, why don't I have a look at you now that Knox is awake?"

Ava takes a step closer to the door, shoving her hands in the back pockets of her jeans like she does when she's anxious. "When I'm finished with the horses. They could use a familiar face and a head rub after the night we've had. Especially Loca."

Again, I frown because I'm missing the entire story. Every nervous tick of Ava's body tells me as much.

"I'll be back soon," she promises. "And I'll bring Lucy in if I can get her to leave the kids that were lavishing her with attention out there." With another forced smile, Ava strides out the door.

"What isn't she telling me?" I pry my eyes from the empty doorway and meet the doctor's dark gaze as she glances away from the monitor.

"Honestly, I'm not entirely sure. She's been so focused on you, she hasn't given me much, but . . ."

"But, what?" My hands fist with apprehension.

"Andrew said she was agitated when they found her. Like she was running from someone, or that something scared her —other than your wounds, of course."

"She was running away from them, most likely. When we

saw you guys in Amarillo, we thought you were dangerous. We were trying to avoid you and the road."

"Perhaps that's what it was," Malia says, and she motions for me to sit up. Gently, she prods the swelling at the base of my head. "Sorry for my cold hands," she mutters, removing the gauze. "The bleeding has stopped, and you could probably use one or two stitches, but I didn't want to tempt fate while you were unconscious. I'll let you decide if you want sutures now that you're awake. Your vitals are normal, though I'd like you to sleep here tonight." She looks at me, expectant.

"Yeah. Sure." I don't know that I have much of a choice or where I'd go otherwise. "Thanks."

"You're welcome. Now"—Malia clasps her hands together again—"the important question. Do you need to use the bathroom?"

All my apprehension vanishes the instant she asks. "Desperately," I admit.

With a knowing smile, Malia removes my IV, covering the wound with a cotton ball from the canister behind her and a piece of tape. The instant she pulls my covers back, cool air accosts my exposed skin since I'm only in a hospital gown and underwear. "The toilet is down the hall. I'll walk you to it."

Carefully, I swing my legs over the bed, noting the socks on my feet, and I'm instantly grateful when they hit the cool concrete. Malia takes my arm and helps me stand as I get my bearings. My head pounds a little, and blood rushes through my limbs, but there are no twinges or shooting pains, no broken bones.

She offers me her arm. "Do you feel nauseous at all?"

"No." I shake my head. "Not at the moment."

"Good. What about increased pain anywhere? Anything fractured or broken that we missed?"

"No," I breathe, clearing my throat again. "I'm good. Sore, but . . . good."

"Glad to hear it. Feel free to lean on me if you need to. The moment you start getting dizzy, let me know."

I grunt instead of nod, my bladder ready to explode, and allow the doctor to help me out of the room. "How long was I asleep?" I scan the walls for a clock.

"According to Ava, you were out about an hour when they found her on the road, and it took us a couple more to get you here and settled. So, about five hours, give or take." I can feel the doctor's eyes on me, and when we get to the restroom, she pushes the door open for me. "Did you see anyone else while you were out there?" she asks, but there's too much caution in her voice for it to be strictly curiosity.

I pivot to face her. "No. Why?"

Malia's eyes squint as she smiles and nods to the bathroom. "I'm just trying to put the pieces together is all."

I really have to go, but I want to know what the thinly veiled apprehension is all about.

"I know you woke up in a strange place, Knox," she continues, "and you have a lot of questions, but I need you to take it slow. Give yourself a few hours to acclimate and assess how bad you're really feeling before you start wandering around. The last thing we need is for you to fall and hit your head again because you're too impatient to wait." She switches on the bathroom light. The overheads flicker a moment as they buzz to life. "I'll wait here for you. Take your time."

"I'll be quick," I tell her, because I don't know how I feel about this place and these people, not yet anyway, and I need answers.

FORTY
KNOX

W<small>HEN</small> I <small>WAKE AGAIN, THE ROOM IS THE SAME AS IT WAS THE</small> first time; only Lucy is asleep on the floor and Ava is gone. I saw Ava fleetingly between her ensuring I ate something and her exam with Malia in another room, and I nodded off again sometime after that.

Spotting a pair of pants and a t-shirt folded on the foot of my bed, I decide to give walking a try. I feel all right, all things considered, which is good because I can't stay in this room with all my unanswered questions for a second longer.

Lucy springs to her feet as I carefully climb out of bed. The back of my head is sore, but my mind feels clearer, and I dress easily enough, taking my time as I measure the lingering pain.

"So—" I meet Lucy's eyes. Her butt swings back and forth with more excitement than should be legal this early in the morning. At least, it feels early. She licks my bare foot, making me twitch. Chuckling, I shove her away. "Where should I start?" I roll on a clean pair of socks. "Find Ava and get some answers, or find Andrew or Dillon since they'll likely have answers too?" I crouch down and tug on my boots that were left by the door with my backpack.

Lucy gives me unsolicited morning kisses, and abandoning my boots, I wrap my arm around her neck, drawing her in for a fierce hug. "You're a good pup," I tell her. "You have horrible morning breath, but I love you anyway." She licks me again, and I nudge her away with another laugh. "Since you can't brush your teeth, why don't I brush mine?"

With a final rub behind her ears, I stand up, grab my bathroom pouch from my pack, and head into the bathroom. It's made with cement bricks, like the other room. There is no glass in the shower, only an inset space you have to step into. A long, narrow window dotted with raindrops faces a field, letting in natural morning light.

It's clean—industrial, and new, and if I had to guess, this is one of the government's retrofitted shelters they spent billions of dollars building over the past decade.

I let the water run as I brush my teeth, waiting for it to warm a little before splashing a handful on my face to chase the lingering grogginess away. The scent of sulfur is nonexistent, and I slurp a mouthful of water from my hand, unable to resist. As it coats my tongue and throat, I think I'll never take drinkable water for granted again.

Lucy waits patiently by the door as I study the reflection staring back at me and shut the water off. Other than the dark circles under my eyes and the three-day-old scruff on my face, I look much like I always do, which is lucky. My fall, Ava on her own—it could have ended much worse than winding up here with a bump on my head, three stitches, water to drink, and Lucy at my side.

I decide to start the day like I would any other and give myself a close shave. When I'm done with my morning rituals, I head back to the exam room and leave my things where I found them. I follow Lucy down the hall, since she's familiar with the place, and we pass two other patient rooms, empty and dark, before the distant drone of conversation reaches my ears.

I step into a scantily furnished reception area and peer around. It's nestled in the corner of a giant, utilitarian building with cement pillars every dozen feet and tinted floor-to-ceiling windows, filling the space with gray morning light.

A young girl, leaning back in a chair behind a curved reception desk, tosses a rock up and catches it, quietly humming. She's a smaller version of Ava with dark hair and tanned skin, only her cheeks are rounder and her eyes are lighter. I can't tell if they're green or dark blue as her gaze darts up and down with each toss and catch of the rock. She's maybe nine or ten years old with a doctor's coat hanging off her that's four sizes too big, and she has no idea I'm standing there.

I clear my throat.

The girl catches the rock with a start and eyes me up and down. "Wow." She pushes a giant pair of glasses up the bridge of her nose, only for them to slide back down. "You look like hell."

My eyebrow lifts, though my expression gives nothing away. "Thanks."

Her ponytail whips her in the face as she tugs herself closer to the desktop, but she barely notices, too focused on the folder in front of her. "Knox, is it?" She sets her rock aside. It's an arrowhead, I realize, and it gleams in the morning light.

"I might be." I step up to the desk as she peers at me over the rim of her glasses. "And you are?"

"You can call me Dr. Robinson. I'm taking over for Malia while she's resting. You're supposed to be asleep."

She has gumption, I'll give her that. "I got tired." She looks at me. "Of sleeping," I say dryly. I glance around for an adult I might speak with. Unless this place is managed by child prodigies? "Dr. Robinson, is it?"

She nods.

"What's my diagnosis?"

"It was touch and go there for a while." The little girl shrugs, flipping through the papers in the folder, though she's not even reading them. "But I think you'll live."

I hum in understanding. "That's a relief." Dr. Robinson has no idea how much of a relief, but any playhouse concern she has for me is entirely forgotten when Lucy abandons all other distractions and prances over to her.

The little girl's blue eyes light up and she jumps up from her seat. "Hello, doggie."

"Her name's Lucy."

She pulls a face—a *that's a dumb name* sort of look only a kid could get away with. "You don't look like a Lucy," she mutters, petting her under her chin.

My eyes narrow on the girl. "And you don't look much like a doctor." The girl ignores me, but I notice the closed laptop on the desk and a walkie-talkie discarded next to an open-faced Stephen King book. "Where—"

"Ah, Knox."

An older man with a trimmed, gray beard and a bald head walks toward us. He looks like a civilian in his Dockers and thermal shirt, but he walks with rigid purpose like a man in uniform would. He takes a slurp from his mug. "I was just getting some chow." He cants his head toward *Dr. Robinson*. "What are you doing over here, Harper?"

She glances sheepishly at me. "I was looking after the patient for Malia."

"I see," the man mutters. "And smudging up my glasses while you're at it." He holds out his hand for them.

Harper begrudgingly hands them over. "I didn't smudge them."

He makes a derisive noise and sets his mug on the desk. "I'm Elijah." He turns to me, offering me his hand. "*I'm* covering for Malia."

"Are *you* a doctor?" I say sardonically, glancing from him to Harper.

Elijah smiles. "No. Well—a medic in the army a lifetime ago, but here, I'm the head of environmental engineering. Malia is my wife and she asked me to keep an eye on you while she gets some shut-eye. You had this place in a tizzy when you arrived last night."

"Funny. I can't seem to recall." It's a joke, a bad one, delivered with skepticism that Elijah's arched eyebrow tells me doesn't go unnoticed.

I glance around the building, eyeing it more closely. There are sofas and sectionals arranged in front of the windows that could serve as a lounge or waiting room, and beyond the sitting area are four rows of cafeteria tables across from an industrial kitchen.

"What is this place?"

"Facility 38," Harper supplies proudly.

"We call it the Watch House," Elijah adds. "We've been monitoring all seismic activity and catastrophes since April. And now SOS calls, it would seem. At least within a hundred-mile radius." He nods toward the people descending the stairs, then those beginning to cluster by the kitchen. "We're not typically an evacuation center, but the last few days have been . . . unprecedented, to say the least."

A few people stride across the second-floor landing, snagging my attention.

"The extra bunkrooms and staff living quarters are up there on the second floor," Elijah explains. "We'll get you squared away with a room now that you're awake. The third floor," he continues, pointing higher, "is our comms room, research lab, and the lookout tower. Civilians and servicemen from all over Oklahoma are housed here. We've been assessing the rapidly changing landscape for months—some of us for years, actually. Facility 38 is one of fifty—or at least there were fifty when the project started. We've since become the only shelter left between San Antonio and the panhandle." He glances around, shaking his head as if he can't really believe the turn of events. "Nearly a hundred people have come in the past few days alone, and I have a feeling we haven't seen the last of them. We're working on an alternate location to send folks because we're nearly at capacity."

I'm not sure if his explanation is unsettling or makes me hopeful, knowing there are other safe houses still standing. "Where are you looking to send people?"

"North."

My heartbeat ticks up a notch since that's the way we've been heading. "What's north?"

"Currently?" Elijah walks to the clipboard on the desk with a sigh that sounds like reluctant acceptance. "With Facility 32 under evacuation in Wyoming, we have six still operational throughout the Midwest and dozens of military bases from here to the East Coast that we're currently in communication with. At least, what's left of them."

"What's *left* of the East Coast?" I say carefully. I'm sure my eyes bulge as I consider the West Coast is submerged in water and all of Texas is a lava bed. But as my gaze darts to

Harper, who's watching me intently, I quash any outward concern.

Elijah gives me a sidelong look. "A lot has happened in the past week," he reminds me.

No shit goes unsaid, and with a nod, I look at Harper again.

Elijah sets the clipboard down, and I don't miss the way Harper eyes it curiously. "Why don't you go grab some breakfast, Harper?"

"But, I'm not hungry."

"Harper—" Elijah says more firmly.

With an indignant sigh, she jumps down from the chair. "No one ever wants me around," Harper grumbles. She grabs her arrowhead, and marches away.

Elijah steps closer, his expression stark and his eyes rimmed with shadows. "I'm sure you have a dozen questions," he says carefully, "and we'll get them answered for you as best we can. For now, there's a whiteboard with a current list of safe places." He points to a wall-length board in the common area, sectioned in a grid. "As well as which states have gone dark."

My eyes snap to his.

"We update it at six a.m. and six p.m. each day with any new information we receive from around the country."

States that have gone dark?

Elijah lets me process that for a moment. "I hear you came from Texas?"

Immediately, I think of Ava, and wonder where she is. "Yeah—Sutton County."

"Texas is—" He shakes his head. "If you have any loved ones still there, it's not good." My dad flashes to mind. So does my brother. I'd started out hoping my brother would find his way home, and now, I pray that if he's still alive, he went nowhere close to it.

"Where's Ava?" I say, clearing my throat.

Elijah raises his hand to chin height. "She's the one about yay-big, long dark hair, and a no-nonsense look about her?"

I huff. "Could be."

He glances toward the cafeteria. "Breakfast, I believe." I scan the increasing number of bodies at the tables for her. "If I may," Elijah starts, and his careful tone gives me pause. "Has she talked to you yet about what happened last night?"

My body stiffens. "Not really, no."

"As far as Malia knows, Ava hasn't talked much to anyone since she's been here, which is fine, but she *has* been asking questions."

I frown, uncertain why that would be a problem if this place is what he says it is.

"Specifically, about learning self-defense," he adds. "I just thought you should know."

At first that surprises me, then my heart sinks. I have no idea what Ava went through last night, and my entire body tenses as I consider *why* that would be on her mind. "Thanks."

Elijah nods and motions toward the cafeteria. "Last I saw your friend, she was sitting at the middle table."

"Thanks," I mutter again. The *why* behind her desire to learn self-defense makes me feel like there's lead in my feet and screws in my stomach as I start toward her.

Lucy is twenty steps ahead, scouting the floor for crumbs. A handful of people gravitate toward the coffee station and another dozen or so stand in the breakfast line. There are twice as many people as when I looked last time, and when I spot the analog clock on the wall, I note it's just shy of eight a.m.

One child clutches a singed teddy bear like it's his life-line. And I notice a man wearing rumpled jeans and a long-sleeve shirt that look to be a few days old, like the clothes on his back are all he has left. Other people are freshly showered or shaven, their clothes pressed or at least clean. All of them, however, have a harried, haggard sheen in their eyes that I feel bone-deep.

I spot Ava sitting with her back to me at one of the tables. She's alone, picking absently at her food. Relief knots with apprehension, and I walk over to her. "Good morning," I murmur.

Ava's head snaps in my direction and she swallows a mouthful of food. "You're up." She licks her lips as I sit beside her and straddles the bench, facing me. "I thought you'd sleep longer." She frowns, eyeing me up and down. "Should you even be walking around?"

"I've barely got a headache. I'm fine." I watch the others in the common area. "I've got too many questions to lie uselessly in bed all day." Ava tosses her napkin on the table. Her hair is damp, straight and loose from a shower. She's in a clean, black long-sleeve shirt and jeans, but her boots are covered in mud. It's her expressive, amber eyes that catch and hold my attention, though. She's relieved to see me, but something else brews behind them as well. "Besides," I hedge, "I actually slept last night. Did you?"

"I slept," she mutters, and she scoots her perfectly propor-tioned breakfast tray away. "A little."

"At least you're eating." I steal a piece of bacon from her plate, eyeing the few bites of egg and toast she has left. It's obvious they are trying to ration, which means they are preparing for scarcity or are already worried about it, all of which is a concern I tuck away to worry about later. "Well, except for your fruit cup." I notice it's not even open.

Ava chuckles. "I've never been a big fan of corn syrup." I must have a wild look of hunger in my eyes because she grins and scoots her tray to me. "By all means. Have at it." She smiles playfully, and I can tell she has rested a little. Her mood is lighter, or rather, her easiness is more genuine than last night.

I take another bite of bacon and hold her gaze. "So . . ." I watch the way the corner of her mouth tugs between her teeth. Even when she's not dwelling on something, she still worries, even if she doesn't seem to notice.

"So, what?" She blinks those big, beautiful eyes at me and I want to kiss her.

"Are you going to tell me?" I ask quietly and probably too gently for it to sound conversational.

"About what?"

"Ava." I can't help my exasperation. "About what happened yesterday. Last night. All of it." I stare at her, anxious and afraid and a little bit angry, even if I don't fully comprehend why. "Tell me. Please."

With a soft, wavering smile, Ava groans and leans in, resting her forehead on my shoulder. "I did something stupid." Her voice is barely audible.

"It couldn't have been that stupid," I tell her, running my hands over her shoulders and down her arms. I'm not sure if it's for her comfort or mine. "We're here, after all."

Ava sits up, picking at her fingernail. "I went back to the farmhouse." Her eyes search mine and I think she holds her breath.

Scrolling through my memory, I revisit our path and the few places we saw on the road. Finally, I remember the gated farmhouse with the warning signs, and my uneasiness drops like a tire iron to the pit of my stomach. I hold her gaze. "And?" I murmur, my blood suddenly raging as I consider every nightmarish, horrible thing that might've happened.

"Ouch—" Ava winces and tugs my fingers from her forearm. I snap my hand away, unaware I was holding onto her at all. "Sorry—"

"It's fine." She waves my apology away. "It's bruising, that's all."

I glare at her arm sleeve. "What's bruising?"

When Ava doesn't answer me, my gaze snaps to hers again. Shame reddens her cheeks, and Ava looks away.

"Ava—"

"You'll laugh when I tell you."

"I highly doubt it," I grit out.

Picking at the edge of her napkin, Ava mutters something.

"What?"

"I said," she annunciates more carefully and with a bite of sass, "an old woman bit me."

"*What?*" My eyebrows shoot to my hairline. "An old woman *bit* you?" I reach gently for Ava's arm, and carefully pull her sleeve up, my teeth grinding with only slightly-curbed abhorrence. A black-and-purple bruise blooms around the indent of teeth.

"She wasn't . . . right."

"No fucking shit, Ava. An old woman *bit* you. Why did you go back there in the first place?"

Ava glares at me. "Are you serious? Because you were unconscious, Knox. For all I knew, you were dying last night." She points toward my recovery room. "You were out cold, and I had no idea where to go or how to find help. So, yes, I went back to the only place I could think of."

Guilt worms its way through me. Or it could be self-loathing for putting Ava in that position in the first place. "Is that all that happened? Was there anyone else—"

"No," she mutters, raking her fingers through her damp hair. It falls back into her face as she looks down in shame. "There was no one else there. Not alive, at least."

"I'm sorry," I whisper. I wrap my arms around Ava, pulling her closer. "I didn't mean it like that. I just—I wasn't expecting . . . *that*. I would have gone back, too." I've never found comfort in someone else's warmth before, not since my mother, and even if I hate that I wasn't there with Ava, that she's sitting here—that I can smell her apple-scented hair and feel her fingers pressed into my back—is all that keeps my firestorm of emotions just below the surface.

Sighing, Ava pulls away and rests her elbow on the table. "I feel like there were a dozen things I should have done differently, but at the same time, I can't think of a single one. At least, not with so many uncertainties."

I take Ava's other hand from her lap and lace my fingers with hers. "What the hell was wrong with her? Was she rabid?" It's a small, horrible attempt at levity, but Ava doesn't laugh.

"Not rabid," she says, shaking her head. "But she *was* sick and . . . she was starving. I don't know the last time she drank clean water or ate a real meal." She frowns to herself. "I don't think she's stepped off her porch in fifty years, Knox. Her husband is still lying on his deathbed."

My jaw ticks as I stare at Ava in disbelief. "You saw that?"

Ava sighs in answer. "She was going to shoot Loca. That's why she locked me in his room."

I tilt my head back and squeeze my eyes shut, my toes curling painfully in my boots as I force myself to stomach every image Ava paints and feel the depth of her fear. For me. For herself. For Loca. I want her to stop telling me these things because I can't bear much more of it, but that's selfish and insensitive, and I swallow a curse instead.

"It was fucked up," she continues, "and I might've put myself in that position, but—"

My eyes snap open. "You did what you had to, Ava. And you got yourself out of there in one piece. Don't play the blame game unless you want to be angry at me for putting you in that position to begin with."

"Rooster, actually," she counters. "Maybe we should ground him."

I huff a laugh despite myself, though none of this is funny. "I'm sorry you had to go through that, and all because of me."

Ava shakes her head with a soft, exasperated chuckle. "You definitely owe me," she teases, and as her gaze lingers on me, her worry alleviates a little. "I would've done everything I had to, Knox. Just like I know you would have. And besides—" Ava runs her teeth over her bottom lip, lost in her thoughts again. "That's not really what bothers me the most."

I fidget with her fingers in my hand, waiting for her to continue.

"That's twice that I've been in a situation where I've felt that kind of fear and borderline helplessness because of someone else, and I don't want it to happen again. Not if I can help it. I thought I was strong before, that I could protect myself because I've been on my own for so long. But this— this is different. I want to learn more about guns. I want to learn how to defend myself so that I'm not scrambling to figure it all out, hoping for the best, because it won't be a feeble old lady next time."

"Next time," I repeat, realizing Ava is right. This isn't likely the last time she'll find herself at someone else's mercy. My size would make anyone second-guess picking a fight with me, but Ava—save for that fiery glint in her eyes—looks like much easier prey. I take Ava's chin between my fingers so she'll look at me. She blinks and runs her tongue over her lips. "We'll find someone to help us," I promise. "And I'm so fucking sorry you had to deal with all of that alone."

Her eyes mist a little and a hint of a smile tugs at her mouth. "I'm glad you're awake," she whispers. The cafeteria rings with voices, but hers is all I hear. She is all I can see, and unbidden, my gaze shifts to her soft lips again, and I kiss Ava because I've craved her since I woke up last night, her body curled around me in sleep.

Her mouth parts, and she grips my arms, kissing me in return. Everyone else falls away as I bask in the heat of her mouth and the caress of her breath against my skin. But before I can get too carried away as we sit in a mass of onlookers, I pull away, leaning my forehead to hers. "Thank you, Ava," I rasp. I swallow the sting of my own failures and steady my breath. My heart is full of gratitude and an almost crippling amount of solace. "For what you did for me last night," I say, squeezing my eyes shut. "And for what it cost you."

Ava pulls back and her lips curve. A true smile fills her face, and her eyes glitter impishly. "You could make it up to me," she says.

"Yeah?" I watch the way she nibbles on her lower lip and admire the dark lashes that frame her eyes. "What sort of payment do you have in mind?"

"Pausing time for a little while would be nice."

"Oh, is that all?"

She grins. "It would be nice to take another mini reality break is all."

A thought crosses my mind. "I have an idea." I kiss her

again, short but unrushed and sweet, unable to resist. "I'll talk to—"

"Tony."

The words die on my tongue. "What?"

"Tony." Surprise lights Ava's eyes, and she turns my face to the breakfast line behind me. "He's here."

I zero in on the stalky, dark-haired cowboy in faded Wranglers and a Dallas Cowboys football jersey and rise to my feet. "Tony!" My voice booms through the space and he glances in my direction.

The moment Tony sees me, his eyes bulge, and his entire face brightens. "Hey, boss." He steps out of line and rushes over. "I never thought I'd be so happy to see your ugly face," he jokes. I pull him in for a hug, and tears fill my eyes as he claps his hand on my back.

A week ago, I thought he was dead, along with everyone else I loved and cared about. "I can't believe you're here." I can barely find my voice through the shock, so I squeeze him tighter. "And I'm no longer your boss, so stop calling me that."

"Fair enough," Tony agrees. When I finally pull away, all I can do is stare at him like he might not be real.

When Tony notices Ava, he stills. It's only a split second of surprise before a shit-eating grin fills his face. "And you're with Ava Hernandez?" He glances between us, then reaches for her, pulling Ava in for a hug. "Color me surprised. I didn't see that one coming either."

"It's good to see you, Tony," Ava rasps. The two of them have always gotten along, so her stilted hug surprises me.

"I hoped you'd gotten out of Sonora before—" Tony's words fall on deaf ears because I see the increasing panic in Ava's eyes as she pulls away from him, and I realize what's happening. Her face pales as she looks at me.

"Knox . . ." Her voice is thick with panic as she looks around, taking in her surroundings with compulsive swallows like she might be sick. "I need to sit . . ."

"Shit." I reach for Ava and pull her into me. "I've got you," I promise as I lower myself onto the seat. "It's okay."

She mumbles incoherently and then her body slackens against me. As Ava starts to slip, I hold her tighter.

"Tony—" I meet his panicked gaze. "Find Elijah or Malia."

FORTY-ONE
AVA

I sit on the edge of an exam table as Malia checks my vitals. My mind is still heavy with fog, but strangely, I feel lighter than I do after most episodes—embarrassed for causing a scene, but safer, I guess, having Knox here with me.

He rubs his chin from a chair beside me, a harried look on his face and his elbows braced on his knees. Our roles today have completely switched and it's exhausting.

"Your vitals are fine, Ava. But you probably already know that, if this is a regular occurrence."

I nod because she's right. I've gone through this a dozen times before, and other than waking up with IVs in my arms during ambulance transport after passing out in public places, I am always "completely healthy" by the end of it.

"How often is 'regular'?" Malia asks, taking a step back.

"A couple times a month while I had my prescription. I ran out a few days ago."

Malia purses her lips. "And how long has that been going on?"

"Well—" I glance at Knox. "The short story is, I've had a

version of these episodes my whole life, but the summer before I started high school, I was diagnosed with petite mal seizures and put on meds to regulate them."

"And you saw a specialist who diagnosed you?"

I nod. "I went through a series of tests, and even though my results were inconclusive, they found 'abnormal synapsis in my frontal lobe,'" I add with air quotes.

Malia takes a seat on the rolling stool and sets her clipboard aside. "And you've been on the same anti-epileptic drugs since and with the same doctor?" She's casual and soft-spoken, and even if I'm currently her only patient, she's attentive and curious, which puts me at ease. There is no side-eye with her. No judgment.

"I've been on a few different prescriptions over the years," I explain. "I had adverse reactions to some of them—prescriptions, not doctors. Well—" I correct with a shrug. "I guess I've had some adverse reactions to my doctors, too, but that's not what you're asking." I loathe the wobble in my voice. It's borne of years of fear and anxious frustration. "I've been on Zarontin, Lamictal, and Topiramate, that I can remember off the top of my head, and I've seen three neurologists in the past six years because of my medical coverage."

Malia stretches her legs in front of her, crossing her ankles. "And these episodes worsened in high school, you said?"

"More or less."

She tucks a loose strand of hair behind her ear. "I know you're out of your pills now, but before this week, do you think they'd been helping?"

Groaning, I run my hands over my face. Not because I'm exasperated with her, but because the more I talk about this out loud, the more I wonder what the hell I was doing all these years, forking out money for pills I couldn't afford.

"The pills didn't stop them from happening," I admit, "if that's what you're asking."

Malia glances at Knox, but he's staring at me and doesn't notice. "One last question," she says carefully, and I can tell I'm not going to like it. "This week aside, have you had significant trauma over the years that stands out to you?"

Instantly, my gaze shoots to Knox, too, lingering on him as I consider where the hell I should start and how much to say.

Malia glances between us and clears her throat. "Would you like to speak privately?"

"No—" I shake my head, snorting a nervous laugh. "It's fine. Knox knows most of my trauma already." I swallow thickly, but this time, I have a question for *her*. "Can I ask why you want to know? I'm sensing you're about to drop a bomb on me that I should prepare myself for."

Malia offers me a cautious smile. "Have any of your doctors ever mentioned vasovagal syncope?"

I frown, barely able to say the term in my head, so I would have remembered hearing it.

"The sensations you experience before you lose consciousness sound exactly like it. The vagus nerve is part of our fight-flight-freeze response system—specifically, the latter—and when it's overstimulated, it can cause heart rate and blood pressure to drop so low that blood flow to the brain is reduced. It's quite common, actually. Lightheadedness, feeling sweaty or clammy, tunnel vision, and the ringing in the ears you mentioned—they are all symptoms. Other people experience the same reaction when they have excessive bowel movements and food poisoning. Or when they faint at the sight of blood. And heat—heat and dehydration contribute to its severity as well."

My frown deepens. It sounds so basic, which only makes

me more confused by her questions. Especially when my doctors have never uttered those words to me before.

"Vasovagal syncope fainting spells can also be known as anxiety attacks—the body's reaction to severe emotional distress and certain triggers," Malia adds carefully, which gives me pause. There's an unnerving certainty in her expression and resolution in her voice, and while I loathe thinking all my doctors have been wrong for so many years, something inside me deflates because I think Malia could be right.

"Why?" I ask, licking my lips. "Why don't you think it's epilepsy?"

"For starters, absence seizures are common in children, not in adults—children usually grow out of them. Add to that the list of neurology meds you've cycled through, your lack of convulsions, and the fact that seizures aren't detectable, yet your spells have been. Epileptic attacks usually come out of nowhere. People can't typically prepare for seizures, which is why some patients rely on animal companions to help alert them."

Malia stares at me as I absorb the weight of everything she's saying. As the dozens of appointments and bus rides and phone calls and bills—as the years of struggling with my brain health is reduced to anxiety.

"I always know when my spells are coming," I say, reiterating out loud one of the biggest reasons I believe Malia is right. "I have seconds to worry about them . . . Sometimes minutes to grow more anxious as I try to stave them off." I stare at her. "Which I assume is why it never works."

"Perhaps. That's why I asked about the trauma in your life," Malia explains. "I'd like to know if you see a correlation with certain events over the past ten years that may have worsened your episodes."

Acute frustration makes it difficult to speak as the pieces

fall into place. "My mother died when I was young," I confess, staring at the cement floor. "And ten years ago, my uncle—my guardian at the time—took someone's life in a car accident and went to prison." Even if that's only the tip of the iceberg, the list in my head continues. I think about Mitch's harassment and threats, Lars's constant bullying, and how every day has been a struggle to keep my head above water, especially since Mavey got sick. And all of it—every extra shift I had to take to help pay our bills, every sleepless night and added worry only compounded it. And it all started ten years ago.

Knox's gaze bores through me, and I squeeze my eyes shut. I can't handle the guilt I'll see on his face if I look at him because he unnecessarily shoulders part of the blame.

"I can't imagine what you have been through, Ava." Malia's voice is kind. "And though I could be wrong, I don't think I am. In fact, *I* think this is good news." My eyes open and fix on her. Malia doesn't look triumphant in the slightest. She seems happy for me. Hopeful. "Anxiety can be handled," she continues. "It's not easy, of course, especially now, but it can be reduced, and learning how to control your anxiety will help you in the long run."

"I don't get it." Knox's voice is loud compared to hers, startling me a little. He stares at Malia. "Why hasn't she had one while we were fleeing wildfires or while she was trying to find help last night? Instead, it happens when she's feeding the horses or making dinner. That makes no sense."

"It may seem that way," Malia explains, "but panic and anxiety are not the same. Ava isn't having these attacks when she's upset because, oftentimes, when we're too busy holding ourselves together, it's the quieter moments when it all catches up with us. Think of anxiety like bottled-up toxins. Once that bottle is full, it overflows or bursts."

Malia's eyes meet mine. "That's why, if you can learn to manage your stress better, it will help. And the good thing about anxiety is there are many natural ways to cope and medicate yourself if needed. You won't have to rely on a pharmacy to manage your health. Especially with the unpredictable state of things. *You* have the control, Ava. It's not an easy path, but it *is* possible. The same can't be said for seizures."

"I have the control," I repeat, shaking my head in disbelief. "I find that hard to believe, seeing as I've been trying to control this for as long as I can remember."

"Yes, but until now you were taking anti-epileptics that changed the chemical balance of your mind. Once they are out of your system, we can focus on what will help you, not hinder you from getting better."

I stare blankly at the wall, my grip on the exam table tightening.

"I am not saying that your doctors didn't know what they were talking about because they *did* find some inconclusive results in your neurological scans. But," she says crisply, "inconclusive to me means they never had a definitive diagnosis."

"Which means you're probably right," I finish for her.

She purses her lips. "I believe I am. But for now, it's all speculation. Our equipment is limited here, but I can run a blood panel to see if you have any vitamin deficiencies, and I'd like to check your hormone levels. The results will help us determine where to start. Only when your body is balanced will you be able to accurately gauge which approaches are working and which aren't."

"Yeah." I nod, suddenly more exhausted. "Sure."

"Perfect." Malia grabs her clipboard. "I'll be right back."

"Thank you," I blurt as she leaves the room. I'm sure she

has better things to do with her time other than cater to me, and she's not even getting paid for it.

Malia flashes me a quick smile. "You're welcome, Ava."

I inhale a lungful of much-needed air as her footsteps grow fainter, then make a pathetic brain explosion noise as I look at Knox. "That was . . . a lot."

He walks over to me, the furrow in his brow deeper. "Yeah, it was." His eyes shift over my face. "Are you okay?"

"I'm good. I'm just—over all of this."

"I can imagine." He shoves his hands in his pockets, assessing me. "You seem convinced she's right, though."

"It's a hard pill to swallow, but I know she is," I admit, and the words feel right. "Or maybe I just want her to be, because nothing I've done this far has worked."

Knox huffs a sad little sound and rubs my arm. "Then, I hope she's right, too."

"Thanks." I stare at Knox, admiring his hazel eyes even in the abhorrent overhead lighting. "And thanks for sitting with me. It's really nice to have you in here with me."

The corner of his mouth lifts, a dimple slightly forming in his cheek. "Thank you for *letting* me be here. I know this is hard for you."

All Knox has wanted since all this started was for me to open up more. Now, he gets to be part of it, whether he wants to be or not. "Welcome to the craziness."

Knox kisses my forehead. "I didn't give you Loca by accident, remember?"

"Har har. Very funny."

He smiles, and straightening, he glances around the room.

"I'll be fine with her if you want to head out. I know you've been itching to check on the horses since you woke up. And now Tony is here." I grin. Their reunion would have been picture worthy if I'd had my phone on me. "You should go. I'll find you when I'm done here."

Knox eyes me skeptically. "You're sure?"

"Yeah, trust me. Malia is far less terrifying than Dr. Singh was. I think I can handle her." I wink at him and gather my hair into a ponytail. "Now, go. Give the horses some love for me."

"I'll come back when I'm finished, if you haven't found me yet."

Despite his reluctance, Knox leaves me to my thoughts, and honestly, I'm happy for the breathing room. I lean back on the exam table with a sigh that feels like my first real breath in the last twenty minutes.

Mavey passed away, then Scott showed up.

Lars killed Scott, and I was stuck with Knox.

Knox took care of me when I thought he hated me.

Mitch showed up, and we formed an unspoken truce.

Knox diverted his trip to Kansas to drop me off in Sweetwater.

Julio died in my arms, and Knox was there for me again.

Now, we're here when I thought last night would end far differently . . .

Mentally, I tick off the events of this week in my head, all of it a mix of dread and surprise. After what we've been through in the past few days alone, I know anxiety is something I can and need to manage better. I'm determined to.

I sit up, catching movement from the corner of my eye. The Hispanic girl I saw in the cafeteria this morning stands in the doorway fidgeting with something in her hand. She stares at me. I stare back.

Since she came into my doorway, I assume she has something to say, but as the seconds tick by, I cave first. "Hello."

She tilts her head. "Hey." Her mouth presses together in

consternation as she looks me up and down without the slightest bit of reserve. "Are you with Knox?"

I grunt at her candor. Something tells me she's not only asking if we're traveling together. "Uh, yeah. I am." My eyebrow lifts of its own accord. "Why do you ask?"

She shrugs, but I get the feeling she's sizing me up. "Knox was in here this morning, too."

I try not to smile. "He had a small accident yesterday," I explain. I don't know if she has a little crush on him or if she's simply curious about me—or us, as newcomers—but she's definitely giving me the once-over. "But he's fine now."

"I know."

I blink at her, pressing my lips together to stop another smile, and glance down the hall for Malia. "So, what brings you to Exam Room One? Are you looking for someone?"

The girl turns what I think is an arrowhead over in her hand and leans against the doorframe. "Not really."

"Just bored?"

She nods, but she looks more than bored. There's something about the way her blue eyes shift to the obsidian—the way she fingers it like it's the most precious thing she has—that resonates with me in a strange, unexpected way. She tucks a strand of loose, dark hair behind her ear and heaves out a sigh.

"I'm Ava, by the way."

The girl lifts her head and shoves the arrowhead into her pocket. "Harper."

"It's nice to meet you, Harper. How long have you been here?"

She wanders into the room, running her finger over the metal shelf until she stops at the glass cabinet. "A few days."

"Are you here with your family?"

I note the way her finger pauses on the glass before she

drops her hand at her side. "No." Harper's mask of boredom and indifference slips as she turns, and her cheeks redden. *Shit.* The flash of what looks like hurt that's there one second is gone the next, tugging at my heart. A hollow pit in my stomach immediately follows. This girl could have lost her entire family this week, and I so casually bring it up.

I clear my throat. "Are you from Texas, like me?"

Harper shakes her head and plops down in the chair Knox was sitting in. "My group home was in New Mexico. We came here when they evacuated Santa Fe."

My heart sinks deeper. It should be a relief Harper hasn't been alone through all this, but for some reason, it isn't.

"Are you going to be okay?" she asks, and this time there is concern in her eyes as she stares at me.

"Ah." I nod with understanding. "You saw my little fainting spell out there, did you?"

Harper blinks at me.

"Yeah, I'll be fine. Thank you for asking. Sorry if I scared you."

She shrugs again, and the tips of her shoes brush the floor as she leans back in the chair. "Is Lucy yours?" Harper folds her hands in her lap.

"No, she is Knox's dog." I smile. "She's a sweet girl, isn't she?"

Harper nods, glancing around the room. "I like dogs, but they never let us have them in the group home. I had one when I was a kid, though."

"When you were a kid, huh?" I grin. "And what was his name?"

"Freckles. He was a Dalmatian. But he ran away when I moved in with my grandma. It sucked."

"I bet it did. I'm sorry you lost your friend."

Harper stares up at the ceiling, drumming her fingers on

the arms of the chair. "I asked Jenny if we could at least get a rabbit or a hamster or something, but she said they stink, and her boss wouldn't let her anyway."

"So, I take it you like animals, then?"

With a head bob, Harper lifts her head and looks at me. "I'm going to be a veterinarian."

I can't help my smile as I imagine her no-nonsense bedside manner delivering any sort of news to her patient's owner. "That's a big job, and a good one. You must like animals a lot."

"I pretty much love them," she confesses.

"Well," I say with a shrug, "maybe Knox will introduce you to his horses while we're here."

Harper's eyes widen to saucers. "He brought *horses*?"

"Two, in fact." I can tell Harper's mind is spinning a mile a minute. "He had a ranch in Texas."

"I've never been to a ranch before. Did he have other animals?"

"Cattle. Pigs. I think that was it. We're headed to his uncle's farm next." I pause. "At least, we were." I realize I'm not certain *what* the plan is now, if we're still going to Ransom, or when. All the questions that have plagued me since we started this journey return and settle in my shoulders, tightening the back of my neck again.

"What sort of animals does his uncle have?"

I force the deluge of uncertainties away for now, refocusing on her. "Uh, I—I'm not sure, actually. I've never been there."

Harper screws her mouth up and drums her fingers on the chair again, thoughtful. "Do you really think Knox will let me see his horses?"

"I do. I'll ask him when I see him again, okay?"

"Harper," Malia says with a hint of exasperation. She

steps into the room with a tray of empty vials and a lifted eyebrow. "You're not supposed to be in here. You know that."

"We were just talking."

Malia gives her a sympathetic smile. "You know the rules."

With a huff, Harper pushes herself up out of the chair. "Fine." Sparing a last glance at me, Harper trudges down the hallway.

"Cute kid," I mutter, though I'm not sure if cute is exactly the right word.

Malia shakes her head with a small chuckle. "Yeah, she's cute and *very* curious. She speaks her mind too."

Harper drags her feet as she disappears around the corner.

"Jenny," Malia continues, "the social worker who brought the children in on Tuesday, mentioned Harper's mother was a founding member in one of the major Moonie militias they busted up six years ago after the researcher kidnappings in Las Vegas. Harper has been moving around from different homes and facilities since she was three. I can't figure out if she's restless being cooped up here—yet another new place— or if it's just another week for her."

A lump lodges in my throat. No family in a world as crazy as this? I can only imagine how alone Harper must feel. "That's really . . ."

"Horrible. Sad. Enraging," Malia finishes for me. She grabs a cotton ball and tape from one of the drawers in the cupboard. "I know. And yet, a part of me wonders if somehow those kids are better off than the rest of us."

I meet Malia's gaze.

She shakes her head, almost thoughtful. "Most people have lost lifetimes of friendships and loved ones in the last few weeks alone. But for kids like Harper, this cruel life is all they've known, and I can't help but think if, in a way, it has better prepared them for whatever comes next. Unlike the rest of us."

Whatever comes next. I stare down the empty hallway as Malia pushes up my sleeve. A little part of me concedes she might be right and wonders if Harper isn't a version of me lost in a spiraling world she's simply trying to exist in. I pray that, whatever does happen next, the little girl will be okay.

FORTY-TWO
KNOX

"I KNOW AVA IS GOING TO BE OKAY AND ALL, BUT YOU DON'T seem as freaked out about what happened in there as I am," Tony says. We make our way out the double doors, into the back lot of the facility.

I nearly bark a laugh, ignoring my headache as we walk shoulder to shoulder across the lot. "I am. Trust me. It's just not the first time I've seen her like that." Nose to the damp ground, Lucy scopes the place out. Remotely, I realize it rained while I was sleeping.

I scan the back lot, which is more like a compound, with storage buildings and a hangar for a garage across from us, a puddle-riddled parking area to the right.

"Honestly, when I saw her with you in the cafeteria," Tony continues, "I was floored. I'm still trying to figure out how the two of you could have possibly ended up here together in the first place. You've been avoiding her for nearly a decade."

I rub my shoulder, realizing how hard I must've hit it yesterday during my fall. "I ran into Scott, and he was helping her until—" I run my hand over my face. "Until he couldn't. That's a story for another time, though." I whistle for Lucy, wandering closer to the newest arrivals.

"Andrew said the horses are tied up by the garden." Tony points to a greenhouse half visible behind a hangar.

As we pass, I note the two fire engines with ash debris on the windshields, a Peterbilt with enough soot that the company logo is indiscernible, and an empty trailer, parked side by side in the hangar.

There's a commotion in the parking area as a handful of people climb out of a white van parked haphazardly in front of a graveyard of dust-covered, beat-to-shit vehicles. As newcomers pile out, I think of the van Ava and I saw in Amarillo.

"This way!" A facility employee motions for everyone to follow him as they adjust their bags and backpacks.

Most people move like zombies, rumpled and dirty, and exhaustion hovers over them like a cloud. A couple walks hand in hand, the packs on their backs so heavy they have to lean forward to stay upright. A teenage boy has his head wrapped and walks with a limp.

"We'll get you checked in," the worker says. "Then we'll answer your questions."

"So," Tony starts, and his stare is like a cattle prod, willing me to look at him, but I don't. "While you were in with Ava, Elijah mentioned they found a room for you guys."

I watch the newcomers filing into the facility and wonder if we've gotten one of the last rooms. "Yeah? That's good news."

"Hmm."

With a sigh, I finally look at him. Tony's eyebrow is raised and his brown eyes twinkle with amusement. "A lot has happened in the past week, huh?"

I laugh—*really* laugh—this time. "You have no idea."

When Loca's tanned rump comes into view, I smile with relief. The horses are tied up at a fence post, grazing on weeds along the garden perimeter. Amidst gorging himself, Rooster's head pops up when he hears us coming, a stem hanging from the corner of his mouth.

"Surprise, surprise," I mutter. "You're eating." I rub his head and pat his thick neck. "What sort of damage did you do to yourself yesterday?" I lift his front leg to check for any injuries he might've sustained when he spooked since I have no idea what happened after.

Tony goes over to Loca, cooing to her like they are old friends. He strokes her belly as he coaxes her front leg up. "Where's Poppy?" The clipped tone of his voice tells me he's braced for the worst; he knows I'd never leave a horse behind if I could help it.

"She stayed back with my dad."

Tony drops Loca's leg, slowly straightens, and stares at me over her back. I pretend I don't notice as I run my hand up and down Rooster's back leg to ensure there are no wounds. I'd told Tony the ranch was likely gone, but I guess I'd failed to mention anything about my father staying with it.

"Your dad was there when you left?"

"He wouldn't leave," I admit. "Even when the fire was so close it was all we could see on the horizon." The memory is gutting, and I try to swallow it all away.

Tony's chin lifts. "Your mom," he realizes. Having been a part of the ranch since he and I were in high school, Tony has learned more than he'd ever wanted to know about my family. He was with me when my mom died and helped me care for the steers and the horses after Kellen left, while my father was making runs to Dallas and San Antonio for the auctions. He was there for our shouting matches and the aftermath and all the bullshit in-between. Tony knows my family better than anyone, so of course he could guess why Mitch Bennett stayed behind.

"Yeah," I murmur, "my mom. He made sure me and Ava got out of there, though."

"That's something I never thought I'd hear you say."

"Which part?"

"Mitch looking out for you, and Ava, all in the same sentence."

I pick a piece of mud from Rooster's coat. "Yeah, that was unexpected. And weird. But—" I shake my head.

"But what?"

Still trying to wrap my head around it all, I meet Tony's gaze. "This is going to sound crazy, but I don't think he minded having Ava at the house." I recall the haunted look in my father's eyes when he got home after all he'd been through. "I thought he was dead—hell, *he* thought he was dead—and I think it changed everything for him."

"I would imagine so. It's not every day you're faced with every wrong and horrible decision you've made in your life, only to come out of it filled with regrets. And I say plural because Mitch would have many." Tony runs his hand down Loca's back leg, drawing her hoof up to inspect it. "Horrific experience aside, though, I'm really glad Ava's okay. She's good people. And I'm relieved neither of you have been alone in all of this. After the news about California . . ." Trailing off, Tony puts Loca's leg down and walks around her, stopping on the other side of Rooster. "I was worried about you— in a purely manly sort of way, of course." He jests with false bravado, as always.

"Of course." I roll my eyes with a grin. Taking a beat to soak in the past seven days, I fold my arms on Rooster's back. "To be honest, if it weren't for Ava, I don't know what state I'd be in now. Then again, we haven't had time to dwell on much. This is the first real break we've caught since we left the ranch. And what Ava had to go through to get us here —" I grit my teeth, groaning as I shake my head. "I'm over this shit, man."

"You and me both." Like the shit friend I am, I realize I have no idea what sort of hell Tony has been through since last I saw him.

He pulls his baseball cap off and scratches his head. Tony is freshly shaven, which is easy for him because the guy can't grow a beard to save his life. He's in clean clothes, which is more than I can say for half the people here. But there's a shadow in his eyes that has never been there. A gauntness to his face that comes from a week of misery and bone-deep weariness.

"What about you?"

He looks at me.

"After the sinkhole, I couldn't get a hold of you. I thought you were dead . . . How did you end up in Guymon?"

"That's a fun story," he grumbles, and inhaling a deep breath, Tony rests his arms on Rooster's rump. "Long story short, my mom's house was beyond repair after that earthquake, so we had already left San Antonio. We were headed back to Sonora when we heard about it, actually. We never made it, though. Traffic was being diverted, so we went to my aunt's place in Fort Worth instead." He draws circles in the dust on Rooster's coat. "We were bused here three days ago. And I'm not sure what we're going to do next. I don't know how long they're letting people stay, but it can't be forever. The only other family we have is in Washington, and I haven't been able to get a hold of them, and I doubt I ever will."

Two facility workers exit through the double doors, chatting among themselves as if it's just another day at work. We watch them get into one of the government vehicles.

"I overheard two analysts talking in the cafeteria yesterday," he continues quietly. "They said they are understaffed as it is. Now, dozens of people are arriving each day, and not nearly as many of them are moving onward. I guess we're all too scared to leave a good thing."

I scratch my jaw, thinking about Kansas. "We were headed to Mason's," I tell him. "I don't know exactly what we'll be walking into in Ransom, but you and your mom should come with us. We should all stick together, if we can help it."

Tony spits off to the side, a hard habit for guys like us to break, who spend all day in the dust and muck. When he looks at me, it's with an expression I know like the back of my hand. Despite the muted daylight, his brown eyes are filled with reluctance. With worry. And I know it's for his mom. "I would go with you in a heartbeat if it was just me," he says, his voice rougher than usual. "But I don't think it's a good idea. All of this has taken its toll on my mom. Losing her house, the fear and uncertainty. We've been lucky, especially compared to you, but she lost her cat on our way here, and let me tell you, that cat was as much a pain in my ass as it was an angel in disguise. It kept her busy and gave her something to smile about and fuss over. But after the evacuation center, at one of the rest stops, the damn thing bolted." He sighs with a ragged breath. "My mom's health wasn't great before, and without that damn cat to focus on, it's like she's aged a year in the last three days. Unless you're certain Mason's place is safe—that he's even still there—I'm not sure I should risk it. She hasn't even come out of our dorm room yet today."

Tony, my brother in all ways but blood, looks at me with

regret and misery and a tinge of defeat, but I can't hide my disappointment. "I understand." And the truth is, I do understand. If my mother were with me, and ailing, many of my decisions would have been different.

"I'd stay here, but if my dad or Kellen—"

"You don't have to explain, Knox. I know why you're going to Mason's, and you *should*. I just—" He shakes his head. "There's no telling what could happen between here and there, and I need to keep her someplace I know is safe."

Blowing out a chestful of uncertainties, I rest my forehead on Rooster's back. His coat is warm from his body heat, and the scent of him—of hay and dust and sweat—is so comforting I can almost pretend I'm back home if I squeeze my eyes closed hard enough.

"Have you been up to the third floor yet?" Tony asks. "They can tell you more about Kansas."

"Not yet. I found Ava the minute I woke up, saw you in the cafeteria, and you know the rest. But I will."

"I spent a couple of hours in there yesterday."

Bracing myself, I stare at Tony. "And?"

He spits again, glancing around the lot. "It's not good, Knox."

"That's why you're so reluctant to go with us."

He nods. "That's definitely part of it. I don't want to risk what I don't have to. Not yet." We stand in silence, both of us petting Rooster as our thoughts consume us.

"There is no such thing as normal anymore, is there?" I peer up at the gray sky that looks like it might burst at any moment and consider what lies beyond Guymon. But as my list of worrisome thoughts grows longer, I push them aside. My head aches enough as it is. For now, we're all okay. And that Tony is here . . . it's more than I could've dared to wish for at the moment.

"Come on," Tony says, in tune with me, like always. "I'll show you around."

I nod when a thought occurs to me. "Actually—I need your help with something. It's for Ava." Because we *do* deserve a break, and I'm not sure when we might get another one.

"Sure."

I turn around and stop. A child is standing directly behind me, looking at me expectantly.

"Harper," I drawl in greeting.

Her gaze shifts from me to Tony and back again. "Ava said you'd introduce me to your horses."

"I'm actually about to go—"

"I'm going to be a veterinarian," Harper explains, cutting me off. "So, it's for science."

Tony chokes on a laugh. "If it's for science, Knox," he titters, "you can't say no." I look at him and a shit-eating grin fills his face. Tony dips his chin at Harper. "Knox is *definitely* your guy. He knows *all* the things about horses." He ignores my glare and crosses his arms over his chest with a smirk. I don't mind kids, but I'm not particularly comfortable around them either. Tony, on the other hand, loves them . . . and loves torturing me, apparently.

"So," Harper says, stepping closer. Her eyes don't leave me. "Are you going to introduce me to them, or what?"

FORTY-THREE
AVA

MY STOMACH RUMBLES AS KNOX LEADS ME UP THE STAIRS TO the second floor. My appetite snuck up on me after spending the morning with Malia, and the afternoon with Knox, getting more familiar with our shotgun and pistol. Then, I learned proper defensive strikes with Annabel, one of the military personnel. That the sergeant took the time to help me when she could have been resting or eating or spending time with her daughter—pretty much anything other than working with me—earned her daughter access to the majestic horses in the back during brushing and feeding time. Harper was there, too, showing her how it was *properly* done, of course.

I glance longingly over the rail at the people in the cafeteria below, plating for dinner. "What are we doing, exactly?" I ask again. I notice a few open doors as we walk down the hall. Each room is teeming with belongings—sleeping bags on the floors, luggage and toiletries cluttering the bunks and desktops, and stacked on top of lockers. The dorms are like cement shoeboxes, especially those without a window. Obviously built for practicality, not comfort.

"Welcome home," Knox says when we stop at room 44-B.

I stare at him, more confused than anything.

"It beats sleeping in the hospital bed again, no?" Without ceremony, Knox pushes the door open and steps aside. Glowing light pours into the hall, and I gasp, an unstoppable smile engulfing my face.

A blanket is spread out on the floor, and a cardboard box and a coffee flask are situated off to one side. A pillar candle flickers on the desk, as does another one on the table beside the double bed, and a bundle of sunflowers in a red solo cup are illuminated beside it. Country music plays so low I can barely hear it; I can't even tell where it's coming from.

"Knox . . ." My gaze sweeps the room again. "You did all this?" My hunger is entirely forgotten as I meet his gaze. His gold-flecked irises twinkle in the flickering light, and a small, bashful smile tugs at his lips. "I had some help," he admits, ushering me inside. The candle flames tremble in the breeze as he closes the door behind us, and shadows dance across the room.

"All of this is for me?" It's a dumb question, but my heart is pounding—so full of emotion I can barely think straight. Even my pack is in here, nestled between the wall and the desk.

"I thought an actual date was long overdue," he whispers in my ear. "And you wanted to escape from everything for a while . . . This was the best I could come up with." He shrugs like it's no big deal. Meanwhile, my heart melts for this man. I've been in domination mode all day, thinking about how I can conquer my fears, my anxiety, and everything in-between. A moment to breathe *and* relax and simply be with Knox is the best date or gift he could've given me.

"It's perfect," I whisper, my voice tight and my chest

swelling with adoration. I brush a soft kiss against his lips. That I can do that now is still borderline surreal, giving me the best type of butterflies. "Thank you."

Knox looks at me with what I can only describe as satisfaction. "I'm glad you like it."

"I love it."

His gaze drifts to my mouth again like he might kiss me back, when my stomach rumbles, loud enough that our eyes widen and we both stare down at my stomach.

Knox chuckles. "Let's get you fed, shall we?"

Before he can move, I grab his shirt. "I'm going to change first. Give me a minute?"

He nods, and flashing Knox a giddy smile, I kiss his lips again, find my night clothes and toiletries in my pack, and head down the hall to the locker room we passed.

I make swift work of undressing, and after piling my hair on top of my head, I jump in the shower and rinse the day off as quickly as I can. I'm barely dry before I tug my leggings on and an old t-shirt, then head back to our room.

When I get to 44-B, I pause in the doorway, unable to resist another smile. Knox is in his sweats and a worn Bennett Family Ranch t-shirt, sitting on the floor with his back against the bed frame, his legs stretched out and ankles crossed in front of him on the blanket like he owns the joint. Only sheets cover the mattress. Our pillows, blankets, and sleeping bags are on the floor in a nest of padding.

Tossing my dirty clothes and accessory bag by my pack, I plop down beside Knox on the blanket. The last time we sat this close—on the floor only a foot apart—it ended with us in bed together, Knox and I lost in the heat of the moment. Lost in each other. I can only hope tonight ends the same.

He takes a sip from his water bottle.

"You're popping my cherry again," I muse.

Knox sputters and his eyes shoot to me. "Wow." He chuckles. "Go me."

I grin. "No one has ever taken me on a date like this."

"No—" He gestures around our cement quarters. "I imagine they haven't."

Grinning, I bump his shoulder. "I'm serious. Our date has only just begun, and it's already the best date ever." I lean in and kiss his cheek.

"Already making moves, Hernandez?" he says huskily. "I haven't even gotten you liquored up yet." His smirk makes my insides melt all over again. It's boyish somehow, and it makes my stomach flutter. Not with lust or because of the sexual tension that always builds between us. But because I like Knox more than he could possibly know, and right now, he's mine.

"I'm afraid it's not very fancy," he says, uncapping the coffee flask with a shrug. "But it's the best we got." He pours the contents into a cup and hands it to me.

Lifting it to my nose, I sniff the tannic scent of wine.

"You seem to be a lightweight when it comes to wine, and last time, that ended well for me, so I figured—"

My head falls back and I burst into laughter. "You're such a dork."

He chuckles and holds out his cup. "Cheers to our first real date." And with a wink, says, "I hope I don't screw it up."

Grinning, I tap my cup to his, and we take a sip. I watch him over the brim. He watches me. We swallow and lick our lips, and his eyes crinkle as he reaches for the box. The air is different—it's charged with something new and unfamiliar. Maybe because this moment between us is intentional when the rest were stolen amid tragedy and chaos. Maybe it's because of what has already happened, and the way Knox's jaw twitches, I think he must feel it too.

"We've had a really long couple days," he muses. "I wanted to spend tonight with you—just us." *Before something else happens.* He doesn't say the last part, but I know what he means. I feel the same way, like we're trying to outrun the hound of misfortune that's always at our backs.

"I'm only bummed I didn't think of it first," I confess.

Knox lifts a shoulder like it's no big deal and rubs his hands together. "Okay—time for grub before something with fangs crawls out of that stomach of yours." Knox opens the makeshift picnic basket. "We've got turkey clubs on a French roll," he says, pulling out two plastic-wrapped halves. "Egg salad. Fruit snacks. Two individual bags of jalapeño kettle chips and a slice of carrot cake."

My eyes bulge. "Carrot cake? That's . . . my favorite." I eye him skeptically.

Knox winks at me. "I actually can't take credit for that part. Tony knew, somehow. Just like he knew where I could find sunflowers for you."

"Tony?" I cover the giddy laugh that sneaks its way out. "You two are dangerous together."

"Tell me about it. We got into far too much trouble our senior year. My dad told me we could no longer be friends, which I ignored, obviously. He was worried I wouldn't graduate."

I watch Knox from the corner of my eye, realizing his mother's death likely had something to do with his rebellion.

"What?" Knox's fingers freeze in the plastic wrap.

"Nothing." I smile wider. "I was just thinking how glad I am that Tony's here and he's okay. And that you never stopped being his friend."

Knox exhales a deep breath. "Me too. It doesn't seem

real, if I'm honest." His eyes lose focus for a second, then he smiles at me and hands me my sandwich. "For you." When Knox's half is unwrapped, we tap sandwiches and take our first bite.

The lettuce crunches, and I don't think Swiss cheese and mustard ever tasted so good. "I'm starving," I admit through a mouthful of food. "Just ignore all the moaning. Okay?"

His eyebrow quirks and a salacious grin lifts his stubbled cheeks. "One can only hope."

I elbow him, worried I might choke if I allow myself to laugh. "You know what I meant." I wipe the corner of my mouth and take another bite.

We eat between our laughter and companionable silence, the low music emanating from a small speaker on the desk, cushioning any awkwardness. It's one thing for Knox and me to have slept together or fought for our lives together. But it's the quiet moments like this that feel the most intimate. The most important.

Knox makes a face when he eats a fruit snack, unim-pressed as it sticks to his teeth. "Here." He hands his packet over to me and I gladly accept. "So, how did it go today after I left you with Malia?" Knox opens his chip bag.

I steal one of his kettle chips before answering. "Fine. She said the blood panel results won't be ready until tomorrow, but she gave me some breathing exercises to practice when I start to feel wound up. She did tell me something I think you'll appreciate," I confess. "She said I should practice talking about things more to expel the negative, pent-up energy. That way, I'm not stewing in all the things weighing me down twenty-four seven."

Knox looks knowingly at me. "Maybe I should be a doctor."

"Ha! You and Harper could open a practice together." I wink at him.

"But seriously," Knox says, licking his lips. "I agree."

"Do you now," I drawl, eyeing him skeptically as he shoves another chip into his mouth. Manly, stoic Knox who likes to pretend he's unaffected by everything for my sake, even if I know how difficult all this has been for him. Especially with the added burden of worrying about me. "It's a two-way street, you know? Just because you don't have anxiety attacks or whatever doesn't mean you shouldn't share your burdens with me, too. You've said it a dozen times— we're in this together."

Knox studies the chip in his hand more carefully than is necessary before popping it into his mouth.

"See?" I can't help my smirk. "It's not easy to be vulnerable."

"I'll do it," he says, his gaze finally shifting to me. He tilts his head. "If you do, I will." This time, when his eyes linger on mine, they are filled with a silent promise and maybe even a plea. There's no humor or machismo, and I believe him.

"It's a deal, then."

"Good."

"Great," I counter, then take a gulp of water from my bottle, completely forgetting about my wine. "Maybe we should have a code word."

"A code word for stress?" Knox's shoulders lift with a chuckle. "It better be something good because we'll be saying it *all* day."

"Wait—" I glance around. "Where's Lucy?"

Knox scoffs. "Lucy who?" He shakes his head with a sigh. "Now that Tony's back, she barely cares about me anymore."

"I highly doubt that's true."

Knox shrugs and balls up our garbage to put back in our food box. "I think it's time," he says, lifting out the carrot cake. "Now, do you mind sharing, or do I need to go down and get my own piece?"

Playfully, I roll my eyes. "I guess I can share."

"You guess?" Knox chuckles again, and the sound soothes my fluttering nerves. He has never been as sexy as he is now, his handsome smile growing, his laughter filling the room.

I shrug. "I'm sort of full, so—"

"So otherwise, you would've told me to screw off and find my own piece—"

I grab his t-shirt and tug his mouth to mine to shut him up. He tastes like fruit snacks and smells like Old Spice deodorant, and all my lady bits perk to attention as I breathe him in.

I don't know when this man became all that matters to me, but I'm struck with the realization that, last night, I might've lost him, and that thought is so devastating I kiss Knox harder. Deeper. I grip his shirt tighter and inhale him until he floods my mind, my chest, and makes my heart swell so much it aches.

"Ava?" Knox pulls away. His gaze shifts anxiously over my face, his lips parted as he catches his breath. "Are you okay?"

I search his eyes for a center of gravity as my heartbeat trips and stumbles, but Malia's advice is what fills my head. Instead of bottling up or suppressing my feelings, I exhale and give them a voice before I chicken out and shove them away to dwell on later. "I could have lost you," I whisper.

The lines in his crumpled brow deepen, and Knox swallows, regret filling his eyes.

"Your fall," I explain. "Being locked in that room. And when I saw the van, I thought my only choice was to give myself over or lead them to you." I shake my head. "Of all the people I've lost, you—" My throat closes. My eyes burn. "I don't want to do *any* of this without you."

Knox's nostrils flare, and he brushes my hair off my forehead. "And I'm going to do everything I can to ensure you don't have to." His words are earnest, his gaze imploring, and before I can respond, Knox's mouth covers mine. His lips are soft, but his kiss is urgent, his tongue greedily seeking mine.

Hot chills travel over every inch of my body down to my toes, and I groan. *This*, I think, *is perfection.*

"Knox . . ." I breathe his name, wrapping my arms around his neck, careful of the back of his head.

Grabbing my hips, he pulls me onto his lap, his fingers pressing into my backside as I straddle him and settle against his erection. We both groan, and cupping his jaw in my hands, I lower my forehead to his and breathe his name again. *I have loved you for as long as I can remember,* I want to say. *When you looked at me at church and when you stopped to help me. When I saw you around town with your friends— even when I thought you hated me.*

We stare into each other's eyes, our noses touching, and Knox's breath caresses my cheeks with each exhale. Instead of telling him any of that, though, I show him how much he affects me instead.

I roll my hips into his, soft fabric all that's between his center and mine. I move my hips again and again without breaking eye contact, more feverishly until Knox squeezes his eyes shut, and his head falls back. "Fuck. Me."

I claim his lips, swallowing his groan as I move faster, intending to do just that. I tease him until his breaths are so ragged I think he might come, and stop. I admire the way his Adam's apple bobs with another gasp of breath. "Why—"

"Don't move," I whisper, and rising to my feet, I pull my shirt off and fling it to the side. Knox drags his teeth over his upper lip as I roll my leggings off. His hand goes to his erection, and he squeezes it through his sweatpants. His gaze rakes down my body, from my face to my naked breasts, then the curves of my hips as I pull one foot free and then the other.

Knox's jaw ticks, only it's not unease that's got him wound so tight this time. "God, you're so beautiful, Ava." His gaze is fire and his words are as terrifying as they are emboldening. With a bashful smile, I lower myself to straddle his lap again. Knox grabs my hips. His eyes dilate. His chest rises and falls with each uneven breath, but I make him wait.

Holding Knox's gaze, I lift the hem of his shirt over his head and study every toned inch of his chest and shoulders. I admire his virility and strength and the way his muscles twitch as my hands skim over his body.

"You're beautiful, too," I murmur, and leaning in, I brush a kiss over his mouth. It's featherlight and my tongue teases the seam of his lips. My hands roam down his stomach, over his taut skin, trailing a line to his waistband.

Knox's breath hitches, he gulps, and my fingers slide beneath the elastic. Lifting onto my knees, I free him from his sweats and lower myself over his length, basking in the rightness of Knox Bennett filling every inch of me.

"Holy fuck." His voice is guttural, raw, and I can't help but moan with pleasure.

Knox splays his hands on my hips, pressing into my skin as I move against him. Slow and steady, up and down. Rolling my hips as my entire body burns for him.

We're breathless.

Our skin slickens, and my thigh muscles burn.

Knox curses again, and as he claims my breast with his mouth, I gasp and every nerve ending ignites. Wildfire ripples through my blood, so consuming my body trembles, and Knox takes over.

He lays me on my back and we move together—a ritual of worship and a joining of souls as we lose ourselves to the rhythmic sound of drumming heartbeats and abandon. The country music croons in the background. Knox rasps my name. And there is no moment stronger than this. No closer we could ever be. And I revel in the delirium that I have my person for as long as the universe will let me.

FORTY-FOUR
KNOX

OUR ROOM IS DARK, AND AVA BREATHES DEEPLY IN SLEEP. Her hair tickles my nose as she nestles into my arm, and I cherish the moment. Unsure when I'll get to hold her like this again, I squeeze her tighter against me.

Unspoken or not, last night we made a promise to one another that it would be us against whatever comes next, and yet, my path leads away from here. Away from safety and farther into the unknown, which is the last place either of us wants to go. As much as I want to keep my promise, I can't stay here wondering who might be waiting for me in Ransom —it would eat me alive. At the same time, asking Ava to go with me puts her in more danger.

I stare a hole through the wall, suddenly too restless and slightly claustrophobic in a cement shoebox without windows. I press a kiss to Ava's temple and gently pull my arm from under her.

She stirs, rolling over so her back is facing me, mumbling.

"What's that?" I whisper, kissing the soft skin of her shoulder.

"Is it time to get up?"

"No." I can barely see her outline in the darkness, but I tuck the blanket around her, willing her to rest. "It's still early. Go back to sleep."

She nestles deeper into the blankets. "Where are you going?"

"I need a shower."

Ava groans. "Sounds like so much work."

I bite back a chuckle as I sit up. Feeling around for the table lamp, I flick it on, blinking as I take in what looks like a war zone in our room. Our clothes and picnic remnants are scattered across the floor, our mostly untouched wine cups and the half-eaten carrot cake discarded on the desk.

Scrubbing my hands over my face, I climb to my feet, tug on my sweats, and grab fresh clothes. I'm not sure how I know it's dawn. Maybe it's my internal clock and the not-so-long-ago routine of livestock to feed and chores to do at sunrise. Tucking my bathroom bag under my arm, I switch off the light and escape the room.

The industrial sconces lining the walls dimly light the way, and I ignore the cold floor on my bare feet. All the dorms are still closed, and the clock above the bulletin board reads a quarter to six. No one is idle in this place, so it's only a matter of time before the facility is teeming with life, and I take advantage of the quiet.

The locker room door creaks as I push it, echoing off the tile and cement. The pungent scent of damp towels mixed with floral shampoo and air freshener hits my nose first. Then the overhead lights flicker when I step inside, reflecting in the row of mirrors above the sinks across from me, causing momentary blindness.

Six shower stalls are partitioned by neck-high walls lining one side of the room, and lockers line the opposite. I bypass the offshoot to the toilets and head straight for the bench at the lockers, making a mental checklist of the questions I need answers to today.

What does the facility know about Kansas?

Is it safe to travel there directly, and are the roads drivable?

I discard my things on one of the benches, grab a towel from the marked closet, and pull off my sweats before heading to the closest shower stall. There are Recycled Water signs, which makes sense for a place like this, and as I step under the lukewarm spray, I hope that means there are other facilities like this all over the country. That this isn't our one and only option.

I turn the water temperature higher and let it run over me, basking in the glory of it. Being warm and clean is a salve on any worry, and I allow optimism to nudge its way in. We're so lucky to be here—things are looking up.

Plus, Elijah said many civilians have already left, which might make it easier to find a vehicle I can take to Kansas—something that was left behind. I could drive ahead solo and check it out, then come back for Ava.

The locker room door creaks open, and I glance over the wall, smiling instantly. "You missed me that much?"

Ava groans. "Your body is like a furnace." She drags her feet over to the bench and drops her bag onto the floor. "It's impossible not to." I use the body wash from the dispenser on the wall and suds up, grateful I don't have to use the stash of soap I brought yet.

Ava mutters as she adjusts the water temperature in the stall beside me. She shrieks and prances in place, and even if I can only see the ridiculous expressions she makes, it's enough to ruin me, and I wonder if I'll ever think of showers without remembering the way her nose crinkles like that again.

"Are you going to tell me?" she asks, stepping under the water as it washes over her hair.

I scrub my head, closing my eyes as I wash the soap away. "Tell you what?"

"What's on your mind."

I smile to myself. "How do you know there's something on my mind?"

"Knox, we agreed," she chides.

I meet her gaze over the cement partition. "You think you know me so well?"

She gives me her arched eyebrow, no nonsense expression and I look away.

"So?" she prompts. Closing her eyes, she tilts her head back beneath the spray.

"So," I start, "I was thinking that after we go to the comms room, I might see if I can get a vehicle to drive to Ransom, check things out. It should only be about three hours from here, if the roads are decent."

Ava snorts. "*Only*?" She looks at me as she rubs shampoo into her hair. The suds drip down her cheek. Ava has never looked so comfortable in her own skin, or so normal, even if we're in an industrial locker room in a facility filled with evacuees. "One hour could be a day's worth of travel these days," she continues. "And you're not going ahead without me."

"Ava—"

"Knox," she growls back.

I have to smile to myself because she's stubborn, if nothing else. "Okay."

Her eyebrow lifts before she dips her head under the spray again. "Try as you might," she says, wiping the water from her face. "You can't get rid of me that easily, Knox Bennett." Ava smirks at me, water dripping from her nose and lashes.

I smile. Not only because having Ava with me makes me the most content I've ever been, but it feels good to have someone who would go up to bat for me like I know Ava would. She'd do more than that, she'd scratch their eyes out, jump on their back—she'd even knock an old lady out to save my horse if she had to.

"Good," I say, shutting off my water. "I wouldn't have it any other way."

FORTY-FIVE
AVA

Kɴᴏx ᴀɴᴅ I ꜰɪɴɪsʜ ʙʀᴇᴀᴋꜰᴀsᴛ, ᴀɴᴅ ᴀꜰᴛᴇʀ ᴄᴏᴍᴘʟᴇᴛɪɴɢ another night shift for Malia, Elijah takes us to the third floor to meet the team responsible for keeping this place running and, beyond that, ensuring our safety.

"Kevin Montgomery is the facility director," Elijah explains as we reach the landing. "He was a lead researcher at one point, but now he's running this place—or rather, he's the one everyone goes to for direction." Elijah glances over his shoulder at us. "Things have a way of changing quickly around here, as I'm sure you can imagine."

"It wouldn't be a normal day if it didn't," Knox mutters. We meet each other's gaze and follow Elijah through the double doors he opens with a key card. As we enter a two-level comms room, my steps falter.

A map of the United States stretches the length of the room, to my left. Throughout the rest of the level, there isn't an inch of wall or window that isn't covered by a map, flip chart, or a whiteboard. A metal supply closet is open, ravaged, and looking bare. The labyrinth of desks weaving throughout the space is cluttered with coffee mugs, stacks of file folders, and paperwork. Even the computer screens are busy with digital countdowns, moving graphics, and blinking notifications. The entire room feels chaotic, and yet, other than intermittent beeping and the garbled static on a radio, I only see four staff on the upper landing, moving languidly around as if it's just another day.

"This is the night crew," Elijah explains, nodding to a man who walks by us with an empty coffee cup. I'm surprised he doesn't look more harried than the rest of us.

Elijah scans the room with a frown. "I thought Kevin would—"

The door opens behind us, and we glance back. A middle-aged black man, bald with a salt-and-pepper goatee and glasses, stops in his tracks. I study his wrinkled, army green uniform as he looks between the three of us. His brown eyes widen slightly. "Visitors," he muses, eyes shifting to Elijah expectantly.

"This is Knox and Ava. They came in two nights ago from Sutton County, Texas."

Kevin's brow furrows at the mention of Texas and he studies the both of us more closely. "Then you two have been through a lot to get here." He takes Knox's hand for a firm shake. Then mine. "Welcome to Facility 38. Currently your one-stop shop during the apocalypse."

Elijah snorts a laugh and drains the last of his coffee. "On that note, I'll leave you to it."

"Thanks," Knox murmurs, and Elijah throws up a wave before stepping out of the room.

We both look at Kevin. He takes another sip from his mug and exhales when he looks at us again. "Well then. If you're up here, that means you're one of the few visitors actually *trying* to leave."

"Hopefully," Knox says dryly. "We've been through hell to get here, so it seems dumb to move on, but . . ."

"But you have family you're trying to get to," Kevin supplies. "And I'm going out on a limb, but I take it we don't have anything on the whiteboard downstairs about it, so you're hoping for some good news."

"Yes, actually," Knox says. "We're headed to Kansas. We have horses, so we don't technically need transport, though if the roads are okay, a truck and trailer would be helpful. And to know what we're up against."

"Horses?" Kevin bobs his head, looking pleasantly surprised. "That's a first."

"For me too," I mutter.

The corner of Kevin's mouth lifts, and he waves for us to follow him to the landing. Knox is hot on his heels, but I linger behind, stepping closer to the wall-sized map of the fifty states. Every capital is starred and noted with a dry-erase marker. What I assume are research facilities are each marked by their number, and every single state has a letter written on it in a different color. Red. Orange. Black. Blue. Green. Pink. Some states have three or four letters.

"State of emergency," a young woman says as she stops beside me. Her blonde hair is frizzy and gathered at the nape of her neck, and there's an ink stain on her white shirt. "Each color and letter is the level and type of threat." She fingers the tea bag in her cup then points to Texas. "In some cases, they indicate which states have gone dark."

Bile rises up my throat as I note a red F, an orange V, and a green E are partially covered by black Xs. I don't know why it triggers me because I know how bad Texas is; I've seen it —lived through it. But seeing each county crossed out like a bad omen is one of the most unsettling things I've seen yet.

Like the state is gone forever; there's no hope and whoever is left there is not getting a rescue.

But Texas isn't the only one. I stare at New Mexico, then California, Louisiana, and Florida.

"The letter is the type of emergency. The red F is for fires," the woman explains. "The Ws are for the floods. E for earthquakes—"

"V is for volcanoes," I guess, noting one written on Texas, New Mexico, and Wyoming.

The woman hums in agreement. "Don't get me wrong," she says. "That doesn't mean there aren't people living there still or that there aren't survivors in those states, but not enough to make them viable. The terrain is too unsteady, and we have to focus our resources as much as possible since they are limited. The entire nation is in a state of emergency at this point."

I nod, but I'm only half processing what she's saying as I take in hundreds of colors and letters scattered across the map. Every single state is suffering from Mother Nature's wrath.

"Plus," the woman continues, "there has been no official communication with them or their facilities in at least thirty-six hours or more. The entire continent is waiting with bated breath to see which regions will be left standing."

I stare at the map, but my eyes glaze over. The years leading up to this, the days, feel like a lifetime ago, and yet it was only last week that I was worried about paying my bills and Mavey's next visit from hospice.

"This isn't real," I murmur, running my finger over San Antonio, which is no longer a city but a hole in the earth.

"I keep telling myself that too," the woman muses. She finally looks at me. "I'm Kylee, by the way." She offers me her hand.

"Ava."

Kylee glances at the map. "Where is it you're running from?"

I point to Texas, and she looks at me, sobering a little. "I'm glad you made it out." She gives me a taciturn smile and glances at her desk. "I've got to wrap things up before I can get some sleep, but I hope you find whatever you're looking for, Ava."

"Thanks." Kylee walks back to her desk, stopping to pick up a rogue dry-erase marker on the floor along the way. She tosses it on the desk beside hers and sits down, setting her mug aside and cracking her neck before she begins clicking around on her computer screen.

"—got seismic activity coming out of my ears."

I peer up at the landing. Knox and Kevin are staring at a giant computer screen among many lining the wall.

With a final glance at the giant map of doom, I join them.

Kevin looks between us as I stop at Knox's side. "Where is it you're trying to go, exactly?"

Knox crosses his arms over his chest as he studies the map with pulsating red, yellow, and orange circles on the computer screen. "Ransom."

Kevin shakes his head. "I'm not familiar with it."

"It's north of Dodge City."

Kevin's eyes brighten. "You might get some luck, then, depending on your friends' setup. Most of Kansas and the Midwest have experienced increased tornado activity but otherwise are relatively unchanged, all things considered. That being said, it's too early to know what the winter months will bring."

"I saw California on the whiteboard," Knox says, his voice an octave lower.

Kevin must note the emotion in his voice, so he treads

carefully. "It's flooded. So is half of Mexico and most of the East Coast." He moves two stations over and wiggles the wireless mouse. He clicks on a moving graph on the computer screen. A different, colorful view of the country pops up, and after clicking a few boxes, it filters out all the areas that aren't flooded throughout the United States.

"The West Coast was hit hard by the Ring of Fire," Kevin explains. "And the rest of us—especially in the areas with the most seismic activity—have had the most extreme upsets. The eruptions, the lightning, and the lack of sun are changing weather patterns everywhere. But with the ash clouds and wildfire smoke drifting north, it's been difficult to gauge what's a temporary side effect and what our new reality will be. Technically, though, Kansas should be okay. And we haven't lost contact with them yet, which is as good of a sign as you could hope for."

I watch Knox's expression closely. He's restless to get to Kansas and see how his aunt and uncle are holding up, but I know a part of him is torn, too.

"So, you think it's okay to head that way?" I clarify. "Based on what you currently know, I mean."

Kevin takes a deep breath and shoves his hands in his pockets. "Look, I'm in no position to give any travel advice with how unstable things are right now. Anything is possible, but I'll be real with you both." Kevin and Knox lock eyes. "As of three a.m. this morning, we've exceeded capacity here. We've got the equipment for surveying and monitoring and only enough supplies to last us another two weeks at the rate we're going with this many people. That's why finding a place to send people is now a top priority. If we can't find somewhere soon, there won't be much we can offer you here either." He points to a relatively open area on the map with only a few markings. "We're waiting to hear news about a larger facility in Tennessee, hopefully within the next day or two, and we can start busing people there."

Kevin looks at me. "All that is to say, if you have a place to go—if you have family still—it might be worth the risk to head that way because it's only a matter of time before you'll have to leave anyway, and it's gonna be soon."

Knox stares at a screen mounted on the wall, his eyes watching the live meter I've noticed jump a few times in the five minutes we've been standing here.

"Are those tremors?" I ask.

Kevin follows my gaze. "Yep."

"Hey, Kev?" Kylee waves him over. She's got a satellite phone pressed to her ear. "I've got Tennessee on the line."

He holds up a finger to Kylee, his eyes shifting between me and Knox. "There's still a Kansas facility that's open and running, and they might be able to help you if something comes up. But it's in Wichita." He purses his lips. "Regardless, if you decide to leave and need anything, let Hanoford know in the processing office."

I frown. "Processing office?"

"Well, the sign actually says Finance Office, but that was last week." With a shake of his head, Kevin heads for Kylee. "Hanoford can help you," he calls again. "Good luck."

Within moments, Kevin is back in boss mode, and Knox and I are left to our chaotic thoughts, staring at the overwhelming amount of information coming in and out of this room.

"It's all a gamble," I realize aloud, and shoving my hands in my back pockets, I turn to Knox, appraising his pensive expression as he stares at the screen. "But at least we know what we might be up against now." The hum of the room grows louder in his silence. "Shall we find Hanoford?"

Knox's jaw tenses before he drags his attention from the

monitor to me, and his expression softens ever so slightly. "It's decided, then?"

I tilt my head. "We have a ranch to get to. It's only three hours away, you know?" I repeat his words from earlier with a wink. "Who knows, maybe we'll be there in time for dinner."

FORTY-SIX
KNOX

"I DON'T KNOW HOW I FEEL ABOUT THE CLUTCH," AVA mutters from the driver's seat. She winces as the gears grind for the dozenth time, and I'm finding it more amusing than I probably should.

"You wanted to learn," I remind her.

"Yeah, well, you made it look so easy. But this—" She shifts into third gear and the '88 Dodge Ram lurches. "Mechanics everywhere are rolling over in their graves."

I laugh and lean back in the passenger seat. The old 4x4 groans a bit, but as long as it hauls the trailer and gets us to Ransom within the next couple of hours, I won't complain.

Ava's eyes flash to the rearview mirror. I know she can't see anything but the horse trailer, but I appreciate her attempt to survey our surroundings. "Thank God the owner won't be needing his stuff back. I can't guarantee the transmission's condition by the time I'm done with it."

Grinning, I shake my head. "That's not really how it works, and you're being too hard on yourself. Everyone has to start somewhere. It was the same for me when I learned to drive the old tractor. You, on the other hand . . . Well—" I huff. "You get a crash course on how to drive *and* shift a manual all in one week. And ride a horse," I add, but I stop my thoughts from trailing there. The list of firsts we've had in the last nine days—good and bad—is endless.

"Lucky me." Ava looks at me from the corner of her eye, but her smirk makes me smile.

"Lucky *me*," I correct. "It's highly entertaining."

Ava heaves out a breath and refocuses on the road. "I just want to be helpful when we get to your uncle's." She locks her arms in place and stretches her back. We've been on the road for an hour, even if she's only been driving for half of it. Between driving against the wind and exiting the on and off ramps, she's had her work cut out for her. "I don't want to be another mouth to feed without something to contribute, you know?"

"What are you worried about? With your toxic positivity" —I reach for her arm and playfully squeeze her muscles— "and your brute strength . . ."

Ava snorts and slaps my hand away. "You're right. You're entirely too amused by all of this." Ava sighs, sobering a little. "What if they don't like me? What if your dad has filled them with poison about me over the years, or they are already worried about supplies? Then I show up and—" Ava bites her inner cheek, refocusing on the road ahead.

"First, Mason is *nothing* like my father," I promise her. "And my dad told us to go there. Besides, Mason was the wild child. The brother who went to college and traveled a little and wanted to live his own life. Not inherit the family business. He's like Kellen was, actually." The thought is saddening, but I continue. "And second, my father would not have ever mentioned you to my aunt and uncle because he barely talked to them."

Ava glances at me, skeptical.

"Mason tried to help out after my mom died," I explain. "And my father was too stubborn to let him. The last time I saw my uncle was at my mom's funeral. He and my father had a fight, and Mason and Beth left." As the past sneaks back up on me, I shake it away. "It went from Kellen and I staying with them for two weeks every summer growing up to never seeing them at all."

I crack my neck and watch the mile markers as we pass. The truth is, our mom was the one who sent us to Mason's for two weeks every year, to get away from the ranch and have fun—so we could be kids and get dirty in a way that wasn't from chores and ranch work. My dad might have imploded when we lost my mom, but he'd always been a hard-ass. A workaholic.

I feel Ava's gaze on me in my silence, but I stare at the open fields that stretch ahead, at the cows grazing in some of the pastures. It reminds me of home.

"Is that why he moved to Kansas?" Ava asks, her voice nearly too soft to hear against the truck's rumbling engine. "Because of the fight?"

"No. They'd moved out there years prior, when Beth's mother passed and her father couldn't keep the place up on his own. He'd built what was probably considered an empire fifty years ago," I explain. "Her parents were hardcore preppers. Her father was in the war and swore the day would come when society would break, and it would be every man for himself. It only amplified after Gerty. I remember the giant tins of grains and powdered foods that lined the shelves in the guest bedroom closet. The dried beans and rice. I thought it was hilarious at the time." I huff a bitter laugh. "It's not so funny anymore." Shaking my head, I mutter about what an ignorant kid I was.

"Then I was too," Ava says. "We all were. We've been

warned about this our entire lives, but it made no difference. Now look at us."

"Yeah . . ." I snap a string from my shirt and peer out the side window. "Now look at us."

Ava and I drive in silence for a few minutes. I glance in the back of the truck to make sure Lucy is still hunkered down and peer out the window again.

"It was nice of Hanoford to help us get a vehicle," Ava says. She wipes a sweaty palm on her thighs. "He could've just let us ride all this way since that was our plan. Even if this is nerve-racking, it's better than dragging this journey out another two days."

"I guess abandoned vehicles are one perk in all of this."

"Maybe the company, too," she counters. Ava winks at me, making my chest warm and my pulse quicken a little, and we fall into a companionable silence again. Ava finally starts to relax until the horses move, torquing the trailer. The whole truck shifts and her eyes fly to the rearview mirror as she grips hold of the steering wheel to steady us.

"It's fine," I say calmly. "They're just restless." I watch Rooster's head move in the side mirror. With open roads and no fissures to speak of this far north, we only have to hang tight for a couple more hours.

"So," Ava drawls, "this is what Kismet, Kansas looks like, huh?"

I peer around the open fields—each one the same but with a barn or silo slightly different from the last. "I guess so."

"I'll take it over Sweetwater," Ava grumbles. "Or Amarillo or Cactus." Leaning forward, she peers up at the dark sky. "Those storm clouds look slightly terrifying, though."

"Looks like it might rain again," I say absently, checking the horses in the mirror once more. Rooster seems to have mellowed, which makes me feel better, but I make it a point to glance back occasionally, just in case. "How is your anxiety?" I glance at Ava, gauging her response. It's been on my mind since her blood test results came back. Malia said her hormone and vitamin levels were off kilter, but it was nothing unfixable.

Ava pats her backpack on the floor between us. "Having those GABA tablets help, but they'll only last so long."

"You'll let me know, right? When you starting feeling . . . off?"

Ava's mouth quirks at the corner and she glances at me. "I promise."

Swallowing thickly, I nod because all I can do is trust that she will, and I stare out the window again.

We drive for another stretch in silence before I find myself snooping through the truck to see what I can find. A flashlight in the door that doesn't work, along with a rusted bottle opener. I open the glove box and find unused napkins, a faded parking pass from the Guymon Gunshow, an old truck manual, and . . . "Wow, look at this." I hold up a cassette tape. I've only ever seen one in the movies.

"Is that what I think it is?"

"Yep." I squint, trying to read the writing scraped off the side. "Eye of . . . the tiger. Ha!" I grin. "You've got to be kidding me." I flip the cassette over and meet Ava's quizzical gaze. "Written and sung by Survivor."

Her brow lifts. "Well, that's ironic." She glances out the window. "Do you know who that is?"

"No idea, but let's find out. Shall we?" I push the cassette into the player on the dash. At first, the tape sounds like screeching gears, but quickly turns into the quick strum of a guitar, followed by the punch of the drums. It's upbeat, a little edgy, and exactly what we need right now.

We drive another hour, barely talking as we listen to the

single a handful of times before Ava makes me shut it off. I watch one sign after another pass us by. More fields. A couple of small towns. We drive through a blip on the map called Plains, and by the time we get to Dodge City, the sky looks like it's about to rain hellfire on us, but we keep driving. With only an hour to go and nightfall approaching, I can tell Ava is as determined to get to Ransom as I am.

The trailer jerks behind us, and as the truck swerves slightly again, Ava grips the steering wheel tighter with a curse—even Lucy sits up in the back of the truck to see what the ruckus is all about. I peer back as Rooster yanks his head up. I can't see Loca, but with as much as the trailer is moving, they are both getting more restless than I'm comfortable with. "We should pull over."

Biting her lip as she downshifts, Ava pulls over in concentration. "You think there's something wrong?"

I shake my head. "I don't know, but I've taken them on drives longer than this."

"Great," she mutters, and the moment the truck stops, I open the door. The wind is lukewarm but sends chills down my back as I slam the door shut and make my way to the trailer. Thunder rumbles somewhere in the distance, and this time, I shiver. Rooster whinnies, pawing hoof against the metal. "Easy," I croon, unlatching the door. "What's gotten into you?" His head shoots up. Rooster's eyes are wide and blinking at me, his ears perked in my direction. "You need to stretch your legs already, or what?"

But as I let the door swing open, I have my answer. I *feel* the color drain from my face. "You've got to be shitting me."

"What is it? Are they—" Ava stops short beside me. We stand a heartbeat in silence. "Harper?"

The little girl's eyes are wide with a mixture of what looks a lot like fear for her life and fear that she's been caught. She's flat against the wall in the back of the trailer, her backpack on the horse blanket bunched under her feet.

"They were fine," she squeaks. "Something spooked them. It wasn't me. I promise."

"You shouldn't even *be* in here," I growl, quickly untying Loca.

Ava stares hard at me as I lead my mare down the ramp.

"Harper," Ava starts, her voice firm but far softer than mine. "What are you doing in the horse trailer? Don't you know how dangerous that is?"

"You said there was a farm where you were going."

I huff. "That's your response?" I don't look at either of them as I untie Rooster and lead him out next. I welcome the wind, because I'm not only livid, my stomach knots, and I feel sick imagining what could have happened to Harper had we not stopped. "This is unbelievable," I mutter, stepping back into the trailer.

Ava crouches in front of Harper. "Everyone will be worried about you."

Even if the girl isn't crying, it's obvious she's second-guessing her decision to sneak aboard. *Good.* But as angry as I am, my insides twist a little as she wipes a silent, stray tear off her cheek. "But . . . I left Jenny a note."

"Oh, well, in that case," I grumble.

"Knox, you're not helping," Ava chides.

I cross my arms over my chest, inhaling a deep, calming breath as I glance up at the roof of the trailer, praying to all the gods everywhere to give me patience.

"I won't get in your way. I can help with the horses and the other animals." Harper's eyes shift between us.

"It's not about the animals, Harper. You have people—"

"The other kids don't like me." Harper's eyes narrow with indignation, even as her voice trembles.

"Harper," Ava sighs, "I'm sure that's not true."

"Yes it is. Grant and Becky are brother and sister and only play with each other, and Jenny only cares about Theo because she's his mom. They don't care about me." Now, her chin is trembling, and I have to look away.

Ava sighs again and rises to her feet. "Stay here, Harper," she mutters, then nods for me to follow her around the trailer.

The instant we're out of earshot, Ava's shoulders slump and she rakes her fingers over her head and through her pony-tail. "What do we do?" Her hair catches in the wind, whipping her in the face, but Ava barely seems to notice. "We're so close. I hate to turn around, but—" She shrugs. "I don't know."

My jaw ticks as I consider which is the least of two evils. We could turn around now and be back in Guymon within a couple of hours, then start out again tomorrow. Or, we could finish the trek to Ransom, scope things out, rest, and make the drive back tomorrow. There's the questionable fuel situation in Kansas to consider as well, and I shake my head. "We turn back, or this is going to turn into a—"

"Knox—"

"Bigger ordeal and drag out for days—"

"Knox!" Ava punches my arm, and I look behind me just as she says, "Is that a funnel cloud?"

My heart might actually stop as a funnel cloud snakes its way into formation, touching down half a mile in front of us.

"Shit."

FORTY-SEVEN
AVA

I'VE ONLY EXPERIENCED ONE TORNADO IN SONORA, AND IT was a baby from what I remember—it barely rattled the walls or cracked the windows. I've never seen one touch down before; the movement and way the clouds circulate are as petrifying as they are mesmerizing.

"We can't outrun it," Knox says, frantically searching our surroundings for another option. "Definitely not with the trailer." His eyes widen and he turns me around. "There—" He points to a loft barn across an acre of pasture. He's already sprinting to our bags in the back of the truck. "We'll ditch them if they slow us down too much."

I heave mine onto my back. "We can ride the horses. It'll be—"

Knox shakes his head. "The barbed wire." He calls Lucy as I stare at the field, registering the fence for the first time. My heart hammers faster. There's no way the horses can get over that unscathed.

Knox rushes to the trailer ramp where Harper stands, gaping at the tornado forming down the road with terrified, round eyes.

"Start running," Knox calls over the intensifying wind. He unties Rooster and smacks him on the butt. "Get!"

"What are you doing?" Harper shrieks.

I run into the trailer for a saddle blanket.

"They're safer on their own," Knox shouts. "Now, go! Follow Ava!"

Harper collects her things in the trailer as I grab her arm. "Come on." Taking Harper's hand, we sprint off the road toward the fence. The wind roars more than howls as the funnel moves closer, but the sky is so dark I can't work up the nerve to see how close it's getting behind me.

Come on, Knox. I silently urge him to hurry as I lay the horse blanket over the barbed wire.

I toss Harper's backpack over the fence and motion to her. "Up!" Holding her waist, I help her over the wobbly wire fence. "Run!" I shout, pointing to the barn when her feet hit the ground. I toss my pack over the fence next. "Go as fast as you can, Harper! Don't stop!" My hair tugs from my pony-tail, whipping me in the face, and I know the terror in Harper's expression mimics my own. But Harper has a steely look in her eyes—a determination I wish I had right now—and she nods, turns, and sprints on her little legs across the pasture.

"Knox!" When I look back, the tornado is close enough I can see a storm cloud of debris thickening around it. Loca and Rooster are halfway down the road, running in the opposite direction.

"Let's go!" Knox and Lucy are right behind me.

Lucy crawls underneath the fence and hesitates on the other side as Knox helps me over. My flannel sleeve catches on a barb, throwing me off balance, and I grab the wire to hold myself upright on instinct. I feel the sting and dampness of blood, but I don't stop as I stumble ungraciously to the other side.

I take Knox's pack as he climbs over, and once his feet hit the ground, we run. The cows pace restlessly around the pasture because, like the horses always seem to, they know what's coming.

Lightning snaps through the sky, and I can feel the twister moving closer. In a matter of minutes, we might be dead, and I'm not sure I've ever been this scared before. Not when Lars was aiming his gun at me. Not when the old woman locked me in that room with her dead husband. Because this is nature, and it's relentless and unpredictable, emotionless, and far more terrifying. My pack weighs me down more and more by the second, but I won't ditch it yet—it's everything I have left. My lungs burn. My legs feel like Jell-O, but the barn is so close I force them to move faster.

"We can make it!" Knox shouts.

The wind is so loud and violent I feel it vibrating through me, making my eyes water.

Harper struggles to open the barn door as it rattles on its hinges, and she frantically glances back at us. Knox practically falls into it, lifts the heavy, rusted latch and tears the door open. Lucy and Harper run inside and Knox takes my hand, pulling me into the barn behind him.

Harper slams the door behind us, and I spin around, helping Knox with the latch as I see the whirling monstrosity through the window, tearing at the northern fields, headed in our direction.

"I think it will miss us!" Knox shouts.

Lucy barks, and Harper's fear catches up with her and she starts to cry.

"The stalls!" I shout, taking Harper's hand. We scramble to the empty feed stalls fortified with wood panels, hoping an extra layer between us and the tornado will keep us safer from debris.

Harper and I fall to our knees and huddle into the corner, and all I can think is if the twister only grazes us, we might stand a chance.

Knox crouches down, straining with Lucy in his arms. Harper latches onto the dog for dear life and Knox and I sit on either side of them, our bodies the final shield and defense.

"It will be okay!" Knox shouts, his eyes meeting Harper's first, then mine. I see his fear, but as always, he's determined to survive this.

I nod, and my heartbeat is drowned out as the wind rages around us so loud it's deafening.

It gnashes at the siding. The walls of the barn flex as the roof creaks and hay whirls around the interior. The tools on the walls clank and clatter as some of them fall from their hooks, and debris, and what looks like hail through the windows, pelts the building, shattering the glass.

Wind funnels through the barn, so violent it burns my face and eyes. I can barely see Knox, but his gaze is on me. It's focused, and somehow, even in physical pain and paralyzing fear, it calms me. Resting his forehead to mine, Knox wraps his arms tighter around the huddle, and I do the same, folding in as we brace ourselves.

Squeezing my eyes shut, I wonder if this is it. After everything, this is how it ends—Knox, me, and a little orphan girl. Even if it's the most terrifying experience of my life, Knox is here, and I clutch onto him tighter, waiting for the end to come.

FORTY-EIGHT
KNOX

THE WORLD IS QUIET, DAMP AND GLISTENING IN THE YELLOW hue of the setting sun. It's been over an hour, and I'm still running on adrenaline, still wound tight and on edge, but I can't shut it off as I survey the pastures.

The power lines snap and sway in the lingering breeze, and the north-facing fence is gone. The cattle are too, likely to have scattered the instant they could flee. The trees are standing, but most of their branches are strewn across the field with wood panels and a glinting road sign in the mix.

The tractor is still here, just like the truck and trailer that rolled farther down the road. I imagine what few supplies we had in the back are in the next state over by now, and I stare at the trailer. The trailer we no longer need because my horses are gone. Safe, I presume, but gone nonetheless, and though I know I should be thankful we're alive, my heart still breaks a little.

Lucy whimpers at my side. "I know," I murmur, reaching down to scratch her head. She hasn't moved since she finally ventured out of her hiding place in the barn.

Clearing my throat, I scan the property again. I can't stop

searching the sky for signs of another storm. Another obstacle standing between us and Kansas.

"How is there such a beautiful sunset after what just happened?" Ava says, walking up behind me. There's awe in her voice as she admires the golds and oranges, and she loops her arm through mine. "Harper finally calmed down," she whispers. "We should stay here tonight."

I glance over my shoulder at the rascal, curled on a bed of hay with Ava's sleeping bag over her. She picks idly at the straw, her eyes glazed over from crying. Her thoughts seem faraway.

"We need to decide what we're going to do next," she continues. "Harper still doesn't want to go back, but we can't keep her with us." Ava pauses a moment. "Can we?"

My eyes dart to her, incredulous. "Do you *want* to?" My heart starts thudding all over again, but for an entirely different reason this time.

Ava blinks at me. "I mean, I don't know." She shrugs. "The poor thing doesn't really have anyone to go back to. Not really. The last thing we need is a child to worry about, but . . ."

"But," I parrot, needing to know what justification she has to remotely consider this.

I don't like the way Ava studies me or that contemplative look in her eyes. "But maybe she would be better off with us."

I don't know whether to groan or curse. "We're not keeping her."

Ava's expression hardens. "She's not another dog, Knox."

I nearly laugh. "I know, she's a fucking kid, Ava." Her nostrils flare with indignation. "You don't think it's hard enough with the two of us already? We nearly died in a tornado five minutes ago." I try not to raise my voice because

I don't want Harper to overhear, but after all we've been through, I'm gobsmacked Ava would be willing to take on a kid on top of everything else. "We have nothing to offer her —no home or—"

"Neither does anyone back at the facility," she counters.

I shake my head. "You're not thinking clearly."

"And you're just scared," she bites back.

"Hell yes I am, Ava. Jesus—" I point into the barn. "That kid wouldn't be in a sobbing heap on a barn floor right now if she was back in Guymon."

"Her name is Harper," Ava says coolly.

"No," I say, ignoring her. "We can't keep a child. Harper's safer with her friends—"

"She might be safer there for now, but she isn't happy. And she doesn't have friends, Knox. Why do you think she ran away in the first place?"

"Because she's a curious kid who gets into trouble."

"It's more than that, and you know it. If she felt like she belonged with those kids, she would have spent her time with them, not off on her own, pretending to be your doctor and a veterinarian."

"She's a ward of the state and now a damn runaway."

"Which state?" Ava asks tersely, her jaw set. "New Mexico, where her grandma's place no longer exists? Nevada, where her mother was arrested for researcher kidnappings?"

I swallow thickly.

"Screw the laws and rules—they couldn't protect us before all of this, and they sure as hell can't protect us or dictate anything now."

My frown deepens.

"Don't look at me like that, Knox. You know it's true. It's not like Elijah and Jenny will think we kidnapped her. If anything, they know where we're going, and if they really want to, they can come get her."

I've never seen Ava so vehement, and as much as I know Harper is a lost little girl, I'm having a hard time grasping how any of this is a good idea.

I stare at Ava, really looking at her. Her rapid breaths. Her fixed stare and pursed lips. Her arms crossed over her chest. This is about more than Harper.

Ava lifts her eyebrow. Even if she *sounds* decided, there's uncertainty in her eyes—uncertainty and desperation.

"This is about you," I realize. "You empathize with her."

She throws her arms up. "Of course I do! This world *sucks,* Knox, and I know what it's like to feel alone in it. She has no one who cares about her, not really."

"And in the two days you've known her, you care enough to look after her *forever*?"

That gives her pause, but only a heartbeat before she stubbornly lifts her chin. "I'd rather try to help Harper than send her back, wondering for the rest of my life what happened to her—if she did something else reckless—and feeling guilty that I didn't do more."

I stare into the inky sky, exasperated and so tired it almost aches to breathe.

"Knox," Ava says more carefully, "can you honestly say that if we took Harper back, you wouldn't wonder what happened to her or if she ran away again? If she was safe wherever she ends up? Because you know as well as I do they're getting people out of Guymon soon, one way or another."

"I'm not a complete asshole." I run my hand over my face. "It's not that I don't want to help her, but we can't. We barely know her. We don't even know what we'll find in Ransom." I turn to face her fully. "Look, I wish this was all easier and I *could* help her. I'm just saying I am not a father. You and I—we're barely—" I stop gesturing between us because nothing between Ava and I is textbook, and I'm certain I'm going to regret whatever comes out next if the look on her face is anything to go by. "I'm barely holding *myself* together as it is. That's all I'm saying."

Ava's eyes soften and she seems to deflate a little. Our heightened emotions fizzle into an awkward void as she averts her gaze, and we just stand there for a moment, staring at the darkening horizon. I get that Ava feels responsible for this girl, but her bleeding heart is blinding her to our very unstable reality.

"You're right," she finally says, tucking her loose hair behind her ear. "I don't know what I was thinking." She stares inside the barn and turns away from me.

I should be relieved Ava finally agrees, but an unexpected twinge of guilt and disappointment needle through my certainty instead.

"Hey, Knox?"

I glance at Ava in the doorway.

"I'm sorry about Loca and Rooster. I know that was hard for you."

Another sharp pang tightens in my chest, and I am so tired of it all, I don't know what to do anymore. "Thanks."

She walks away from me smaller than she was before, and it reminds me of how it used to be between us, the air tenuous and cold. As always, it's my doing, and as much as I hate it, I don't think I can bear one more burden. Not when I have no idea what is coming next.

I walk the perimeter with Lucy for a while in the darkness. I have my flashlight, but I don't use it. I've memorized the path I've worn around the barn while considering what daybreak will bring. Certainly, more tears from Harper. Maybe the cold shoulder from Ava. The longer I turn the idea over, the more it dawns on me what this little girl really means to her.

Ava is a caregiver—it's all she's known. If she wasn't raising herself and her uncle, she was caring for Mavey. So, as surprising as her hell-bent determination is, I can understand it too. She wants to help the girl, and I can't begrudge her that.

I talk myself in and out of what to do as I check on the truck, telling myself I need to be the voice of reason in this, and when I'm tired of thinking and ready to sleep, Lucy and I make our way to the barn. Since all our supplies were gone from the back of the truck as expected, we not only go back empty-handed, but I brace myself for glares and cold shoulders.

The door is partially cracked open.

"—I had jerky or something in here." I pause when I hear them murmuring and peer inside. The barn is dark save for the halo of lantern light surrounding the girls. A couple of gnats flit around the light, and the draft that whistles through the barn catches wayward strands of their hair as it passes.

Ava's crouched at her bag against the wall, searching for something in her pack. Her hand is freshly bandaged from her barbed wire wound.

I'm about to step inside, out of the wind, when Harper holds a granola bar out to Ava. "You can have mine." She's cross-legged on the hay beside her with her backpack.

Ava's face crumples, but she quickly catches herself and smiles. "You keep it for when you're hungry. I'll be fine."

Harper shrugs and sets the mangled bar between them.

"It's okay. I always hide extra snacks in my bag, just in case." The wrapping has seen better days, like it's been in there for a while.

"How about," Ava says, picking it up, "we share? That way, you can save the rest of your stash for when you really need it."

Harper considers her proposal and nods. "Good idea. I hate being hungry," she murmurs, and my heartstrings tug more than I care to admit.

"Me too," Ava whispers, and she sits down beside Harper and breaks off a piece. I swallow thickly. "Thank you for sharing with me. My stomach gets angry when it's empty."

Harper smiles. "Mine too. Sometimes I scare myself."

Ava chuckles and breaks off another piece. Harper resituates herself on the sleeping bag to face Ava better, and winces. Leaning forward, Harper pulls the arrowhead I've seen her with from her pocket and tucks it into her backpack.

"That's a pretty arrowhead. Where did you get it?"

Harper pulls it out of her pack again and hands it to Ava. "Officer Swiftwater gave it to me last year when my grandma died. He said it holds all of my worries so that I don't have to. So I can be brave."

A small smile pulls at Ava's lips. "You *are* very brave," she murmurs. "So, I think it's working."

Harper's eyes gleam with pride, making my eyes sting.

Shoving the arrowhead back into her backpack, Harper pulls out a tiny flashlight, a stuffed duck, and a bruised apple.

Ava tilts her head. "It might be time to get rid of that."

Harper nods, staring at it with a wrinkled nose. "I don't really like apples."

"Then why do you have one in your pack?"

"Because—" Harper licks her lips. "Because my grandma

told me it's rude not to keep things people give you. I didn't want to tell Malia I don't like them."

"Here—" Ava holds out her hand. "I know who will eat it." Harper blinks at her but hands the apple over. "Tomorrow, if we see the cattle, we'll leave it for one of them. How's that?"

Harper's cheek lifts in a half smile, and she bobs her head with a nod. "Or the horses."

"Or the horses," Ava says wistfully, and the knot in my chest balls tighter.

Harper pulls a roll of clothes, mittens, and two pairs of socks from her pack and sets them beside her before reaching in for a notebook and colored pens.

Ava offers her the last pieces of the granola bar, but Harper shakes her head. "You can have it. You're bigger than I am." Opening her notebook and turning to a blank page, Harper starts writing.

"Drawing something?" Ava balls the wrapper up and pulls out her water bottle.

"It's a note," Harper explains. "Well, more like a card."

"A card?"

"For Knox."

My shoulders stiffen, and I'm suddenly aware I'm spying on them and that if either of them looked my way, they'd know it.

"That's nice of you."

I glance down at Lucy to find her staring up at me, judging.

"Well, he did save us. I figure it's the least I can do. Wait —" My gaze darts up. "How do you spell his name?"

"It's an X, even though it sounds like a CKS," Ava explains, pointing to the notebook, and Harper continues writing.

"You know, he'll really like that, Harper. That's a very nice gesture."

Harper shrugs. "Maybe he won't hate me if I say thank you. And he won't be mad anymore about me sneaking into the trailer."

Hate her. Jesus. I pick at a splinter in the doorframe, swallowing thickly. This kid is gutting me, and she doesn't even know it.

"Knox doesn't hate you, Harper. He was worried about you getting hurt by the horses and surprised to see you. That's all."

Harper holds her mouth just right in concentration. "I heard you guys fighting."

Staring up at the ceiling, Ava takes a deep breath. "We weren't fighting," she lies, and she scoots back against the wall. "He wants you to be safe. And he's not sure the two of us can guarantee that you will be."

"There is no safe place," Harper whispers.

Impatient, Lucy walks into the barn, giving us away. My face heats a little and I step fully inside. I feel the shift in the mood instantly and shut the door behind me.

I clear my throat. "It will be cold tonight." My voice is louder than I mean it to be, and I feel my ears redden as Ava's eyes linger on me. "The wind hasn't let up. I'll cover the—" Burlap is already tucked around the broken windowpanes.

"Harper and I took care of it," Ava says. Her voice isn't cold so much as subdued. Maybe she's exhausted like me, or maybe she's still upset, but the tension between the three of us is there nonetheless.

Thankfully, Lucy sidles up to Harper for attention and the disquiet in the barn dissolves. Lucy is the focal point as they lavish her with affection, and if I didn't love my dog so much, I'd be jealous.

I grab my pack by the wall and pull out a bag of jerky. "Have at it," I say, tossing it between the girls.

"Thank you," Ava says, and she offers Harper a piece.

I crouch on the stretched out sleeping bag beside Harper and unclip my own. Each time I move, so does Harper, like she's trying to keep me from seeing her notebook. When I realize she's staring at me, I meet her gaze. "Are you going to sit down?" she asks.

I pull a flannel shirt from my pack. "In a minute." I lift a skeptical brow. "Why?"

Harper shrugs. "Nothing you need to worry about." She refocuses on her card, and I bite back a grin as I zip my bag shut.

"Here." I hand the shirt to Harper since she doesn't have a jacket. "Your long-sleeve shirt won't keep you warm tonight. You can sleep in this."

Harper's brow twitches with confusion before reaching for it a bit reluctantly. "What about you?" Her deep blue, curious eyes glint in the lantern light.

"I'll be fine." I set my pack off to the side and pull my beanie over my head to keep my ears warm. Suddenly, my muscles ache, and I'm not even sure why. I just know I need sleep if I'm going to get through tomorrow, whatever it brings.

Ava must have the same idea I do because she maneuvers things in her pack to use for a pillow, and I unzip my sleeping bag.

"In case I fall asleep," Ava starts, moving the lantern closer to Harper, "turn this dial off when you're finished, okay?" Ava stretches out on the other side of her. "And crawl under here to stay warm with me."

Harper nods, intent on the page in front of her.

I guess that answers that. Ava is sleeping over there, so I

guess that means Harper will sleep between us tonight. I don't take it personally since Harper will be warmer that way, but I can't help but wonder if that's the only reason.

Scooting closer, I lay the sleeping bag out over Ava's for extra warmth, take out my pocketknife and my wallet, which is likely obsolete at this point, toss them on the ground next to me, then stretch out where I am. Using my folded arms as a pillow, I watch Ava get settled in across from me.

I know we're bound to have differences of opinion, but I don't want it to change things between us, not when she's the only person keeping me sane. I silently plead for her to look at me. To reassure me that whatever tomorrow brings, she and I will be okay. We will still *be* a we. Still be us. Even if she's mad at me.

I finally exhale when Ava's eyes meet mine across the four feet between us that might as well be a mile. But her gaze is softer this time, almost apologetic, and she mouths a "good night" to me as the draft whistles through the barn.

"Night," I whisper, and the rasp of Harper's pen and the crinkle of paper becomes a distant melody as I fall asleep.

FORTY-NINE
KNOX

I WAKE WITH A SHIVER TO THE BLUE DAWN FILTERING through the poorly covered windows. I rub my eyes and blink the world into focus. A folded piece of paper sits by my head, and it takes me a few seconds to grasp what it is. Rising on my elbow, I glance around the quiet barn. Ava and Harper are asleep, huddled together under the sleeping bag. Lucy is curled up by me, the flannel I gave Harper covering her.

I look at the card again.

For Knocksx.

I flip it open to find a drawing of two horses next to a letter.

I am sorry I sneaked away and made you mad. Thank you for saving me from the tornadow, and I am sorry you had to let your horses go. I do not want to go back to Jenny. But it is okay if you want me to. From Harper.

Tugging my beanie off, I run my hand over my face. I'm not awake enough for this yet. I rake my hand through my hair with a sigh and look back at the girls again. Harper did as Ava asked. She shut the lantern off and moved it aside.

Damn this kid. I stare at Harper, folded into a little ball with her stuffed duck as her pillow, and try to swallow the lump in my throat. Her mitten-covered hands are clasped under her chin and her beanie is pulled down so far I can't see her eyes. Fully clothed and under the sleeping bags with Ava, Harper is scrunched up like she's still cold. *And she gave the extra shirt to my dog.* I know at that moment that I'm a goner.

Resigned to the fact we'll have a little girl with us for the rest of our trip—maybe forever—I get to my feet as quietly as I can manage. My body is stiff from sleeping on the cold ground, but I have to piss like a racehorse, so there's no time to dawdle.

Horses. Another painful realization stirs the rest of the morning fog from my senses, but I push it away and snatch my pocket knife and wallet from the floor.

Lucy lifts her head, but she doesn't follow as I slip outside with the creak of the door.

The morning is cool, the wind still rustling what's left of the leaves on the oak trees in the pasture, but the sun peeks through the clouds, a sight that makes me feel instantly lighter. My bladder screams at me to pick a damn tree, and I round the corner of the barn and hurry about my business.

Toothpaste. I need toothpaste and water. A hot shower. And what I wouldn't give for a cup of freshly brewed coffee. I groan, fleetingly lamenting the morning routines that no longer exist.

I zip up, forcing myself away from the rabbit hole of self-pity and wishing things were different, and head back in for my water bottle, toothbrush, and the promise of a fresh mouth.

I glance at the straggling cattle who have meandered their way back into the vicinity and think of Harper's apple. An amused huff escapes me as I really look at the cattle, and I freeze when I see buckskin coloring in a group of black cowhides.

"Loca?" I can barely believe it as I stride closer, scanning the pasture for Rooster. I grin so wide my cheeks hurt when I spot him grazing away from the herd over by the water trough. It's the thickest patch of grass, of course. "Son of a bitch," I mutter.

His head snaps up as he chews his breakfast, and tears fill my eyes. Not only because they are alive but because they came back, a part of my past that isn't gone, leaving me with only a painful memory.

Rooster walks over, his tail swishing and his head bobbing in excitement. "You devil, you," I say, patting the side of his sorrel neck. Never one to snub affection, Loca ambles over too, her ears shifting between me and the rustling by the barn.

"They came back?" I can hear the smile in Ava's voice.

"Yay!" Harper runs closer. "Oh!" She stops and looks wide-eyed at Ava. "The apple!" She disappears into the barn again.

"Hey, girl," Ava coos, rubbing Loca's nose. The mare leans in and rubs her head against Ava.

"Here!" Harper chirps. She reappears with the beat-up apple from last night, Lucy trotting at her heels. *Traitor.*

I can't stop smiling, though, as the horses assess the sudden chaos surrounding them. Lucy sniffs Rooster. A curious cow inches closer.

Harper holds up the apple, her nose pink in the chilly

morning, and suddenly, her smile falters and she frowns. As both horses move closer, she drops her hand, taking a step back. "I only have one."

"Here—" I hold my hand out. "May I?"

Harper hands me the apple, and I pull my knife from my pocket and carefully cut the apple in half. "There. Problem solved."

Harper's grin returns.

"Remember what I showed you at the facility." I hold out my palm flat. "Feed them like this."

Harper's eyes widen with a mixture of excitement and maybe a little bit of fear, and holding her breath, she lifts a palm out to each horse, grimacing as if she's only hoping for the best. I watch the horses closely, trusting them to be gentle, but her hand is much smaller than they are used to.

"It tickles." Harper giggles, and in the blink of an eye, the battered apple is crunched to nothing and gone. Harper wipes her palms on her pants, and I grab hold of Rooster's halter, then Loca's, realizing the day just got a hell of a lot brighter. "Well, then," I start. "If everyone's here, we should load up before something else happens between here and Ransom."

Ava's smile twitches, and her brow lifts a little. "Ransom?"

Harper looks at me, confused.

"I figure we're too close to turn back now. We'll figure everything else out later." I wink at her, and Harper's freckled cheeks lift. I don't think she even realizes she's smiling from ear to ear as she straightens.

"I'll get my backpack!" She runs for the barn, shouting something excitedly at Lucy, who lopes after her.

I can feel Ava's eyes on me and have to force myself to look at her because I know what I'm going to find. She's smirking, her amber eyes glittering in the morning sunlight.

"It was the card that did you in, wasn't it?" She nods, so self-satisfied I could kiss her.

"Meh." I shrug. "That was only the icing on the cake," I admit, and whatever reservations I still have are overshadowed by the beaming smile on Ava's face, the relief in her eyes, and the sound of Lucy barking and Harper laughing in the barn.

For as shitty as life is, right now, everything feels pretty right.

FIFTY
AVA

THE DRIVE TO RANSOM FEELS LONGER THAN IT IS. HARPER sits between us on the bench seat, Knox at the wheel this time. The horses are loaded in the trailer, and Lucy holds her head to the wind in the bed of the truck, like nothing has happened. And best of all, there aren't many clouds in the sky. That means no smoke or tornados, at least for now, and a much-needed reprieve.

Flat land stretches as far as the eye can see, the landscape in areas riddled with debris. The fields that are still intact alter between corn and wheat. Some are unkempt, some still tended to by the looks of it, but many are decimated. Phone poles are uprooted, fences are torn up, gone, or mangled, and scars mar the earth, just as they did in Texas, only these are wind-made and carved by tornadoes.

The anticipation of whatever awaits us has hiked my anxiety up a few notches, but Harper's constant chatter helps distract me. We started our drive with a game of I Spy and a hopeful, anticipatory charge in the air, which has since downgraded to silence in the cab of the truck and a thick apprehension about what happens next.

Malia was right. There's something freeing in telling Knox when I feel strange, like earlier when we got back on the road. Giving it voice makes it feel like the burden isn't all mine, and I've been able to breathe a little easier. His frequent glances of reassurance help too.

Knox leans forward, downshifting as a telephone pole blocking the road comes into focus.

"That's . . . big," Harper says, and Knox slowly drives around it, onto the dusty shoulder.

"Let's hope they are all that easy," he mutters, and we continue in more silence. If people were still living here, wouldn't they have cleared the road? Then again, as we pass an overturned car on the shoulder a quarter mile down, I decide they have more urgent things to worry about.

"Kevin said it's still viable to live here," I remind us out loud, in case Knox is worried about his uncle's place. The debris scattered along the road is a near-constant reminder that we don't exactly know the state of things.

"It's Tornado Alley," Knox says with a shrug. He veers around snapped branches on the shoulder. "It might be worse than it once was, but people here are used to this, at least to a certain degree. Most people have storm cellars here."

We drive by what's left of a farmhouse and then an old warehouse and toppled water tower that looks like it was picked up and tossed across a pasture. We pass another house set back at the edge of a wheat field that's unscathed, but the building on the lot next to it is nothing but crumbled bricks and debris.

"A horse!" Harper points to a man riding a horse down a dirt road off in the distance, and then we pass a pasture of sheep.

"What do we have here?" Knox mutters. The windshield of an approaching car glints in the sunlight, and Knox slows the truck as it gets closer. It's a golf cart on steroids, not a car, and it pulls to a stop, idling loudly beside us. An older man with tanned, wrinkly skin, a scraggly gray beard, and hair poking out from under a John Deere ball cap peers inside the cab of the truck.

Knox rolls his window down and dips his chin in greeting.

The old man cants his head, glancing between the three of us in the cab. "Mornin'. You folks just passing through?"

"Sort of," Knox says, scanning the horizon. "I'm here to check on some family."

"Whereabouts?" He combs his gnarled fingers through his beard.

"Just outside of Ransom."

The man's face falls a little, but he shrugs. "I wish I had better news, but as you can see, we've had our share of storms lately. We've had two tornadoes in as many days. Ness County hasn't had it easy, that's for sure. But some folks have been lucky."

Knox swallows audibly, and I exchange a wary look with Harper, offering her a forced smile of reassurance.

"Who you here to see?" the man continues.

"The Bennetts. Mason and Beth."

The man shakes his head. "'Fraid I don't know 'em, but it's a straight shot from here to Ransom."

"Thank you. Any idea what the fuel situation is around here?"

"There's a station a mile down that is still in service, but outside of that, I'm not sure. Most folks in this area are stocked up or have had to leave. You can have a storm cellar, but rebuilding isn't as easy as it used to be. Folks are friendly, though, as long as you are."

"Understood."

The old man nods. "I've got a burst water pipe and a birthing cow to tend to." He grabs the bill of his ball cap politely. "Good luck."

"Thank you!" I call as he drives away. I watch the man disappear behind the horse trailer, and the sound of his engine grows more distant as he speeds down the road. Only when my neck hurts do I turn forward and realize Knox is staring out the windshield, his hands tightening on the wheel. Harper looks at me and then at Knox again.

"They're okay," I tell him, hoping with every fiber in me that it's true.

He inhales a deep breath and puts the truck into gear. "There's only one way to find out."

We drive for another thirty miles before we see the sign for Ransom, and Knox's eyes linger on it until we're completely past it. "They live a mile outside of town," he explains. I'm not sure if it's worse to drive in anxious silence or to fill the quiet with nervous chit-chat.

"Whatever happens," I say softly, and reaching over Harper, I rest my hand on his thigh to physically remind him he isn't alone. "We're together. We can get through it—whatever it is."

The column of his neck moves with a thick swallow, and his eyes dart to me. They are sad already, like he's bracing himself for the worst. "I know." Reaching forward, Knox pushes the cassette into the tape deck. "Eye of the Tiger" starts playing, and despite how tired I am of this song, I'm glad there's something other than dread to fill the silence. After the first riff, Harper taps her thighs with the beat of the music like she knows it.

Knox and I stare at her, but Harper is oblivious as she strains her neck to see out the windshield.

As soon as the slightly garbled male voice starts to sing, Harper hums.

"You know this song?" I ask, dumbfounded.

Harper makes a duck face as she shrugs. "It was Larry's favorite."

"Larry, huh?" I glance out the window. "And who is that?"

"He lived next door to my grandma. He would let me hang out with him in his garage when he was working on cars. Larry sang into his beer bottle and pretended he was playing the drums. He said they're underrated."

Knox and I smile at each other. "Who?" he asks. "The band or the drums?"

Harper shrugs again. "I have no idea."

"Well, if you know the words, then you can teach us." Knox smiles at me since we already know the song by heart, having listened to it on repeat from Guymon to Kansas.

"Sure, I can teach you, but it's not about the words," she explains. "It's about the passion." Harper starts beating on her thighs again, her face contorted like she actually knows what she's doing, and I burst out laughing because kid energy is good energy, especially now.

"Yeah?" Knox chuckles. "And what do you know about passion, Harper?"

Her eyes get wide. "I know that the more scrunched up your face is, the more passionate you are. And the more you can *feel* the music."

Her nose scrunches and she pretends she's strumming a guitar, even if I think it's actually an electric keyboard in the background. I look at Knox. "We have much to learn."

"Yeah, we do." Our eyes meet, and gratitude fills his hazel depths. I recognize it because I feel it, too, this new energy with the three of us together.

As the song plays on, Harper gets tired of being passionate and settles in, tapping her fingers sporadically to the beat instead.

My amusement fades as Knox's expression sobers and the truck slows. Knox downshifts and comes to a complete stop at a dirt road turnoff. A small wood sign is etched with Bennett and a road number.

I peer farther down the road, past the open gate to a white, two-story house with a wraparound porch. I can barely see it through the sparse elms.

"It's still standing," Knox rasps. So is the barn and a few sheds. There's even a draft horse and goats in the field. Harper looks between us, but I watch Knox, waiting for him to take the lead.

Harper wiggles in her seat, growing restless.

"The moment of truth," Knox murmurs, but he doesn't move.

FIFTY-ONE
KNOX

My hands are sweating, and it's not because of the Kansas sunshine beating against my skin. My heart is pounding. I should be elated that the farm is here. That the place looks lived in and not abandoned. But all I can wonder is whether my dad or Kellen are here. And *that* is what I've hoped for since the day I saw what little remains of San Francisco. Even if I told myself not to.

"Are we going?" Harper whispers.

I look at her.

Her face contorts a little. "I have to pee."

Ava asks her to be patient a moment longer, but I shake myself out of whatever paralysis starts inching its way in and shift into first. The truck and trailer lurch into motion, like even they are hesitant, but the crunching gravel beneath the tires is a proclamation that we're doing this. It's happening. There's no turning back. In a matter of minutes, I'll have all the answers I've wanted, whether I'm ready for them or not.

I roll the window down for fresh air.

"We're finally here," Ava says, and whether it's the relief

in her voice or the fresh air hitting my face, I feel a sense of peace, too.

A black lab runs down the gravel drive, barking as it trots alongside the truck, tail wagging with barely restrained excitement. Lucy yips in the back, whining as she paces the length of the truck bed. "Stay," I tell her out the window. A newer heavy-duty truck is parked on the side of the house, as well as an ATV and riding mower.

I've barely shut the truck off when the screen door opens. I can only see the outline of someone, but I know my aunt and uncle well enough to assume they've got a gun beside the door if it's not already aimed in our direction.

The door opens farther, and a woman steps onto the porch. I don't expect it, but tears fill my eyes as my aunt steps into the sunlight, her blonde hair braided back, a brown t-shirt tucked into her jeans. She's dirty from hard work, vibrant with life, and as beautiful as ever.

Her entire face softens when she realizes who I am, and I climb out of the truck.

"Knox Bennett!" she squeals. "I prayed you'd come." She meets me in the driveway, looking me up and down in disbelief. "Mason knew you would." With a tearful smile, my aunt pulls me into her, clinging onto me with a stifled sob before she pulls away to stare at me like I might be an apparition. "Thank God he was right. When I heard about the sinkhole and the fires, I tried to call, but—" She stifles another sob and clears her throat. "I'm so happy you're here."

"It's been the longest ten days of my life, but we finally made it." Straightening, I peer around the property and watch the front door. "Where is he?"

My aunt frowns and her face falls. My heart drops as her chin starts to tremble. "Oh, sweetheart." She shakes her head. "I lost him months ago."

"What?" I feel the blood drain from my face. Feel my heart lurch and my knees weaken as I shake my head. "That's —no. Dad would have told me."

She smiles sadly. "His cancer came back. It was fast, though. He didn't suffer long."

My jaw clenches so tight my teeth might crack as the vision of her blurs behind a veil of tears. "Came *back*?" I can barely say the words.

She curses under her breath. "You didn't know." Aunt Beth rubs her temple and shakes her head. "Pancreatic cancer, sweetheart. Two years ago. He was in remission, but—" She stares at me, shaking her head with more rage than sadness. "Those stubborn-ass men," she grits out. "He told me he talked to Mitch, but I knew better than to believe him. Those two have barely talked since, well—" She huffs a breath. "Your mother."

I exhale a long, shaky breath and turn away from her for a modicum of privacy as I process everything. The tightness in my chest eases, but only slightly as memories filter through my mind. Uncle Mason showing me how to fish for the first time at the creek running along the edge of the property. Helping him chop firewood alongside my brother. Our campouts under the stars with s'mores and hot cocoa. Suddenly, my summer memories are as painful as they are precious.

"You've been alone this whole time?" I rasp, turning to face her. The lines around Beth's brown eyes are deeper, but they still gleam with that light she has always emanated—it's what Mason said drew him to her in the first place.

She offers me a small, reassuring smile, sad and resigned as it is. "I grew up on this farm, Knox. And I'll die here. I've been managing just fine." As capable as my aunt is, relief escapes through the crack in her voice, and her eyes shimmer brighter as she wraps her arms around me. "I'm so glad you're here now, though."

I squeeze my eyes shut, holding her tighter. "I take it you haven't heard from anyone else, then," I ask.

With another squeeze, Aunt Beth lets go and takes a step back to look at me. She wipes a stray tear from her cheek. "No one." Her gaze catches on something behind me. "But it looks like you brought company."

The passenger door creaks open, and Ava and Harper murmur as they climb out of the truck.

My aunt smiles instantly.

"Aunt Beth," I croak, clearing what emotion I can from my throat. I readjust my ball cap. "This is Ava—"

"And I'm Harper."

I huff and shake my head, smiling. "And that is Harper," I repeat.

"Well, aren't you two a breath of fresh air? It's one thing to have a strapping young man here, but two more women—it's been a very long time." Ava smiles as Beth pulls her in for a hug, but Harper offers her hand instead.

Aunt Beth's brow raises. "Old school," she muses, shaking Harper's hand. "I like it. It's nice to meet you, Harper. Welcome to our farm. My family settled here three generations ago, and despite my effort to flee, here I am." She takes a deep breath before nostalgia can settle in too deep. "Now—" Beth's gaze sweeps over the three of us, then she notices Lucy in the truck and the horses in the trailer.

"Mind if I let her down?" I ask, eyeing the black lab sniffing around the horse trailer.

"Yes. Yes, please. Shadow is harmless."

"Luce—" I barely say the word, and she jumps over the side of the truck, sniffing her new friend so excitedly her butt wags back and forth.

"So." Aunt Beth looks carefully at me. "How long do I have you for, Knox?" Her question sounds almost fearful, like I might turn around and leave. That my arrival gives her comfort makes all this even more worth it. I can't imagine what she's been through—dealing with my uncle's death only to have to survive the earth tearing to pieces all on her own.

"For as long as you'll have us," I say, realizing the words have never been truer or hurt my heart so much. This farm was our one destination, and we've *finally* made it.

Aunt Beth pulls me in for another hug, and her body shakes with silent sobs. "You don't know how happy I am to hear that."

I embrace her like I would my own mother, soaking in her vitality and warmth. She smells like promise and hope and biscuits, and I squeeze her tighter.

"Um—" Harper squeaks. "I really need to pee."

With a choked laugh, Aunt Beth lets go and wipes more tears from her face. "Well, there's no reason for you to go in the driveway." She puts her hand on Harper's shoulder. "Let's get you to the bathroom, sweetie."

I thumb the tears from my eyes and blow out another shaky breath as I try to collect myself. I'm not ready to feel it all, not yet. Instead, I stare around the property, a list of things to do already forming in my head as I take in the broken barn door and the sagging barbed wire fence.

"We're finally here," Ava whispers. She shakes her head like she can't believe it.

"Finally." It's all I can manage to say because we might've made it, but we're the only ones. No Dad or Kellen. No Uncle Mason.

Ava steps closer and rests her hands on my waist. "You got us here, Knox. You did it. You promised your father you would, and you did." When her voice cracks and her nostrils flare, the tears start dripping down my face again.

I shake my head, unable to speak. I wish I could tell him we're safe. That my dad knew we've made it. That he hadn't died worrying about me.

Ava wraps her arms around my neck and pulls me to her for a hug. She holds me tight, like she's sending me her strength. Turning my face into her neck, I clear my throat. "Thank you." I let my silent tears drip down my face. "I couldn't have done it without you."

"Sure, you could have." She pulls away enough to look at me. "It just wouldn't have been as fun."

I choke on a laugh. "Fun is a word for it." Sniffling, I wipe my nose on my long sleeves, overheating in the afternoon sun.

"And," she says, her voice more incredulous than anything. "We have Harper now, too."

Harper's voice fills the inside of the house, followed by the patter of running feet and barking dogs, and I can't help my smile. "I guess we do, don't we?"

Ava lifts onto her tiptoes, her eyes locked with mine. The longer we look at each other, the more that everything broken seems to soothe a little, and everything scary feels farther away. All I see in her beautiful brown eyes is hope and happiness, and I bask in it for as long as I can before she presses a kiss to my lips.

I melt into her, delirious with relief. The brush of her fingers at the nape of my neck sends shivers over me, and the press of her chest against mine is solid and grounding, and I kiss her deeper.

"Now," she murmurs breathlessly, and as she pulls away, I groan. "It's my turn to pee."

FIFTY-TWO
AVA

I STAND NEXT TO THE FIREPLACE, STOMACH FULL OF cornbread and chili as I stare at photos of Beth and Mason on the wall. I don't know what I expected Mason to look like. Perhaps a younger version of Mitch? He was tall and broad-shouldered—rugged in an understated, stoic way that is consistent with the Bennett men—with the same twinkle in his eyes that I see in Knox sometimes too. A kindness that even his sharp features can't distract me from, with a smile that could light up a room. Somewhere in a fleeting thought, I can hear the timbre of Mason's laugh, and imagine it resounding through the house.

Grinning, I admire the rest of the photos cast in the glow of the setting sun. Beth and Shadow sitting on a tractor together. Mason fishing at a creek with a little Knox and a young man I assume is Kellen. He's tall and leaner than Knox. His hair is much darker, almost black, and his features more angular. I see bits of Mitch in him, but there's a familiar gleam in Kellen's eyes—or perhaps it's the shape of them—that is all Knox. Their mother, I realize. I can barely remember her, but there are splashes of memories that surface. Me on the monkey bars in the schoolyard and her calling her students to form a line. The dresses she always wore and the way her hair escaped her ponytail.

"That was the last time my brother and I came here," Knox says wistfully, and I stir from my thoughts.

"What was he like?" I ask without thinking. I know it's hard for Knox to speak of his brother, but in my sporadic memories, I never see Kellen.

"Serious," he says easily. "A man of few words most of the time. Until he wasn't." Knox snorts and shakes his head. "He internalized a lot of things. I think that's why he left— he'd finally had enough." Knox studies the other pictures on the wall, sighing despite the lifting corner of his mouth. They are good memories, I realize, and I smile too.

"Kellen's twelve years older, so we weren't close growing up, but I always looked up to him. He stood up to our dad when I would cower. He was his own man—never wanted to run the ranch or muck cow shit for the rest of his life. He had a path much different from mine." Knox shrugs. "Kellen was out of college by the time I got to high school, so I never really knew him outside of the house. When I realized what being gay meant and why my dad was so angry, I was more surprised than anything. Kellen *never* wanted to be like my dad, and sometimes I think my dad only resented Kellen for being gay because it made him that much more different. One step further away from the future my dad saw for the ranch. For his sons. Mitch Bennett liked to control things, and the irony of it is, he never could. Not a single thing." Knox runs his hand up the back of his head. "I guess that's why I was mad at Kellen, too. I had an older brother, and it felt like he was never there. He was always running in the other direction."

"I can't imagine what it would have been like for him," I muse.

Knox adjusts the skewed frame. "Me neither," he whispers. The lights flicker, and while it's only a matter of time before we lose power, with the windstorms Beth has been telling us about, that seems like the least of our worries. *"Our sunshine doesn't come without a cost,"* she'd said, because while the near constant wind keeps the ash clouds away, the weather here is anything but stable.

Knox nods to the mantel clock. "It's time."

"I'm clean!" Harper chirps as she runs down the stairs. Her hair is wet, and she has on fresh pajamas. Dread and hope burn a hole in my chest.

Beth comes down just behind her, an apologetic smile on her face. "We're just sneaking down to make some popcorn," she explains, knowing the heaviness of the transmission we're about to make.

"Why do we have to *make* popcorn?" Harper asks, leading the way to the kitchen.

"Because it won't pop itself."

"It actually pops?"

"Yes, and it's fascinating to watch. We grew the kernels ourselves."

As Beth does her best to keep Harper busy in the galley kitchen, Knox and I settle on the couch for our first attempted radio call with Facility 38. *"It's right before their nightly communication with NWA,"* Georgie, a retired Navy vet and Beth's neighbor had explained. *"My contact in Wichita says Guymon should be there."*

Knox ensures the transceiver is on and tunes the console to 162.500, the National Weather Service broadcast frequency. Then he meets my gaze. The fact of the matter is, even if Knox is on board with Harper staying, and Beth loves the laughter of a child in her home, there is no telling what, exactly, Facility 38 is going to say or request we do when we check in with them. We're talking about a living, breathing child, after all, and there's more than ourselves to consider.

This, I think, is what Knox was really worried about. I see the same look in his eyes that was there yesterday when we had this discussion. Apprehension as he considers the possible aftermath. Fear of how sticky the situation is about to get and the difficult decisions we might have to make. And the dread, of course, considering the look on Harper's face if we have to tell her we're taking her back.

I lace my fingers with his free hand, squeezing in reassurance, and Knox clears his throat as he presses the mic. "This is N0KAN calling Facility 38. Is anyone on the air? Over."

Radio silence.

Knox tries again. "This is N0KAN calling Facility 38. Is anyone there? Over."

"N0KAN, this is N5STORM." My heart races at the sound of a familiar voice. "We copy you loud and clear. What's the situation? Over."

"N5STORM, good to hear from you. We made it to Ransom," Knox says. "Over."

There's radio silence again, and then, "Copy that, N0KAN. It's good to hear your voice." Kevin sounds relieved. "What's the situation there? Over."

"N5STORM, Ness County has clear skies but has been hit by massive tornadoes. The locals say it's been chaos in surrounding cities now that food is scarce, with widespread crop damage and disruption of supply chain deliveries. They expect power outages will be next, but most of the citizens remain hunkered down for now. Over."

"Copy that, N0KAN. Please be advised, whatever happens, Tennessee is open. Over."

"Affirmative, N5STORM. And . . . there's more." Knox looks at me and braces himself. "We had a stowaway," he says. "Over."

"Copy that, N0KAN." Kevin's reply is almost immediate. "I heard there was a missing child. Over."

That Kevin seems to have so little to say about it is surprising but gives me hope.

"N5STORM," Knox hedges, "we have no plans of returning to Guymon. Over."

Knox holds my gaze. We blink at each other and my heart pounds with each drawn out moment.

"Roger that, N0KAN. I'll relay the information to the team. Over."

Knox frowns. "N5STORM, is there someone we need to speak to about our situation? Over."

Once again, Kevin's response is immediate. "N0KAN, the first caravan left this morning for Tennessee. By the time you get here, there may be no one to bring her back to. Over."

"Are they saying Jenny already left?" I ask Knox. I don't know if I should be livid that she cared so little about Harper or relieved.

He shifts a perturbed gaze back to the transceiver. "Roger that, N5STORM. Over." Knox shakes his head, glancing at me as he opens his mouth to say something when the radio clicks.

"Hey, Knox?"

His attention snaps to the radio "Tony?" Knox stares at the transceiver in his hand like he's holding his breath.

"You got room for two more?"

A grin engulfs Knox's face. "We could use another good worker," he says, and the smile in his voice is contagious. "We'll keep an eye out for you. Over."

"Roger that, N0KAN," Kevin says this time. "Stay safe out there. Over."

"You do the same, N5STORM." And just like that, all of our fears and apprehension were for nothing. Jenny is gone. The only government we have left is too busy trying to save the world to worry about a little girl who ran away. And now Harper stays with us. Indefinitely. And Tony and his mother are coming this way.

"It couldn't have been that easy," I murmur. There's a moment of hesitation when I'm not sure what else to say or how to feel. This is big. I don't think I knew just how big until now.

For a minute, my entire world stills. The noise and overwhelm and constant tension I've felt each moment since I ran home to Mavey after that first big earthquake at Scott's is vacuumed away, a quiet clarity forming in its place. This is bigger than Harper. It's scarier and far too unknown.

Whatever the future is, it's with Knox, with these people here at a farm I didn't know existed two weeks ago. With Beth, who I met only hours ago, and Harper—a child to care for. A child *we* have to care for, to worry about and raise, and we don't even know how long we'll have power. It's the most insane reality and should be utterly terrifying. But it's not . . . not for me.

Knox huffs an incredulous laugh and rubs his head. "You know this is crazy, right?"

I nod, searching his expression for a sliver of truth; a sign or indication that it's too much for him. That he can't do this, that Knox is not all in, because no one should have to make decisions like this and take on so much in a matter of days. I would totally understand, even if it would break my heart too.

"Yes," I whisper, my voice hoarse. "It's crazy—unbelievable if I think too much about it." I stare down at my hands, at my fingers that tremble a little with emotions too big to shove away. "And scary," I admit.

Knox laces his fingers with mine. "But you're good with this?" he asks, and his eyes shift over my face like he's assessing every nuance of indecision.

"I am," I say easily, realizing how true it is. I feel purpose and direction for the first time in my entire life. "You?"

Knox's brow furrows ever so slightly. "I think," he starts, staring down at our joined hands, "it's a good thing we're used to crazy." When he meets my gaze, there's a smile in his eyes I don't expect. "It wouldn't be a normal day without another life-altering decision to make."

A slightly deranged laugh bubbles out of me and I feel lighter. "True."

Knox stares at me, and the humor in his eyes softens. "I'm glad I get to make them with you."

A lump thickens in my throat. "Yeah?" It's barely a breath.

He dips his chin. "I need all the toxic positivity I can get."

With a smile, I lean in and kiss him. And as the playfulness thickens to something more potent and reassuring, the lump in my throat and the tremble in my hands dissipates.

The floor creaks and Knox and I glance over his shoulder. Harper peeks around the doorjamb in the kitchen, her gaze shifting between where she picks at the wood and us. Whether she understood what we were talking about or not, Harper knew we had to reach out to Guymon, and her dread is palpable.

Beth walks up behind her, resting her hands on Harper's shoulders. I hadn't noticed the scent of popcorn filling the house or both dogs sitting patiently by the dining room table, butts wagging and hoping for a treat from the kitchen.

"Well, kid," Knox says, and both of us stand up. He

sounds cool and collected, but I'm holding my breath, even if I'm not sure why. "It looks like you're stuck with us," he drawls.

Beth sighs with relief, but Harper seems reluctant. "For how long?"

"Forever," he explains. "And ever. You're our family now. Which means," he adds more sternly, "there's no more running away. No more—"

Tears burst from Harper's eyes, and she covers her face with her hands.

"Oh, sweetie." Beth squeezes Harper's shoulders, and I hurry over, my heart so full it hurts to breathe.

"It's okay," I whisper, pulling Harper into me. "You have all of us now. We aren't going anywhere."

She nods, sobbing into my shoulder, and I meet Knox's watery gaze. I can't help my own bleary vision, imagining how different this all could have ended. How this little girl could be lost out in the world and never have found us.

"I swear," Knox croaks, and he runs his hand over his face. "You're all going to be the death of me." He wipes the tears from under his eyes, and I smile, holding Harper tighter. All things considered, that's not a bad way to go.

FIFTY-THREE
AVA
TWO WEEKS LATER

I'VE GROWN SO USED TO THE WINDSTORMS AND THE DISTANT peal of tornado sirens that I struggle to sleep without the howl of the wind or the creak of the roof above my head. Tonight, the cricket songs, beautiful as they are, drift through the upstairs window like an echo in a steel drum. It's warm, and I inhale long and deep before my eyes flutter open. It's nearing dawn, anyway. I can get coffee going and feed the animals before everyone wakes.

Resigned, I roll onto my side. Instead of Knox beside me, the bed is empty, and the covers are hastily drawn. I lift onto my elbow and scan the shadows of our room. He's not standing by the window like he sometimes does on sleepless nights, and our door is cracked open.

Flinging the covers back, I lower my feet to the cool floor, forgoing slippers in the late-summer morning. I reach for one of Knox's flannel shirts draped over the chair by the window and pad out the door.

Harper's room across the hall is quiet, and her door is closed. So is Beth's at the end, and the faint scent of coffee wafting up the stairs makes me smile.

Knox is most definitely awake.

I tiptoe down the steps and through the living room, past Beth's art room and into the kitchen to pour myself a mug of coffee. It's not hot, which means Knox has been up for a while, but it's warm, and we've just gotten our rations from the swap meet yesterday, so it's a morning treat I'll revel in all the same.

My senses spark to life as I take a sip, and I have to cover my mouth so a snort doesn't ricochet through the house. I swallow thickly. Yep, Knox's specialty—strong-ass coffee.

As I pass the wall of pictures, I nod a silent thank you to Mason for providing this safe place for us. Beth's parents thought of nearly everything when they updated the place, and she and Mason did all they could to keep it up since their passing. Because of that, Harper, Knox, and I have a chance as this world around us continues to shift. So do Tony and his mother, Kate.

Supplies and food stores might be hard to come by some weeks, depending on what new upset has triggered whatever turmoil and where, but we're self-reliant here in all ways that matter. Meat and milk and water. A small variety of vegetables grow in the garden, and we've started new sprouts in portable containers in case we have to leave in a hurry. We've enough grain from an abandoned farm to plant wheat in the spring, now that there are more hands to work the land and harvest.

Cracking the screen door open, I peek outside. The motorhome Tony and Kate arrived in is dark and quiet on the side of the house, and Knox sits in one of the chairs on the porch, staring out at the farm. I take another sip of coffee and lean against the doorframe, watching him for a minute.

I'm still learning about Knox—something new every day—but I know he never stops planning. He never stops anticipating and thinking ahead. Not after all we've been through. All of us do that, to some degree. Preparing for what-ifs and bracing ourselves for each new day. Even Harper won't leave the house without ensuring both dogs, the horses, chickens, pigs, goats, and the cattle all have food in their bowls and water in their troughs, just in case we don't make it back to care for them. It's heartbreaking, really, but that's the way of things.

Perhaps Knox is contemplating the winter garden we'll need to plant as soon as autumn hits. Or maybe he's thinking about the canned, pickled, and dehydrated goods we need to rotate from the storm cellar. Or that Kevin reported Montana going dark.

The breeze picks up, and I close Knox's flannel over my camisole and step onto the porch.

He glances over. "Hey, beautiful." His voice is quiet and rough from disuse.

"Hey back," I whisper. I climb into the seat beside him, curling my legs under me. "You're up early." I offer him a sip of my coffee.

"The crickets," he explains, and glancing at his empty mug—probably drained hours ago—Knox takes a long sip of mine.

I smile, leaning my head back as I rock to the sound of the cricket symphony. "Same. It reminds me of Texas when it's quiet here."

He nods, his thumb absently brushing the handle of the mug. "Do you miss it?"

"Sonora?"

He dips his chin.

"No," I whisper. "I don't miss it at all."

Knox's gaze lingers, and he hands my mug back to me. Loca's tail swishes in the paddock, and I consider what she and I went through together. "Despite everything," I start, "I am happier here—I feel safe and comfortable—more than I ever was in Sonora." I meet Knox's gaze. "Even living with Mavey always felt like a holding pattern to whatever came next. Like I was treading water."

The chickens muddle around in the coop over by the garden with a flutter. "I've thought about it a lot, actually." I turn the mug around in my hand and take another sip, anxious to swallow the lump forming in my throat. "I don't think you or Beth could ever really know how grateful I am to be here. If it wasn't for you—"

Knox rests his hand over mine.

I don't finish because Knox already knows. We've had this conversation, or at least many just like it, and it's still hard to fully comprehend, even now.

Our chairs creak on the old porch in an off-beat rhythm that's soothing.

"I can say the same," Knox murmurs. "So, let's call it even."

Rooster snorts, shaking his head as he clomps closer to the fence line to sniff for wandering weeds. "I never asked you—" I tilt my head. "How did Rooster get his name?"

Knox leans his head back and continues rocking. "My brother."

"Kellen named him?"

"Renamed him, actually. His registered name was Midas, but when he first came to the ranch, he would mimic the roosters in the morning and wake Kellen up. It pissed him off so much I seriously thought I might wake up one morning and my horse would be gone. But that never happened, and Kellen started calling him Rooster. It just stuck, I guess."

Even though Knox doesn't talk about Kellen much, I know he thinks about his brother a lot. One of the blessings of this place is that it's filled with happy memories Knox can't seem to escape, even if I know they make him sad too.

Knox's eyes glint in the pale moonlight, half covered with clouds. "One of my first memories is of Kellen making my lunch for school. He always snuck me a piece of candy."

I grin. "What a good brother."

"He took me trick or treating once when my mom wasn't feeling well or had to work late—I can't remember. He took me to the posh houses on the hill—"

"The ones with the full-sized candy bars," we say together.

Knox huffs a laugh. "I thought he was the coolest brother when he did stuff like that." We continue rocking as a golden hue lines the horizon with daybreak.

"I was thinking," he says, which only makes me smile again.

"Of course you were."

His eyes shift to me in question before he continues. "I want to talk to Aunt Beth about building a bunker. Not just a cellar but a place we'll all be comfortable in when the time comes, because it will. Sooner or later." He exhales a deep breath. "I'm not sure what to do about the animals yet, but we have to start somewhere."

"It's a good idea—a huge undertaking, but you're not wrong. Beth will agree. In fact, she's made a few comments about having one."

He nods. "It definitely won't be easy, and we could use more hands to help, but—" He shrugs. "We know where procrastinating gets us."

I nod in silent agreement and finish my coffee as we watch the sunrise. The sky turns from indigo to gray, then teal, before the sun peeks through the intermittent clouds, casting the cornfields in gold. I lose myself to the rustling stalks and the way they sway back and forth in the breeze.

When I glance at Knox again, that pensive expression of his makes my heart sink a little. His mind rarely rests. "Maybe," I start, cocking my head slightly. "Maybe we spend the morning doing a bit of planning."

Knox's gaze shifts away from a vague point on the horizon to me. "Planning?"

"To see if this bunker idea will really work. We can brainstorm what we think it will take and if it's even possible before we speak with Beth about it."

The furrow in Knox's brow lessens minutely, and the corner of his mouth lifts ever so slightly. "You know me too well," he mutters.

"Ha. I'm getting there," I concede, and I climb to my feet and head inside to grab a notepad and pen.

After a break for breakfast, a couple more hours walking the property, and taking stock of what's at our disposal for such a project—as well as a lengthy list of what we still need—Knox and I regroup on the porch again, sipping on our cold cups of lemonade.

I lick the sweetness from my lips, content. "How many pollywogs do you think Harper will bring back this time?" Setting my glass down, I straighten my back after leaning over my horribly drawn, disproportionate sketch of our fantasy bunker.

"Too many," Knox murmurs. He sets his pencil down on his measurements and chicken scratch and glances at the water trough Harper's last batch are thriving in. "I prefer the sound of crickets to the croak of toads."

Smiling, I pull my cap off and wipe the perspiration from my brow. "*Frogs*," I correct, punctuating the word like Harper always does when Knox teases her.

"Toads," he counters, and winking at me, he sits back in his seat and takes a hearty gulp from his lemonade glass.

I heave out a contented, slightly tired sigh and stare at the land that disappears into the hills, connected to an abandoned neighboring farm. "Maybe we're thinking about this the wrong way," I say thoughtfully. "Beth and Georgie were saying the other night that their neighbors left their farm weeks ago. Whatever its condition, it has the infrastructure we need at least. Running water, wiring for power and reworkable space . . . Maybe we can use it to our advantage somehow."

"We could," Knox agrees. "The only problem with that is the distance. If there's an emergency, the Mayberry's farm is a lot farther away than twenty feet." He nods to the barn and storm cellar.

"True." I exhale a weary sigh.

"But you might be on to something." Knox rubs his brow, shaking his head with discontent.

"At least we have options," I remind him. "We'll figure it out." And I say it with truth because, despite my constant worry and pessimism, I've been feeling uncharacteristically optimistic lately.

Knox huffs with amusement and his eyes flick to my *Toxic Positivity* hat. And finally, as he rocks back in his chair a genuine smile tugs at Knox's cheek. "Thank you," he murmurs.

"Pssh." I shrug as if it's in my nature to be a positive ray of sunshine. "You know where to come if you need an unhealthy dose of positivity for the day."

"Since when?" he jokes.

"Since—" I glance around. "This place. It has a way of making anything feel possible." Because we're all together. Because we're so far removed from utter chaos and destruction at the moment. Because Knox and I can tackle anything, we've proven that already. Whatever the reason, everything feels as if it's exactly as it should be, and there's a sense of relief in that.

Knox stops rocking, straightening in his chair. "Do you —" The furrow in his brow returns. "Do you hear that?" The careful way he says it gives me pause, and my heart pounds harder in my chest.

"Hear what?" I ask nervously, and we both rise to our feet. His attention snaps to the gravel drive.

Knox grips the porch post, straining to listen. "A car engine."

FIFTY-FOUR
KNOX

I STARE DOWN THE ROAD, SQUINTING INTO THE LATE MORNING sun as Ava turns for the door and grabs the loaded shotgun just inside the screen. I can't see the gate from here, but I hear it squeak as it opens, and my body goes rigid.

I hold my hand out for the gun, eyes fixed on the vehicle rolling down the dirt road.

"Wait," Ava gasps. "Didn't we—"

"Lock the gate," I finish for her. "Yeah. I did it myself." I step to the edge of the porch. If this car got onto the property without ramming the gate down, they know the code, and as a white sedan slowly draws closer, I hold my breath.

I grip the shotgun tighter in my hand. No one gets out of the car for what feels like the longest moment of my entire life, and I step off the porch into the gravel.

"Knox—"

"Get Tony from the barn," I say as the driver's side door of the sedan opens. A tall, dark-haired man steps out. A *familiar* man.

I take a step toward him, and only as my knees nearly buckle do I realize my entire body is trembling with a toxic, nearly paralyzing sense of anticipation. I take another step, then another—each step less hesitant than the last as I stare at my brother's features. His eyes glisten in the bright morning, and his tussled black hair catches in the breeze.

"Am I imagining this?" I murmur. My heart is thrumming, and my chest is so tight I almost can't breathe.

"Hey, little brother," Kellen says. It's a voice I have missed for years and have longed to hear for days. It's achingly familiar and soothing all at once. Kellen's eyes gleam and his chin trembles, and all my apprehension melts away.

In two slow strides, Kellen pulls me into his arms.

"I'd hoped," I choke out, but it's all I can manage as my brother squeezes me tighter. "I'd hoped," I repeat. I can't form words—I can barely form a coherent thought in my astonishment and relief.

Remotely, I register a guy standing on the passenger side of the car, younger than my brother but as equally disheveled, and relief washes over me again, knowing Kellen hasn't been alone through all this.

He squeezes me tighter and exhales a deep, soul-stirring breath. "I knew I'd find you."

EPILOGUE

AVA

ONE MONTH LATER

A FARM FULL OF PEOPLE. OF LAUGHTER AND CHATTER AND bodies always moving. There's never an empty room, and even nights are filled with creaks in the house for those staying in the living room. Or Kellen and his partner Tyler's soft murmurs in Beth's old art room below us or hushed voices that drift through the window from those nestled around the pump.

The temporary chaos since Kellen arrived has been strangely gratifying and comforting—the friends he and Tyler made on their harrowing journey, as well as Tyler's brothers, who are now part of our lives. Part of our home.

"Ava—" Kellen grunts behind me. When I glance back, wiping the sweat from my brow, Kellen's lifting a rafter beam over his head in the newly framed living room. "Can I get an assist?"

Smiling, I rise from mixing cement with Harper. "Of course."

It turns out the Mayberry farm was damn near in ruins.

Whether that's the reason the family departed or the storms caused the damage afterward, the farmhouse is only bare bones now.

In a roundabout way, it works out for the best. We might not be ready to build a bunker large enough for over a dozen people, but we can remodel and reinforce the farmhouse and expand the cellar so it's more than a hole in the dirt.

Grabbing the other end of the beam, I heave it up to Knox on the ladder for him and Tyler to secure.

"I think your muscles are bigger than mine now, Ava," Kellen teases.

Though I laugh at the joke, Harper is practically offended. She drops the half empty bucket of water she was pouring into the cement mix. "What about mine?"

Knox winks at me, barely containing a grin. He has found immense entertainment observing Harper's interactions with so many personalities over the past few weeks. Jesse, Tyler's smartass younger brother being Harper's favorite to verbally combat with. Even if she'd never admit it. Not to mention, a giant weight has been lifted from him since his brother's return; it feels like I'm learning a whole new, light-hearted part of Knox I didn't know existed.

"Wow." Kellen whistles. "They *are* big." He shakes his head with mock concern. "You should probably stop eating Beth's spinach salad before they get *too* big."

Harper's haughty expression slackens to a frown. "What do you mean?"

"Spinach," Jesse pipes up, grabbing a jug of water from beside our snack box to sate his thirst. After a few glugs, he gasps for breath and winks at Harper. "Everyone knows that your muscles will get *so* big, you won't be able to pull your shirt sleeves over them." He cocks his head to the side. "Or is it only canned spinach?" He looks at Tyler, who shrugs, biting back a smile of his own as he wisely decides not to get involved in their teasing.

"No," Harper says, "that won't happen." But there's a tinge of uncertainty in her voice as she glances at Knox for reassurance.

He shrugs. "It happened to Popeye."

"Who's that?"

"A guy from my childhood," Knox says, a grin lifting his cheeks.

"Well—" Harper huffs. "I'm a girl, so it will be different for me."

"Hmm." Jesse taps his finger against his chin, thoughtful. "I don't know . . . I had a friend once who—"

"She's a doctor, Jesse," Knox tells him. "Or, at least she used to be. I think Harper would know best."

Jesse is a good actor, and his crumpled brow and concerned expression douses any certainty Harper might've had that he was teasing her. "If you say so."

I shake my head. When I was younger, the tall tale was that beer or coffee would put hair on your chest. I might've believed it, but Harper—well, the way she's staring at her arms, I think she might never touch a green vegetable again.

I'm about to chime in to ease her panic when Beth walks up.

"Enough, you three." She sets a few fresh jugs of water down to replace the empties. The loose blonde wisps of her ponytail catch in the breeze. "Don't listen to them, sweetheart. They are only teasing you."

Harper's eyes narrow slightly, and Jesse grins, tossing his hands up. "My brothers told me that when I was your age. It only seemed fair."

"Interesting," she muses, and with a harrumph, Harper straightens her shoulders and follows Beth toward the horses, where they nibble on the dry grass sprouting along the cement slab. Her sassy walk gives Jesse pause.

"*Interesting*?" he repeats. "I'm going to regret that little lie. Aren't I?"

"Oh, you definitely will," I say with a laugh. "Harper is the queen of storytelling."

"You mean *Dr. Robinson*," Knox counters.

Chuckling, I flash Jesse a warning look. "She's clever, that kid. And you've not only given her more fuel but more ideas too."

With a quiet curse, Jesse walks back to where he and his eldest brother Aaron are working on one of the room extensions, his head shaking the whole way.

"It's weird," Kellen says, his eyes flicking to his brother as he crouches down to help me finish mixing the cement.

Knox takes the nail from between his lips and hammers it into one of the beams above him. "What is?"

"Seeing you like this, teasing her. Teaching her how to ride horses. Tucking her in at night." Kellen is thoughtful for a moment and pivots on his feet to meet Knox's gaze. "It seems right, and yet, I don't think I could have pictured it. Until now."

Knox shifts his tool belt on his waist and climbs down the ladder. "I never imagined it either. I've never had a sister, but she doesn't feel like a sister. Then again, she doesn't feel like a daughter either," he realizes. "I guess I'm whatever Harper needs me to be." Our gazes flick to each other.

"For now," Kellen says. Knox frowns. "You're whatever she needs you to be *for now*. When she meets a guy, your parental side will take over."

Knox pauses, mid-grab of a jug of water, and frowns. "Christ," he mutters as if he hadn't thought of that. "A guy in this world? No way."

"Ha!" Kellen and I both bark a laugh. "As if you'll have a choice," he says. "She won't be alone forever."

I hold up my finger. "In all fairness, you and I wouldn't be speaking now if it weren't for *this world*," I remind Knox. "And Harper will be smarter than us. She's lived through more and knows what this world is capable of." I say it in full confidence.

"It's not her I'm worried about," Knox explains, as if his mind is already whirling, and Kellen winks at me with a smirk.

"How about," I start, rising to my feet. I step up to Knox, peering into his eyes. "We worry about the farm right now, and we'll worry about Harper when the time comes."

With a glance at his brother's smug expression, Knox nods and a wicked gleam lights his eyes. "You laugh at me, Kel," Knox warns and he picks up a stack of two-by-fours. His arms flex under the weight of the wood. "But you're her Uncle Kellen and second-in-command when she meets said guy."

Kellen's eyes widen, I laugh, and with the sounds of chatter, laughter, and hammering around us, we get back to work, rebuilding our lives. Together.

THE END

Be sure to read Kellen and Tyler's story in *Waves of Fury* by K Webster.

ACKNOWLEDGMENTS

A huge, heartfelt thank you to my amazing readers whose monthly support contributed to the production of Knox and Ava's adventure.

Natasha, Deanna, Conrad, Sabrina Hatfield,
Laura Price, K Webster, Mindi Travis, Martha,
Angela H, Charlei, Katelyn Bobbitt, Katie Rose,
Fred Oelrich, Helen, Katie K., Amanda Schmidt,
Amanda Eide, Debbie, Stephanie E., Shannon B.,
Jennie, Jenny Ganzberger, Dawn, Michele Morgan

Here's to the next one!

ALSO BY LINDSEY POGUE

THE ENDING WORLD

SAVAGE NORTH CHRONICLES

(Reading order)

The Darkest Winter

The Longest Night

Midnight Sun

Fading Shadows

Untamed

Unbroken

Day Zero: Beginnings

THE ENDING SERIES

After The Ending

Into The Fire

Out Of The Ashes

Before The Dawn

The Ending Beginnings

World Before

THE ENDING LEGACY

World After

The Raven Queen

FORGOTTEN WORLD

(Stand-alones, suggested reading order)

RUINED LANDS

City of Ruin

Sea of Storms

Land of Fury

FORGOTTEN LANDS

Dust and Shadow

Borne of Sand and Scorn (Prequel)

Earth and Ember

Tide and Tempest

ABOUT THE AUTHOR

Lindsey Pogue is a genre-bending fiction author best known for her soul-stirring survival adventures and timeless love stories. As an avid romance reader with a master's in history and culture, Lindsey's series cross genres and push boundaries, weaving together facts, fantasy, and romance set in rich, sweeping landscapes of epic proportions.

When she's not chatting with readers, plotting her next storyline, or dreaming up new, brooding characters, Lindsey's generally wrapped in blankets watching her favorite action flicks with her own leading man. They live in Northern California with their rescue cats, Beast and Blue.

Visit Lindsey's website for newsletter signups, premium memberships, exclusive content, bookshop discounts, and all the socials.

ALL THE LINKS TO ALL THE PLACES

SCAN ME!